A Flock of Swirling Crows

KUROSHIMA DENJI

A Flock of Swirling Crows

and Other
Proletarian
Writings

Translated by Zeljko Cipris

University of Hawai'i Press
Honolulu

Library of Congress Cataloging-in-Publication Data
Kuroshima, Denji.
    A flock of swirling crows and other proletarian writings /
Kuroshima Denji ; translated by Zeljko Cipris.
       p. cm.
    Translation of "Uzumakeru karasu no mure" and others.
    Includes bibliographical references.
    ISBN 0–8248–2855–0 (hardcover : alk. paper)
    ISBN 0–8248–2926–3 (pbk. : alk. paper)
    I. Cipris, Zeljko. II. Title.
    PL832.U7.A6 2005
    895.6'344—dc22
                                        2004022009

Designed by the University of Hawai'i Press production staff

Printed by The Maple-Vail Book Manufacturing Group

*To Ljubomir Ryu Cipris
and Shane Satori Cipris
and to all who are building
a worldwide community of
sharing and peace*

CONTENTS

CONTENTS

Preface

THE OFTEN ENCOUNTERED dissonance between official truth and intractable reality may make one not only bracingly skeptical but also highly appreciative of those who are able to break through tranquilizing modes of thought, confront and depict appallingly grim conditions, and indicate a rational path toward emancipation from an entrenched system of institutionalized cruelty and falsehoods. It is quite a challenging task. Yet in an unassuming and powerful way, proletarian writer Kuroshima Denji does just this.

I developed an interest and affection for Kuroshima as a graduate student at Columbia University after reading about him in a book by one of my professors, Donald Keene. A search for Kuroshima in the stacks of Columbia's Starr East Asian Library led to the discovery that his collected works—three volumes—had never been checked out in all the fifteen years they had spent on the shelves. Their author gazed at me intently from one of the photographs as if to say, "Get me out of here!" Readily assenting, I translated one of Kuroshima's stories for a class with Professor Keene and then two more for a one-man seminar with another of Columbia's greats, Edward Seidensticker. Both professors made encouraging comments for which I am still very grateful. "Kuroshima Denji and Three Stories of the Siberian Intervention" became the topic of my MA thesis and marked the beginning of the work that has led to this book.

One summer evening in New York, Japan's hugely popular historical novelist Shiba Ryōtarō asked me to name my favorite Japanese writer, and I promptly replied: "Kuroshima Denji." Shiba-san and the *Yomiuri Shinbun* journalists accompanying him exchanged bewildered glances, then smiled and shook their heads. Kuroshima remains virtually unknown even in his native land. I certainly hope the readers of this translation will not conclude that the obscurity is richly deserved but decide instead that it is a good time for his works to become better known. The narratives translated here are taken from *Kuroshima Denji zenshū,* edited by Odagiri Hideo and Tsuboi Shigeji and published by Chikuma Shobō in 1970.

In addition to Professors Keene and Seidensticker, my other distinguished teachers at Columbia, and the wonderful Chiba Sen'ichi Sensei (presently at Hokkai Gakuen Daigaku) who taught me so much about Japanese literature, I would especially like to thank my friend and colleague Shoko Hamano who painstakingly read the entire first draft of this book and saved me from a number of creative but undeniable mistranslations. My warmest thanks go also to Professor Norma Field of the University of Chicago who as a reader for the University of Hawai'i Press made many helpful suggestions and enthusiastically recommended publishing the manuscript. I also thank the other, anonymous, reader for the press and my sterling editors, Pamela Kelley and Jenn Harada. To the entire illustrious staff of the UH Press, I direct a deep bow of gratitude and admiration.

I would like to thank my parents Divna and Marijan, who did indeed make all things possible, and my good wife Etsuko who has cheerfully been putting up with me for a quarter century. Many thanks also to my talented sons Shane and Ryu, to whom the present book is cordially dedicated.

In transliterating Japanese names, terms, and places into English I have relied on the commonly utilized Hepburn system. For Chinese names and places I have used the Wade-Giles system, which was prevalent in the 1920s and 1930s. Except for authors of Western-language publications, Japanese and Chinese names are written in the East Asian sequence—family name first and personal name second. The macrons encountered in some Japanese words (such as Ichirō) indicate that the marked vowel is doubled in length. In a few cases, such as the names of well-known Japanese cities like Tokyo or Osaka (properly pronounced Tōkyō and Ōsaka), macrons have been omitted. The inclusion of several words that were censored from the original manuscript is indicated by square brackets (as in "Those were their [enemies]"). Regrettably the dialect and class-marked speech that so flavor Kuroshima Denji's prose are lost in translation.

Introduction

Rise, like lions after slumber,
In unvanquishable number,
Shake the chains to earth like dew,
Which in sleep had fall'n on you—
Ye are many—they are few.

Percy Bysshe Shelley
The Masque of Anarchy (1819)

Broadly defined, proletarian literature is any creative writing in which the author identifies with the working class and champions its cause. In this comprehensive sense proletarian literature may embrace a poem by Percy Bysshe Shelley or William Blake as well as a memoir by Domitila Barrios de Chungara or Rigoberta Menchú Tum. A more specific usage of the term denotes the great worldwide upsurge in the production of left-wing literature that followed the Russian Revolution of 1917 and includes such writers as Jaroslav Hašek in Czechoslovakia, Bertolt Brecht in Germany, Maxim Gorky in Russia, Lu Xun in China, Yi Ki-yŏng in Korea, Kobayashi Takiji in Japan, Pablo Neruda in Chile, Josephine Herbst and Meridel Le Sueur in the United States, and hundreds more.

Reaching its productive zenith during the 1920s and 1930s, proletarian literature formed a prominent part of contemporary proletarian art, a diffuse and largely spontaneous international movement represented by a variety of artists like the German graphic satirist George Grosz, the Mexican painter Diego Rivera, the Soviet filmmaker Sergei Eisenstein, the Italian photographer Tina Modotti, and numerous others. Some of the cultural workers of the period accepted the tenets of "socialist realism"—a Soviet artistic

1

doctrine officially promulgated in 1934 and prescribing a formula of anti-modernist realism, sunny optimism, and idealized depictions of the working class. A great many, however, did not. Brecht, for one, explicitly rejected it as an obstacle to imaginative experimentation; most other artists who were free to ignore it tended to do so.

Although proletarian literature is characterized by a diversity of genres and styles, its political stance has been consistently anticapitalist. Insofar as they were acquainted with Marx's critique of capitalism, most proletarian writers active since the second half of the nineteenth century have considered it valid. Be they communists, anarchists, or rebels of a less identifiable sort, proletarian artists generally regard the capitalist socioeconomic system as incorrigibly alienating, oppressive, and exploitative. Skeptical or contemptuous of the dominant representations of capitalism as natural, eternal, and in the best interests of all, they view it instead as a heartless and hypocritical regime that ostensibly promotes freedom and prosperity while in fact depriving the majority of humankind of both.

According to Marx's analysis, capitalism splits humanity into two major classes: the relatively few who own and control the society's productive resources and the dispossessed many who are compelled to sell themselves on a daily basis in order to survive. Although capitalism is more dynamic and infinitely more productive than the feudalism out of which it evolved, its endless quest to accumulate wealth and maximize profits renders it more destructive of the natural environment, highly aggressive economically and militarily, and intrinsically detrimental to human equality, liberty, and happiness. Its supremacy, however, is not unassailable. There does exist a life-affirming alternative: once the disinherited majority fully awakens to the true nature of the capitalist system and effectively organizes to reclaim the earth from its usurpers, it may at last be able to create a humane world —a cooperative commonwealth "in which the free development of each is the condition for the free development of all."[1]

Proletarian literature, along with other forms of politically radical art, has played a vital role in the ongoing struggle to construct a more rational and compassionate way to live. It has done so by taking a penetrating look at our current mode of life—with its myriad unnecessary tragedies, tireless efforts at resistance, and intimations of a better future—and by striving through powerful portrayals of the reality it sees to galvanize its audience into thought and action. Variable in aesthetic quality, at times more noted for passion and political commitment than for artistic virtuosity and refinement, proletarian literature has persevered in its task without worrying much about critical approbation, especially that of mainstream critics. As *The Anvil,* a North American proletarian literary magazine edited in the 1930s by Jack Conroy, proclaimed through its motto: "We prefer crude vigor to polished banality." [2]

The wave of proletarian literature marking the 1920s and 1930s subsided amid repression and the chaos of a world war but resurfaced in a more scattered form shortly after. Continuing to draw strength from, as well as to inspire, radical mass movements, left-wing writing has since then fluctuated in scope and influence while continuing to constitute a significant current in world literature. In the early twenty-first century, the work of such literary artists as Eduardo Galeano of Uruguay, José Saramago of Portugal, Ngugi wa Thiong'o of Kenya, Arundhati Roy of India, and Ahuti of Nepal suggests that rebellious independent-minded writers will keep on endeavoring to interpret the world and—together with a burgeoning movement for global justice—to change it for the better.

Kuroshima Denji

One of the best—though least known—practitioners of proletarian literature in Japan was Kuroshima Denji. Born on Shōdo Island in the Inland Sea on December 12, 1898, he was the eldest son of a poor rural family who had been farmers for many generations. Denji completed elementary and vocational schools and then worked as a sardine fisherman and as a laborer in the local soy factory. In the autumn of 1917 he went to Tokyo where he found employment with a construction company, leaving it shortly to become an editor of a poultry journal. A chance meeting with his childhood friend Tsuboi Shigeji, then studying literature at Waseda University, contributed to Denji's decision to become a student himself. His academic background was quite inadequate, however, so he resorted to having his entrance examination taken by a substitute. The trick worked: in the spring of 1919 he began his studies at Waseda University. Among his interests at the time were literature and French—he had been trying to learn the language since coming to Tokyo—and he might have entered the university intending to make them his field of study. Kuroshima enjoyed reading Dostoyevsky, Tolstoy, and other Russian writers, reserving his greatest admiration for Anton Chekhov and his own compatriot Shiga Naoya. But whatever academic plans he may have had were cut short by a conscription notice received late the same year. As a vocational school graduate, Denji was ineligible for deferment and in December 1919 he was inducted as a medical corpsman into the Himeji Tenth Infantry Regiment. A most unenthusiastic conscript from the outset, he prefaced his army diary with a dedication: "To the day of discharge from military service."[3] He spent the next sixteen months stationed in Japan, but then in April 1921, with his discharge date drawing near, his unit was sent to Siberia to take part in the Japanese armed intervention there.[4]

The term Siberian Intervention (Shiberia shuppei) refers to the role played by the Japanese military in an international effort to reverse by force the recent political victory of the Soviet revolution. In the autumn of 1918, Japan sent some seventy-four thousand soldiers to cooperate with French, British, US, Canadian, and Czech troops fighting against the newly formed Red Army and communist guerrillas. By June 1920 all other foreign troops had withdrawn in the face of the Soviet advance, but the Japanese troops fought on for more than two additional years before finally pulling out of Siberia in the autumn of 1922.[5] It was only in 1925 that a humbled Japanese military evacuated entirely from Soviet territory.

Kuroshima spent a full year in Siberia. While still in Japan he had begun to show symptoms of tuberculosis, and the harsh Siberian climate made the illness worse. He was hospitalized in March 1922 and repatriated in May. After separation from the military he returned to his island village and, while recuperating, began to write stories of rural and army life. In the early summer of 1925 he went to Tokyo for the second time, taking along the stories he had written. Tsuboi Shigeji and some friends were then putting out a small magazine called *Chōryū* (Current), and it was with Tsuboi's help that Kuroshima published in its pages his story "Denpō" (The telegram), translated in the present volume. For the rest of the decade, Kuroshima's work continued to appear in various literary outlets, including the Marxist journal *Bungei sensen* (Literary front), which was the prime promoter of proletarian literature, and the highly influential liberal magazine *Chūō kōron* (Central review).

The political and cultural atmosphere of 1920s Japan was relatively liberal, especially if compared with what was to follow. The prestige of the military was so low that army officers were said to have trouble finding women willing to marry them and wore their uniforms in public as seldom as possible.[6] Young and vigorous social movements proliferated—among them a labor movement, women's movement, student movement, farmers' movement, and a movement for the emancipation of social outcasts (Burakumin kaihō undō). Enthusiastic dissident artists and authors produced a wealth of posters, paintings, poetry, plays, and prose with antimilitarist, anti-imperialist, antiracist, antisexist, and anticapitalist themes.[7] Dozens of proletarian writers were active, including Maedakō Hiroichirō, Nakano Shigeharu, Kobayashi Takiji, Miyamoto Yuriko, Sata Ineko, Hirabayashi Taiko, Tsuboi Shigeji, and Oguma Hideo. The authorities watched the surge of socialist and feminist activism with a wary eye but resorted only sporadically to repressive action. Censorship existed; anticapitalist agitation was made illegal in 1925; but the harshest laws were not yet being heavily enforced.

Japan of the 1920s was a constitutional monarchy with an elected parliament. Wealth and power were concentrated in a relatively few hands. Large family-owned financial/industrial/commercial combines dominated the nation's economy and largely controlled its politics by supporting the major political parties. Big landowners dominated the economy's agricultural sector. The country exercised colonial rule over Taiwan and Korea and maintained cooperative relations with Western powers. Alongside the United States, Britain, and several lesser European hegemons, Japan assiduously exploited the natural and human resources of a politically fragmented China and backed whichever of the Chinese warlords it deemed the most compliant. It was in China that Japan's foreign policy began to swerve out of control—with tragic consequences for the people of China and Japan alike.

As Chinese resistance to foreign economic aggression intensified, Japan's governing elite responded to the threat to its freedom of action with increasing reliance on military force. One of the early "incidents" *(jihen* or *jiken)* that would eventually lead to a full-scale war between Japan and China occurred in the spring of 1928 in Tsinan, the capital of Shantung province, during a northward advance by Chinese nationalist troops attempting to reunify the country. Possessing considerable commercial and industrial investments in Tsinan, and faced with a collapse of its favored warlord in the area, Japan rushed in its own troops, ostensibly to safeguard the Japanese residents of the city. After a tense standoff the Japanese units clashed with their Chinese counterparts. The Japanese army, needing reinforcements, claimed that more than three hundred Japanese residents had been massacred by the Chinese troops. Although the Japanese who were killed were in fact some thirteen suspected opium smugglers, Japanese newspapers reacted to their deaths with inflammatory outrage and called for armed intervention. Japan's prime minister dispatched an additional division to the region, and the Japanese troops launched an attack against Tsinan, killing and wounding thousands of Chinese civilians.[8]

Japan's military response in such cases, though supported by the major-

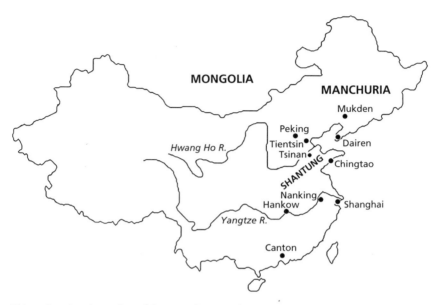

China, showing the region of Japanese intervention.

ity of the Japanese public, deepened the Chinese hatred of Japan's imperialism and strengthened the popular resistance to it. In Japan itself, not everyone subscribed to the official story: a small but energetic anti-interventionist movement called for an end to Japanese militarism and for solidarity between the people of China and Japan.[9] Kuroshima Denji, who knew war at first hand, traveled to China to see for himself what some of the realities of the new war looked like up close. His research resulted in a novel called *Busō seru shigai* (Militarized streets), published in November 1930. Kuroshima's novel was instantly banned, censored again fifteen years later by the US occupation authorities, and not reprinted in full until 1970, four decades after its initial publication. The poet and essayist Tsuboi Shigeji, Kuroshima's lifelong friend who was instrumental in publishing the work, has commended its uncompromising anti-imperialism.[10] The novel remains little known in Japan even now, although according to a leading literary historian "it may well be the most absorbing work to have been fostered by the proletarian literature movement."[11] The present volume contains a complete translation of *Militarized Streets*.

By the beginning of the 1930s Kuroshima Denji had written and published several dozen narratives depicting the stunted lives of impoverished peasants and workers and detailing the misery of soldiers (most of them conscripted from that same wretched population) who are shipped overseas to kill and die for the master class.[12] As may be expected in a writer influenced by Chekhov and Shiga Naoya, the narratives are unadorned in style and simple in storytelling technique. Their content conveys a sense of authenticity, grief over the unnecessary suffering, and above all the urgent need for change. Despite occasional flashes of humor and lyricism, the tone is seldom cheerful and happy endings are rare: Kuroshima refrains from accomplishing in fiction what is much harder to attain in actuality. Devoid of easy optimism, his stories are open-ended chronicles of abuse and resistance. If his protagonists fail to survive and prosper despite strenuous effort, his readers are all the more impelled to seek a way out of the brutal labyrinth. How can the human race emerge once and for all from poverty, oppression, racism, sexism, nationalism, and war? Kuroshima's work may implicitly point to an answer. A clear-sighted, courageous, and profoundly compassionate writer, Kuroshima recognizes that, however long it may take to materialize, only a vast international movement based on grassroots solidarity stands a chance of replacing the present hell on earth with a sane, livable world of justice and generosity.

Kuroshima's literary activity diminished rather abruptly after 1932. A story he had published in February of that year was sharply criticized on doctrinal grounds by a young but influential Communist Party leader and self-appointed literary critic.[13] That the attack should come from within the proletarian movement, rather than from the authorities, was symptomatic of the internal dissensions afflicting the leftist circles—dissensions which would make it that much easier for the government shortly to crush them. Kuroshima was undoubtedly stung by the force of the criticism, but he might not have withdrawn from the literary world had his health not taken a sudden turn for the worse. Early in 1933 he began to cough up blood, and that summer he returned to Shōdo Island. Apparently intending to stay on the island only long enough to recover, he left his furniture and other possessions in the care of his younger brother in Tokyo.[14]

Around the same time that Kuroshima's health deteriorated, Kobayashi Takiji, a prominent young proletarian writer, was arrested and beaten to death by the police. The event signaled a marked change in the nation's political climate. In the 1930s, as Japan moved ever closer to an all-out war with China, the intensifying aggression overseas was matched by increasing domestic repression. Arrests grew more numerous and sweeping, sentences harsher, censorship more heavy-handed. Dissidents were accused of being un-Japanese or anti-Japanese *(hikokumin)*.[15] Through a combined reliance on force and persuasion, the government succeeded in neutralizing the social movements and even converted some of their former members into ultranationalists. With the population largely under control and the production of heavy armaments strong and growing, the governing elite felt free to extend its economic and military hegemony over the continent. Sporadic armed clashes continued until, in the summer of 1937, the conflict exploded into a major war engulfing a large portion of China. Many of Japan's journalists, academics, and other manufacturers of public opinion supported the war and echoed the government's consistent claim that the aim of the conflict was not conquest but liberation. By the time it ended some eight years later, the alleged war of liberation had killed more than half a million Japanese and perhaps as many as thirty million Chinese.[16]

"In war, truly good literature can probably do nothing but disappear," wrote Kuroshima Denji to a friend in the late summer of 1937, shortly after the outbreak of full-fledged warfare.[17] The only literary outcome Kuroshima expected for the duration of the conflict was a profusion of shallow war literature. About a year after Kuroshima made his gloomy prognosis, the Japanese government invited a number of prominent Japanese authors to travel to the front as members of its newly organized Pen Corps (Pen butai) and write about the fighting.[18] The response was so enthusiastic that not all the writers who wished to join could be accommodated. In September 1938 a contingent of twenty men and two women was flown overseas and nine additional members followed two months later. Not surprisingly, the work they produced was supportive of the war and, as Kuroshima had anticipated, very superficial indeed.

Kuroshima spent the final decade of his life living quietly with his wife and children on the island of his birth. He read widely and wrote letters and articles but no works of fiction. The house had very few visitors and Kuroshima rarely left his room except to work in the garden or stroll among the nearby hills or by the sea. Though he grew weak and had to walk with a cane, he remained intent on recuperation. At the slightest sign of a cold he would take to bed and stay there until the symptoms disappeared. The children—two girls and a boy—regularly walked several miles to the nearest hospital to get the medicine that he conscientiously drank. Despite his best efforts, his condition began to worsen in the spring of 1943, and he succumbed on October 17 of the same year, eight weeks short of his forty-fifth birthday. His wife Yuki, who survived him by ten years to die at the same age as her husband, managed to keep the impoverished household together and raise the three children to adulthood. Encouraging them to persist in their studies and to help her and each other, she often spoke of their father's stubborn optimism, recalling his unwavering conviction he would get well and his joyful anticipation of the day he could once again go to Tokyo.[19]

It may be surprising that a man whose works are seldom cheerful should be described as such an optimist, yet he undeniably was one. His strong will to live recalls the characters in his narratives who struggle to survive against all odds. Kuroshima believed, both as a human being and as a committed proletarian writer, that things were bound to get better in the long run and devoted his life to the creation of an egalitarian and peaceful world. The best contribution he could make was by writing, he felt, and he intended to continue. In a letter dated March 19, 1940, he writes: "I have been feeling much better this year. I am sitting at the desk for the first time in a long while and although I have not been writing for five or six years, let me only regain health. For I find myself able to write better than before, more subtly and deeply—and I am happy."[20]

ASSESSING THE NARRATIVES

As Kuroshima would have been quick to recognize, conditions in Japan and indeed in the world have changed greatly since the time he lived and wrote. Rural poverty within Japan has been largely eliminated, Japanese militarism appears to be extinct, and China is no longer a victim of imperialist depredation. Given all this—as well as the fact that Kuroshima himself had no illusions about being a "great writer"—do his writings possess any value today beyond the historical?

Indeed they do—because the ongoing changes, dramatic and important as they are, have been taking place within the context of that same global socioeconomic system whose multiple facets Kuroshima explored in his writings. True, the level of misery in the Japanese countryside has been sharply reduced thanks in large part to a program of land reform. Yet conditions as painful as those he described, or even worse, still plague hundreds of millions of people in dozens of countries throughout the world.[21] True again, tens of thousands of Japanese youths are not currently being shipped overseas to kill and die for the ostensible sake of the nation. Yet similar operations by other world powers continue unabated, and their full-scale resumption by Japan itself may only be a matter of time and popular acquiescence. Targets of imperialist plunder have definitely shifted. Yet imperialism remains as alive today as in Kuroshima's lifetime and even more attractively advertised.

Convinced that poverty, exploitation, and war cannot possibly be eradicated within the framework of a system based on organized greed, Kuroshima nonetheless recognizes that many people do not share his conviction, do not consider the system surmountable, or simply do not give the subject much thought. His writing addresses a broad spectrum of readers, making its appeal both to their emotions and to their intellect. In detailing the anguish and indignities that are systematically and relentlessly inflicted on human beings whose only offense is a lack of wealth and power, Kuroshima evokes a potent sense of sympathy and anger at the sheer injustice of it. At the same time, he attentively examines such diverse topics as the mechanics of oppression and obfuscation, tactics of resistance and rebellion, impediments and catalysts of international unity and revolution.

Kuroshima's narratives explore a number of significant questions:

- Why is education potentially subversive? ("The Telegram," "Their Lives")
- How can a worker be induced to turn against a fellow worker? ("The Sugar Thief," *Militarized Streets*)
- Can a rebellion succeed if some decline to join? ("A Herd of Pigs")
- Does a highly motivated and diligent individual working alone stand any chance of effecting meaningful change? ("Their Lives," "Land Rising and Falling")
- Is submissiveness a satisfactory strategy for survival? ("Siberia in the Snow," "A Flock of Swirling Crows")
- Is spontaneous rebellion effective? ("Siberia in the Snow," "The Sleigh")
- How does ethnocentrism support an oppressive status quo? ("The Hole")
- Does militant unionism give rise to sufficient change? ("The Cape")
- How do exploiters justify their conduct? *(Militarized Streets)*
- Whom does a war allegedly benefit, and whom does it actually benefit? *(Militarized Streets)*
- How do the mass media generate support for war? *(Militarized Streets)*
- How does the military maintain control over a powerful body of armed men? *(Militarized Streets)*

The presence of such questions, and others, does not by any means suggest that Kuroshima's narratives offer nothing more than a sort of revolutionary catechism disguised as fiction. But since their author is after all wholeheartedly committed to fundamental social change it is hardly surprising that such issues should arise as integral components of the work. Although a reactionary reader would be unlikely to enjoy the pages that follow, one certainly does not need to be a Marxist to discover considerable interest in them.

The artistically accomplished oeuvre of Kuroshima's nonproletarian literary contemporaries—Akutagawa Ryūnosuke, Tanizaki Jun'ichirō, Kawabata Yasunari, Nagai Kafū, Yokomitsu Riichi, and others—continues to merit and enjoy a wide readership in Japan and abroad. One hopes that increasing notice will soon be taken not only of writers such as these, who poignantly celebrate the beauty and sadness of human existence, but likewise of those who strive to promote the kinds of transformation that diminish the province of sadness and expand the realm of beauty. At any rate, faced with the daily tragedies of an irrationally structured world, radical artists everywhere are bound to persevere in their oppositional work. As Kuroshima Denji writes in a 1929 essay: "So long as the capitalist system exists, proletarian antiwar literature must also exist, and fight against it."[22]

Notes

1. Karl Marx, *Karl Marx: Selected Writings,* ed. Lawrence H. Simon (Indianapolis: Hackett, 1994), 176. The quoted words conclude Part II of the Communist Manifesto.

2. Mary Jo Buhle, Paul Buhle, and Dan Georgakas, eds., *Encyclopedia of the American Left* (Urbana: University of Illinois Press, 1992), 163.

3. Kuroshima Denji, "Guntai nikki," in *Kuroshima Denji zenshū,* ed. Odagiri Hideo and Tsuboi Shigeji (Tokyo: Chikuma Shobō, 1970), 3:247.

4. Inagaki Tatsurō, "Kuroshima Denji no rinkaku," in *Puroretaria bungaku,* ed. Nihon Bungaku Kenkyū Shiryō Kankōkai (Tokyo: Yūseidō, 1971), 7.

5. Janet E. Hunter, "Siberian Intervention (Shiberia shuppei)," in *Concise Dictionary of Modern Japanese History* (Berkeley: University of California Press, 1984), 205.

6. W. G. Beasley, *The Japanese Experience: A Short History of Japan* (Berkeley: University of California Press, 2000), 239.

7. For a sampling of radical posters from the period see the website of Ohara Institute for Social Research, Hosei University, at www.oisr.org.

8. Mikiso Hane, *Modern Japan: A Historical Survey* (Boulder: Westview, 1992), 237–238.

9. Dissident groups included the Alliance Against Intervention in China (Tai-Shi Hikanshō Dōmei) and the National Antiwar Alliance (Zenkoku Hansen Dōmei). See Kobayashi Shigeo, "Kaisetsu," in Kuroshima Denji, *Nihon puroretaria bungaku shū 9: Kuroshima Denji shū* (Tokyo: Shin Nihon Shuppansha, 1989), 442.

10. George T. Shea, *Leftwing Literature in Japan: A Brief History of the Proletarian Literary Movement* (Tokyo: Hosei University Press, 1964), 184. As Shea notes on the same page, the literary historian Odagiri Hideo considers Kuroshima's novel to be a model in illuminating the essence of war.

11. Donald Keene, *Dawn to the West: Japanese Literature of the Modern Era,* vol. 1 (New York: Holt, 1984), 608.

12. The original publication sites of the narratives translated in this volume are as follows: "The Telegram" (Denpō): *Chōryū,* July 1925; "A Herd of Pigs" (Tongun): *Bungei sensen,* November 1926; "The Sugar Thief" (Satō dorobō): *Bungei shijō,* December 1926; "Their Lives" (Karera no isshō): *Bungei sensen,* March 1927; "Siberia in the Snow" (Yuki no Shiberia): *Sekai,* June 1927; "The Sleigh" (Sori): *Bungei sensen,* September 1927; "A Flock of Swirling Crows" (Uzumakeru karasu no mure): *Kaizō,* February 1928; "The Hole" (Ana): *Bungei sensen,* May 1928; "Land Rising and Falling" (Fudō suru chika): *Keizai ōrai,* June 1930; "The Cape" (Misaki): [unpublished during author's lifetime] *Shin Nihon bungaku,* September 1949; *Militarized Streets (Busō seru shigai): Nihon Hyōronsha,* November 1930. Source: *Nihon puroretaria bungaku shū 9: Kuroshima Denji shū,* 457–460.

13. Keene, *Dawn to the West,* 610. The critic was Miyamoto Kenji, who would become the durable head of the Japan Communist Party. Years later he expressed regret for the sharpness of his criticism.

14. Moroi Shirō, "Kuroshima Denji nenpu," *Kuroshima Denji zenshū,* 3:392.

15. Junichiro Kisaka, "Detour Through a Dark Valley," in Harry Wray and Hilary Conroy, eds., *Japan Examined: Perspectives on Modern Japanese History* (Honolulu: University of Hawai'i Press, 1983), 247.

16. Japan's war against China is thought to have killed between fifteen million and thirty million Chinese, the vast majority of them civilians. For one estimate see James C. Hsiung and Steven I. Levine, eds., *China's Bitter Victory: The War with Japan, 1937–1945* (Armonk, NY: M. E. Sharpe, 1992), 295–296. According to Hsiung and Levine, about four million Chinese soldiers and eighteen million civilians were killed in the war.

17. *Kuroshima Denji zenshū,* 3:359 (Letter to Kawanabe Kōichi, September 2, 1937). See also Kobayashi Shigeo, *Puroretaria bungaku no sakkatachi* (Tokyo: Shin Nihon Shuppansha, 1988), 87.

18. Richard H. Mitchell, *Censorship in Imperial Japan* (Princeton: Princeton University Press, 1983), 295.

19. Kuroshima Kazuo, "Chichi," Monthly Bulletin 1, April 1970, in *Kuroshima Denji zenshū,* 1:7–8. This is a terse, affecting account by Kuroshima's only son of his father's final years and the decade following his death.

20. *Kuroshima Denji zenshū,* 3:373.

21. The land reform in Japan was implemented during the US occupation. The United States did not see fit to carry out a similar land reform program in the course of its decades-long colonial occupation of the Philippines, where desperate rural poverty still prevails.

22. *Hansen bungaku-ron* (On antiwar literature) may be read in Japanese online at www.aozora.gr.jp/cards/000037/files/1424.html. Aozora Bunko has also published over a dozen other works by Kuroshima, including six of those translated in this volume, and more are being added. A complete English translation of Kuroshima's essay on antiwar literature will be found in a forthcoming anthology of Japanese proletarian fiction and criticism edited by Norma Field and Heather Bowen-Struyk.

A Flock of Swirling Crows

The Telegram

1

The rumor that Gensaku's son had gone to take the entrance examination for the town's middle school spread throughout the village. Gensaku was an independent farmer in the village, but so poor he did not even own enough land for a single household. When it comes to the sons of landlords or soy brewers, it is deemed natural and not in the least surprising for them to enter a university in Tokyo. That causes no gossip at all, but the news that a dirt-poor farmer like Gensaku was sending his son to a school in town aroused the villagers' curiosity.

When Gensaku's wife Okino went next door to take a bath, or to the temple to pray, she was taunted by the other wives: "So you're sending your child to middle school? With all that money you've got, you can get him into any school you like. He-he-he-he."

2

Okino herself did not utter a word about having sent the child to take the examination. But the day after the son's departure, all the villagers she met in the streets already knew of it. At first she felt proud to be told by others, "Well, you must be sending him to school to make him a great man." She was even happy.

"Did you tell people that he went?" she asked Gensaku at lunchtime.

"No. I didn't say a thing," Gensaku replied curtly.

"I see. . . . And yet everybody already knows."

"Hmm." Gensaku grew thoughtful.

After losing his father at sixteen, Gensaku had begun to work on his own and managed to acquire about an acre of land and some two thousand yen. He was a year short of fifty. He had spent his youth in work, even going hungry in his determination to save up twenty or thirty thousand yen. Yet despite his best efforts he had barely accumulated two thousand yen and seemed to have no prospect of earning any more. Already he was feeling well past his prime, declining in energy and ability to work. He saw that whereas all his hard work since the age of sixteen had gotten him a negligible sum of money, soy brewers and landlords were earning great amounts of money and living in splendor without working particularly hard at all. There was the landlord's third son, same age as himself, who had no special aptitude for learning but who thanks to money had gone to school and was now a priest at the Konpira Shrine, adroitly squeezing the parishioners for money. People the same age or younger who had shown far less ability in school than Gensaku but whose education went on slightly longer became skilled in reading and writing and presently became soy company managers, brewery clerks, or elementary school principals and swaggered around the village. He had to bow his head to such people. He had to submit to their rule. Such people became village assembly members and arbitrarily set the household tax.

The farmers these days were forced to go hungry despite working all year round. The prices for the crops they raised were low, the taxes and living expenses high, leaving them chronically short of funds. Even if one became a worker at a soy brewery, the work was heavy and the wages low. It was too late for him to quit farming and transform himself into a merchant, nor could he become a brewery clerk. Yet he could not bear the thought of trapping his own son in the sort of hopeless position he had come to.

Gensaku had married off his daughter the previous year to a man in a neighboring village. Only her younger brother remained. Lucky to have just enough money to send the child to middle school, Gensaku planned to have his cousin who ran an umbrella shop in town take care of the boy allowing him to attend classes at no great cost.

"I hope it goes well," he said, putting down his teacup.

"I'm sure it will. Ever since the first grade, he's been the best," Okino said, gazing at Gensaku's broad forehead. His salt-and-pepper hair, untrimmed for over a month, was getting long and shaggy.

"Still, there are many talented people in town, so one never knows."

"I'll pray to the Goddess of Mercy every morning and it'll surely go well."

Gensaku made no reply. He was imagining his son graduating from middle school, entering a higher technical school, and having completed that becoming an engineer at an industrial laboratory and earning a hundred and twenty yen a month.

3

A postcard came from the cousin in town. The son was well and in good spirits. The number of applications for the prefectural middle school was extremely high. The children from the urban elementary schools, having had their teachers prepare them for the examinations six months in advance, confidently wrote everything they knew and turned in their test forms, but the rural children's chances of acceptance were twenty or thirty percent lower. Even so, this child was very capable and would most likely pass, wrote the cousin.

"It will be wonderful if he passes," said Gensaku after reading the postcard to his wife.

"I will pray even harder."

Though long convinced that praying for such things to gods and the Buddha was useless, Gensaku did not at that moment have the heart to contradict her.

While Gensaku was out working, Okino's uncle came. "I hear you've sent the child to middle school. What on earth for?" the uncle asked Okino, seating himself on the veranda that was worn smooth with scrubbing.

"Even if we made him quit school and sent him back to work," Okino replied, "he wouldn't make much money and would only have to live out his life as a pauper keeping his head down. But if we spend a little now to send him to school he might become something, don't you think?"

"Hmm. That's fine. But just finishing middle school won't get him very far, you know."

"Gensaku says he'll let him go higher."

"Hmm." The uncle inclined his head awhile. "The village head hates the very idea of poor folks sending their children to the town school, so you'd better keep it a secret," he said, his voice low and forceful.

"Is that so?"

"Best tell anyone who asks that you've sent him to town to be an apprentice."

"I see."

"You have to be very careful, . . ." he stressed. Then he stood up and went to take a look at the pigpen.

"This female's getting outrageously fat."

The two adults had been sold about a month earlier, and only a pair of piglets remained. The uncle was pointing to one of them.

"Yes," said Okino accompanying him.

"If you raise about ten pigs, you should be able to pay for the child's school expenses. . . . Anyway, poor folks here don't go for higher schooling so you have to say you've sent him to be apprenticed," the uncle reiterated.

Complying with the uncle's admonition, Okino told anyone who inquired about her son that he was sent to be an apprentice at the umbrella shop. The villagers, however, did not believe her. Yet she stubbornly insisted, "What would be the use of sending him to the town school? We barely have enough to eat, so of course we sent him to be an apprentice." But the people responded all the more sarcastically, "Being so very rich, why would you send your only son to be an apprentice? You've sent him to school, you liar. . . . Well, your child is so great he's likely to become a gentleman, he-he-he."

Subjected to withering sarcasm from nearly everyone she met, Okino said to Gensaku, "Would it be better to call it off and really make him an apprentice?"

"An apprentice?" Gensaku smiled a trifle mockingly, then sullenly said, "Our life is just about over, but his is only beginning. Rather than leave him a bit of money, it's much better to see he gets educated. It doesn't matter what the villagers say. I'm not having the village head pay for it. I'm spending my own money to send my child to school, so there's no need to apologize to anyone."

Listening to her uncle's warning and the villagers' sarcasm Okino had felt that sending her son to school might have been a mistake. But Gensaku's words struck her as reasonable, simple and clear, leading her to conclude that the others had no grounds for complaint.

4

On the day her son was expected to return having taken the examination, Okino went to the train station to meet him. In order to avoid the eyes of the others—the village head's maidservant, the soy brewer's wife, the clothier's son—who had come to greet the young masters returning from the examinations, Okino stood outside the station building waiting for her son. Since her family's status was low, she was humbly refraining from mingling with the rich. And she was indeed looked down upon as a lowly peasant's wife.

The train presently arrived, and the sons of the village head, the soy brewer, the clothier, and the like alighted.

"Mother!" The soy brewer's son, locating his mother soon after stepping down onto the platform, ran up to her with a shout. Observing the scene from a corner, Okino thought how happy she would be if her son called out to her so freely.

"Welcome back, young master." The village head's maidservant bowed politely to her employer's slightly daft son, whose mouth always hung open, and took his cloth traveling bag.

Okino looked carefully at each of the arriving passengers as they came out of the ticket gate, but her son was not among them. He was definitely supposed to return with all the other boys after taking the test. They had left the village on different days, but all were headed for the same school. Worried that he might have traveled past his station, she remained standing and gazing around the station grounds.

"I couldn't do two arithmetic problems. In language, I got a perfect score." Thus informing his mother in a childish voice, the soy brewer's son led the way down the prefectural road that runs to the village. The other passengers followed, each heading toward their own home.

"Tanimoto said he solved all the problems, . . ." she overheard the child saying. Tanimoto was Gensaku's family name. Okino wanted to run up and ask about her son. But remembering her husband Gensaku had gone to work for the brewer, she felt even more humble and gave up the idea.

No one remained at the station except the staff. Okino turned toward home disappointed. She thought of inquiring about her son from the clothier's child who was walking slowly in the rear. The boy was talking with his elder brother about something, perhaps the examination, and laughing. Okino thought she would approach and ask once their conversation ended. Her son was not the type to miss his stop absentmindedly, she thought, and yet . . .

She did not let her attention stray from the face of the boy who was eagerly talking while looking up at his brother. Taking advantage of a momentary pause in the conversation, she hastily drew near and asked about her son.

"Tanimoto said he'd stay on," the boy told her.

"The examination is over, isn't it?" she inquired very politely.

"Yes, the one he took with us is over. But Tanimoto said he'd take another one."

"Is that so? Thank you very much." Okino bowed. Having her face seen by the boy's elder brother made her feel strangely embarrassed.

A postcard from the cousin arrived the following afternoon. The son had most likely passed the prefectural middle school examination. But in order to take a private middle school entrance exam in case he had not, the cousin would have him stay on until they learned the result.

"If he doesn't pass, there's no need to make him take the private school exam," said Okino to Gensaku. "Besides, the higher-ups might frown at a poor family like ours sending a child to the town school and raise our taxes, and we'd be in trouble."

Gensaku was silent. He too was rather reluctant to send his son to a private school.

5

A tax collection notice arrived from the village office, but since the twenty-eighth happened to be a Sunday, Gensaku withdrew his savings from the bank on the twenty-ninth and took them to the office. Most of the villagers seemed to have paid a day or two earlier; no one else was going there. The treasurer read out the amount and two clerks attacked their abacuses. Gensaku was waiting for the calculations to finish.

Suddenly a hoarse and thick voice forcefully rang out.

"Hey, Gensaku!"

The voice was familiar. It was Ogawa, a village assembly member, who had come up and taken a seat next to the assistant village master.

"Yes," replied Gensaku upon noticing Ogawa. Ogawa was a man who delighted in utilizing his influential position within the village to harass the poor and those he disliked. When Gensaku had applied for a loan from the mutual financing association and pledged a half-acre field as a guarantee of repayment, he had been stiffly rejected by Ogawa on the pretext of insufficient security. Ever since, he had feared Ogawa.

"Gensaku, come here a moment."

Gensaku nervously approached.

"Gensaku, I hear you've recently sent a son to middle school," the corpulent, steely-eyed assembly member said in a burly voice.

"Yes, I did."

"I won't press you not to do it, but I'll tell you that it isn't good for workers to send their sons to middle school. When people go to middle school and such, they just get impertinent, lazy, and argumentative, making it all the worse for the village. At any rate, people who don't work, who loaf around and argue about everything, are the worst. What's more, you yourself haven't got enough land in this village even for a single household. You're not even paying a respectable man's worth of tax. Rather than sending your kid to school and making him impudent, it's more important for you to pay a decent man's share of tax. That way you'll be doing something for your country." Ogawa said it at a measured pace, clipping his words, and directing a piercing gaze at Gensaku.

Gensaku's lips trembled. He tried to say something. But what Ogawa had told him made it seem as though his long-held conviction that no one had the right to interfere with his sending his son to school with his own money was utterly indefensible.

"You've brought the tax money?"

"Yes, I have . . ."

"Right. It's outrageous for someone like yourself who doesn't pay his tax by the due date to be sending his son to middle school. Sending a child to school and such is something that's done only after properly and decently fulfilling one's duty both to one's country and to one's village. . . . Well, do as you like. But I'll have you know that from this year on you'll be paying the full household rate."

Ogawa fixed his stern look on Gensaku for a moment longer, and then, as if angry, abruptly turned away toward the assistant village master. The treasurer and the clerks had stopped fingering the abacuses and were looking at him. Gensaku felt numb.

After paying the tax, Gensaku left the village office and went dejectedly home.

"Do you have a headache today?" asked Okino during lunch, seeing his gloomy and strained expression. He made no reply.

When they had finished lunch and gone to the field, Okino said to Gensaku, "There's talk all over the village about poor folks like us sending our child to a town school. We should never have done it."

Gensaku was thinking of something.

"If he doesn't pass the prefectural test, don't send him to the private school. We'd better call him back soon."

"Mm."

"We forgot our place. So even if he does pass, we'd be better off not sending him . . ." said Okino to herself.

After a while Gensaku said, "In that case, shall we call him back?"

"We'd better," Okino promptly agreed.

Gensaku left off working in the field and went to the post office to send a telegram: *"Father sick return soon."* On his way back he felt relieved as though he had laid down a heavy burden.

His son, startled, came rushing home by the eleven o'clock night train. Three days later a notice arrived from the prefectural middle school informing the boy that he had passed the entrance examination, but the parents did not enroll him. The son is now serving as a brewer's apprentice.

MARCH 1923

A Herd of Pigs

1

The sow was walking slowly and breathlessly, dragging her red tender belly over the dirty floorboards. As if exhausted by eating, having walked a while she climbed onto the bedding of short barley straw and lay down. Her belly was heavily swollen. From time to time piglets could be made out moving about inside it. There seemed to be very many of them. Leaning on the fence and watching them steadily, Kenji was wondering whether it would be all right to release her into the fields. If she fell into a ditch, her belly might get ripped on the stone edge. That would cause difficulties for the family. . . .

It was not clear whether it would take another year or two to resolve their financial problems, but anyway until that time they would have to make a living from pigs. Pigs were nothing to laugh at. The sale of a two-hundred-and-sixty-pound pig to the butcher enabled a family to feed itself for a month.

For about the past six months Kenji, with the help of his father, had been devoting all his energies to raising pigs. He spent all his days taking the cart to go buy the feed, cleaning the pigpen, and trying to increase the number of offspring at breeding season. As a consequence, his very body grew saturated with the smell of pigs. No matter how hard he scrubbed at the bath, he could not expunge the strange stench from his skin.

Originally they had had a small pigpen with only a few pigs, and Mother had been taking care of them by herself. Father had mainly been working in the fields. Kenji had been traveling to work at a soy brewery some seven miles away. But because of the high farm rent, fields were left uncultivated following last autumn's harvest and were overgrown with weeds. In the valley, blackened stumps remained where the rice had been cut. Almost none of the village land was being tilled. Tenant farmers had all transformed themselves into pig farmers.

Only those who owned their own fields had sown them with barley. The plants were now some three feet tall and heavy with grain. In the expanse of arable land grown hard and wild that stretched from the valley to the hills, those small barley fields stood out freshly green and seemed proud of their success.

2

With the piglets due any day now, would she be all right if he released her into the fields or would it brutally kill her? Kenji watched the sluggishly moving sow and worried. At any rate, would the present plan work? For if it failed, there would be trouble. . . .

Father came up the hill carrying a swill bucket. "I hear from Uhei that Uichi's at a neighbor's pen now, saying he won't let his pigs out so they don't get mixed up with the others," he said.

Kenji looked at his aged, withered father. The bucket of swill seemed heavy.

"Uichi seems to be going around telling everybody not to release them," said Father, lowering the bucket and pausing to catch his breath.

"What! . . . He's double-crossing us, the bastard!" Kenji burst out in disgust.

"Even if we do release them, those to be taken will most likely be taken." Father did not seem to bear much animosity toward Uichi. If anything, he too appeared to think it better not to release the pigs.

"Do many people seem to be listening to him?"

"Well, quite a few. After all, if their own fat pigs get mixed up with other folks' scrawny ones, they'll lose out."

"If they get greedy like that, it'll all come to nothing. . . . In that case, it would've been better not to have gone on strike at all," Kenji muttered angrily.

After a pause, gazing at him with bleary eyes, Father asked: "Are you planning to let her loose too in that condition?"

"Yes."

"If she falls into a pond or a ditch, you'll kill both her and the piglets after all that work. . . ."

"If that happens, I'll put up with it," Kenji said, as much to himself as to his father.

Father sighed. The two unfastened the fence gate, took out the shit-stained straw, and were replacing it with a fresh layer when the grinning and habitually fawning Uichi arrived. Taking pleasure in the fresh straw, the pigs romped about stamping against the floorboards.

"Are you ready to let them go?" Kenji asked looking at the arrival.

"Ah," Uichi vaguely replied.

"If any fences are still up when the time comes, it'll be disastrous. We're quite ready," Kenji said with deliberate exaggeration. By observing the other's reaction, he hoped to learn his intent.

Uichi was avoiding Kenji's gaze. After a while, he looked up at Kenji with oddly gloomy eyes and half muttered, "If we go against the master, it'll only do us harm."

Now that the market price was high, the landlord was trying to seize the pigs, the farmers' only means of livelihood, instead of the farm rent. In response the farmers planned to release the pigs into the fields when the officials came to impound them, making it impossible to identify the owners. They decided to do so at a meeting. At the time, no one opposed the plan. Afterward, however, two or three switched sides for reasons of private profit or personal ties to the landlord.

Uichi's family had its own field growing tall with ripe barley. They also owned about twenty stout pigs of good stock. He worried that if he released the pigs, his own field would be trampled. He also begrudged exchanging his own good pigs for the others' inferior breeds. Moreover, having accumulated a sum of money, he was lending it to a number of villagers at fifteen percent interest. He was different from the tenant farmers who might be unable to pay the farm rent even if coerced. But since his entire family was greedy, Uichi had until the previous year been going to work at the soy brewery in town, along with Kenji and others, in order to accumulate still more money.

The tenant farmers of the village could not make a living by farming alone. Leaving the fields for the old men and the women to till, the young people mostly went to work in town. Kenji was one of them. For three years or so he had been going to town to work while his father, younger sister, and the rest of the family remained at home depending on the money he brought back. The soy brewer also held most of the land in the village. And in town, he was Kenji's employer.

It had happened at the end of last year. Kenji had drawn the heated soy sauce into a pail and was carrying it to the storage tank when an office boy came to summon him. Wiping the sauce from his arms with an apron, he walked to the office and was abruptly told by the chief brewer that the master no longer required his services. Something seemed to be the matter.

"What happened?"

"Go home and you'll soon find out, I guess. . . ." The chief brewer smiled good-naturedly. "The master's angry and says there's no need to explain, but I hear the trouble has to do with the rent."

"In what way?" Kenji thrust his face forward. Because the year's harvest had been poor, the tenants were trying to get their rent reduced. He knew the subject had come up soon after the crops were gathered. It had caused considerable trouble. But he did not yet know the outcome.

The chief brewer's tone of voice was rather mild. He said, "It seems the master does intend to pay the wages after that affair is settled, so you might as well go home and take it easy until then."

"That's no good. We have to get paid!"

It was already the twenty-fifth of the month. Since money is needed at year's end, he had been working nearly every day in December. In addition, he had not even been paid half the previous month's wages. To throw him out now without paying a penny was utterly unscrupulous. Kenji argued with the chief brewer a while, but failing to dissuade him withdrew in the end to the men's dormitory. There, gathering up his clothing and a few scattered articles, he stuffed them into a cloth bag and prepared to leave.

"Hey, you been fired too?" Uichi walked in wiping his hands.

"Yeah. . . . You too?"

"What a mess. And without even getting paid. . . . I wonder whose idea it was to strike." Instead of hating the employer, Uichi resented his striking comrades.

"If I'd known he'd pull a dirty trick like this, I'd have been ready for it. . . ." Kenji was vexed by his own carelessness.

A little later, two or three more men from the village walked in looking puzzled and foolish. "Hey, everybody, are you thinking of just pulling out like this? That's ridiculous!" exclaimed Tomekichi whose wife and child lived in the village. "Let's all together pay the boss a visit. We won't let him get away with this underhanded blow!"

Venting their spleen, they flung their clogs against lockers and smashed the frames of the sliding partitions with their rough hands. A fifteen-year-old boy named Keikichi, who had only started working that autumn, was rubbing his eyes and sniffling in a corner of the room. His mother, a widow, was waiting alone in the village for her son.

"Who had the crazy idea to start the strike? All the rent that's due to be taken will be taken anyway," Uichi grumbled. "This way everyone's just wasting his time. It's much better to stay quiet and don't make trouble." Since he had no immediate need to send his earnings to his family, he simply lent them to the soy brewer and collected interest. If the situation turned ugly, he might not be able to get the money back. Uichi fretted about that too.

Kenji, who knew this, felt all the more disgusted. Suddenly, familiar voices rang out beyond the soot-stained lattice window. "Hey, everybody, how's everything?"

"Damn, you been fired too?" Tomekichi, standing by the window, peered through a rip in the paper screen and shouted in surprise. Six or seven men from the same village who worked for a different soy brewer were standing there, cloth bags over their shoulders. They had been thrown out in the same way, without getting paid.

3

A grove flanks the village shrine that directly overlooks the highway from town. One morning, two youths who had been keeping watch concealed in the grove came back running and out of breath.

"They're coming! Watch out!"

A short time later, three uniformed bailiffs conversing with each other walked into the village. They had come to seal the pigpens to prevent the farmers from letting the pigs out of the enclosures and trading them at will. As soon as the youths came back to warn them, the farmers had agreed to release the pigs into the fields all at once.

Kenji hurriedly opened the fence and drove ten or so pigs out of the pen. Some, afraid of going out, cowered by the corner of the fence. These he lashed with a whip. Thereupon the stolid animals resembling cement barrels grunted thunderously and rushed out knocking over the water buckets. The big-bellied sow, twitching her snout at the grunts of her fellows, got up and lumbered over to the exit. With the fence open, she sluggishly stepped out, dragging her big belly along the ground and uttering deep grunts of her own.

Tomekichi, surveying the valley from the top of a cliff in the back, called out to Kenji in the pen: "Hey, no one's letting them out. That Uichi really let us down! Not even twenty are out yet. . . ."

"Damn it!" Kenji hastened to get his own pigs out.

"Neither Sahei or Genroku or Kanbei's letting them out. . . . Come out and look!" Tomekichi continued to relay the bad news. "This won't do us any good!"

A project of this sort cannot succeed unless, at the very least, everyone carries it out at once. If only a few take part, it will be all the worse for them. And yet half the villagers did not seem to be letting the pigs out.

Kenji hurried out for a look. A mere handful of pigs was romping about over the hills and valley, kicking up dirt and weeds in delight at having been suddenly released into the open fields.

"This is bad!"

"Uichi betrayed us!" Tomekichi was grinding his teeth. "That worthless son of a bitch!"

There was no time to lose. The bailiffs were just about to enter the first pigpen. Beside themselves, Kenji and Tomekichi sprinted down a narrow path toward a jumble of houses at the bottom of the hill.

One of the three bailiffs was a thin old man who walked with difficulty. The other two were men with splendid mustaches, explosive tempers, and a tendency to swagger. At the first pen they entered, the pigs were still within the enclosure. The men broke off their conversation for a moment and averted their noses from the foul stench of the pigpen.

Startled by their footsteps, the pigs, which until then had been listlessly lying on the dirty floorboards, suddenly sprang up. And then, kicking wildly against the floorboards, they rushed up to the fence. Shoved by the tips of the pigs' snouts, the fence toppled over with a clatter as though crumbling. Doubly surprised by the noise of the collapsing fence, the pigs jumped up even more violently. And as they did so, they bounded over the fence and out. The three men dressed in valuable suits recoiled from the shit-stained pigs and fell back two or three steps. Taking advantage of the passage thus offered, the pigs burst out into the field.

As one pig commenced to hop and squeal, so the pigpen's entire population followed suit. Knocking down what was left of the fence, they dashed between the officials and into the open. Realizing at last that they must not let the pigs get away, the men with splendid mustaches waved their white hands and gave chase. Being pursued, the pigs fled even further.

"Pshaw! It can't be helped." Deciding it would be better to have the farmer round up the pigs, the men in suits smiled uncomfortably and moved on to the next pigpen. The second pen was completely empty, not a pig in sight. Nonchalantly they proceeded to the third. There some ten stalls were empty except for a reclining sow nursing her piglets. In that pen they spent about twenty minutes, applied the first seal, and stepped out. By this time, however, a herd of pigs was grunting and frolicking over the hills and valley, digging up the soil with tough snouts, and madly running about. Pigs appear dull-witted and seem likely to tumble into ponds and ditches. Yet even rushing around at random as they were, they no sooner approached the edge of a cliff than they stepped back and withdrew to safety.

Eyes wide open with astonishment, the three stared at the gamboling herd of pigs. But after a moment the necks of the able-bodied two flushed red in anger. Their arms began to twitch. They had fathomed the reason why the pigs were running loose over the fields.

Some thirty minutes later, the two had removed their jackets and, in their shirtsleeves, sticks gripped in hand, plunged into the herd of pigs. They were cursing heartily. Struck on the rump, the pigs squealed and trotted around the field like mad.

At first the two seemed to be trying to drive the pigs back to the pens. But when approached by men with sticks, even the meekly grazing pigs suddenly tossed their heads awkwardly and commenced to leap about. Forgetting that their precious trousers and shirts were getting stained with sweat and dirt, the two grew enraged and blindly began to swing at the pigs.

Contrary to the men's efforts to drive them back, the pigs, grunting and squealing, surged away from the pens and toward the distant fields like savage beasts on the trot. Far off, in the vicinity of a barley field, someone was waving a stick and driving away the approaching pigs.

"Shoo! Hey! Don't you trample my barley!" That was Uichi, defending his field.

"Shoo! Hey! Get away!"

Since none of the pigs were his, he thrashed with all his might any pig that drew near. Hammered by his heavy blows, the pigs turned back toward the dress shirts.

In spite of the turncoats, the number of pigs released was tremendous. Within a short while, the two shirts grew dead tired, flung away their sticks, and hung their heads. . . .

"Look, here comes Grandpa!" Back on the hilltop at last and resting among the weeds, Tomekichi had spotted the old bailiff.

"Which one? Where?" Kenji asked, having been watching the valley.

"Down there, look," Tomekichi pointed to the side of a pen.

The thin old man, skeletal and with fierce eyes, a bowler hat hitched to the back of his head and a bamboo stick gripped in hand, had arrived at the foot of the cliff. "Hey, move!" Discovering the big-bellied sow sprawled on her side, he stiffly prodded her rump with the stick.

"Ooh," moaned the pig and made not the least attempt to rise.

"Hey, move!"

"Ooh, ooh." The sow remained resolutely recumbent.

"Hey, move!" Again the old man plied the stick. Concealed in the grass, Kenji and Tomekichi were chuckling with delight.

At the end of the day, having sealed only two or three pens that had been firmly bolted from the outset, the three officials headed back utterly exhausted. They were in no mood to notice that those pens belonged to the turncoats who had given in to them. Convinced they were obstructive farmers like the rest, they treated them with deliberate severity.

4

One day about two weeks later, as Kenji was climbing the uphill path carrying a bucket of feed, some twenty pigs from Uichi's pen that had received the official seal began all at once to grunt and clamor loudly at the sound of his footsteps. The grunting was that of hungry and thirsty animals demanding to be fed.

Putting down the bucket and stepping into the pen, he saw the traitor's pigs stumbling about with restless eyes, emaciated, and blackened with shit. Thinking they would be taken by the landlord anyway, Uichi had stopped feeding and taking care of them. The pigs were desperately propping their forelegs against the fence, stretching toward Kenji, pleading frantically for food. Their cries echoed to the village two or three hundred yards away, assaulting people's ears. . . . For another week or so those neglected pigs continued to cry night and day, but in the end they began to succumb one by one. The pigs that had been freed to romp in the fields are now feeding tranquilly in the pens.

What happened to the ringleaders? Well, although they defied the officials, in the end nothing was done to them. Their action was thoroughly worth it.

OCTOBER 1926

The Sugar Thief

YOSUKE'S WIFE was having a baby. The couple had two children, the elder a girl of five. The coming child would be their third. One day Yosuke slipped into the sugar storehouse and scooped out some granulated sugar into a canvas apron, but the master saw it.

The master had just passed through the gate of the soy sauce brewery. The sugar storehouse was just beyond the gate to the right. It was guarded by a sturdy lattice door. The master was frugal and demanding. He scolded the workers severely if they so much as swept away or burned a single bag or a few feet of rope. Such being his nature, he kept a close eye on every little twig whenever he set foot in the workshop. He seemed to possess a special talent enabling him to see in minutest detail.

Pretending not to notice Yosuke, he returned to the mansion and summoned his chief brewer. The chief listened to the master's words respectfully with bowed head and downcast eyes.

"How much does Yosuke owe?" asked the master.

"Sir," the chief brewer bowed again. "For all of this month, I believe."

The master's face grew troubled for a time. "Fire him as of today!"

"Sir . . . if we do . . . what shall we do about what he owes?"

"Make him pay it."

"But he doesn't have a penny, sir."

"Doesn't he, the useless bastard! Well, even if I lose twenty yen or so, it's better than employing a thief. Throw him out right now!"

"Yes, sir." The chief brewer bowed once more.

After the chief brewer left, the master recalled that as he made the workers save five percent of their monthly wages, the money he was keeping for them included nearly forty yen belonging to Yosuke.

On returning to the workshop, the chief brewer called Yosuke to the office and, sliding the paper-screen door shut, told him in a low voice that could not be heard outside what the master had said.

Thinking there was enough sugar to sprinkle on the New Year's rice cakes, Yosuke had hidden it among the piled up bags of wheat and was just about to take a short rest. He was sure he had not been found out. Yet he grew uneasy, for his being summoned seemed to be connected with what he had done. He looked worried. He had been born into a farming family but in recent years could no longer make a living as a farmer. Formerly he had been tenanting a farm of nearly two and a half acres, but he had stopped and returned the rice field to the landlord. Now his wife was growing vegetables and barley alone on a half-acre plot inherited from his parents.

"If I'm fired it will be terrible, what with another child and my wife lying in." He was downcast and imploring.

"Your third already?" The chief brewer's tone was bantering.

"Yes."

"When was it born?"

"Confinement's just ending today."

"Hmm."

"We need money for childbirth expenses, and now if I'm thrown out of work without a penny it will be awful. New Year's coming, too. . . . Won't you please ask the master once more to reconsider?"

Reluctantly the chief brewer went to see the master. The master's decision was the same as before.

"Well, it's no use," said the chief brewer upon his return. "On the other hand, I got him to write off the twenty yen you owe him," continued the chief, pretending to have gone to considerable trouble on Yosuke's behalf.

Yosuke's face grew even more bereft of hope.

"You know what you've done!" the chief brewer said rudely.

Yosuke's heart gave a sudden start. After a while he said, "Eh, if I stop working I can get the monthly savings back, can't I?"

"Well, I don't know."

"I'm sorry, but could you please talk to him and ask to have it back?"

"Wait a minute!" Once again the chief brewer started off for the main house. This time, however, he was slow to return. Cold wind blew sand through the rips in the paper-screen door. It was a harsh west wind. The feeble sunlight falling on the iron-latticed southern window reminded him of the approaching winter solstice. He wondered what would become of the glutinous rice needed for the New Year.

"It's not going well." Back at last, the chief brewer spoke sympathetically.

"Oh."

"The savings agreement's like this." The chief brewer thrust before Yosuke a mimeographed copy of the bankbook kept by the master. According to the agreement, the principal and interest would be returned upon discharge or retirement—or in situations of special need occasioned by unexpected adversity—to the workers who had wholeheartedly worked for the master. But there was a clause stipulating that the money would not be returned when a worker was dismissed due to dishonest or disorderly conduct. Masters everywhere tend to draw up such self-serving contracts. Yosuke had never heard anything about it. Looking utterly lost, he went on standing before the chief brewer.

"It's too bad, but there's nothing to be done," said the chief brewer, waiting for him to go.

"But I never knew anything about that at all. Can't something be done?" He kept repeating the same words over and over.

The chief brewer had already seen five or six workers leave in this manner, deprived of two or three years' savings because of a minor infraction. And he felt rather foolish as it occurred to him that he too, with thirteen years of continuous service, might in time come to the same end. In the present situation, however, he knew that it was his role, as the one the master relied on, to drive Yosuke away. Consequently he paid no attention to Yosuke's pleas.

Yosuke thought of his wife sleeping with the baby in her arms. The second child who had finally started to walk was not yet able to wear sandals, so he needed to buy him some shoes and socks to keep him from getting chilled by going barefoot. He had been thinking about that for a full month. Getting fired without receiving a penny left him completely helpless.

He had stolen sugar and soy sauce two or three times before. "This would cost thirty or fifty sen if you had to buy it, so it'll be a big help," Yosuke's wife had said to him with delight. Sugar and soy sauce were not goods that could possibly be made at home.

The two children, having been given a small amount of sugar two or three times, had gotten to like its taste and expected to receive something from Yosuke when he returned from working in the soy sauce storehouse. Catching the sound of his footsteps, the two shouted "Pop!" and, holding out both hands, immediately ran up to the doorway.

"Pop, sweet." The little boy, tottering over with uncertain steps, clung to Yosuke's knees.

"Look, look! Here you are!" As he wrapped the tiny quantities of sugar in pieces of newspaper and gave them out, the girl and her little brother jumped around the room with joy.

"Setsu, you mustn't tell anyone that you got sugar from Pop!" The wife glanced sternly at the little girl who was hopping about.

"All right."

"Kei, come to Pop." Stepping into the room, Yosuke would pick up the little boy and set him on his lap. Seated there, Keiichi would unwrap the paper and, sticking out his little tongue, lap up the granulated sugar.

The children liked sugar the best. Once the wrapped contents were gone, they asked their father for more. But the mother did not let them eat to their hearts' content. Coming up from the side, she nimbly snatched away the sugar package from her husband. "This is enough." She put just a little onto the pieces of newspaper the children had spread out expectantly. "The rest you'll eat with the dumplings I'll make when we celebrate the end of winter."

The children hoped for something every day. When there was nothing, they looked disappointed and complained.

"Well, well, here's something good." One time Yosuke stuck a hand in his pocket and, stirring the children's expectations, was slow to pull out the important object.

"What, Pop?"

"Something good."

"What? . . . Give it quickly please!"

"Something very, very pretty." He pulled out one of the labels that is pasted on barrels of soy sauce. It was a showy lithograph colored red, blue, black, and gold. "Pretty, isn't it?" Seeing the children looking forlorn with the inedible piece of paper in their hands, Yosuke tried to cheer them up.

"This paper's no good!"

"Look! See how pretty it is? . . . Over here's the sun coming up, and a crane is standing in the river." He explained the picture.

"Which is the crane?"

"This. A crane is a bird with a long neck."

The children gazed at the crane with interest. "What's a real crane like?"

"Just like this, only bigger."

"Where does it live?"

"There are some at the Konpira Shrine. When you children get bigger, I'll take you to the Konpira Shrine to see them."

"Yes, take us."

"We're happy, happy, Pop will take us to Konpira and we'll see cranes. We'll see cranes." Setsu bounced around over the straw mats, then playfully ran up to her mother. Yosuke looked on with a big smile.

"Stop that, calm down." Still pregnant at the time, the wife seemed listless and annoyed.

After some time, the master came to the brewery to see whether or not Yosuke had left. Seeing the master, Yosuke implored him for the return of his savings.

Without changing his expression, the master said gravely, "Surely you remember why you've been fired."

Yosuke's legs trembled painfully.

"Well, then," the master said, putting an end to the matter. "I would prefer to have you leave without an investigation. But if you object, I'll turn you over to the police right now."

Yosuke suddenly grew alarmed. "No, never mind the savings. Just pardon me and don't tell the police anything!"

"No, there will be no pardon!"

"No, please. Just pardon me and don't tell the police anything!" Yosuke bowed deeply.

In the end he went back empty-handed, conscious of having had a narrow escape. Two or three days later, as young workers were transshipping the bags of wheat, a canvas apron containing granulated sugar emerged from among the bags. Laughing they divided up the sugar and licked it up. The chief brewer shared in the treat.

The dirty canvas apron remained flung away in an empty barrel for about a week, but presently the chief brewer had an old woman who worked in the kitchen wash it for him and made it his own.

DECEMBER 1923

Their Lives

I HEARD THE STORY from an elder cousin just the other day, after returning to the village of my birth. The story's protagonist Shinzō is distantly related to my cousin and lived in a village some seven miles away, but I vaguely remember his face. We are not blood relatives. There have long been many soy sauce breweries in that village; at present the place looks almost like a factory town and no longer like a farming village. It seems the house and field Shinzō inherited from his ancestors have been demolished without a trace and replaced with soy storehouses. Be that as it may, let us get on with the story.

It was about eleven o'clock in the evening. Carrying a lantern, Shinzō entered the fermentation building to check whether the malt cultured in the daytime was ready. It was winter, and a large brazier burning a half bag of charcoal was heating the room. After a certain time, the fermenting malt would grow hot and rise up with yeast. Burning the charcoal aided the heating process. Because the windows and the door were tightly shut and all gaps sealed to keep out the draft, the glowing charcoal consumed the oxygen and the carbon dioxide accumulated stiflingly within the building.

It was just then that he walked in. He thrust his hand into the malt spread out on the straw mats and felt it. If the mixture of soybeans and finely crushed wheat was hard and parched, the malt was not well done. If it was soft and uniformly warm, that was good. A single building contained some one hundred eighty to two hundred shelves covered with malt spread over mats. He walked around among the shelves, thrusting his hand into the malt here and there to check its condition. After a while, he began feeling lightheaded and unwell. Alarmed he ran toward the door. But on reaching it, he collapsed. The lantern he was carrying flew forward, blazed up where it fell, and began to burn brightly. He realized this. He knew he had to get up and put out the fire. But he lacked the strength to rise. In front of him, the red flames burned on.

Yet he no longer cared. He had lost consciousness.

His father too had once walked into a fermentation building and passed out. Shinzō was fifteen then and had just begun to work at the soy brewery, drawing half of an adult's wages. Father was chief brewer and the master's faithful employee. For twenty-three years he had worked for the master keeping careful watch over the entire brewery. After midnight, Father pulled himself out of bed and, shivering with cold, went out to check the malt.

It was warm inside the shed. Father, grown sensitive to cold as he aged, stepped in hoping to warm himself. And he never came out.

At that time Shinzō, along with two or three companions his age, was enjoying a night out at a girl's place in a neighboring village. They were chatting away, sipping tea, and gazing at the girl's face: entertaining themselves in the manner of all village youths. Thus they passed the time every night, from twelve until one or two in the morning. Shinzō had not told his family where he was going. Hence it was quite a while after his father collapsed that his younger brother came to summon him.

He snatched away the brother's lantern and ran back alone ahead of him, but his father had already been carried out and lay in front of the office lifeless. His mother, her hair in disarray and face flowing with tears, was frantically calling the father's name, but Father remained rigid and utterly still.

He vividly recalled that time as he was losing consciousness. Often he had been frightened by the thought that what had happened to his father would, for good or ill, be repeated by the son and repeated yet again by the grandsons. And for him, in the end, this seemed to be coming true.

He was forty-seven. His father had died at the age of fifty. Grandfather had died at forty-four. Grandfather too had worked at the brewery. And he had died while at work for the brewery. The extraction vat rod had flown out, and he was struck down by the overhead weight. Grandfather's death had been the most miserable. Flattened from hip to thigh by a two-hundred-fifty-pound stone falling from a height of six feet, he died like a crushed crab.

Grandfather, Father, himself—three generations in a row losing their lives working for the brewery. It was because he had had a presentiment that it would eventually come to this that he had hated working at the brewery. And indeed it was turning out just as he had feared.

That both his father and grandfather had worked at the brewery was not itself a reason for him to work there. He was free to engage in a safe job, no matter how poorly paid. Yet it was impossible to exist without food every day. That being so, there was no choice but to do the same work one's father had done. As far as he could remember, nearly all the villagers, excepting two or three, had been doing the same work their parents had done. Somehow things were organized in such a way that they did so automatically and inevitably. He had the foreboding that if it continued like this, it would be impossible for his sons, his grandsons, and their own grandsons ever to become anything other than brewery workers. It was unbearable to think that perhaps the grandchildren too, like the grandfather and father, would lose their lives working at the brewery. One way or another, they had to escape such a life.

It happened quite some time ago. Shinzō was conscripted and enrolled in an infantry regiment. Applying to become a noncommissioned officer shortly after, he was made a lance corporal in the second year, assigned to a corporal. Nearly two years had passed and he was three months away from promotion to an NCO. He realized that he could not spend his entire life in the army. Eventually he would have to go back to "the provinces." Army life was crammed with activity utterly useless for "the provinces." Finding it difficult to speak to his officer about withdrawing his NCO application, he wrote to his uncle asking him to come to the regiment.

The uncle set out. He had always been convinced that being drafted as a soldier meant going to war and getting killed. Indeed, seven of the men his age who became soldiers all returned home as bones.

The uncle spent some time looking hard at his nephew in the visiting room. All of a sudden he asked accusingly, "Why did you apply to be an NCO without consulting anyone?"

Shinzō's eyes were blinking. "Because I didn't want to work at the brewery again! I thought I'd try to stay in the army a while."

"Work—that's something you've got to do pretty much anywhere."

"That's true, but . . ."

For about an hour Shinzō gazed at his uncle's rather pale and sickly face and asked about the work at the brewery, if any workers had been injured, and about the effect of dust on the lungs. Then he edged up to the uncle, smelled the odor of unrefined soy permeating the uncle's body, and sighed. Looking at his uncle, ravaged by working at the brewery, his resolve to withdraw the application seemed to weaken.

"What are you going to do?" the uncle demanded.

"Well, I'm not sure."

"I took off from work and paid boat fare to come!"

"Maybe I should think about it some more," he said as though to himself. "It's just that I hate cutting my life short like Father and Grandfather!"

"Well, whatever happens, I won't be responsible!" the uncle warned him. "If you go to war, you'll be killed like a puppy. You could all die, and the people high up won't give a damn about it."

The uncle stood up and turned to go. Looking reluctant to part, Shinzō accompanied him to the barracks gate. There he said, "Please, wait a while!"

"You'll quit after all?" the uncle said. "Good, you can work at the brewery, or be a farmer, or whatever."

"Yes."

On the third day he was relieved of his assignment to the corporal. After that he was assigned to one work detail after another. "He applies to be an NCO just to become a lance corporal, and then he quits." The company members viewed him with contempt.

Suddenly he seemed to lack the ability to function even as a lance corporal. He forgot sentry regulations. One night on maneuvers, he scorched the soles of his shoes at the bonfire and was severely reprimanded by the company commander. He had never before been so absent-minded. All at once he appeared apathetic. He bought books with titles like *Raising Tangerines, How to Grow Peppermint,* and *A Guide to Profitable Crops* and eagerly read them while on duty.

The story jumps forward to the time when he was about thirty.

He purchased a sailboat holding some twelve thousand gallons and began to make the runs. Having only worked at the brewery, he had hardly ever been aboard a boat before. Nonetheless, within just half a year he had learned to navigate the boat, to forecast the weather by the look of the sky, and to estimate the ebb and flow of the tide by consulting the lunar calendar. When tying up the boat in a storm, he would wind the rope around his waist and swim to land through high waves. He rejoiced in having been able to escape from the storehouse that reeked of unrefined soy. Hazards of the sea did not strike him as dangerous. Like an acrobat pleasurably crossing a perilous tightrope, he too felt nothing but pleasure.

But wherever one may go, mishaps are bound to occur. One rather calm evening as he was leaving Osaka, a merchant steamer cut ahead of him. He was gripping the helm and thinking the steamer would leave him sufficient space.

"Will she pass?" He called out to the boatman who was standing at the prow holding a lantern.

"Yes, she'll pass."

The steamship, like a black mountain, was steadily bearing down on them.

"Will she pass?"

"Yes, she'll pass."

But soon the boatman exclaimed, "Oh, she's too close! Too close! Turn away, turn away!" And then he frantically shouted toward the steamship, "Look out! Please! Look out!"

Hurriedly he spun the wheel trying to alter course. Yet the boat inexplicably continued to draw ever closer to the steamer. Later he realized that in confusion he had been turning the wheel in the wrong direction.

With a great thud, the stricken boat tilted violently as if about to capsize, and then creaked loudly as the bow facing north was thrust eastward. The steamship passed by like a charging bull without so much as a quiver.

"Hey! Wait, wait!" His face upturned, he yelled at the rushing mountain. There was no response whatsoever. The steamship proceeded serenely on its way.

He was all right. Though the badly damaged boat was taking on water, he managed to get it to a nearby island. The repairs cost a prohibitive sum of money. All the same, the boat was better than the brewery. He did not get rid of the boat.

The third year, he brought Osono with him. She was his mistress. He rented a room in the village for her. Although somewhat unrefined, she was a plump and pretty woman with a fresh aroma. He already had a wife. Although Okiyo knew he had brought a mistress, she not only remained outwardly unperturbed but even went to the woman's place taking some bean paste, vegetables, and two or three household utensils to give her.

When their men are away, sailors' women often take lovers. About seven months after Shinzō brought Osono, the village head began visiting her room. He was a dark-complexioned man whose face was still free of wrinkles though he already had a young grandchild. According to rumor, he was the richest or the second richest man in the village. Within two weeks,

Shinzō was aware of what was going on. He had grown extremely sensitive regarding Osono's conduct.

As he acknowledged later on, he knew even before he brought the woman that he could not be negligent with her. He had decided to bring her here thinking he might rest a little easier if she came to live in his own village. On the contrary, that made it worse. A woman follows the one who has money. Being stingy, the dark-complexioned old man did not hand out money easily. But he had mastered the skill of enticing a woman by displaying bundles of banknotes. Just as a cat rises up and stretches its paws to grab a handball suspended from the ceiling, the woman grew desperate desiring what was out of her reach.

He could no longer set out on his boat feeling free from anxiety. The fifth year, he sold the boat and stopped leaving the village. He did not wish to part from the woman, no matter what.

The old man too grew zealous about the woman. Through an intermediary, he inquired whether Shinzō might be willing to yield the woman to him. He brusquely refused. The intermediary came again. He gave it some thought. If the proposal were reasonable, he might consent. That was his reply. The intermediary tactfully sought to learn how much money he was demanding. Every last penny the old man had hidden away, he responded. "Those eyes alone are worth ten thousand yen!"

The next day came the old man's offer of two hundred yen. Shinzō demanded two thousand. After five or six days of confusion, the matter was finally settled by his taking one thousand yen from the old man and the intermediary receiving fifty yen. At that time, his wife was pregnant with their first son.

He reverted to being a brewery worker. Even though his wages were low, Okiyo was happier to have him working at the storehouse and smelling of soy rather than spending most of the year aboard a boat. She was a woman who enjoyed saving money little by little even if it meant eating the same sort of plain food that cows or pigs ate.

Shortly he decided to try starting his own brewery. The wife tried hard to talk him out of it. "If you do that, as soon as you make a little money you'll drag that woman in again."

"Don't talk nonsense. What makes you think I'm thinking about that?"

"I have no idea what you're thinking about!" She was hoping he would go on doing ordinary work. Sudden riches would bring nothing good. In the end, she thought, they would only lead to misery.

He paid no attention to her words. He strove to become the master of his own brewery. The premonition that so long as he worked on at the brewery he would come to the same end as his father and grandfather menaced him constantly. In fact, the brewhouse was unsanitary and damp and smelled of rotting vegetation. Breathing there made you feel that your lungs would rot.

It became increasingly clear to him that if he and his fellow workers continued to labor meekly at their allotted tasks in the customary way, they were ultimately bound to die working. Unless he somehow escaped from such a life, not only he but his children and grandchildren too would be forced to relive the same conditions. He could not bear to think about it. Relying on his own power, he had to extricate himself from this predicament whatever the cost.

He built a soy storehouse, installed the vats, hired people, stocked the cereals, and produced unrefined soy. He attempted to become a capitalist. But it did not go as expected. The time had already arrived when small, independent breweries were being swallowed by the large ones. He had not realized that. After about two years, he secretly withdrew his wife's savings and fled from the village. Both the storehouse he had built and the plot of land remained gloomily behind to be auctioned off.

The master for whom his grandfather and father had worked until their deaths, and for whom he too had worked, was a man who liked to donate money to the elementary school and the shrine. Once, when making a pilgrimage to the Honganji Temple in Kyoto, he had tossed a hundred-yen bill into the offertory box.

Whenever the villagers caught sight of his rugged face and heavy eyebrows, they promptly recalled his offering a hundred yen. A certain old woman wondered every time she met him whether he might toss her, not a hundred-yen bill, but one or two yen. The old woman earned small amounts of money doing errands for people and drank. On meeting the master, her wrinkled face broke into a smile and for some reason she bowed. The master smiled too, knowing somehow that she was about to address him.

"It's a cold day, Master. . . . If, thanks to your kindness, I were to enjoy a warm cup . . ." hinted the old woman.

"Mm, mm," responded the master. But he only smiled and passed her by. That happened every time. Nevertheless, whenever the old woman saw him coming, she inexplicably felt that he was about to give her money and kept up her baseless hope.

This master bought Shinzō's storehouse. Shinzō's assets had consisted of the damaged sailboat, which had cost a prohibitive sum to repair, the hillside woods inherited from ancestors or perhaps purchased by Grandfather or someone, the tiny quarter-acre field where they grew barley and millet, the building lot carved out of a rice field, the money taken from the old man in exchange for Osono of the precious eyes, and five or six debt bonds. These items all formed the capital that Shinzō invested into building the storehouse, hiring the workers, and producing the soy. He had thrown his whole might into it.

Okiyo, being a good wife and an honest, hardworking woman, resigned herself to the loss of the storehouse and land. But to avoid inconveniencing others, she wanted to repay the debts Shinzō had left behind. With this in mind, she thought the storehouse ought to have fetched a higher price. Its value was considerable. Someone else was likely to buy the remaining property for a pittance. It would be good if the man who threw a hundred-yen bill at the Honganji Temple, which was nothing to him, were to come to the aid of a chief brewer whose family had served his for generations faithfully. That would only be proper.

When the master came to look over the storehouse he had bought, she took the opportunity to speak to him about it. The master was fully aware he had paid much less than the storehouse's actual value. He thought he might be asked to add a little more and was willing to comply. Hearing what Okiyo had to say, he exclaimed with surprise: "What? You're planning to repay everyone with interest?" This will not do, he thought. Being asked to buy the storehouse at such a high price will not do.

"That's absurd! That's absurd!" he kept repeating. "No one does anything so absurd. Pay fifty percent of the debt, and have the rest written off. Why, you don't have to say a thing. I'll work it out with the backers for you."

"Well, but is it right to do that?"

"Why, of course it's right. Leave it to me. I'll work it out for you."

"Well." Okiyo drew a heavy sigh. She was breathing hard. Her second child was due to be born in a month or so.

The master continued: "And I'll also see to it that you and the child have enough to eat. Shinzō will most likely be back before long."

"Well, thank you very much. I don't mind losing the storehouse, but I cannot help worrying about the debt and about the two children."

"Mm, mm. You're already anxious about the child in your belly." He extracted a bill from his pocket.

Shinzō had gone off in pursuit of Osono. The old man who had acquired Osono through purchase had been enamored of the woman and thoroughly addicted to her, but shortly, during the summer, he had contracted dysentery and died in the quarantine hospital.

The village head's son, displeased by his father's indulging of the woman, threw Osono out after the old man's death without a penny. Even the kimono the old man had bought for her was taken away. Yet for Shinzō, that was ideal.

Once the debts were settled, the master urged Shinzō to return home, thinking of employing him at the brewery, but he did not even reply.

Okiyo thought that the master would provide her with food and clothing. Still thinking so, she gave birth to the child. She sent her mother, who had come to care for her in childbirth, to tell him that a boy had been born.

Dragging her clogs, the elderly woman walked slowly to his place. The master's wife looked at the mother and retorted suspiciously, "Did she send you to tell him that?"

"Yes she did, madam."

"No, it can't be. Haven't you come to the wrong place?"

"Okiyo said to go tell the master."

Impassively the old lady took a seat on the veranda.

Okiyo thought that if she informed the master that the child was born, he would send her a small sum for the childbirth expenses. (He seemed likely to do that much if only to make up for having bought the storehouse so cheaply.) After ten days or so had gone by, she began to think that her mother might have made a mistake in conveying the message. And so she gave the mother a detailed account of what had happened, including the promise, and sent her over once more.

Again the master's wife came out. Hearing what the mother had to say, she replied: "Why, Granny, you've already grown senile!"

"Beg your pardon?" asked the mother loudly, unable to make out the words.

"It's as though she were deaf." The wife looked back at the maid in the living room and sniggered.

Around the time Okiyo had finally recovered sufficiently to be able to do light work, the maid came to tell her to start working at the storehouse.

The promise to provide for her had meant, in other words, to have her work at the brewery.

Strapping the baby to her back, she went to the storehouse and worked. She was assigned tasks like washing bags, tanning them, and washing the vats. Her three-year-old son played by his mother's side as she labored. Picking up a stick, he banged on an empty barrel as though it were a drum.

"Where did your dad go?" Young men came up to him and inquired with a laugh.

"He sailed away on a boat."

"Where did he go?"

"He sailed away on a boat," he repeated. "He went far away to make money."

Three years later, Shinzō came back. Okiyo, anemic from overwork and malnutrition, had grown pale, withered, and fleshless. Her hands, now large and rough, stained with scrubbing and tanning, hung at her sides.

In the three years she had not seen him, Shinzō seemed to have aged ten years. There was after all nothing for him to do but work at the brewery. He seemed resigned to being tied down. His former vigor and spirit that strove to liberate him from a fettered life had apparently vanished. Quietly he began to work for the master.

He was skilled at the work and possessed a kind of talent for it. He made good malt and flavorful soy sauce. The soy he produced was sold by the master to be served at the tables of ladies and gentlemen of fastidious taste. The money he earned was brought back to the smoky dwelling roofed with dilapidated thatch. There the pale wife was sharply scolding the children for peeling the potato skins too thickly. The small children poured tea over boiled barley and rice and, hardly even chewing, swallowed it with delight.

He had not yet lost hope, however. Every month the crumpled, brown banknotes were set aside for the children. Now he was working for the children's sake. He only wanted to liberate the children from this life in chains. His sole hope was linked to that. . . .

The concrete corridor of the fermentation building stretched far into the distance. Five similar buildings, each hardened with mortar, were adjacent to it. There were more on the opposite side. At the end of the concrete corridor was the processing area. In the daytime, cauldrons parching the wheat revolved there and rollers groaned. Large vats boiling the soybeans emitted steam like craters. They worked there coated with dust, their nostrils blackened. At night, however, the broad complex of the brewery was utterly, eerily silent. From time to time, far off in the extraction room, the pressing rods made a snapping noise like trees breaking deep in the mountains.

He had lost consciousness upon entering that corridor. There was a hush all around; everything was asleep. The wax collected at the bottom of the lantern blazed like a bonfire, brightening the surroundings.

Suddenly a woman's voice rang out from somewhere. "There's a fire! There's a fire! There's a fire!" It was a maid who was washing the next morning's barley in the kitchen.

Shinzō awoke abruptly to the clamor of young people gathered in front of the building. He had been saved.

He continued to work at the brewery. The fine sauce he made added zest to the meals eaten by ladies and gentlemen and lavishly pampered their stomachs. His own body, however, had begun to deteriorate. The back of his head often felt oddly numb. Prolonged work caused him pain and shortness of breath. Coming near the fermentation building made him so nauseated he thought he would vomit.

One time he threw open the windows to let a breeze into the building, but he grew faint all the same. He had lost his health. Yet the master demanded that he work and kept on making him produce the splendid sauce in order to maintain his brand's status as the customers' favorite. Shinzō had no choice but to work. For food, for the children, for his wife.

Nonetheless, a battered machine cannot keep working forever without repairs. The loose screws need to be tightened. Not even given time to rest, he lacked the strength to recover. His lungs had been afflicted. Even if only a single part of a machine has begun to give way, forcing it to keep running will cause the entire apparatus to break down. Less than two full years after he had lost consciousness, Shinzō died.

At the time of his death, his older son was attending technical school. By not eating enough, he had managed to save up a small amount for the boys' school expenses. Aware of his approaching death, he asked the master to take care of his children and wife. He wanted the children to graduate from school and find a way of escaping their present lives. The master consented. Thereupon, he closed his eyes.

My cousin's story contained additional episodes and went into greater detail, but I hope you will forgive me for not narrating all of it. I rather doubt that I could. At any rate, that is the gist of the story my cousin told. As the story drew close to its conclusion, my cousin's big round eyes began to glitter with passion.

Then he put a question to me: "Well, then, what do you think? After Shinzō died, how did the master take care of his wife and children?"

I did not have a reply.

"Because of his father's death, the boy who was at school returned home for a while. But after that, the master would not let him go back to the dormitory. His pretext was interesting. It was not for the poor to go to school. Even if they graduated, they only grew insolent, lazy, and worthless. You're to come and work at the brewery instead, he told him, and not waste your time playing around when you're already fourteen. It was also unprofitable to keep Shinzō's savings deposited at the bank, which paid low interest. Hand it over and he'd put it to good use. So the wife trustfully gave him the passbook. What foolishness! The money Shinzō had shortened his life to earn has no doubt been converted by the master into soybeans and wheat and is now shortening the lives of others.

"The child—well, the child is working quietly at the brewery. He's getting half an adult's wages. That isn't enough for food, so the wife is once again washing the vats with her big rough hands. Needless to say, she was never given a receipt for the money she had handed over.

"Even though Shinzō spent his entire life squirming and struggling to escape from his plight as a worker, in the end he could not escape. Like his father and grandfather, he too had his life cut short by his work. His sons might sooner or later end up the same way.

"But this isn't just about other people. It holds true for me also. And for our uncles and fathers as well! Their lives are our lives too, you see. If we go on acting as meekly as we do now, it will even happen to our children. They won't be able to escape either."

The cousin clamped his mouth shut and, with glittering eyes open wide, stared at the cracked wall before us as though there were something there.

FEBRUARY 1927

Siberia in the Snow

1

After seeing off their third-year unit, which was returning home, the two walked back from the station, stretched out on the barrack bunks, and for a time sighed and said nothing. No going home for them—they would have to bear it for another year.

The past year in Siberia had been unbelievably tedious and long. Their second year in the army they served a stint in the garrison hospital and then were sent to Siberia. Over a hundred soldiers boarded the steamship at Tsuruga with them. Upon their arrival, the fourth-year men already in Siberia were sent back along with some men in the third year.

Siberia was blanketed in snow as far as the eye could see. Workhorses pulled sleds across frozen rivers. To keep from slipping on the ice, soldiers wrapped woolen rags over their arctic boots. They ventured out into the fields only after donning fur hats and greatcoats. Crows with white beaks swarmed over the snow pecking intently at something.

When the snows vanished, there emerged an endlessly changeless, desolate steppe. Neighing and bellowing, herds of horses and cattle ambled over it. Before long the wayside grass was putting forth green shoots. The distant meadows, the nearby hills—everywhere shimmered the fresh grass. The utterly dreary fields turned emerald within a week. Grass was sprouting, trees stretching their branches, geese and ducks waddling to and fro. In the summer the two men were moved, as part of an infantry corps, close to the Russo-Chinese border. October saw a clash with the Red Army. An armored train helped the men pull back from the front line. Fog covered the entire plain and for about a week you could not see even fifty yards ahead.

They occupied a hilltop brick building that had been the Russian army barracks, cleaned it, subdivided the rooms with wooden partitions, installed

50

the operating tables, brought in the medical supplies, and nailed up a board in front saying Army Hospital.

In November it began to snow. That snow did not melt; it piled higher and higher with each subsequent snowfall. There were the paths that the coolies climbed carrying water from the valley spring to the hospital: the water they spilled froze, and since accidental spillage occurred daily, tall masses of ice hedged the paths and ran in lines like mountain chains.

The men kept the Manchurian stove lit and shut themselves up indoors. Both thought over the past year. Though they had personally seen wounded soldiers, men with severed legs and arms, and the dying, they had always kept thinking of home and waiting for the day when their replacements would come and they would be free to go.

The replacements came. It was precisely a year after they themselves had been dispatched here. The fourth-year men and most of the third were to be repatriated. But two men from the third year had to remain behind to instruct the new arrivals who had only just completed their basic training.

The army surgeon and the chief orderly talked it over. They wished to send back the ill-mannered and violent soldiers who were a nuisance to handle. The mild-mannered, hardworking Yoshida and Komura were made to stay on by order of the army surgeon.

2

No one wanted to stay long in Siberia.

There was a man named Yashima who sported a closely trimmed mustache and was fearless, murderous. It gave him positive joy to brandish a bayonet and skewer Russians with it, as he often did. Lacking human victims, Yashima liked to jab to death the cows and pigs that roamed the plain.

"See, you can't do any of this if you ship back home. There's no law here in Siberia, so I'm going to have all the fun I can."

He was in the habit of defying both the army surgeon and the chief orderly. Once he snatched up a handgun and chased after the army surgeon. The officer had demanded he carry out his duty as prescribed by the regulations and this had touched a raw nerve. Yashima aimed at the fleeing surgeon's backside and squeezed off a thunderous shot. The shot missed and punched a hole in the storm windows.

Everyone was convinced it was Yashima's intent to remain in Siberia. "Looking at it from the point of view of a nice long lifetime, what's it matter if you stay in Siberia a year or two longer? It's nothing to get worked up about." He spoke in such a carefree way in front of all.

And yet when the army surgeon and the chief orderly drew up the list of returnees, Yashima's name was at the top. Nothing but trouble could ensue from detaining a man prone to slashing a bayonet about and discharging a pistol.

A man named Fukuda had volunteered to come to Siberia. Fukuda had some knowledge of Russian and had enlisted with the intention of practicing in Siberia. He was a forward sort and once he engaged a Russian in conversation, he threw away whatever work he had been assigned and kept on talking for two or three hours. His wish was to go back to Japan after becoming fairly proficient in Russian. Nevertheless, Fukuda's name was on the roster of those to be repatriated.

And there were other cases. A man had left the hospital without leave and spent three days at a Russian's home. This was desertion from the barracks—punishable in wartime by death before a firing squad. The affair was hushed up, however, and the man escaped the penalty. Everyone, himself included, expected that instead he would be detained in Siberia until his fourth year. But this man's name too was clearly inscribed on the list of those going home.

Only the industrious, tractable Yoshida and Komura were left behind. The two had always exerted themselves thinking that as a reward for obedience and diligence they would be sent home early. Even when coming down with a cold or at times when they found their duties most irksome, they forced themselves to carry them out without a trace of negligence.

As a reward they won the privilege of an extra year's sojourn in Siberia for their country's sake. The two felt themselves victims of abominably foul play and in their fury no longer gave a damn about anything and found fault with everyone.

3

Yashima had said it while waiting for the train: "You guys turned out to be idiots. If you want to get sent back in a hurry, do like me. Who wouldn't want to keep on subordinates who act like little sheep? Even so, if you look at it from the viewpoint of a long lifetime, what's a year or two in Siberia or wherever? Well, anyway, take care."

Yoshida and Komura listened dejectedly. Already the soldiers spoke brightly of life after return to Japan. What were the girls they knew up to? Who would come out to meet them? They spoke of nothing but this, utterly forgetting the prostitutes so zealously frequented up until moments ago.

"I'm going to get me a wife posthaste as soon as I get home."

Even Fukuda who had volunteered for Siberia was in a rush to return. "Who needs to know Russian, anyway? If I inherit what my old man's got I won't starve. I've had it up to here with this Siberia where at any fine moment you can expect a partisan to pick you off."

Yoshida and Komura, cut off from their returning comrades, lingered like shadows in the corner of the waiting room. The two had never been particularly close. Komura was shy. And though he conscientiously did as he was told, he was not the type to do things on his own. Yoshida was outgoing. But because he was a good sort, he would invariably end up having to do himself the various things he had poked his nose into. When the two were together it was always Yoshida who made the decisions. He acted the adult. Although Komura did not say so, this grated on his nerves. But now both felt it was incumbent upon them to be friends. They were determined to put up with whatever irritated each about the other. In the coming year they had to help one another.

"Thanks for coming to see us off!"

As the train pulled in, the soldiers picked up knapsacks crammed with Siberian curiosities and, each struggling to be first, clambered aboard. They scrambled for seats, doffed the arctic hats, and pressed their faces against the windowpanes.

No platform had been erected alongside the tracks. The two men stood between rails looking up at the giant train. Beyond the glass the returning men were laughing, every one, and saying something. But as the two tried to laugh in reply, their cheeks twisted strangely and they looked about to cry. Not wanting such faces to be seen, they fell silent and looked grim.

The train began to move. Faces in the windows drew back at once. Try as they might, the two could not stop the flood of tears they had been holding back.

"Let's go back to the hospital," said Yoshida.

"Yeah." Komura's voice was tearful.

To put an end to this, Yoshida challenged: "I'll race you to that bridge."

"Yeah," replied Komura as usual.

"Right. One, two, three!"

Yoshida taking the lead, the two ran about a hundred yards, but before they were even halfway to the bridge they became dispirited and stopped. Dragging their legs they trudged back to the hospital. For five or six days they left all the work to the second-year soldiers and slept in the barracks like dead men.

4

"Hey, let's go rabbit hunting." It was Yoshida's idea.

"Whatever makes you think there are rabbits around here?" Komura was lying with the blanket drawn up to his nose.

"Sure there are. Look, you can see them hopping around over there." Yoshida pointed through the window. He had been lying on his belly looking past the storm windows at the distant hills.

The undulating hills stretched all the way to the mountains on the horizon. The grass, clumps of shrubbery, and piled stones dotting the hillsides were all covered with snow now, forming a white seamless surface. Rabbits would emerge running from places where there had been grass and vanish in the snow only to reappear after a few moments hopping about in a different spot. First you noticed the big ears. But unless you watched very carefully, their coloring rendered them indistinguishable from the snow.

"There he is!" exclaimed Yoshida in a low voice. "Jumping as full of life as can be."

"Where?" Komura rose sluggishly and joined him at the window. "Can't see a thing."

"Open your eyes. Look at him jump! See, he's running toward that heap of rocks. You can see the long ears, right?"

The two were tired of sleeping. Yet the idea of work seemed absurd and they could not bring themselves to take it seriously. Most likely their unit had already reached Tsuruga. Soon their term of duty would be up and they could go home. The two thought of nothing but this. They remembered their own night in Tsuruga prior to boarding the ship for Siberia. That port town glowed sweet and radiant in their memories! How many years had it been since they had last seen the sea? It felt as if they had been cooped up in Siberia more than three, no, more like five years. What made it so necessary to send troops to Siberia and have them suffer? The soldiers killed the Russians and in turn the Russians killed them. If only they hadn't shipped troops here to start with, the third-year men would not be trapped in a place like this. The two regretted their past sober and exemplary conduct. You had to be wild and irresponsible or you were lost. They were bent on spending the coming year doing just as they pleased. Such was their plan. Yoshida donned the arctic uniform, grabbed the loaded rifle, and flew out of the barracks.

"Hey, is it all right to use live ammunition for shooting rabbits?" Komura, putting on his own arctic gear, was doubtful.

"Do I care?" said Yoshida.

"I wonder if Oink will be mad?" By Oink Komura meant the chief orderly.

Rifles and ammunition had been distributed to the hospital, but it was forbidden to use them except in emergencies. In other words, only in the event of an enemy assault. Not caring, Yoshida went out. Komura, too, thinking that things would sort themselves out, grabbed a rifle and followed him.

Yoshida vaulted over the fence enclosing the hospital garden, walked twenty or thirty paces, stopped, and pulled the trigger. He had often gone deer hunting at home and was accustomed to firing a hunting gun. At target practice with infantry rifles they were told to relax and fire only after taking a deliberate aim, but a hunt allowed no time for this. It presented you with a target running for its life. A mere instant of aiming had to suffice. Used to firing right after raising the weapon, Yoshida was consistent in hitting the mark. No sooner did the shot ring out—identical to a shot heard in battle— than the rabbit described a five-foot arc through the air. A sure hit.

"Got him! Got him!"

Yoshida lowered the rifle, turned to wink at Komura, and ran forward. The rabbit lay like a small child, its entrails exposed, blood dyeing the snow crimson.

"Oh, I could do that! Wouldn't it be great if one more came along?" Komura exuded competitive spirit.

"There are plenty. I saw two or three."

The two climbed a hill, descended into a valley, and started up another hill. A clump of bushes grew in a hollow along the way. As the two approached, their boots crunching the snow, a long-eared creature dashed out from behind a root just ahead. Yoshida saw it first.

"Hey, let me! Hey!" Komura shoved his friend's leveled rifle aside.

"Sure you can do it?"

"I'm sure."

Komura was slower than Yoshida in taking aim. But the shot did not miss. The rabbit flew four or five yards through the air and lay still.

5

Taking care not to be seen, the two pilfered ammunition from the magazine. Secreting some ten cartridges each in their pockets they set out for the mountains daily. And every time they returned with their catch.

"At this rate, there won't be any rabbits left in Siberia," observed Yoshida. But the next day they would go out and again the sound of their boots would startle some rabbit into dropping its long ears and flying from its patch of grass. Once they saw their game, they never let it go.

"Where are you getting all this ammunition?" The chief orderly made an indirect attempt at stopping the excursions of this pair who had grown indifferent to work and addicted to hunting.

"We get it from the regiment," replied Yoshida.

"Partisans are around. Be careful you don't step in the wrong place."

"If any partisans come around, we're going to bag them like rabbits."

Winter had deepened. Hunting dispelled the two men's rancor and helped them cope with the boredom. Rabbit tracks gradually became fewer. Fresh snow obliterated the ravaging tracks of the men's boots, but hardly any new traces of rabbits were to be seen imprinted on it.

"Well, the Siberian rabbits are just about through," laughed the two. They began to go farther and farther afield each day, climbing far-off hills, crossing valleys, and slipping under the barbed wire perimeter put up by the regiment. The snow was deep, reaching up to their knees or as high as their hips. The two found it great fun and strode ahead kicking up vast quantities of white powder.

Their catch continued to dwindle. Often it took them half a day just to shoot a rabbit each. At such times the two would pause at a mountain summit on their way back, turn, and in frustration fire off all the remaining cartridges at random.

One day the two scraped under the barbed wire and went down into the valley. Leaving it behind they climbed up the mountain beyond. There was nothing but snow bathed in a pale, feeble sunlight as far as their eyes could see, and the only sound reaching their ears through the still air was that of their own boots crunching the snow. Both the town where the regiment was stationed and the hill where the hospital stood were cut off by mountains and could not be seen. After walking along the summit for a time they descended into the next valley. A bog spread before them, swollen high with ice. On the opposite side they could see two or three houses covered in snow.

The two had not shot a single rabbit yet. They had succeeded in rousing one from its lair, but both had missed. Though they pursued it and searched the area where it vanished, the rabbit did not show its ears again.

"Let's go back." Komura had stopped. He did not like the look of the unfamiliar houses.

"Without even one? Not me." Yoshida advanced steadily toward the marsh. Reluctantly Komura followed his friend.

It was a deep valley. A river that flowed into the marsh seemed frozen. Apparently it resumed its course at the far edge of the marsh and ran on down an incline. As they were walking down the slope, abruptly a large rabbit started up from under their feet. Instinctively the two aimed and fired. The rabbit somersaulted less than a dozen yards away.

Their bullets appeared to have hit almost simultaneously. The handsome animal had been devastated, its long-eared head lay torn from the body. Most likely the shots had struck the neck rather close to each other. The two rested briefly in front of the trophy whose blood streamed into the snow and froze. They were tired and thirsty.

"Let's go back," urged Komura.

"Let's go as far as that swamp."

"No, I'm going back."

"Why, it's right in front of us."

Yoshida took up the catch still dripping blood, and as he started to rise he glanced back at the hill they had just come down. "Ah!" he exclaimed with alarm.

At the summit where until a moment ago not a living being was visible amid the boundless snow, brown-bearded Russians in fur overcoats and rifles in hand stood watching them. These, without any doubt, were either outlaws or partisans.

Komura's legs seemed to grow paralyzed and he could not get up.

"Run for it," called Yoshida.

"Wait, just a second!" Komura's legs refused to budge.

"Nothing to be scared of. It's all right," said Yoshida. "If they come near I'll shoot them." But he himself panicked and broke into a run. Though they thought the slope facing them, being devoid of houses, offered an escape route, they were soon confronted by six or seven dwellings that had sat there hidden by snow. Clearly Russians lived in them.

The Russians on the hilltop spread out. Then they began to close in from the four directions. Yoshida grasped his rifle, aimed at the approaching men, and fired. Komura too gripped his rifle and raised it. But the two found it impossible to shoot easily or smile inwardly as when shooting rabbits. Even as they took aim, their fingers trembled and their weapons refused to perform as they wished. The fewer than ten cartridges they each had were soon spent. The two wielded their rifles like clubs and commenced to strike at the men crowding in on them, but their arms were presently seized by powerful individuals descended upon them from all sides and the rifles were wrenched away.

Young men smelling like gunnysacks pinned Yoshida to the ground so hard he could barely breathe. In a loud, spirited voice a brawny old man with an awful gleam in his large eyes issued what sounded like a command to the men who had overpowered the Japanese. The youths astride Yoshida spoke two or three words in reply. Yoshida was made to stand up.

The old man stepped up to the two, who were held so tightly by pairs of viselike hands that they could not so much as stir. Peering at them a long moment with eyes that seemed to demand they confess everything, he then asked something in Russian.

Neither Yoshida nor Komura knew Russian. But they could gather from the look in the old man's eyes and his gestures that he suspected them of having come to reconnoiter and wanted to learn such things as how many Japanese troops were quartered in town at present. The old man seemed genuinely alert to the possibility that, even as he spoke, the Japanese army might come pouring over the hilltop.

"*Neponimayu*," said Yoshida, using a word he had picked up. "I don't understand."

The old man fixed them with a hard, lengthy stare. A young man in a dark-blue hat then put in a word of his own.

"*Neponimayu*," repeated Yoshida. "*Neponimayu*." A note of entreaty had unwittingly crept into his voice.

The old man spoke to the youths. As a result the young men began to strip the two of their arctic gear, uniforms, undershirts, underpants, boots, and even socks. The two stood in the snow stark naked. It dawned on them they were about to be shot to death. Two or three youths were methodically searching the pockets of the confiscated uniforms. The others, carrying rifles, started to walk toward a spot a short distance away.

They are going to kill us, thought Yoshida. And suddenly a fragment of Russian he had once heard floated up to his lips. "Mercy! Mercy!" he cried out. But the word he remembered was incorrect. He was trying to shout "*Spasite*"—Mercy—but it came out "*Spasiba*"—Thank you.

There was no indication the Russians would heed the two men's pleas. The old man's eyes had grown indifferent to them. The two young men who had removed themselves to a slight distance lifted their rifles.

Yoshida had up to this instant been docilely standing in the snow, but now he darted forward. Komura too began to run in his wake.

"Mercy!"

"Mercy!"

"Mercy!"

Screaming the word, the two raced across the snow. But the Russians heard it as "Thank you! Thank you! Thank you!" Two rifle reports reverberated through the valley.

The old man, leaving it to the young ones to collect the rifles, uniforms, arctic gear, boots, and whatever else had been wrested from the Japanese, withdrew in the direction of the snow-buried houses.

"And don't you forget that headless rabbit, either!"

6

When on the third day they were located at last by the combined force of officers and men of two companies, it was seen the two were frozen looking precisely as when alive. The only visible injury was a small hole, no larger than the tip of a little finger, in the back of each man. Their faces, grown hard with the eyes still open, looked as if they were calling out to something.

"And didn't I warn them? If only they hadn't gone rabbit hunting, it wouldn't have come to this!"

The chief orderly stood before the two bodies surrounded by a multitude of soldiers and held forth as one free of all blame. If only he had let them go back with the rest of the third-year unit, it would never have happened—but this he was not thinking. He was thinking that he must write an explanation concerning the loss of two pieces of ordnance and clothing for two.

MARCH 1927

The Sleigh

1

Icy, nose-freezing wind whipped across the steppe. The village was totally immersed in snow. Roadside trees, hills, houses—all was glittering whiteness.

Halfway up the hill a sleigh was parked in front of a farmhouse. From what served as the living and dining room came the voice of a Japanese speaking crude, atrocious Russian.

"It's cold. Why not come in?" The entrance door opened and a housewife wearing low-heeled shoes showed her face.

The driver sat in the sleigh buried up to his waist in hay, head hunched between his shoulders. He was a young man of small build. His cheeks and the tip of his nose were red with frost.

"Thank you."

"Really, do come in."

"Thank you."

But the young driver merely moved to draw the hay closer to his body to try and keep the wind from penetrating his clothing and made no attempt to rise from the sleigh. The blinkered horse, blowing vapor from his nostrils, waited meekly for the purveyor to come out. As the vapor left the animal's nostrils it rapidly turned to frost. This adhered to the hair on the horse's face, to the leather trappings and blinders, like a sprinkling of powdered sugar.

2

Old Peter was in no hurry to accede to the purveyor's request.

A growth of beard concealed the purveyor's face from cheeks to jaw.

He spoke primly with what he considered an air of importance. His form of address was excessively familiar and his discourteous use of the personal pronoun *"ti"* extended even to the women. He had picked up his Russian by ear.

Listening to the conversation between his father and the purveyor, Ivan turned to his younger brother. "There might be fighting."

"Certainly not!" The purveyor's eyes were quick to blaze up. "We are to transport provisions and clothing."

"Why do you need so many sleds to carry provisions and clothing?" asked Ivan.

"Because we do. Soldiers all need clothes to wear and food to eat." The purveyor wanted Peter's two sleighs to be put at the regiment's disposal. He proposed to pay any sum asked.

Peter had no liking for the Japanese army. On the contrary, he thoroughly detested it. His house had, for no reason, been searched by the Japanese. Another time, insisting all the while they would pay for it, the Japanese had brazenly requisitioned and carried off his sow heavy with young. His field had been ravaged. And his family never knew when a stray shot from a nearby skirmish might come flying their way. With all his heart he cursed the Japanese who had gone out of their way to come to Siberia when they had no business there.

The purveyor, whenever regimental orders sent him to farmers' houses to transact business, could perceive on the basis of minute details just how much antagonism they bore the Japanese. Some displayed it openly, but such were extremely few. For the most part they said nothing hostile. They simply offered diverse pretexts for turning down the regiment's money and requests. Some claimed the horseshoe nails were loose, others that the horses had colds. But the purveyor, who could read their motives and was intent on concluding business, soon penetrated to the heart of things. And he made his proposals accordingly. That the sleighs were in fact to be used in a military action, he kept absolutely secret. Within fifteen minutes he had obtained Peter's consent to hand over the two sleighs to the regiment and have the two sons serve as drivers.

"Very well, then," he said. "Get the sleighs ready and take them over to the regiment right away."

"Just a minute," said Ivan. "We'd like the money first." Ivan glanced at his father.

"What?" The purveyor, who had started to leave, turned his head.

"We want the money."

"Money." The purveyor chuckled knowingly. "What do you say, Peter Yakovlevitch? With these two young tigers aboard, you'll be making money hand over fist."

Muttering under his breath, Ivan pulled on his arctic boots and a torn, dirty fur overcoat. "There may be shooting," he said in a low voice. "And if it starts, I'm clearing the hell out of there."

Outside, the young driver was freezing. The purveyor stepped out and cheerfully called to him: "Right! Take me to the next one!"

The sleigh glided pleasantly and lightly down a slight snowy incline. At the next house the purveyor, having spotted a horse and sleigh in the yard, stepped into the entranceway. Here too he offered as much money as they liked. The deal concluded, the sleigh drove him on.

Every place he went, hatred of Japanese was pitted against his skill and his money. And invariably his skill and money won.

3

The sleighs had pulled up in front of the company quarters. Horses neighed to each other and the bells on their backs jingled.

All the companies were busily occupied with preparations for moving into the field. But at the battalion mess hall five or six soldiers were freely chatting without a thought for the preparations. The stench of pork fat, cabbage, burned bread, and rotten pickles mingled in the air and assaulted the nostrils. It seemed to permeate the very skins of the men who worked here.

"Pigs and chickens—we're the ones who requisition them. And who do you think eats ham and bacon? The officers, of course. We just do the dirty work." Yoshihara was mouthing off next to the stove. He had often seen the heartbroken expressions of the Siberian peasants as their requisitioned animals were being led away. He grew up a peasant and knew what it was to rear a cow or a pig. The affection a man felt toward the animals he had cared for since their birth was comprehensible only to one who had done it himself.

"Tormenting these Russians, dragging things away from them by force though they're crying and begging you not to—it's plunder, it's evil!"

He was hoarse but had a rich, resounding voice. It virtually rattled the windows. He had once been the battalion commander's orderly. Thus he had seen that the meals of officers and enlisted men differed so drastically the two might as well be disparate species.

When the battalion commander set out in the evenings, Yoshihara had

had to polish his shoes, brush his uniform, lay out his arctic gear, and, what is more, shave his barely visible stubble. To accomplish the latter it was essential to draw hot water to wash his face. Properly decked out, the major would depart.

But he sometimes returned late at night, after one, in the foulest temper. Had the woman sent him packing? Yoshihara did not know. Throughout the following day his mood would remain terrible. Soldiers were ferociously rebuked and the unlucky ones struck with a whip.

No superior had the right to do such things, Yoshihara thought. He began to feel foolish about his own servile bowing and shining of shoes. The major had chosen him as his orderly for his smart appearance and good looks. Thanks to this he had never once been struck. And yet he could not help resenting being treated like a toy by the officer who had selected him for his looks just as a man might favor a beautiful woman. Who can tolerate being a plaything?

"Doesn't matter if it's pigs or chickens. We're sent out to get them. We kill them and cook them. But the big shots take all the best parts," repeated Yoshihara. "Fine work we're stuck with!"

"Hey, cut the blabbing and let's go back. You can gripe all you want—won't do you a bit of good," said Abe. "Everybody is armed and about to move out." Abe had a dark, gloomy face. He was anxious to get back to the company quarters and get ready. Still, he could not very well leave everyone and go back ahead of them, so he fretfully waited.

"Into the slaughter again, hmm? Damn sickening." Kimura spoke to Asada in a low voice. The two sat facing each other straddling their chairs. Kimura coughed lightly, a cheerless sound.

"I hear Russian soldiers don't have much will to fight," said Asada.

"Well, that's good to hear."

"But fighting has little to do with a soldier's will to fight."

"I wonder if the army commanders are bent on fighting forever?"

"And why not? They're safe in Japan."

"It's a nasty business. They drag us all the way to this frozen desert just to make us shoot each other to shreds."

Kimura cut his words short from time to time to cough. When his throat filled up with phlegm, he had to spit it out or he could not talk. Before he came to Siberia his lungs had been clear. Nothing had interfered with his breathing, no trace of pulmonary murmurs. But the snowed-in winters and summers spent inhaling powdered horse manure and roadside dust had taken their toll. Before he knew it he had started to cough and lose weight.

It was an unhealthy climate. In the past year and a half he had been killing Russians and seeing scores of men killed who had been drafted the same year as he. He himself had shot a man dead. It had been a pale youngster whose lips had contorted in a way that made him seem on the verge of bursting into tears. His cheeks had been barely shaded by a thin red beard. Looking at him lying prostrate at his feet, Kimura had realized for the first time that he neither hated him nor bore him any sort of a grudge. This surprised him. He secretly felt then that there was someone who demanded he do such things against his will.

Yoshihara, speaking in his hoarse, resonating voice, turned to Kimura. "You've got a good excuse. Why not report sick so you won't have to go with us today?"

"Until I'm spitting blood they won't even look at me."

"Ridiculous! Tell them you're so worn out with fever you can't move."

"They'll call me a slacker and I'll just get bawled out by the doctor." Kimura coughed. "Military doctors aren't here to cure patients. They just came to Siberia to scream at us."

Yoshihara gazed at him unhappily.

"Hey, let's go back," said Abe.

A confusion of tense shouts and angry words reached them from the company barracks.

"Come on, let's go back," repeated Abe. "What choice do we have, anyway?"

The air shifted. The odor of grease, scorched bread, and putrid pickles renewed its attack on everyone's nostrils.

"I did report sick twice," said Kimura and coughed. "Both times I got a week's rest from drill and was sent back on duty."

"They ought to take a proper look at you."

"It wouldn't make any difference." He coughed.

"What in hell are you men doing?" The special-duty sergeant-major yelled from the doorway. "You don't know the order's been given? Get back on the double and into your gear!"

"Well, Porker found us."

4

Several dozen sleighs filled with soldiers glided over the snowy plain. The bells had been removed from the horses' backs. The snow was deep, the plain endlessly broad. The creaking of runners and the sound of hooves striking frozen snow was all that could be heard. And even this sound evaporated as if absorbed by the silence of the plain.

Peter's son, Ivan Petrovitch, drove the sleigh carrying the commander and his adjutant. The whip cracked the air and snapped across the horse's rump. The animal trotted over the hardened snow on spiked horseshoes that kept it from slipping. The battalion commander was doing mental arithmetic regarding the salary in his pocket. He had received the money just the previous night.

In order to catch up with the company speeding ahead, Ivan snapped the reins and continued cracking the whip. The sleigh swept along like the wind, its runners imprinting a steadily lengthening pair of parallel lines. Two more sleighs raced behind Ivan's. These too carried officers. When driving across an indentation in the landscape a sleigh would plunge in with a jolting thud; in a moment the horse would have it up again on level land. As one sled made the jarring passage, others in succession jounced and recovered. Metal fixtures on the runners creaked. With his voice Ivan signaled to the driver behind him.

The battalion commander was a man whose corpulent body contained an excess of blood enriched by the ham and bacon he ate. "Let's see. . . ." He was sorry that right after receiving the money, last night in fact, he had given the daughter of the old tsar's colonel nearly as much as he sent to Japan in a month. He would not have given it had he known they would be getting into a fight today. If only he still had it—his wife, mother, and two children could live comfortably on it for a month! However, he did not remember that in his enchantment with the sheer lusciousness of the colonel's daughter he had even thought of taking out the last notes left in his pocket and giving most of them to her.

"Major Chikamatsu!"

He continued his calculations deaf to the voice calling him from the rear. What a stupid thing he had done. He had almost nothing left!

"Major Chikamatsu!"

"Battalion Commander, sir, the lieutenant-colonel is calling," said the adjutant.

Wind whistled by his ears. Ivan Petrovitch eased up speed. Like confectioners' sugar, frost clung to his mustache, eyelashes, and eyebrows.

"Major Chikamatsu! What's that swarming at the foot of that mountain on the left?"

"What?" Taken by surprise, the battalion commander could see nothing.

"It's the enemy, isn't it? Swarming at the foot of the mountain on our left?"

"Eh?"

The adjutant took out field glasses and looked. "It is the enemy, Battalion Commander, sir. . . . Oh, God, what are we doing, parading a column before the enemy—our underbelly's exposed!" The adjutant gasped on the edge of despair. "Should we halt the company and have them wheel around?" But in that instant a puff of smoke arose and from nearby came the sound of firing.

"Hey! Hey!"

In a voice that bore no resemblance to that of a senior officer but sounded like the frail cry of a patient calling his nurse, Major Chikamatsu shouted at the company in front. It seemed that company had spotted the Russians at about the same time. As the battalion commander began yelling ahead to them, soldiers were jumping from sleighs down into the snow.

5

The fight lasted about an hour.

"These Japanese are like mad dogs. Biting all over and won't let go," said Petya.

"Still banging away!"

The Russians had lost their will to fight. They had lowered their rifles and were fleeing to a safer place. Whizzing bullets stubbornly pursued and overtook them.

"I'm worn out."

"Can't we get a truce somehow?"

"Try it and we'll all get killed."

"Run! Run!"

A man named Fyodor Lipski was fleeing with his two children. The older boy was eleven, the younger eight. The little one was exhausted, dragging his heavy shoes through the snow that seemed about to devour them. Father and sons were gradually falling behind.

"Papa, I'm hungry. Can I have some bread?"

"Why'd you bring such little kids out in the snow?" asked someone overtaking them from behind.

"Nobody to look after them," replied Lipski grimacing.

"Your wife?"

"Dead five years. We had her brother but last year he died. Starved to death."

He groped to the bottom of a bag and handed his son a slice of black bread. The younger boy reached for it with a gloved frozen hand. The same instant Lipski groaned and pitched into the snow still holding the bread.

"Papa!"

"They hit him!" said someone running past.

"Papa!"

The older son hugged the massive head of his father, once likely a farmer, and tried to lift him up.

"Papa!"

Another bullet flew at them. It struck the smaller boy. Blood flowed onto the white snow.

6

Shortly the Japanese troops arrived at the spot where father and son lay.

"They ever want us to stop chasing them?"

"I could use some food."

"Hey, let's take a breather."

They too were tired of fighting. Winning brought them no benefit. War ate up their physical and mental energy as an express train burns coal. The ill Kimura, coughing and out of breath, caught up at last, dragging his rifle. The thin hard surface of the snow kept caving in under their weight. Whenever they shifted their feet, the snow threatened to snatch off their boots.

"Ah, I'm worn out." Kimura spit out phlegm mottled with blood.

"You'd better go back."

"I can't even move."

"Take him back on the sled," said Yoshihara.

"Yeah, that'd be better. What is this, even making sick men go out and kill!" Two or three nearby voices burst out at the same time.

"Ho, I may have killed them myself." Asada looked at the fallen Lipski and shuddered. "I pulled the trigger two or three times back there."

Father and son lay a few feet apart in the snow, their heads pointing in the same direction. There was a small piece of black bread by the man's fingertips as though he was shot at the moment he was about to eat it. The boy lay face down, his left arm thrust into the snow. The small shoes were torn, and the snow all around him was dyed with blood. It was a pitiful sight. Little pale lips pressed against the snow seemed on the verge of shouting something to the soldiers.

"It's heartless, this killing!" A mighty emotion welled up in their chests.

"Hey, I've finally got it now," said Yoshihara. "We're the guys making war. Nobody but us."

"Other people force us to do it," said someone.

"Still, we're the ones making war. When we stop, it stops."

Like a stemmed tide, the soldiers stood before the father and son. All were utterly weary. What are we doing, said some. Some sat on the snow to rest. Others flung away their still smoking rifles, scooped up the snow, and ate it. They were thirsty.

"There's no end to this."

"I'm hungry."

"Isn't it time to pull out? I've had enough."

"If we don't quit, I'm telling you, it'll go on forever. Those jokers are out for medals and they'll drive us on and on and on until we're all dead! Let's stop this, let's quit! Let's get out of here!" Yoshihara was as agitated as a man in the midst of a brawl.

The battle-fatigued troops wanted to get back to barracks as soon as they could and rest in the warm rooms. Better yet, they wanted to go all the way home and throw off the stifling uniforms for the rest of their lives. They thought of the men who had escaped conscription relaxing in warm beds, their pretty wives beside them. Same age as the soldiers, these men had remained in Japan enjoying the right to choose the most beautiful and appealing women. They had *sake* too, and all manner of good food. Viewing snow-clad scenery was a diversion to them, something done while sipping cups of warm *sake*. All this while the soldiers themselves were condemned to exist in Siberia engaging in mutual slaughter a people they did not hate!

"Advance, you bastards! What do you think you're doing in the presence of the enemy!" The company commander stormed up to them clutching his sword.

7

Like tired schoolboys on a picnic crowding around a spring to rest, the soldiers, completely listless, crouched or sat in the snow. A dispute was in progress.

"Hey, take me over there." The battalion commander was addressing Ivan Petrovitch. "Toward that crowd."

To keep whipping a horse who was worn out from racing all over that snow pained Ivan as if he were lashing himself. It would have been better to carry regular soldiers. As soon as the fight had started the regulars had all jumped from the sleighs and walked through the snow on their own feet. Only the commanders never abandoned the sleigh. The purveyor had deceived him. The sleighs were being used to murder Russians. Without the sleighs they could have done nothing!

Leaving the solid surface of frozen road, the horse's long slender shanks sank deep into the snow. Each time he withdrew them the kicked-up snow scattered, hitting Ivan's face. And the further the horse advanced through the tough terrain, the wearier it became. When the sleigh was a mere hundred yards from the crowd of soldiers, they abruptly rose in a body and breaking up into clusters began to advance. But five or six men remained seated in the snow exactly as they had been. An officer was facing them saying something. Then one of the group, a dark smart-looking man, rose to his feet and in an excited tone commenced to talk back. It was Yoshihara. The officer appeared to be losing ground, the soldier seemed ready to strike him. One of the seated men spit blood as he coughed.

"What is it? What's going on?" demanded the battalion commander of the lieutenant walking unsteadily up to him.

"A man is saying soldiers are going to take over and stop the war, sir. I think he's got the others all stirred up." The lieutenant straightened his arctic hat. "I don't know, sir. Somehow even soldiers seem to go Bolshevik when they come to Siberia."

"What company is he?"

The lieutenant told him. When he got closer the battalion commander confirmed that the man in question was his own former orderly Yoshihara. He glowered as he recalled the man's incorrigible backtalk and, as well, the fine pair of spurs he had permitted to rust.

"This is a flagrant breach of military discipline!" he shouted furiously. Ivan, startled by the sudden violence of the officer's voice, thought it was directed at him. But the rage was aimed at that same Yoshihara who had nosed out the major's infatuation with the colonel's daughter and spread it abroad.

"A flagrant breach of discipline! I'll make him an example to be remembered!" The battalion commander alighted from the sleigh and, boots stamping into the snow, started with great strides toward the spot where

Yoshihara was contending with the company commander. The commander, sensing the major's approach, regained his dignity and slapped Yoshihara across the face.

Now that his sleigh had lightened, Ivan resolved to take no more passengers. He tugged the reins to turn the horse around and began his withdrawal from the front. Having carried the officers he had worked the longest. The sleighs that had transported the soldiers were already three versts to the rear and vanishing fast.

Proceeding at a moderate pace to avoid tiring the horse, Ivan looked back at the arguing men and officers. The fat battalion commander was standing close to the dark-complexioned man. The commander's lips were distended in anger. Some twenty yards away from them knelt an officer with a rifle at the ready, aiming at the soldier. The soldier did not seem aware of this. He will be shot in the back, realized Ivan. These men are vicious, he thought. The battalion commander took a few steps back and signaled.

A puff of smoke left the muzzle of the officer's rifle. The dark-complexioned man toppled onto the snow like a felled log. At the same time a sound like that of a bean bursting open reached Ivan's ears. Once more the officer's rifle belched smoke and a man collapsed. It was the frail-looking soldier with the sharp cheekbones who had been spitting bloody phlegm. A man with an intelligent face, who had been quietly watching everything, abruptly shouted something, tore off his hat, and sprinted forward. Without doubt he was one of those who had been arguing with the officer.

Ivan felt a wave of horror ripple across his skin. He turned back to his horse, swung the whip, and hastened to flee the vicinity. He could not bear to turn and watch what would become of the running man with the pale face. He whipped the horse on. How could they kill people so lightly? Why was it essential that the man be slain? Were they so desperate to fight the Russians? He could not stop thinking about the pale man. Was he alive? He could not bear to see the killing.

At last, having driven a while and unable to speculate about the outcome any longer, Ivan turned around. The man was still running through the snow. The snow was deep and he sank in to his knees; yet he plowed on pawing at it with his hands. The man screamed and swore.

Ivan could not watch any longer. It was unendurable. They will kill him in cold blood. As he faced forward, from behind him came the sound of a shot like a bursting bean. He did not look back, however. He could not bear to.

"Mad Japanese dogs! Lunatics!"

8

After unloading the soldiers, the drivers had slowly withdrawn to the rear. They were enraged at the purveyor's deception. Russians had been tricked into transporting Japanese to murder Russians!

"A splendid swindle! Sons of bitches!"

Having driven at a leisurely pace for a time, they suddenly increased speed. Before long the sleighs had streaked beyond the range of bullets. The drivers pulled from their pockets the prohibited bells, attached them to the horses, and drove merrily on. The bells, having had their rest, rang cheerfully from the horses' backs. Blowing steam from their noses, the horses cantered off across the snowy steppe.

The crowd of battling soldiers was a wriggling mass growing gradually smaller on the horizon behind them. Finally they came to resemble ants and then disappeared from sight.

9

The snowy wilderness rolled interminably on like an ocean. Snow-covered mountains rose in the distance. But walk as one might, the mountains grew no larger, no closer. There were no houses, not so much as a watchman's hut. Crows with white beaks did not fly here. Like a disabled ship with neither compass nor propeller, the battalion was floundering.

The soldiers, afraid of being shot, had held their tongues. Major Chikamatsu had intimidated every subordinate into doing as he wanted. The soldiers spent the last of their energy charging headlong against the Russians. It was either kill or be killed. Because of it they had killed, but were now unbearably tired.

The battalion commander could not turn the soldiers into a sleigh for him. He blamed the sleighs' disappearance on his subordinates' carelessness, bellowed at those around him, and beat on the snow with his sword. His boots stuck in the snow. The spurs Yoshihara had to his great anger allowed to rust were a constant hindrance to his movements.

There was nothing to eat and the water in the canteens was frozen. Rifles, boots, and bodies were heavy. The soldiers, seemingly about to collapse, trudged aimlessly through the snow. They knew they were going to die. No one was likely to bring sleighs to their rescue. Why must they die in the snow? Why had they been forced to come into this wilderness to kill Russians? Defeating the Russians brought the soldiers no benefit at all.

A deep gloom enveloped them. The people who had dispatched

them to Siberia had known all along they would die in the snow like this. Sprawled cozily at home under stove-heated quilts they were no doubt praising the beauty of snow. Even if they were to hear of the soldiers' deaths, they would merely say "Is that so?" Nothing more.

They struggled on through the snow. They had not lost their consciousness, though, nor their rage, resistance, or hatred. The soldiers' bayonets, as if of their own accord, swung toward the chest of the man who had abused them, the agent of those who had sent them here—Major Chikamatsu. Wildly the blades converged.

The snowy wilderness rolled interminably on like an ocean. Snow-covered mountains rose in the distance. But walk as one might, the mountains grew no larger, no closer. There were no houses, not so much as a watchman's hut. Crows with white beaks did not fly here. In the extremity of hunger and exhaustion they staggered aimlessly on. Boots were heavy and the cold pierced through to the core of their bodies.

JULY 1927

A Flock of Swirling Crows

1

"Sir! Leftovers . . . please!"

The children had blue eyes. They were bundled in threadbare, torn overcoats, heads buried in the collars, girls and boys. Needlelike ice stuck in the gaps of their cracked shoes. In his arctic boots, Matsuki stood in the mess hall entranceway, hands thrust into trouser pockets.

Windblown snow piled high, pressing against the windowpanes hard enough to break them. Water gushing from a valley spring had frozen here into great slabs of ice. They rose in tiers from below, yesterday higher than the day before, today topping yesterday. This is Siberia all right, Matsuki thought. Ice rising layer on layer from ground level was something you never saw back home.

The children, in their clumsy Japanese, pleaded for Matsuki's sympathy. The faces of all five expressed a determined effort to be endearing. There was open fawning in the way they said "sir."

"No leftovers?" repeated the children. "Please, sir, please!"

"Here, take it."

Matsuki took the pail of scraps by the rim and rolled it to the door. In it were the remains of rice boiled with barley that the company had left unfinished. Lumps of bread had been tossed in. On top of everything someone had slopped the remnants of bean paste soup. The children, grunting happily, scraped each other's hands shoveling the leftovers into the enameled basins they had brought along.

The mess hall smelled of ancient rotten pickles with a mingled stench of rancid butter and jute sacking. Yoshinaga, who had been chopping burdock root at the kitchen table, strolled over to the entranceway still wearing his jute-sack apron. Takeishi was tossing white birch logs into a pot-bellied stove. Inside it birch bark crackled in the flames. He too walked to the doorway.

"Kolya," said Matsuki.

"What?" Kolya was a boy with eyes round as marbles that continually rolled in circles in a rather pointed face.

"Is Galya at home?"

"Yes."

"What is she doing?"

"Working."

Kolya stood there cramming his mouth with fragments of soup-soaked bread and munching. The other children too clutched and gulped bread or boiled rice streaked with soybean paste.

"Is it good?"

"Um."

"Must be cold by now."

When they had transferred the very last grains from the bucket into their own basins, they hoisted them under their arms and ran up the snowy hill leading to their homes.

"Thank you."

"Thank you."

"Thank you!"

The children's overcoats and trouser hems flapped and twisted in the wind. The three men stood in the mess hall entrance watching them go. Thin, long legs vigorously stamping the snow like powerful springs, the children were climbing the hill.

"Nasha!"

"Liza!" Takeishi and Yoshinaga called out.

"Whaat?" The girls called back from the hilltop. The children all stopped for a moment and looked down at the mess hall in the valley.

"You'll spill your rice," said Yoshinaga in Japanese.

"Whaat?"

Yoshinaga beckoned the girls with his hand. Yells and shrieks of laughter resounded from the summit. After a while the children scattered, each to their home.

2

The mountain's low easy slope parted into two hills running gradually into a steppe that unfolded into the distance. The barracks lay in the ravine between the two hills.

Here and there on the hills, and at their foot where the steppe starts to spread, the landscape was dotted with the houses of Russians, some of whom had fled their native regions terrified by the revolution. There were also indigenous inhabitants of Siberia.

All had a struggle feeding themselves. Their fields had been devastated and their livestock plundered. There was no way for them to work unmolested or make a living. They lived in wooden houses whose sides were held together by rusted, dangling nails. The roofs were low. Straw and trash lay strewn around the buildings. In places, haystacks had been piled high. Carts stood parked under the eaves. Inside the rooms were old tables, samovars, embroidered curtains. From within, however, as if from a stable, exuded the odor of strange furs and animal fat.

To the Japanese soldiers, this was unmistakably the smell of the white man. This is where the children came from, hugging their enameled washbasins, every day. At times it was the old men or women who came. And, sometimes, young women.

Yoshinaga was from the first company. Matsuki and Takeishi were privates in the second. The three no longer threw away the white sugar that had gotten mixed in with bread crumbs but put it aside on plates. They made sure the leftover soup was not dumped atop the half-eaten bread. Then, when the Russians came, they gave it out.

"Would it be all right to come to your house?"

"Of course!"

"Will there be some kind of treat?"

"Absolutely nothing. But you're free to come any time."

The words, vivaciously spoken, brought the soldiers a sense of heartfelt welcome. Their knowledge of Russian was almost nil. But they instantly recognized the notes of hospitality. That evening, mess hall duty done, they left one by one to avoid the officers' attention and breathlessly clambered up the snowy hill. The air they exhaled turned to ice and adhered frostlike to the heavy fur of their winter hats.

They hungered for the warmth and magic of a home. How many years had it been since they'd arrived in Siberia? Only two. But they felt as if ten years separated them from their families and country. As sailors long for a harbor and its solid footing, they yearned for homes and their parents and wives.

Their present surroundings consisted of nothing but a snowy wilderness, angular brick barracks, and sporadic exchanges of gunfire. For whose sake, they wondered, must they be buried in the snow of such a place? It was not for their own benefit or that of their parents. It was for the sake of men who did nothing. Nothing except exploit them. Those men were their [enemies]. The soldiers were simply rendering free service to their own enemies.

Yoshinaga felt as if his lungs were about to disintegrate. He was gasping for oxygen. If he could have fled the barracks forever without being shot, he would not have wanted to stay a minute longer. Even a brief respite was fine with him. He wished to get out for a bit and taste the flavor of a home. With this desire, he hurried up the sloping, snow-covered path.

Liza's house was on top of the hill. He stopped in the entryway. Weather stripping had been applied to the door to keep out the draft. He took his hand from his pocket and knocked on the door.

"*Zdravstvuyte*." It was a greeting. A stove was blazing away in the middle of the room, filling it with warmth. He sensed its presence even outside the door.

"Good evening. Come in." A woman's voice, clear and full of life, floated to the door. "Ah, Mr. Yoshinaga! Do come in." The young woman, happily smiling, put out her hand.

At first he hadn't known about shaking hands. He had never done it. It made him feel nervous, as if he were about to do something illicit. But he soon got used to it. Not only that, he came to understand a woman's emotions through her handshake. What did a firm squeeze mean? What did the way she used her eyes while shaking hands say? If she proffered her hand limply there was no prospect of anything. And so on.

While Yoshinaga was being shown into a room containing a table, chairs, and samovar, Takeishi, emitting steam from his nose, was banging at another door. And Inagaki, Ōno, Kawamoto, Sakata, each two or three minutes after the other, were pounding on still more doors.

"*Zdravstvuyte!*"

And as the women took their hands, they gauged the response levels and watched the eyes. The eyes told some of them they would be granted a certain something they desired. Their hearts thumped in anticipation.

"Right. Today I'll kiss her hand and see how it goes."

It sometimes happened that two men, or even three, would converge upon the same woman. In such a case, on their way back down the hill, the men would halt in their tracks, spin around to face each other, and burst into happy laughter.

"*Sopernik*, aren't you?"

"What's a *sopernik*?"

"*Sopernik*—rival! Competitor in love! Ha, ha, ha."

3

Matsuki was one of the men struggling up the hill. He had no competitor to laugh with. Nor had he met with a bright voice of feminine welcome. His love, if indeed it was love, was riddled with frustration. Before ascending the hill he made sure to wrap up and take along some bread, dried noodles, or sugar. Although the goods were meant to be distributed to the soldiers, he had quietly hidden away a portion. Holding it close, he now climbed the hill and skidded down the other side.

Barely thirty minutes later, empty-handed and dejected, he emerged from the opposite direction, tramping up the identical slope he had just gone down. The other men's hearts were still throbbing in rooms made hot by burning stoves.

"I've had it. No more." He trudged the snow exhausted. "This is ridiculous."

At the foot of the hill ran a broad thoroughfare thickly covered with snow. The snow, compressed by sled runners and boots, was frozen hard. On the way stretched the barbed wire entanglements enclosing the company. Each night Matsuki ducked under this wire, cut across the treacherously icy road, and came to stand under a certain window.

"Galya!" He tapped on the glass with his fingertip. Freezing wind blew through him as if to coat his lungs with ice. He waited under the eaves.

"Galya!" Once more he tapped on the windowpane.

"What?" A woman's face appeared on the opposite side of the glass. White teeth peeked out between her lips—terribly attractive.

"Can I come in?"

"What's that?"

"Bread. I'll give it to you."

The woman opened the window just long enough to take in the paper-wrapped package.

"Hey, open it a little more!"

"I can't. The room will get cold. Every time I open it I lose three pieces of firewood."

She had light pink skin. When she laughed childlike dimples showed in both cheeks. She wasn't a bad woman. She merely had to do what she could to get money. Her parents and brother were short of food. Her sister, who had children, had come to get tobacco for her husband.

Matsuki brought bread. He brought sugar. He brought what he could buy with his salary of five yen and sixty sen. But he was much too poor to support her entire family. Someone with a higher salary was needed. It wasn't only the soldiers who were starved for sex. There was a certain big shot with a salary more than eighty-five times greater than Matsuki's who lusted after female flesh too.

"I have something to do," said Galya. "It's rude of me, but won't you please come back tomorrow?"

"It's always 'come back tomorrow.' If I come tomorrow, then it'll be the day after tomorrow."

"No, really, tomorrow. Tomorrow I'll be waiting."

4

The snow had gotten deep. The road packed solid by those who came to the mess hall in search of leftovers had disappeared under fresh drifts. Though the children tramped through and restored it, their effort was erased by new carpets of snow. Houses on the hill looked like rocks buried by snow.

From a mountain some way off, partisans were tirelessly watching the village. Not only that but wolves frequently attacked sentries by night. The wolves came running nimbly over snow deep enough to swallow their whole bodies. The wolves found no food in the mountains. Spotting a chance, they would raid a village and make off with chickens, puppies, a pig. They formed howling packs and rushed in with such force it seemed they would kill and devour anything they met. The sentries hated to face them. Sentries had guns, true, but there were only two of them. The beasts would duck the bullets and close in on the men. It was terrifying. The soldiers had to join forces and grapple. If luck failed them, the wolves' fangs would pierce their armpits or throats.

It continued to be overcast. Days were short, nights long. Not once did the sun show its beaming face. Matsuki was spending his second winter in Siberia. He was tired and melancholy. It seemed to him sun had abandoned the earth and flown off somewhere. He was certain he'd fall sick if things continued like this. Nor was it only Matsuki. His fellow soldiers were all gloomy and exhausted. So they went to visit women. Only women had the power to excite their interest any more.

Galya, bearing up under the public gaze, came to the mess hall. Her bleached white skirt gleamed beneath an old coat made of good material.

"You don't let a man come anywhere near you. Even if I had leftovers I wouldn't give them to you."

"Oh, I see." She spoke in her agreeable, crystal-clear voice.

"Serves you right."

"Fine." She spun around smartly on the high heels of her black polished shoes and commenced to walk toward the hill.

"No, I was only joking! Someone else was just here and took everything we had." Matsuki called out from behind.

"Never mind, I don't need it." Her slender long legs bounding like resilient springs, she climbed the hill.

"Galya! Wait! Wait!"

Clutching a package of dried noodles he ran after her. Soldiers stepped out of the mess hall and watched laughing. Matsuki, breathless, caught up with the woman and threw the pack of noodles into her empty washbasin.

"Here, it's yours."

Galya stopped and looked at him. Then, revealing her dazzling white teeth, she said something. He couldn't understand her words. But he knew from the soft, rounded tone that she was eager to have him think well of her. He felt he had done a good thing to come running after her. Turning around on the way back, he saw Galya slipping on the snowy path as she climbed the hill.

"Hey, don't overdo it!" Takeishi hollered from the mess hall entrance. "If you keep at it like this, I'll go after her myself!"

5

Yoshinaga's company was to be detached from the battalion and sent to guard Iishi. Between H. and S. lay a broad stretch of forested land. A mountain and a large valley formed part of it. A river flowed through the forest. The area's topography was not precisely known.

A railway bridge in the zone was constantly getting blown up. Without anyone's noticing it, sleepers were being ripped up. A military train would suddenly be ambushed. Telegraph wires were repeatedly severed and communication between H. and S. repeatedly cut. It was safe to imagine the region was a partisan hideout. The mission of the company sent to garrison Iishi was to secure communications.

Yoshinaga was putting his belongings together on Matsuki's bunk. He was to move out of the mess hall and return to his company. He reflected on how often he had been exposed to danger. A great number of men had already been dropped by bullets, lost their eyes, had arms torn off. A man he had stood sentry with one evening suddenly spouted blood from his chest and toppled over. His name had been Sakamoto.

He remembered the scene vividly. The shot had come out of nowhere. The two had been standing on a mountain ridge. It was time for the relief sentries to line up and march out of the guardhouse. In fifteen minutes they could return to the guardhouse and rest. A bright red sun was about to slip beneath the horizon. A herd of cows and horses, hides bathed in sunlight, ambled lazily across the steppe. It was the middle of October.

"I'm hungry," said Sakamoto yawning.

"If I were home this time of day, I'd be ready to toss the hoe on the shoulder and head back from the field."

"That's right, isn't it? It's potato season."

"Um."

"Wouldn't I like to eat one!"

With that Sakamoto had yawned once again. Was his mouth still stretched open when he was knocked over into the grass like felled timber? Yoshinaga leaped up. Another shot zipped past him, grazing his head.

"Hey! Sakamoto! Hey!"

He had tried calling him. The uniform was stained dark with blood. Sakamoto merely moaned, "Ooooh."

They had sailed from Japan and landed at Vladivostok. Ever since the instant of their arrival everyone had been oppressed by the danger. The locomotive burned firewood. He boarded it to travel some thousand miles into the interior. At times they'd jump off to exchange gunfire, then reembark and boil their rice. The kindling smoldered. It was winter. Since it ran on wood, the locomotive frequently slowed to a halt. For two months he didn't wash his face. He looked black by the time he arrived. It was too cold to breathe. To top it off there was an epidemic of influenza. Enemy airplanes roared over the barracks. Streets fluttered with red flags.

What did they do there? Conditions eventually turned grim, spelling defeat, so they burned what they couldn't take and fell back. The Reds cut their line of retreat. They fought and continued to withdraw. Like influenza germs the Reds were everywhere. Again they fought. So what did they do next? There were days when they slept in the swamp of melting snow and mud and woke up only to start firing. More than once they were sprayed from above by machine gun bullets. Yoshinaga thought it quite amazing he was still alive. If he'd strayed even a foot or two to either side he might be dead.

But how was he to know what would happen from now on? How

could anyone know? Nobody cared a fart if he died. The only human being who worried about him was his mother who sold firewood in a village. Next to his skin he wore the amulet case she had made for him. It was a large pouch sewn out of new white cotton. Grime and sweat had turned it black and smelly. He thought he'd open it and replace the pouch. He slit it open with scissors. An indecent profusion of charms had been stuffed in. Konpira Shrine, Nanzan Hachiman Shrine, Tenshō Kōdai Jingū, on and on they came, from every possible source and denomination. Evidently his mother felt the more there were, the greater the likelihood of obtaining divine favors.

The talismans were so frayed the original paper shapes were nearly unrecognizable. There was more. Something had been wrapped separately in paper. He opened it. It contained banknotes. A five, ones, fifty-sen bills— all in all about ten yen. She'd slipped in the money she'd saved peddling firewood.

"Hey, hey. There's money in my charm pouch," Yoshinaga said happily.

"What?"

"Money in the charm pouch!"

"Really?"

"Would I lie?"

"Ho! The man's rich."

Matsuki and Takeishi came running from the table. The notes were black with sweat and dirt too. "Look at that, bills from back home!" Matsuki and Takeishi held up the notes and gazed at them tenderly. "It's been a while since I've seen these."

"Mother must have put them in for me on the sly."

"It took you long enough to find out! What a great find!"

"Hmm, I struck it rich. I'll share it."

Yoshinaga thought that at best he'd have to go to Iishi day after next. He'd be forced to cross a snowed-in valley and then a mountain. Partisans hid there. Once again shooting was inevitable. Would he live, he wondered. Who knew? Who the hell knew?

6

At the canteen Matsuki purchased bean-jam buns, sugar, pineapples, tobacco, and more. When night fell he wrapped them all in newspaper and went up the hill. Rock-hard frozen snow clacked against his boots. Air cut into his nose. He reached the summit and went down the opposite slope. A light was burning in that window by the foot of the hill. Silhouettes flitted across the pane. Walking, he tried out the words.

"Galya."

"Galya."

"Galya."

"What a lively woman you are!"

How would he say it in Russian? Voices seemed to float up from the base of the hill. The voice of a woman over thirty. And what seemed to be that of a Japanese. What were they saying? He paused. It sounded somewhat like Galya's mother, he thought. Abruptly it stopped. Soon blue curtains swept across the nearby window, blocking the view.

"What's this? They don't go to sleep so early. . . ." He ducked under the barbed wire and stalked up to the window. "Good evening, Galya." The stepstone he had strategically placed to help him reach the window had been removed.

"Galya."

A lump of snow came flying at him. It struck the edge of his arctic coat and disintegrated. Another flew at him. It hit his back. He noticed neither but kept looking intently up at the window.

"Galya!" He called with his face upturned. Bright stars shone crisply against the winter night.

"Hey you!"

The man who had been hurling snowballs made a scraping noise with his boots and jumped out from behind a white birch. It was Takeishi. Matsuki started. He almost dropped his newspaper bundle onto the snow. Surprised by an officer or someone unknown, he was ready to throw everything and run.

"You've come back," laughed Takeishi.

"It's you. Don't do this."

It took a while for Matsuki's heart to resume its regular pace. As soon as he realized it was Takeishi, he flushed with embarrassment at the thought he'd been in such a hurry to please a woman with Yoshinaga's money. He wished he'd come without the sugar and pineapples.

"Someone got here ahead of us." Takeishi lowered his voice and pointed to the window. "I thought it might be you so I was waiting to see how things stood."

"Who is it?"

"I don't know."

"Noncom or officer?"

"I didn't see. I don't know."

"Who could it be?"

"Want to go in and see?"

"No, no. . . . Let's go back."

Matsuki had no desire to come face to face with an officer or anyone else. It could do no good. Takeishi disagreed. "It'd be cowardly just to go back like this." He rapped loudly on the windowpane.

"Galya, Galya, good evening!"

An annoyed male voice sounded from the next room.

"Galya!"

"What d'you want?" Her younger brother Kolya thrust his face past the curtains. Although he'd had to quit the army prep school in Vladivostok, he wore the uniform with its white shoulder badges.

"Where's Galya?"

"She's busy."

"Tell her to come here for a second."

"What is it? That?" Kolya was eying Matsuki's bundle.

"Drink." Before Matsuki could reply Takeishi produced a pint-and-a-half bottle of Masamune. "We've got lots of good things." Tearing off the wrapping Takeishi held up the bottle before Kolya's eyes. Matsuki noted a touch of experience in the gesture.

"Let me have it," said Kolya putting out his hand. But there was something uncharacteristically limp in his manner. He faltered. This was highly unusual for someone as assertive as Kolya.

Takeishi had brought things too and was giving them away, thought Matsuki. No reason then to be ashamed of his own purchases. Seeing Kolya so hesitant made him feel especially generous.

"Here, have this too." He took out a can of pineapples.

Kolya was fidgeting.

"Go on, take it."

"Thank you."

This oddly sharp-faced, somehow disheartened boy seemed an intriguing character to Takeishi. "Would you like more?"

His reserve suggested he wanted it but felt it would be bad to accept.

"Tobacco and sugar." Matsuki raised them up to the window.

"Thank you."

As Kolya left the window with his presents, Takeishi whispered to Matsuki: "Someone is definitely here."

"But who? I've no idea."

"I think I'll go in and see for myself."

The two strained their ears. They sensed something happening in the room beyond the next. A door creaked open. A saber sheath rattled. Takeishi placed his hands on the windowsill, pulled himself up, and peered in.

"Can you see?"

"Only a boiling samovar. . . . Hey, the people in this house couldn't possibly be selling their own daughter, could they?"

Kolya came through the door. When he spotted Takeishi seemingly trying to enter the room from the window, his expression changed at once. "No! You mustn't! Don't do that!" The voice was hoarse and thick with rebuke. Instantly convinced by its desperate quality that he'd broken some rule, Takeishi slid down from the window. Kolya started for the window, turned back, slammed shut the door.

For several minutes the two men remained beneath the window. Lights glowed and twinkled in snow-covered houses. Women lived there too, thought Takeishi. In one of them Yoshinaga would be sipping hot tea and mourning his imminent separation from Liza. Maybe he was urging the slender little Liza to go with him to Iishi. No doubt he too had bought her something she would like. Takeishi recalled Yoshinaga's good furrowed face and was moved to smile. Yoshinaga would be going to guard Iishi, a dangerous mission.

Lights on the hillside were vanishing behind curtains one by one. "Good night." Three or four soldiers emerged from Gudkov's house nearby. They spoke animatedly as they walked and their conversation resounded to the bottom of the hill. They were returning to barracks.

All of a sudden Matsuki and Takeishi heard Galya's cheerful voice directly overhead. Both felt instantly resurrected. "Boo!" Laughing she showed her face in the window. "Won't you come in?"

From the entrance Matsuki scanned the kitchen, bedroom, and workroom. "Who was here?"

"*Maiyor.*"

"Who?" Neither of them knew the word.

"*Maiyor* was here."

"What's that? What's a *maiyor?*" Matsuki and Takeishi stared at each other. *Maiyoru* in Japanese might mean "stop by to dance." Had someone come to dance?

7

To Matsuki, a major was not a rival he could joke with. The two men stepped into the room. At that very moment the major was departing by the kitchen door choked with fury. He was a fleshy, bearded man weighing nearly two hundred pounds. His boots kicked the hardened snow into fragments. His flared nostrils drank in the freezing air and expelled it as dense clouds of steam.

He was burning with humiliation and rage. At length he managed to control himself. Taking enormous strides, he struck out for the headquarters. Then suddenly he turned and retraced his steps. The major marched up to the window Matsuki and Takeishi had been standing under moments earlier. He was robust and tall. Through a gap in the curtains he could see into the room even without standing on tiptoe.

Two enlisted men, a bottle of Masamune between them, were facing each other across a table. Galya was chatting with them, her face a little flushed. Her white teeth glistened. Lips, pungent as mint, were parted in a smile.

His jealousy and wrath exploded within him. He had the overpowering urge to roar out in the gruffest voice he kept in reserve for commanding the battalion. The growl forced its way to the uppermost part of his throat. It took an immense effort to suppress it. Then, with greater strides than ever, he rushed back to the regiment. "Guzzling liquor at a woman's place. Unspeakable insolence!"

The sentry who presented arms at the barracks gate had an angry bark hurled at him. Beholding the battalion commander's terrible visage, the commander of guards panicked into thinking he'd come to strike him with a whip.

"Adjutant!" He bellowed upon entering the room. "Adjutant!" As the adjutant appeared, the major flung himself into a chair without bothering to unfasten the sword and snorted hard: "Immediate emergency roll call. Now! This instant!"

"Yes, sir."

"And the mess hall is off limits to the Russians. Absolutely no leftovers are to be given them. Not a crumb. Strictly forbidden."

"Yes, sir."

"That's all."

As the adjutant withdrew to the adjoining room to issue the order, the major shouted again: "Adjutant!"

"Yes, sir."

"About the roll call. If there are any latecomers, the company they belong to is to be sent to Iishi garrison duty instead of the first company. They will not be permitted to remain here. That's the penalty. Do as I say. At once."

8

A company of soldiers walked mutely through the snow. They were tired and dispirited. The big arctic boots sinking into the snow at every step felt extremely heavy and cumbersome. Snow frequently reached up to their shins. All were dejected and uneasy. The company commander's face looked profoundly troubled. The steppe, the road, the river, all blotted out by snow. There was nothing to be seen except for scattered clusters of five or six withered trees with branches so laden with snow they looked exactly as if they'd borne icy fruit. In every direction the only visible object was the expanse of dazzling white snow. There was no audible sound, not a solitary shout. The crunch of soldiers' boots crushing the snow faded instantly as if absorbed by the sky. They had been plodding through this wasteland since early morning. For lunch they had nibbled bread and dried noodles and moistened their throats with snow. Which way was Iishi?

From the top of a smallish hill on the right a scout came running down with a rifle in one hand and clutching a scabbard in the other. His arm seemed stretched to the limit by the weight of the gun. The weapon trailed in the snow. It was Matsuki. Out of breath, he raced to the company commander's side, made a great effort to lift up the rifle he'd been dragging, and strove to present arms. His hands were frozen and didn't move as he wanted them to. He couldn't elevate the rifle straight and properly in front of his nose.

The company commander regarded him with a disgruntled stare. His eyes brimmed with silent contempt for the bungled greeting. Shortness of breath prevented Matsuki from uttering anything for a time. From his nostrils to his larynx everything was parched and stiff like after running a marathon. He tried to produce some saliva to wet his throat but it refused to come up. He wanted to fall in the snow and rest.

"What happened?" The company commander was looking daggers at him.

"The road. There's—" Matsuki lacked the breath to go on. "There is no sign of the road."

"What does the Russki say?"

"Yes, sir. Smetanin." Again he fought for breath. "He says he has no idea because of the snow."

"He's useless. There's supposed to be a big river, and on the other side of the road a fir wood. Find the spot. If we come out there, we can get to Iishi in no time."

"Yes, sir."

"Get on the Russki's back and make damn sure he's guiding me straight." The company commander fumed as he walked. "If need be, prod him with a bayonet for all I care. The snake is probably in cahoots with the partisans and leading us wrong on purpose. Don't you dare take an eye off him for a second!"

"Yes, sir."

Matsuki, secretly hoping to be relieved, marched side by side with the commander. He was deathly pale. All his muscles ached as if they'd been pummeled. He was in a daze and his ears kept ringing. But the commander had no intention of letting him rest. "Hey, get going. Use your eyes."

The tottering Matsuki, like an old horse spurred by the whip into wringing out his last ounce of energy, broke into a trot, again trailing his rifle.

"Hey, Matsuki!" The company commander called him back. "You're not just looking for a road, is that clear? I want to know if there are partisans, if there are any houses, and if you can see the railroad. So keep your eyes peeled."

"Yes, sir." The scout scrabbled up the hill and vanished over the ridge. Takeishi and the guide Smetanin were waiting for him on the other side. Ever since they'd left the main force at daybreak, Matsuki and Takeishi had been made to reconnoiter.

The company commander had showered them with a storm of abuse. "Who do you think is responsible for this company being sent to guard Iishi? It's the fault of you two bastards who scraped under the wire to go play with a woman!" He had fixed them with a ferocious glare. "Does a company commander want to expose all his men to danger? This company is precious! And you two idiots made sure we're all stuck with facing hell knows what kind of risks! Soldiers don't do such things!" And then he had put the two of them on the most backbreaking, hazardous duty.

Matsuki and Takeishi tramped through the piled up snow more than a thousand yards ahead of the company. Taking in the situation, they ran back on the double to make the report. They delivered it only to be ordered out in front again. The snow was deep and it blinded them. They had to keep glancing forward and to both sides. Every time they returned to gasp out their reports, the company commander found something wrong and bawled them out.

"He still won't relieve us?" asked Takeishi sitting in the snow to rest.

"No." Matsuki's voice too lacked spirit.

"What a mess. . . . I might as well stay here and freeze to death." Takeishi drew a sigh and seemed about to burst into tears.

The two resumed walking with Smetanin. Coming down the hill they reached a shallow valley. There followed a sluggish ascent. On their left rose a precipitous mountain. On the right, the snowy wilderness unfolded far into space. Smetanin suggested they try climbing the mountain. Looking down from the top might help them grasp the lay of the land. The trouble was, they'd have to climb up, survey the position, and rush down all in the time it took the company commander to arrive at the foot of the mountain. If they failed, they'd catch hell from him again.

In the folds of the mountain the snow was even deeper. Matsuki and Takeishi struggled upward using their rifles for support. They came across bear tracks. Footprints of small, unknown animals were inscribed in all directions. Wormwood bent under the snow. The men's boots tangled in shrub roots. The two felt dizzy as if with a fever. The desire seized them to unfasten all their equipment, throw themselves in the snow, and rest.

At its crest the mountain linked up with the next. That mountain in turn connected with the succeeding one. And on they ran into the distance like a string of prayer beads. As far as the eyes could penetrate there was only the whiteness of snow. Smetanin had no idea where he was after all. Like a column of ants, the company was inching its way over the hill. In the wide, infinite snowy waste it truly looked no more significant than a few insects.

"Take us anywhere you like, just take us," pleaded the two desperately.

"You keep pushing me so hard I'm getting even more confused." Smetanin swept off his fur hat and mopped the sweat on his forehead.

9

A thin, whitish dusk descended over the entire region. Which way to go?

Matsuki had often heard of exhausted people simply dropping into the snow and freezing where they lay. Fatigue and hunger robbed the body of its resistance to cold. Was it possible for a whole company of men to die of cold in the snow? Could it be permitted to happen?

The soldiers had been [sacrificed] to a major's lechery. But they didn't even know it. Why had they been compelled to come to Siberia? Who had sent them? The answers, hidden beyond clouds, were of course a mystery to them.

"We didn't want to come to Siberia. We were forced to come." Yet even these simple facts they were now on the verge of forgetting. I don't want to die, thought each. One way or another I just want to get out of this snow alive, nothing more.

It was Matsuki and Takeishi who had gotten them mired in the snow. And it was Matsuki and Takeishi who had lost the way. This is how the men reasoned. They didn't understand it was from much higher spheres that the demons' hands reached down to wield such power over them.

No matter how the men hurried only snow lay ahead. Their limbs were getting numb. Consciousness began to lapse. A ruined hut or anything— just a place to spend one single night! But however far they walked there was nothing but snow.

Matsuki was the first to collapse. Takeishi followed him. Matsuki still knew enough to realize his senses were getting blurred. But soon his mind was in a whirl and he could no longer distinguish the sequence of events or remember where he was. As in sleep, his consciousness slipped away.

His limbs grew stiff. Shortly his entire body turned hard as wood and just as still.

Snow fell. Its white shroud drifted down to settle in successive layers on horizontal human flesh. It draped over the fallen soldiers so that before long the rucksacks, boots, and hats all were concealed under the snow and not a trace remained to show where they lay. Still it continued to snow.

10

Spring came. Bright sunlight poured through gaps in the clouds. The bare trees had, unobserved, shaken off the oppressing snow. Flocks of sparrows chirped among the bushes and hopped happily around. Even the rumble of a troop train crossing the steel bridge rang exhilarating.

Snow was melting and the water formed a delightful sound as it trickled ceaselessly through rain ducts. Yoshinaga's company had been detailed to Iishi. At the moment, they were occupying a wooden hilltop building. Water dripping from the barracks eaves ran across a wilted lawn and, swelling into a minor torrent, flowed into the valley.

At the time Matsuki and Takeishi's company had strayed out of contact, the battalion commander had mobilized another company and conducted a search. The commander made it a point to appear worried. He went so far as to say he was inexpressibly sorry for the men's families. Inwardly, however, he felt no concern whatsoever. He was relieved, in fact. The one thing that weighed on his mind, the sole consideration, was what sort of report he should submit to the division commander.

The search went on for a week but the company's whereabouts remained as mysterious as before. The major seemed to have forgotten all about it. From the second floor of the headquarters he gazed in the direction of Galya's house and whistled "The Red Setting Sun." Spring had come. And still no one knew where the company had so utterly vanished or why. Not a trace had been found.

From the hilltop barracks Yoshinaga looked out over the immense plain where the snow had not yet totally thawed. He marveled that he had survived. His own company had been detailed to go. One day before the scheduled departure their orders had unaccountably been changed. Had his company been forced to go on foot rather than by sled, some unknown dog would probably be chewing his bones by now.

Proceeding by foot through snow of that depth amounted to sheer suicide. Those who had sent them to Siberia did not give a damn whether the men were ripped apart by [bullets] or [devoured] by wolves. They took it for granted a handful would die. If two hundred disappeared, that too was nothing. A soldier's death meant less than a puppy's. There were plenty more to be had. A single written notice would be enough to drum up more.

To the left of the hill a train was passing. There was a river still coated with ice. Cows shambled over its frozen surface. To the right stretched the savage, boundless plain. Withered trees stood there. The snow was taking a long time to melt.

Black as spilled ink, a flock of crows circled in midair. Their raucous, melancholy cries could be heard all the way to the barracks. There were so many they seemed to have gathered from all points of the horizon and, like a storm cloud, appeared intent on obscuring the sky.

Presently the crows began a clamorous descent. Alighting, they searched, scratching tenaciously and pecking at the snow. The flock had been there the previous day. It was there again today. Three days had passed. But the number of crows, the noise and the gloom, kept increasing.

One day a soldier patrolling the village came across a Russian peasant returning home with a rifle over his shoulder and a knapsack slung from its barrel. Both the gun and the knapsack were Japanese.

"Hey, hold it! Where did you swipe that from?"

"Over there." The heavily bearded peasant raised a big arm and pointed toward the plain where the crows were flocking. "It was just lying there."

"Liar!"

"There are a lot of them in the snow over there. . . . A lot of dead soldiers, too."

"You lying son of a bitch!" The soldier slapped the peasant hard across the cheek. "Move! I'm taking you to headquarters."

It became clear Japanese soldiers were indeed buried in the snow. The insignia on the knapsack indicated it was Matsuki and Takeishi's company. The following day a company of men marched out to the spot where the crows had been circling since early morning. Already the crows were swarming over the snow, striking greedily with their rapacious beaks. As the soldiers approached, the crows, in a crescendo of cawing, soared cloudlike into the sky.

Partly eaten bodies lay scattered over the field. Their faces had been hideously mutilated and rendered unrecognizable. Snow was nearly half melted. Water seeped into boots. Screeching wildly, the flight of crows swooped to the ground a hundred yards away. The soldiers saw them pecking and tearing in the snow and started after them.

Again the crows whirled up screeching and dropped down two or three hundred yards off. Corpses sprawled there too. The soldiers ran toward them.

The crows were gradually fleeing further and further—two miles, five miles—touching down in the snow all along the way.

OCTOBER 1927

The Hole

The five-yen note he had handed out was counterfeit. This was discovered at the field post office. The event took place in P village, which lies along the U-L railway line.

Noisily treading the ground, the military policeman with a leather strap running diagonally from shoulder to holster walked up to the hospital. His face was tense and arrogant, and his large boots seemed to assert the right to trample anything in their path. Awashima—that was the suspect's name—was a first-rate soldier. He was not a cunning man capable of forging banknotes. He had no memory of having made a five-yen note himself or having received such a note from a dubious character. Nevertheless, seeing the fierce countenance of the approaching MP, he could not help feeling shaken as though he were indeed a criminal.

Looking stern and angry, the MP called out his name. Although inwardly rebelling against such pomposity, the soldier unwittingly uttered a docile, nervous reply.

"Come as you are." The ferocious-looking corporal had a long jawbone and was standing erect.

Why should I, he tried to retort. But the MP's superior tone, as though he were dealing with a criminal, strangely defeated him. Forgetting even to hide the photograph of the big-eyed woman from town that he kept in his pocket, he entered the office as ordered.

At the army hospital where he worked they were forced to save one yen every month. The military surgeon who directed the hospital had ordered them to save. The salary at that time, even with combat pay, amounted to five yen and sixty sen. The soldiers had to live on this niggardly sum for a month. On top of that, one yen was deducted for savings. Personal rights notwithstanding, once soldiers are commanded to do something, they have no choice but to obey. That is their duty as soldiers. He had taken out the five-yen note received as salary to have part of it saved. And the servant who collected the money and took it to the field post office had given him four one-yen notes as change. It was a post office clerk who discovered that the five-yen note was counterfeit.

It had been most carefully and elaborately printed. It appeared to be the work of someone who worked at a printing office and knew how it was done. At first glance, the note seemed old and crumpled with use. But closer observation revealed that the grime from being handled had not permeated the paper. The crumpled look too had been intentionally produced.

At the post office, a telegraph corps soldier standing nearby promptly came over, held the note up to the light, and snapped it with his fingers. He gazed at it in wonder. "Some people are sure good at this. It's amazing how every detail's been copied."

"The watermark doesn't seem perfectly sharp," said the savings clerk, a skilled calligrapher.

"Maybe."

"It's because of the paper's origin. Paper for banknotes is made by Ōji Paper Mill, but this seems to come from somewhere else."

"If you take a quick look it's almost the same, isn't it?" The telegraph corpsman pulled a note of his own from his wallet and compared the two. "It's the same. . . . In fact, the 'Five' is perfectly identical."

"Let me see, let me see." Two or three settlers who had come to the post office to read newspapers from home stepped up to the reception desk, eyes shining with curiosity.

The servant was a man over thirty who had not been able to remain in Japan due to a shady past and had come to Siberia where those with criminal records gathered. Something murky and corrupt now appeared in his face and bearing. He was conscious of it. Immediately and sharply, he sensed that in a situation like this, suspicion would soon swing in his direction. "That's funny," he said. "This bill came from Awashima, the medical corpsman. I remember it well. He's the only one who pulled out a five-yen bill, so he must've had something to do with it." He spoke with a feigned ease and in a deliberately loud voice, the better to imprint the information on the ears of everyone present.

"The banknote's from Awashima?" the clerk shot back. His voice was filled with doubt.

"Yes, that's right."

"Are you sure?"

"Yes, I am. No doubt about it."

The postmaster, a bespectacled man with malevolent eyes, emerged from a room in the back. He cast a suspicious glance at the servant over the top of his glasses. "Who does he say the note came from?" The postmaster shifted his glance from servant to clerk.

In the postmaster's shining eyes the servant saw even more clearly that he was under suspicion. He grew defiant and sullen. Pretending not to have heard the postmaster, he loudly told those assembled that there had always been something inscrutable about the medical corpsman Awashima. Before long, people from the street began to pour in attracted by the noise. Quickly the turmoil spread from the post office to the hospital.

Hearing that his banknote had been found to be a forgery, Awashima was inexplicably assailed by a strange feeling that he might indeed have unknowingly made such a note. He felt terribly frightened. Even if a person has no intention of committing a crime, it sometimes happens that a crime is committed unawares. He thought he had experienced something of the sort somewhere in the past, but he couldn't quite remember where. In elementary school, he had been punished by the teacher. It seemed to him that he had not intended to do anything bad at the time, yet the teacher had regarded his behavior as bad. Indeed, that was certainly how it occurs. It often happens that something a child does prompted by a spontaneous impulse is viewed as bad by a teacher. The child must then be punished. Moreover, this did not apply only to children; it applied to everyone. People never know when they might be charged with a crime. There are those who make it their business to pin the blame on the vulnerable. Thinking about it, he grew afraid.

2

"Take out your wallet."

"Yes."

"Got any other money?"

"I don't."

"Was this banknote yours?" With an air of importance, the MP corporal extracted the forged note from his pocket and displayed it.

"Well, I don't remember. . . . It may have been."

"Where'd you get it from?"

There was no reply.

Guarded by a lance corporal, Awashima spent two hours shut up in the office sitting blankly on a chair. On the desktop, the big-eyed woman in the photograph was smiling. The lance corporal picked up the photo and, looking at him, smirked. He was sneering at Awashima for treasuring the photograph of a prostitute, and Awashima found it unpleasant to think that the lance corporal recognized her from his own excursions into town. Falling in love with the woman was neither bad nor shameful. When a soldier was under investigation, however, such an event was treated as though it were contemptible and repulsive. It was magnified into dissolute conduct. Like venereal disease, it was despised.

When he first pulled the photograph from his pocket along with two or three folded postcards, the corporal had asked him with a derisive smile: "And what's the meaning of this?"

"Nothing."

The corporal had contemptuously flung the photograph on the desk. "You must be spending quite a lot of money on this one. . . . Without forging the bills you wouldn't have enough." He spoke as though Awashima had clearly forged money to hand over to the woman.

Awashima had no desire to defend himself. Convinced that the truth would come to light in due time, he remained silent. Yet to wait patiently was unendurable. It was not unusual for MPs to contract a venereal disease and surreptitiously come to the hospital for treatment. At such a time they bowed, grinned, and spoke ingratiatingly to medical corpsmen. Like an open hand that changes into a fist, that attitude was nowhere to be seen now. The lance corporal's expression, malicious and cruel, was that of an utter stranger who had never been treated by the hospital.

Such a sudden change in attitude is common among both military and regular policemen. Nor is it limited only to policemen. Such inconstancy is common among ordinary people as well. Even he understood that much. Even so, his anger did not subside. He wanted to insult the MP to his face by reminding him of the time he had limped into the hospital with a venereal lesion. But if he did so it would only redound to his own disadvantage. So he forced himself to hold his tongue.

While he sat blankly on the chair, the corporal and another lance corporal were at the barracks ransacking through his personal belongings, knapsack, bunk, straw mattress, and everything else in sight. Not only that, they made the other medical corpsmen put their wallets and personal effects on top of the bunks and peered at the banknotes they found to ascertain whether or not they were forgeries.

The discovery of a single counterfeit banknote did not affect the MPs' interests in the least. Had it not been discovered, there would have been no need for a strict and thorough inquiry even if a hundred or a thousand notes were circulating. But once the news of its discovery got out, it was their duty to investigate. Unless the criminal were sought out and apprehended, that duty would not be fulfilled. And not fulfilling a duty was a serious matter that affected promotions and employment.

From their first year, the soldiers got used to being lined up in front of their bunks and having the squad leader inspect their account books and the money in their wallets to see if the accounts balanced. (They were ordered upon enlistment to keep such records.) If the accounts did not balance, the soldiers were grabbed by their collars, shaken, and harshly reprimanded. And if someone's money was missing, the man whose account did not balance would find himself under suspicion. No one could conclude he had stolen it—it was a shortcoming, but no proof of theft. Nevertheless, the careless good-natured man who did not balance his accounts ended up making a great fool of himself.

As expected, it was such shortcomings that the eyes of the corporal and the lance corporal searched for as they conducted the investigation. If they could arrest someone whose numerous shortcomings made him look like a criminal, they would fulfill their duty.

Allowed to leave the office, he returned to the barracks to find all his fellow soldiers grumbling. "Awashima, did you really forge that note?" Matsumoto asked.

"Quit joking, will you," he replied with a laugh.

"The MPs say it looks like you did."

"Don't try to scare me."

On top of his bunk lay scattered notebooks, books, picture postcards, and other items dumped from the box holding his personal effects. The bankbook the servant had taken to the post office lay open without a single yen's deposit recorded in it. He was accustomed to the humiliation of having the box holding his personal effects ransacked. But he could not help feeling scorn for the servility that would drive military policemen to focus such prolonged attention on his own shortcomings although it was obvious that a soldier had no means of obtaining banknotes from any other source than his salary, which was issued by the regimental accounting office. They dare not raise their heads before the paymaster, so they swagger in front of the enlisted men. Such were his thoughts.

"Hey, Awashima." The corporal, who had been making some arrangements with the army surgeon, thrust his ferocious face through the half-open barracks door. "Did you really use it without knowing it's a forgery?"

"That's right."

"You'd better not lie!"

"It is not a lie."

"You're to stay exactly where you are. It may be necessary to investigate further."

3

The MP unit was stationed just above the railroad tracks in a three-story building of red brick. Prior to being occupied, it seemed to have served as a Russian brigade headquarters. Not a single ray of light entered its corridors. It was dim and damp, like a cellar. Led by the lance corporal, he climbed the staircase following a grimy banister. About a week had gone by. On reaching the second floor he finally felt he had ascended from the cellar to the first floor. Yet he knew well it was the second floor. On the way back, he would have to descend the stairs and pass through the dark corridor. He would flee. From the doors on both sides, the hands of military policemen would lunge forth to clutch at him. He had been brought from the outside world into an utterly isolated place. The atmosphere of a heartless dungeon permeated it. "It's nothing. They just want to talk to you. Come along." The nonchalant manner of the lance corporal who came to the hospital to summon him had struck him as all the more sinister. Countless innocent people had been cast into gloomy dungeons. The same, he thought, might happen to him.

He was led into a room containing a long desk flanked by two long benches. A sergeant major entered the room holding a pencil and took a seat opposite him. Looking younger than the ferocious corporal, the sergeant major appeared childlike. Awashima braced himself for the interrogation. Whatever he might be asked, he had nothing to hide! The sergeant major inquired how much Russian he had studied. His manner was mild and friendly.

"I began to study it after coming to Siberia, so only a little." The instant he said it, surprise flashed through his mind: how did the sergeant major know about his dabbling in Russian?

"Can you speak it?" the sergeant major lightly asked.

"How did you find out I've been trying to learn Russian?"

"I've heard you talking with Varushnya at the station. She's a beauty."

"That woman's nothing special. There's nothing going on between us." Recalling Liza Lipskaya, he grew flurried. "I know her because she comes to get free treatment for pleurisy."

"You don't need to explain. I'm not saying there's anything wrong with it." The sergeant major laughed.

"I see." Mustn't lose composure, Awashima thought.

The sergeant major kept up a rambling conversation for an hour or so, asking him about his siblings, the kind of work he hoped to do after returning home, his acquaintances in P village, and talking about his own plans to take the second-class civil service exam. The sergeant major had volunteered for active service. He was young for his rank. His manner of speaking readily revealed his dream of becoming a low-grade success. So that's the kind of man he is, thought Awashima.

While they were talking, an interpreter entered bringing in a flat-faced Korean whose eyebrows sagged at the end. The smell of opium assailed the nose. He had a thin mustache and a body saturated with the odor of squalid lodgings. The man was grimy and old. The interpreter said something in Korean and gestured. Awashima understood him to be telling the man to sit down. The Korean's upper body weaved back and forth like rice jelly, but he made no move to be seated.

"Sit down, it's all right."

The old man said something in a stifled, pained voice. The interpreter sat down next to him. Once again he gestured in the same manner as before. The old man placed his thick fingers with their round nails onto the edge of the desk and, supporting himself with his arms, sat down timidly and quietly as though the bench might break were he to sit on it all of a sudden.

The conversation in Korean, as overheard, appeared to consist of shrill, coded exclamations. The old man spoke seriously in a tone that sounded comical. Yellow, dirt-flecked teeth peered through withered lips, and his foul breath spread outward as if through a horn to penetrate the noses of everyone present. Awashima felt the filth as though he himself were being breathed upon.

"Wait here a moment." Interrupting his own monologue on the foremost authorities in criminal law and similar matters pertaining to the civil service exam, the sergeant major left the room as if going to the toilet.

Awashima shifted his seat as far toward the edge of the bench as possible to avoid the old man's breath. He watched the lip movements of the interpreter and the old man as they continued their shrill conversation. The old man's tongue seemed cramped and he moved it with difficulty. After a while, the interpreter too went out. The aged Korean and he were left in the room by themselves. They scrutinized each other. The old man's face wore a dispirited expression common to Koreans. Awashima had had so little contact with Koreans it seemed to him they all had the same profiles and expressions. Invariably manifested in their faces was the melancholy of human beings who continue to be subjected to one humiliation after another. The old man seemed about to burst into tears. He looked wretched.

Awashima only knew how to say "I don't have any" in Korean. He could not communicate with the old man. "Where do you live?" he tried asking in Russian.

The old man showed his yellow teeth and said something. His tone was sorrowful and dejected. The thin mustache rose and fell with the movement of his lips. The reply was spoken in Russian, but he could not catch the meaning.

"Why did you come here?" Once more he asked in Russian. The old man puzzled over the question as though mystified and continued to look at him timidly with wretched, doubting eyes. He gazed back at the old man.

4

Without understanding why he had been brought to the MP headquarters, he was sent back through the damp, subterranean corridor. He was irritated, felt he had been made a fool of. One of the doors in the corridor that led to the outside was open. Peering in, he saw a military detention cell.

As Awashima returned to barracks, Matsumoto, who had taken out a shogi board and was moving the pieces about alone, raised his head and asked: "Did you see the man who seems to have been arrested for forging that banknote?"

"No."

"I hear he's a Korean. They say he had three or so five-yen notes stuck in the pages of a book."

"Who did you hear it from?"

"An MP who came to get a shot for his urethra was saying it just now. An undercover agent found him out."

The undercover agent was Korean. Quite fluent in Japanese and Russian, the man was employed by the military police for thirty yen a month. The commander had announced a reward of ten yen to expedite the criminal's arrest. Enticed by the promise of ten yen, the undercover agent had gone sniffing about in search of the culprit like a dog. And he received the ten yen with delight. The military policeman had laughingly told Matsumoto the story.

"Well, then, maybe it was that Korean. We were sitting at the same desk at the MP headquarters just now." The image flashed across his mind.

"What's he like?"

"A grimy, miserable old man."

"You were asked if you knew the old man, right?" Matsumoto inquired suggestively.

"No."

"Weren't you going over to the Korean place pretending that you're off to study Russian?"

"When?"

"Recently."

"Why are you asking?"

There was a Korean hamlet about a mile away, close to a swamp. A fair-skinned young woman with an oval face lived there. She was unusually refined compared to the other Koreans in this area. Don't you know that? asked Matsumoto.

Awashima recalled being pestered by the sergeant major about the layout of the Korean hamlet, the appearance of the houses, the structure of their interiors, about the beautiful girl.

"A woman's a fearsome creature. There's no limit to the money she's capable of sucking in." Without pointing to anyone in particular, Matsumoto was alluding to the big-eyed woman from the town.

When his fellow soldiers walked into the barracks with cold, doubting eyes, he realized for the first time that they suspected him of having received the counterfeit notes from that Korean. He felt exasperated beyond measure.

5

A hole had been dug beneath a white birch in the valley. About ten soldiers were standing beside it. They had dug the hole just now with the shovels held in their hands. An officer was pacing round and round under the birch, his hand on the hilt of his military sword. He was a young man with a tight mouth and angry eyes. The soldiers' faces were colored with the anticipation of something. The officer, though conscious of the hole, the white birch, and the soldiers' glowing faces, had separated himself from it all and was apparently attempting to pursue metaphysical ideas.

Crossing a brook and passing behind a haystack, an old man slowly approached, urged forward by three military policemen. He was sunk in gloom, head drooping. It was the Korean who had been locked up in the MP detention cell. "Ah, here he comes, here he comes." From the hilltop hospital, four or five medical corpsmen ran down in their slippers.

The old man's pace was as slow as if his legs could no longer carry him. The military policemen flanking him had taken his arms and were marching him ahead. The old man's expression had darkened. A flat face with eyebrows sagging at the ends. The smell of squalid lodgings and opium. Twisting his withered lips, showing yellow dirt-flecked teeth, he seemed about to burst into tears. His arms were moving forward, dragged by the military policemen, but his trunk and legs remained behind aslant. A man struck his backside with a sheathed sword. Still the old man, like one who had lost all sensation, did not stir. Instinctively he was avoiding going to the foot of the white birch.

"Ah, it's him, it's him!"

The medical corpsmen who had descended from the hilltop came to the space the old man was crossing. One of them spoke. On approaching the Korean, they fell back a few steps as though they might be infected by a contagious disease and gazed with curiosity at the old man who was trying to stick to the ground like malt syrup.

"Corporal, sir." The corpsman who had just spoken to his comrades now boldly addressed the man striking the old man's backside. It was Awashima. "Did you come across any evidence that I forged the note?"

"Wait, will you!" The corporal glanced back at Awashima.

"Did this Yobo say he gave me the note?" he asked with malicious sarcasm.

"This one's the criminal for sure. There's nothing more to say," remarked the lance corporal pulling the old man's left arm and turning around.

"How can you say that? Old farmers like him don't counterfeit money! This is some sort of mistake."

The old man was brought to the foot of the white birch and made to stand facing the hole. The interpreter coming up after him said something in Korean. "There's nothing to worry about. Just stand quietly and keep looking over there," he told him. But the old man was terrified and sensed he was being lied to. His face was contorted with grief. "I don't want to be killed. When did I do anything to deserve being killed?" his eyes were appealing. "I want to live as long as I can! Koreans have a right to live too!" So he seemed to be saying.

The soldiers grew deathly silent and stood on each side of the old man. Their eyes all turned toward the hilt of the officer's sword.

The military sword was unsheathed and raised high behind the old man. The sturdy-looking arms, and the eyes that had been pursuing metaphysical matters, concentrated on a single spot above the old man's back.

The old man moved with a shudder.

An icy chill shot through the soldiers' bodies like a jolt of electricity. Their blood ran cold. Awashima could not keep his thighs from trembling. The military sword had swiped downward.

At the same moment, a desperate, piercing roar of lament broke from the old man's body. Far from a cry emitted by an oppressed, dispirited old man, it was powerful and defiant. "What are you doing!" he seemed to be shouting. "What have I done to justify this?"

The next instant Awashima saw the old man jump into the hole. Maybe he didn't jump. Maybe he stumbled. The old man leaped about inside the hole like the severed tail of a lizard. With large, dirty hands, he clawed wildly at the earth. And blindly he kept trying to scramble up and out of the hole. "I don't want to die!" his whole body was shouting.

The bloody military sword lowered, the officer stared vacantly at the old man as though a second stroke of the sword were beyond him. Shivering with horror, the soldiers fell back a few steps. As the old man came crawling back up, the corporal kicked him down in the hole with his boot.

"I want to live!" The old man was asking for simple compassion.

"Die, will you!" The words fell from the interpreter's lips in Russian.

"I want to live!" Knocked back down, the old man leaped about in the hole like a lizard's tail. And then once more he tried blindly to scramble up. Again he was kicked down hard by the boot. Desperately he thrashed about mightily within the narrow hole.

There was a foot-long gash on his right shoulder where he had been cut. Awashima saw the blood from the old man's wound soak into the dirty clothing smelling of opium and drip stickily down onto the hem as though he had been drenched with water. His light blue clothing turned dark. The blood never stopped flowing. The blood was the old man's driving power. As he leaped about, that driving power was draining out of his body moment by moment. Like a discarded head of lettuce, he began to wither and wilt. He summoned up the last of his strength. Again he tried to climb up.

The officer could not bring himself to strike with the sword. The idea of inflicting little cuts on the old man's hands and face, like nicks from a kitchen knife, disgusted him. He had cut the man to test the sword's sharpness. It did not cut too well. "Aah, to hell with it. Bury him as he is! What a nuisance." The officer smiled wryly to hide his embarrassment.

The soldiers holding the shovels hesitated.

"Do it! I don't care. Bury him!"

"Is it really all right? Sir!" The soldiers' hands shook and they could not wield the shovels. Each looked questioningly into the eyes of the man beside him. The officer barked out the command.

Soil began to slide down on the old man floundering about at the bottom of the hole like a half-killed snake. "Help, . . ." the old man groaned in his struggle. Indifferently the soil poured down over the old man's cries for mercy. The soldiers shivered at hearing the old man's groans. They plied the shovels wildly and piled on the soil to cut them off.

The soil filled in the hole and rose foot by foot until at last it formed a mound.

6

This was no more than an insignificant incident. Their attention diverted by the frequent appearance of partisans, the destruction of railway lines, the transfer of units, and a succession of other events, the soldiers quickly forgot about the old man.

The white birch in the valley and the mound covering the hole could be seen from the hospital on the hill. The brook flowed quietly. Awashima sometimes stepped out into the hospital garden and gazed down toward the white birch. Even now he could almost hear the groans from that pit under the heap of soil. The old man, desperately and mightily thrashing about within the narrow hole, was still there before his eyes. He shuddered.

Days passed. The next payday arrived. The soldiers received their salaries from a clerk dispatched by the regimental accounting office. They were convinced that the maker of the counterfeit banknotes had vanished after the old man's liquidation. The cruel manner of that liquidation seemed to make it all the more effective. They affixed their seals under the spot where their names were written and collected their five-yen notes and the rest of the pay. With that money, they thought, they would go to town in search of entertainment.

"Hey! This note is counterfeit too!" Matsumoto suddenly shouted in a startled, cracked voice.

"What is it? What is it?"

"This note is counterfeit too. . . . It really is counterfeit!" His voice was desperate with grief. His plans for going to town in search of entertainment had been ruined.

"Which one? Which one?"

The note was definitely counterfeit. Once again it was extremely skillfully printed. The "Five" was exactly like the real thing. A closer look revealed, however, that S, and H, and Y, and Awashima had all been handed counterfeit money. So had the army surgeon himself. Moreover, the counterfeit notes were not only foisted on the hospital but on the regiment, the military police, and the Russians as well. And now counterfeit notes were flowing on, spreading boundlessly, across the wasteland of Siberia. . . .

MAY 1928

LAND RISING AND FALLING

1

Mountains in May, when it starts getting warm, are sinister and demand caution. Snakes bask in the sunshine, lizards and geckos suddenly dart out.

Of all the animals, I hate reptiles the most. There are folks who say that people's hatred of snakes comes from an unconscious awareness that their ancestors, in ancient times before becoming human, were cruelly tormented by reptiles. I do not know whether my ancestors were birds or horses. But I do hate those weirdly slippery, clammy, vindictive-looking cold-blooded animals.

Nonetheless, snakes aside, no place is as fresh, delightful, and fragrant as a mountain in May. The old decayed brushwood leaves, the budding young chestnuts, the oaks, and the candlelike pine cones give off a pungent, bitter aroma. Mornings are transparent, like polished silver. At such a time, pheasants and bush warblers cannot help getting excited. Pheasants emit a special kind of cry different from the calls of autumn or summer. Bush warblers start to sing as they fly from valley to valley. Theirs are male voices, each calling for a female. Humans too feel the blood dancing throughout their bodies, stimulated by nature and the mountains.

Kōkichi—my elder brother—was running after a girl. I was still six or seven. Pricking their feet on bamboo stumps and scraping their shins, he and his future wife Toshie were romping about, playfully fighting, competing in picking bracken. A chance touch showed that not only Toshie's face but even the hidden parts of her body were delicately smooth. Both her hair and eyebrows were black and thick. Her lips were as red as if she used rouge. She had white, well-shaped ears. Her eyes were lively, and round as pebbles. The only flaw was her nose, which turned up toward the sky, as though cut aslant. Viewed favorably, though, even that was charming.

There was a large, tree-covered hill by her house where bracken, knotweed, matsutake mushrooms of autumn, and other vegetation rose up from the earth in profusion. "There are wild pears in the mountain . . ." When children from the hamlet, four or five of them, at times even seven or eight, each carrying a handbasket, went to the mountain to pick the wild fruit, Toshie, looking scornful, tried to keep them off her family's mountain.

Being a child, I felt humiliated that my family owned neither a mountain nor so much as a quarter acre of land. I remember that even now. At that time, the only rice field my family had was one my father had bought three years earlier for two hundred and eighty yen from a man in a neighboring village who had gone bankrupt. Everything else we grew on land rented from others. Even on the purchased rice field there was a two-hundred-yen debt to the credit union. So-and-so is poor and such-and-such is rich. Some own so many acres of rice fields. Such things were always talked about among villagers. People envied those who owned more land than they did.

As might be expected, that wounded a boy's tender and vulnerable feelings. I grew depressed and exasperated. "If only our family had a mountain with so much bracken, and knotweed, and wild strawberries." I suddenly wished for it with all my heart.

When autumn came, a rope with bells attached cordoned off the place on Toshie's family mountain where the matsutake mushrooms grew. It was to try to keep others from taking the mushrooms. That is where we stole in. And we looted the mountain from one end to the other. As we touched the rope while creeping in, the bells would ring further off. And then the watchman would roar and rush out of his hut clutching an oak staff. But by the time the watchman reached the spot, we had already plucked five or six mushrooms and tossed them into our baskets and were hiding with hushed breath in the dark bamboo thicket or in the shade of the big black pines.

"Damned brats! Where the hell have you gone? I'll break your bones for you!" With his oak staff, the watchman struck a rock covered with green moss. His foulmouthed shouts echoed against a facing mountainside, the same voice bouncing back from a distance. "Damn you, you penniless brats! You're good for nothing! Damn you!" The watchman was employed by Toshie's father for eighteen sen a day during the mushroom season. He was an old man named Utarō. He too owned no land except for a rice field of half an acre in S town. All the rest of his farming was done as Toshie's family tenant. He was definitely poor. Yet when swearing at a person, he always used the word "penniless."

"Go to hell, penniless paupers! Thieving bastards!" Utarō spat. Picking up stones, he hurled them at random toward the nearby bamboo thickets. The stones rattled against pine trunks and bounced off in different directions. Thieving truly seemed to infuriate him.

When the watchman returned to his hut, we popped up one by one from our hiding places. Shikatarō, Ushimatsu, and Torakichi emerged together. They looked at each other and giggled.

"Let's make old Utarō mad again."

"Better let's quietly cut the rope. That'll be fun."

"Oh, yeah! Let's, let's."

2

Seven years later, Toshie became Kōkichi's wife. Kōkichi was twenty-two. I, the younger brother, was fifteen. It was spring. In family terms, the marriage between a landlord's daughter and the son of a small farmer who doubled as a tenant was not a good match. Toshie herself, despite becoming Kōkichi's wife, cherished no desire to become a bride in our family. But her altered physiological condition made it all unavoidable.

"What a stupid thing that fool Kōkichi has done!" My mother said not a word of reproach in front of my brother, but she criticized him behind his back.

"It's because you hadn't got a bride for him sooner," said I as Mother and her elder sister, my aunt, happened to come to the veranda.

"You're a cheeky child, aren't you?" my aunt, who still gave me copies of *Gun Bullets,* said with a laugh. "It's too soon for a twenty-two-year-old to be taking a bride. It's only in the last year or so that Kōkichi finally managed to shoulder a hundred-and-fifty-pound bag of rice." I couldn't stand being called cheeky.

The aunt's husband was a powerfully built man capable of walking in his clogs while clutching a hundred-and-fifty-pound rice bag with each hand or crossing a narrow and flimsy wooden bridge spanning the river with three such rice bags atop his shoulders. That uncle often said that once a man took a bride, his strength increased no further. Even sumo wrestlers declined in prowess after getting married.

From my fifteen-year-old's viewpoint, my twenty-two-year-old brother had become a full-fledged adult. My brother had only finished higher primary school, nothing beyond. Nonetheless, among the people his age he was second to none in being well informed, even more so than an agricultural and forestry school graduate. That sufficed to make me respect him. Kōkichi had grown healthily and fast—like a black pine amid beeches. He had become a mature man.

Village girls kept leaving home for S town or K city one after another, as though sucked out, so that no more than two or three girls of marriageable age remained. Among the girls who went to the towns there might have been one or two Kōkichi seriously thought of marrying. But the girls who went to the towns returned before two years had passed, coughing and looking like pale, withered pears. Six months later, they spat up blood and died.

Afterward, more girls would come back coughing. They too lingered on for six months or a year and died. Some of the girls returned with their legs swollen—pressing a finger against their shins left a dent in the flesh— and unable to walk. The girls who did not get sick were very slow to return from the towns. Year after year, their younger sisters and female cousins headed for the towns as well. They could not afford to let the fear of losing their youth and health stop them. Young men too left little by little, trying to earn money, trying to live colorful lives. The village lost its charm and brightness. Needless to say, those who strolled through the village in flower-patterned muslin were the prosperous Isaburō's Toshie, Tokuemon's Ishie, and other girls who had no need to go to the towns.

Such were the conditions in the village. Recruiters from knitwear factories made annoying rounds of the houses where young men and women lived.

3

The day after she came to our household, Toshie began suffering from morning sickness. The frogs in the rice paddies croaked noisily night after night. Summer was approaching. Toshie came from her parental home after having plucked the summer tangerines from trees that bore fruit so densely the golden skins were tinged with green. She devoured them greedily, oblivious of the acidic juice that set her teeth on edge and burned her mouth. Tangerine rinds piled high outside the window. Gloomy rains pelted and drenched them.

One night, returning from the toilet that stood on a lower level opposite the storage shed, I was raising my foot onto the stone step when suddenly I heard my brother's wife painfully trying to throw up what she had eaten. She had thrust her face through the window and was struggling desperately to expel the nauseating matter from her throat. Yet quite unable to do so, she kept spitting onto the tangerine peels. She was no longer glossy or beautiful. Somehow she looked unclean and foul.

Soon the rice-planting season arrived. The planting and the preparation took my father, mother, brother, and me into the paddies where the muddy water spattered our foreheads and cheeks. We worked with the ox, built the ridges using hoes, leveled the soil. Once the rains stopped, the sun scorched our heads and bodies amid the humid heat of June.

My sister-in-law did not work. My father, mother, and brother were all satisfied with that. Father was satisfied because he had become the in-law of the wealthy landlord Isaburō. Mother was satisfied because Toshie packed each drawer of the two triple sets of chests she brought with Kohama, Kinsha, Akashi, and other expensive silk kimonos. Kōkichi was satisfied because his amorous instinct had so swiftly borne fruit.

From five in the morning till noon the four of us—parents and children—kept working in the fields like thick-skinned animals. We thought of nothing but work. I felt as though the rice mill's steam whistle at last turned us back into humans. We went home for lunch. Afterward we would go back to work until seven in the evening.

Toshie had hung up a mosquito net in her room to keep the flies away and was lying within it. New magazines, half-read, lay abandoned around her head. She did not prepare meals. "I wonder if she'll change and start to work a little once the child is born," said my mother after eating lunch and returning to the field. My brother was still dawdling in his wife's room. "Most likely she grew up playing at Isaburō's and never learned to work."

"I've no idea."

"Won't Kōkichi say something to her?" Mother frowned angrily toward Kōkichi who was pampering his bride.

"You say that but you were delighted when she brought so many belongings they stuffed the house," I said laughing.

"Why, belongings are belongings, work is work. Not working and being useless is the worst."

My brother treated his wife kindly. He shielded her from Mother and Father who had grown up always working and gobbling down rice mixed with barley. Her waist widened. The flesh of her smooth, soft cheeks grew somewhat reddish. And her lips became chapped. From within her belly, the child was stretching her skin and making her plump.

4

A farmer treasures land more than life itself.

Even a dead farmer will have no place to rest his body unless he buys land. Such was the farmer's thinking. Therefore, some money was placed in the coffin. That way the dead farmer could take out the money in hell or in heaven and buy a resting place.

Once when Mother was burying a dead cat, I even remember her tying a straw string with two small coins around the cat's neck and telling it to buy itself a place.

Money can always be stolen. A burned house turns to ashes. When a person dies, that's the end. Only the land lasts forever.

Thoughts like these led Father to purchase paddies and fields bit by bit with borrowed cash and money withdrawn from the financial cooperative. It filled him with triumphant joy to haggle over a bankrupt person's land and be able to buy it below the current market price. For seven years he lived as neither fully a tenant nor a fully independent cultivator, but rather a mixture of the two. Even the purchase of a mere fifth or sixth of an acre would make Father and Mother glow with pleasure.

"From this year on, we'll be paying a little bit more in taxes." Delighted to possess land, Mother even looked forward to paying taxes. My brother and I were listening nearby.

"That strip of land you bought is so small a cat can barely walk through it, and you're acting like you're big landlords," said my brother making a wry face.

"Maybe so, but we don't have to pay rent on that land any more or on the half-acre paddy in Nogami."

"Instead of rent you have to pay interest to the credit union."

"No, without land of your own it's hopeless," Mother repeated. "Why, it's so much better than having to fret over the land being taken away or the rent going up. You can be a lot calmer."

Gradually the village kept changing. Mr. Take, a farsighted independent farmer, sold all his land and moved to the city. The landlord Isaburō too sold a portion of his mountain and fields. The money he gained would cover the cost of sending his son to the agricultural and forestry school. And my father was not the only one struggling to work his way up from tenant to independent cultivator. There was Utarō, too, the mushroom watchman, who owned a rice paddy near S town and snatched up over five thousand yen by selling a portion of it as a site for a pharmaceutical factory.

The one who worked as intermediary in transactions of this sort was a man called Mr. Kuma. Every single one of his thirty-two teeth was wrapped in gold. This was a man who, once he poked his nose in a deal, never failed to extort a five percent commission. People feared him and did their best not to fall into his hands. They avoided him. But Mr. Kuma possessed a doglike nose for sniffing out any incipient business. Somewhere, somehow, he would get wind of it and never missed thrusting his head in and offering his services.

Electric lights came to the village. It was Mr. Kuma again who urged that electric lights be installed. Rattling old horse carriages and ancient pipe-smoking coachmen were replaced by omnibuses and stylish drivers. Cars scattered foul-smelling exhaust along the roads. And leaving behind crowds of children watching curiously from the roadsides, on they rushed toward the neighboring villages.

5

November came. One night Toshie gave birth to a child. My brother entered his wife's room. But the baby uttered no cries. Her labor done, Toshie was lying on her back looking slender and smiling brightly. The child, wrapped in cloth and absorbent cotton, had soft and fine black hair and was eerily cold. It neither screamed nor cried at all.

"It's flown free from the troublesome yoke."

Rather than sad, Toshie looked startlingly cheerful. Her face recalled the time before she became Brother's wife, when she still danced freely in the fields, and loved freely. The look of modesty and utter dependence on my brother vanished from Toshie's face. The baby was dead.

A month later, she was walking along the main street of S town murmuring soft words of affection and accompanied by a different man who was pale and slight and incessantly swinging his walking stick.

Kōkichi too left home.

6

It was my turn to take my brother's place in helping my parents and worrying about the household. This was an unprofitable and cheerless task.

7

Both the shades and bulbs of the sixteen-candlepower electric lights were stained black with soot and fly droppings. Before you noticed it, the lights were glowing with less than sixteen-candlepower brightness. In order to continue with the ten-percent shares, the electric company was playing tricks with the fuel.

When a moving picture began at the cinema, our electric lights would flicker. The powerful light suddenly snatched by the cinema meant that the lights in people's houses dimmed abruptly as though about to go out. When the projection ended, the lights suddenly brightened. When the next feature started, they abruptly dimmed again. The light waxed and waned countless times in a single evening.

Motorcars sped in and sped away every day without exception—even if it rained, even if the wind blew, even on a holiday. They arrived loaded with goods from town: canvas shoes that made straw sandals obsolete, fashionable parasols, Taishō zithers, hydraulic pumps, and the like. And from the village they took, crammed into their secondhand boxes on wheels, every last boy and girl fresh out of higher primary school.

The motorcars brought in newly patented wooden frames to replace the old rice-planting ropes that were marked at eight-inch intervals with pieces of cloth. Well buckets on poles gave way to water pumps. When rice insects bred, incandescent lamps were used. These took the place of the oil lamps that the children, after spilling oil while lighting them, would use to search the undersides of leaves for nits, sloshing ankle-deep through the paddies that reeked of rotting bog moss.

The cut rice had been threshed by a threshing machine, sifted through a sieve, hulled in a mortar, winnowed with a winnowing basket, and turned into unpolished rice. Such endless drudgery grew unnecessary. With great speed, unhulled rice poured out of a rapidly spinning machine. And when the unhulled rice was next tossed into a motorized automatic huller, the husks were blown off by the wind and the grain flowed into a receiving tub like a waterfall.

The spinning wheel, which on rainy days long ago whirred as Mother spun yarn, was now in storage above the ceiling beams, blackened with soot. Sometimes, when mice climbed on top of it, it made a clattering noise.

"What is that?"

It was nighttime. My mother, who had grown somewhat deaf and did not hear my question, continued talking to herself. "Takei came to collect the fee for the huller at noon, but I wonder if we have the money for it."

"What's that rattling sound?"

"It's good to be able to leave the hulling to a machine and not have to bother passing the mortar around, but it does take money."

"I'm asking you what's that strange sound under the roof?"

"What? Are you saying there's money up there?" Mother was starting to grow senile.

To buy canvas shoes and toss out straw sandals that used to be home-made at night, you need money. The pump, the incandescent lamp, the motorized thresher, all require money. The price of rice, on the other hand, was anything but rising. And so Mother, who once thought of nothing but land, land, land, now began to mutter to herself about nothing but money, money, money.

8

Magoshichi's daughter Oyae stepped out a car exchanging affectionate laughter with an unknown man. Though they might look like lovers, they were husband and wife. Tasuke's Omasa too returned home bringing a different type of a man whose face was equally unfamiliar in the area.

In the past, people did not come together unless they were from the same locality and of known origins. You married a person from a neighboring village or the village next to that. Moreover, it was not the young people who chose their marriage partners but rather their faultfinding and obstinate parents.

Nowadays the young women who went to the towns formed relationships as they pleased with the men they met there. They would return to the village briefly, then set out again for the towns. The next time they returned to the village they were with different men. People seemed to think of it as only natural. Though they saw it, they said nothing.

Even those who stayed in the village sensed the times were changing. Those who clung exclusively to the old-fashioned, outmoded ways were gradually nearing ruin. Aggressive, farsighted, shrewd men flourished. Firewood wholesalers became wholesalers of coal, poultry buyers shifted to buying pigs. They made out like bandits. Wholesalers who continued selling only firewood were in the end forced out of business as trees disappeared from the mountains. Wholesalers are speculative by definition. Even so, they were not impervious to certain forebodings.

As ever, Father went on purchasing land bit by bit. Land dropped in value. When independent cultivators went bankrupt, when someone put land up for sale because there were no tillers left, when Isaburō again sold part of a field for his son's school expenses—with each sale people found that the price of land dropped lower and lower, just as in autumn it grows cooler with each rainfall.

Such was the land Father scouted around for and purchased. I did not like that. Father used the purchased land as security, borrowed more money from the credit union, purchased another field. The five or six shares in the financing co-ops were useless. A share in a financing co-op had to be paid twice a year. Consequently, every month an installment notice arrived from one co-op or another. It put a squeeze on Father's purse. For all that, Father did not quit buying land. Taken in by Mr. Kuma's skillful persuasion, he even bought Yamane's barren field that no one wanted, sunless in the shadows of a pine grove. In this respect Mother, even if senile, was wiser than he.

"Do you plan to become a landlord by buying worthless fields and paddies?" To me it was so stupid and exasperating, I could not take it seriously.

"There's no way I can become a landlord. I'm just trying to leave our family a little land. When you use up money, that's that. But land stays for the coming generations." Father was simple and earnest.

"If you're buying the land for us, we don't need it."

"If you don't need it, when Kōkichi comes back I'll give it to him."

"You think Brother's coming back? . . . That's stupid. He's never coming back. No matter how many rice fields you buy, nobody needs them!"

Interest to the credit union, payments to the financing co-ops, and opposition from his wife and son began to cause Father pain. The three of us devoted all our energies to farming, yet the harvests could not catch up with the interest payments. If this continued, it was clear that we'd have to repay the debts by selling off the land for less than we paid for it. We asked someone to make inquiries at a mortgage bank with lower interest rates.

It was a spring day. "It's turned out great." Father arrived home cheerfully and at a brisk pace, as though rejuvenated. As always, he spoke simply and seriously: "They're building a train line from K to S, and it looks like we'll be able to sell a lot of our land for them to lay tracks on. We can sell it for at least a little over a yen per square yard, so it's wonderful we bought as much as we could dirt cheap. It sure was good to buy as much as we could. Now we'll make a big profit."

9

Young barley, wheat, and rye were growing taller day by day, covering all the village fields. Returning swallows crisscrossed over the plants flying so low their breasts nearly touched the green leaves.

A group of surveying engineers moved back and forth through the fields carrying measuring tape, poles painted alternately red and white, levels, and other instruments. They stretched the measuring tape, peered at the painted poles through telescopes mounted on tripods, made notes on maps, and shouted. Square posts, numbered and marked in English, were driven into the fields one after another.

Tenant farmers could not refrain from grumbling about the grain-bearing plants being trampled and broken. Father was delighted by the trampling and breaking. To the landlords and independent farmers, the trampling of the plants signified the arrival of money. Negotiations over the purchase of land began.

The opening offer was sixty-nine yen for a field of a hundred and twenty square yards Father had bought for twelve yen and sixty sen. Father held off. He wanted to cultivate the land, he said. They bid up the price to eighty-seven yen. Father repeated he wanted to cultivate that field because it was so fertile. He held off from selling. The price inched up.

I listened quietly nearby and was impressed that Father, despite his simple nature, was skilled at bargaining. Although the offer of eighty-seven yen was highly tempting, nothing in Father's manner revealed it. In the end they settled on a hundred and five yen.

There were three places where the proposed railway line crossed our land. One of the paddies, it seemed, would be cut straight down the middle. The price of land running alongside the proposed railway rose as well. The outlook was ideal. Father was not the only independent farmer who mortgaged his paddies and fields or had them seized in lieu of debt. Shōbei, Sakuemon, and Fujitarō, along with half the independent tillers in the village, resorted to same agonizing measures. They now felt restored to life. Landowners were delighted. Utarō, who had sold a paddy near town for five thousand yen, used eighty-five yen from his income to buy a field about to be traversed by the railway.

"Serves you right, penniless beggars. Everything I do turns out right. Eat my dust." He swaggered about saying whatever entered his head.

"What is that worthless Utarō braying about?"

Tenant farmers whose wheat and barley were trampled underfoot, those who owned no land the railway would cross, expressed open hostility. There were also the disappointed who ruefully said: "They just barely missed my rice paddy. If they'd only swung those rails thirty feet to the west, I would've made a killing too!"

"Somehow they missed Isaburō, even though he has so much land, almost as if they planned it." My mother was happily talking about her neighbor. She felt as though she were exacting revenge for Toshie's running away. "They only snag one patch and graze one corner, that's all."

"Well, that's interesting." I too found it gratifying.

"And they also have debts from sending their child to school, and their tenants are slow to pay rent, so it's frustrating for them."

"That's what they get. Ask me if I care."

Once the grain was harvested from the land where the stakes had been driven, that land was no longer plowed or planted. When the summer came, weeds grew there in wild green profusion. At the end of autumn, those weeds turned gray and withered. A strip of dead-colored cloth seemed to be stretched straight down the middle of a golden expanse of ripe grain. Starting in the fall, some people stopped the unprofitable sowing even in the fields next to the projected line and let them grow wild.

Winter came. Once again a group of surveying engineers arrived carrying measuring tape and red and white poles. They peered through the level telescopes, shouted, carried the square stakes to a different place, and drove them in. This time the line connecting the stakes turned and twisted somewhat, like a snake.

"Are they going to build yet another railway line?" Father's expression was worried as he returned from watching the surveyors work.

"They wouldn't build two lines in an out-of-the-way place like this."

"Hmm. That's true."

With nerves increasingly on edge, people followed the progress of the new line of stakes. The projected railway line had been shifted from the initial site to the new one. There were landlords and independent farmers whose property was traversed by the original survey but missed by the present one. The land of some was initially crossed in as many as four places, but now in none at all. People were seized by panic. Confident of obtaining a fine profit, they had been looking forward to it and letting the rice fields go to waste. Now their hopes were dashed. They were dumbfounded. Those who lucked out again with the new survey were delighted. People who owned land—landlords and independent farmers—were gripped either by joy or by sorrow. Only the tenant farmers, who owned nothing, could look on without concern.

"This time too, luckily, they cross us in four places," said Father breathing a sigh of relief. "But the first time they took only the worst land, while this time they'll get some of the best. On top of that, it's going to be hard clearing the fields we've let run wild so we can work them again."

It was odd that they would deliberately let the rails wind this way and that. A straight line made much more sense. I was a little puzzled by that until someone said: "They made it snake around like that on purpose to cross Isaburō's fields." Indeed, this time none of Isaburō's fields were left out.

"They're going to move the station away from the Gongen Shrine and bring it over to his field, aren't they?"

"He's been handing the executives quite a sum in bribes using that Kuma. Since last summer, Kuma's been brazenly traveling to K town over and over again."

"Is that right? So that's what he's been up to. I thought Kuma and Isaburō were chummy these days, and no wonder. Damn!"

Those bypassed by the railway site were in an uproar. Whether or not the line crossed people's land had a bearing on whether or not their families would be ruined. Not surprisingly, their eyes grew bloodshot with anxiety.

"Well, then, let's all go to negotiate personally with the other executives too. If that's what Isaburō's been doing, we can't just quietly walk away."

"Yes, that's right. That's right. We can't just calmly put up with this!"

The group that set out for K town made no progress. "Sure enough, a cunning person with money will be a success." I felt this keenly as I watched events. Those who operate secretly behind people's backs get lucky in every way. The stupidly honest always end up the biggest fools.

One night Kyūsuke's wife, screaming at the top of her voice, set fire to Isaburō's house. The flames, however, were smothered before they had a chance to spread. The tenant farmers too had joined the losers. Starting with the June planting, two-thirds of Isaburō's rice fields remained uncultivated and overgrown with weeds. It happened shortly after.

"Oh, this is terrible. Everything's fallen through!" Stunned, Father was sitting on the ground in front of the shit-stained chicken coop.

"What? What happened?"

"It's fallen through. Everything's completely fallen through. Come here! What'll we do? What'll we do?" Father's legs had given way and he could not stand up. He had been about to feed the chickens when a man from the village arrived to tell him that officials of the KS Electric Railway had been detained on charges of corruption and the railroad had been canceled.

"Is that all? That's nothing to get paralyzed over!" Watching my father who still was unable to rise, I felt oddly invigorated.

The villagers, ecstatic, enraged, or chagrined, were plunged one and all from the top of a cliff to the bottom of a ravine. Rejoicing had been easy. Dropping from the heights to the depths was awful!

The ravaged fields remained overgrown with weeds, and in the autumn the grasses withered into gray and rotted.

10

Before long, Father died. Born in the village toward the end of the Edo period, Father had all his life eaten nothing but rice mixed with barley. Unconcerned with malnutrition or premature aging, he thought only of acquiring some land and leaving it to his children.

In his final months, Father grew weak. The flesh that in his youth he so mercilessly overworked in the fields refused to obey him in his old age. Tasks like carrying the night-soil buckets or putting the ox to work began to cause him great weariness and difficulty. He could no longer shoulder a bag of rice. At night he could not sleep. His limbs were sluggish, and his lower back was racked with a violent pain. Long ago his entire body had moved so freely he was scarcely aware of it. Now, strangely, the whole body was listless and painful and even the simple act of standing up felt heavy and troublesome. At daybreak he shouldered a hoe and set out unsteadily to clear the land whose devastation he now regretted. The work made little headway.

This time it was the land that deserted him. The paddies and fields had all been mortgaged. After the electric railway was canceled, the price of land plummeted like a well bucket. Father must have realized he could not fight the current any longer. Still he strove not to release his hold on the land. He borrowed more money to pay the interest. But Mr. Kuma, who a few years earlier had come pressing him to buy land, now rushed in with the speed of an arrow to collect the debts. Wasting no time on civilities, he bluntly told Father to sell off all the land and bring the matter to an end.

In the same way that long ago Father had enjoyed knocking down the land price of men who had gone bankrupt, now other young men playfully beat down the price of his land. It became dirt cheap. He must have felt that his entire life as a father was a pointless failure, the story of a simple, dull-witted fool. The final settlement of his lifetime had been made. And what remained was zero. Like a tree that provides whatever shade it can during its life span and then gradually and irrevocably withers, he died.

I was glad that the land and the debts disappeared at the same time. I grew cheerful. Kōkichi came back from K city. And then Mother died.

Mother had been upset that a policeman occasionally came by, under the pretext of taking a census, to ask about Kōkichi. The policeman's inquisitive questioning focused solely on Kōkichi. Was he married? What was he doing? Might he not come back in the near future? That was the one question he never neglected to ask: might he not come back in the near future? Mother had even begun to worry that her son may have become a thief.

We felt relieved. Paddies, fields, money, family ties—all had vanished. We could do what we liked. The estate of Toshie's father Isaburō, overgrown with wormwood, hay, and rushes, was ignored by all. Kōkichi and I took Mother's ashes to the spot where Father was sleeping and buried them at his side. It was autumn. Over the tomato fields the sun shone clear and cold as a razor. Above the village assembly hall, and beyond in S town, with its white pharmaceutical factory and its power plant outlined sharply beneath the brilliant sky, something seemed to be crumbling and something else to be stirring.

I knew what my brother was doing. The day following our mother's burial, Kōkichi hurriedly set forth from the village.

MAY 1930

THE CAPE

1

Covered with black pines, the semicylindrical mountain thrusting into the blue sea sheltered the village from the roaring westerly winds. Where the sloping red earth turned into a steep cliff and dropped into the sea, rugged red reefs rose out of the water. Secluded deep within a cove, protected by a breakwater, stood a landing place. The mountain forming the cape rose up behind the village and stretched on to link up with various other distant mountains. At the base of the mountain, near the village, there was an oak grove. The acorns grew in tight clusters on pointed branches arrayed against the blue sky.

Tossed about by the west wind, the soot and smoke rising from the soy sauce factory blew against the oak grove. With its soot-blackened roof tiles beneath a dozen brick chimneys, its dozens of buildings standing in rows, the factory occupied the level part of the village. It emitted a salty stench of unrefined soy and a damp odor of heated malt. The banging of coopers' mallets tightening the hoops, the rattle of cartwheels transporting casks of soy to the waterfront, the songs sung by workers churning unrefined soy, all endlessly mingled, rose into the air, and echoed against the mountainous backdrop. Encircling the soy factory, small tumbledown houses roofed with dirty thatch were scattered along the terraced hillside that rose between the flatland and the mountain. They looked like pigpens. Neither rethatched nor repaired in years, they seemed about to collapse. Nets of braided rope covered the roofs to keep the rotten thatch from being blown off by the wind. Senkichi grew up under such a roof.

His father Sōkichi had an aged, wrinkled face. Ever fearful of being late for the factory's morning bell, Father would push open the rickety door while it was still dark and hurry down the narrow path. Father did not use a toothbrush. He merely wet his hands with water drawn from the well and wiped the sleep from his eyes. At night when it was so dark neither the cape nor the pine grove could be made out, he listlessly carried his body home, his stomach filled with pickled greens and warm rice that was seven parts barley.

Wrapped in a dirty hand towel, a hot rice ball lay concealed within Sōkichi's clothing. The freshly boiled food was hot enough to scorch the skin of his stomach. Senkichi, meanwhile, sat on the threshold, his mouth blankly open, hugging his empty stomach. Father was coming home with rice he had swiftly ladled into his towel when the master was not looking and thrust beneath his clothes.

Senkichi was waiting for him. His mother and elder sister were wait-ing too. With earth-stained hands they picked up the rice ball and devoured it down to its last grain of barley, paying no attention to the sweat and dirt of the hand towel. Sometimes sugar, soybeans, or bottled soy sauce came tucked in his garment. At times it was a teabowl or a plate. But there were times when for some reason Father returned without any food. At such times Father's wrinkled face seemed sad to Senkichi. When no food arrived, it was not only he and his sister who could not keep from groaning. Mother called Father an incompetent worker and criticized him mercilessly. Sōkichi groaned in pain and snuffled through welling tears.

Although he worked without thinking, Father could not forget about food for his children. For years Sōkichi had been repeating the same action. Burned by steaming rice, his belly was red and inflamed. Yet he could hardly speak to a physician about it. He kept on putting the hot rice against the red burn on his stomach. After countless repetitions, the festering red skin turned black. Soon he ceased to feel the heat of the food, and the wartlike charred spots left a permanent mark on his body.

The thatch roof, disintegrating over the years, went unrepaired and neglected. The soot and smoke, blown about by the wind every day of the week, rose over the village defiling the air and scattering against the oak grove.

2

Every year the factory grew larger. The eaves of the buildings joined to form an odd, narrow space too cramped even to contain a vat of unrefined soy or be turned into a malt room or storeroom. This space was fitted with floor-boards and bed frames, walled with straw mats, and converted into a men's dormitory. There were no doors. Hanging straw mats took the place of windows. The nostril-scorching smells of unrefined soy, malt, and the sulfur used for fumigation penetrated the area. At times, raindrops blown astray by the wind splashed over the rain gutters and fell onto the heads sleeping side by side.

As a newcomer, Senkichi left his house to live in the dormitory. His sister Koyoshi was hired as a kitchen maid by another factory where, arms bared like a man, she washed barley. The dormitory was jammed with men: single men, married men from neighboring prefectures leaving their wives at home, old men whose wives had fled in disgust from their soymaking husbands, and farmers who came to work during the slack season. Senkichi lived in their midst. In midwinter they were given only a thin and threadbare cotton quilt for every two men. The quilts were cold and slippery with grease and dirt. In summer, they became nests for mosquitoes and fleas. In winter, lice the same color as the quilts crawled along the creases.

As the fragrance of fresh wood used in the new construction faded from the factory in less than a year, the salty odor of unrefined soy soaked into the pillars and mats. It soaked into people's skins too. Within ten days, Senkichi became a part of that smell. Among the soy factory workers it was the brewers who worked the longest and hardest and were paid the lowest wages.

It was while making a fire in the hearth, one cold evening in late March when Senkichi had finished the sixth year of primary school, that Father suggested he become a cooper. Senkichi was gazing intently at the yellow moisture on the skin of the bamboo scraps blazing in the fireplace. "Not a cooper!" He shook his head.

Sōkichi's lower lip stuck out with displeasure. "No matter how much a brewer works these days, he gets no more than a set annual pay. But a cask maker gets that much just for making eleven large casks. For all the ones you make after that, you get paid extra."

But Senkichi declared: "No, I don't want to." It was not that he had a special dislike of cask making. There was another reason, but it was hard to bring it up. His sister, who happened to be present, suddenly cut in with an explanation: "Sen wants to go to middle school. The other day he secretly borrowed Father's seal and sent out an application." The father's hand, thick-skinned, huge, and rough, descended explosively upon him along with a burst of angry words from his mother's sharp mouth. Mother's cheeks flushed red: "Doing such brazen things at your age! You'll grow up to be no good!" The sister, having broken her promise of secrecy, looked proudly at her parents and stole a grin at her brother who was trembling and holding back the gathering tears.

Father had gone to the factory and would be away all day. Mother had gone to the field. During that time, Senkichi took out an empty petroleum can serving as a desk and wrote the application in the manner learned from his teacher. Koyoshi, wet from washing barrels, came in to take a dry kimono and quietly peeked over her brother's intently hunched shoulders. After making her promise to keep it a secret from their parents, Senkichi showed his sister the application.

He remembered that evening well. Before graduation, in an essay on his future goals, he wrote about becoming a great scholar, but he gave that up. Feeling that he could not honestly face his teacher, he had spent the entire night in thought. The next day his life in the men's dormitory began. His grandfather had worked in the warehouses, and so had his great-grandfather. He had lived in the men's dormitory until the master helped him to find a wife. It was to be expected that both his own son and grandson would inherit his warehouse job.

Thirty single men older than Senkichi were idling about the dormitory. Once the number of workers grew and the business structure changed into a corporation, the master had stopped helping the men find wives. Local girls longed to go to town and looked down on brewers as men who stank of soy. Among the male workers there was one in his thirties who was serious and interested only in working hard, one in his forties who wore a red loincloth and enjoyed visiting prostitutes, and various others. Those who lacked the money to go drinking cheap alcohol or buying women formed a circle around a scooped-out hearth and swept the wood shavings from the barrels into it. Only the fire was cheerful. If its sparks ignited the hanging mats, they snuffed them out.

Every evening, a man named Hatta from workshop number six came by. He was brusque, and craggy like a rock. Whenever they saw Hatta, the men warming themselves packed tightly around the fire changed their attitude somehow and broadened the circle to make space for him. Senkichi took note of this. It was the attitude taken only toward a very close friend or a superior. On his arrival, the obscene stories and idle chatter ceased and the focus spontaneously shifted to Hatta.

Senkichi could not really understand what Hatta was saying. Judging from his accent and face, Hatta was not from the region. Senkichi could not comprehend at all why Hatta evoked everyone's friendship and trust. One evening after Hatta had gone back, he quietly put a question to a distant relative who was nicknamed Yatchin.

"Where is he from?"

"He's really great. Still young, but he's already been to jail."

"Gambling?"

"Don't be stupid! They threw him in jail for being a labor activist. When you have the nerve to demand what's your due, the bourgeoisie throw you in jail."

There were times when Senkichi could not understand Yatchin's words either. But just the tone of his voice sufficed to make him respect Hatta. As much as Senkichi could not clearly make out what Hatta was saying, he seemed to be a remarkable person. Not only that, but Hatta's words stimulated his own desire for knowledge:

"They're now doing research in laboratories on adding yeast fungus to unrefined soy. When you toss that in, the soy ferments quickly and the sauce can be squeezed out in seven or eight months instead of the year it takes now. That way, the circulation of capital speeds up. They can cut down on the labor for mixing—and besides there are mixers being made around Tokyo that run on compressed air. In time it'll be done that way here, too, so we have to give it serious thought. Using machines is good. But if we go on strike and two or three stokers betray us, mixing will get done by machines and we'll lose."

Such were the things Hatta spoke of. Senkichi tried hard not to miss any of what Hatta said. But worn out from the unaccustomed labor of the day, he was overcome by a stubborn drowsiness and his head kept dropping forward unawares. Hatta's talk elicited profuse agreement, sighs, and excitement from Yatchin. Whenever Yasukichi asked a short question, Hatta would expend hundreds of words in a detailed and clear explanation. People at the factory called each other by nicknames formed from fragments of their actual names: Makichi was "Maki," Sadaji was "Sada," Tōtarō was "Tokkon," and so on. "Yatchin" derived from Yasukichi. Only Hatta was called by his formal name. This too was a sign of everyone's respect.

After Hatta left, everyone faced each other and crept under their thin quilts. The pillows were four-inch-high blocks of hard wood shiny with grease. Wind that reeked of raw soy blew whistling through gaps in the straw mats. They talked and commented in various ways on what Hatta had said. The most senior—and the most arrogant—of the dormitory residents was the man in his forties who wore a red loincloth and appeared to resent the other men's respect for Hatta.

"Senkō, watch out that Hatta doesn't take your sister. If you're careless, Hatta's going to steal her." Red Loincloth took up his position in the corner where there was the least wind and spoke so that all could hear him.

"That's a lie."

"A lie, is it? You'll see, he'll steal her."

3

Sōkichi was over fifty. Upon starting at the factory, everyone was forced to undergo a painful probationary period. Sōkichi knew that. At the age of twelve or thirteen, his bones not yet fully formed, he was shouldering buckets of soy twice his weight and being rushed along the wet and slippery deck that formed a narrow path between the giant vats. Older and stronger men, accustomed to the work, pressed him from behind running so close their buckets collided. Sōkichi had no room to take steady steps. Often he slipped and fell into the soy. When the carrying pole slid from his shoulder, the soy-filled buckets would strike the deck with a loud crash, the buckets shattered, and the soy splashed all around. At times, the buckets missed the deck and plopped straight into a vat.

"Hey, watch what you're doing!" Hearing the sound of the breaking buckets, Ueki the master paused in his factory rounds to peer from the staircase. Thereupon the other men would piously upbraid Sōkichi for his misstep. The master laughed as he glanced over at Sōkichi, thoroughly soaked in soy, clinging to the vat's edge and clambering out like a wet mouse. He did not scold him for breaking the buckets. To become a full-fledged worker, he had to fall into the sauce any number of times. The soy buckets were heavy as lead and pulled the shoulders down toward the ground. Sōkichi had to brace his maturing bones and resist that pull. As time went on, his legs acquired a separate set of knots below the kneecaps. At present, it was his son Senkichi who was receiving the baptism of soy.

Just now his daughter Koyoshi had been crying after a scolding for some blunder in the kitchen. Sōkichi could not detach his gaze from the painful work his two children were doing. Forgetting there was a time when he too had been treated as badly, or worse, he longed to protect them. Koyoshi had recently managed at last to keep up with the other women and girls. She was starting to handle not only the kitchen work but also the rough chores like washing barrels and straw sacks. She did this in addition to cooking. With a hand towel covering her hair twisted at the back of her neck, and wearing clogs with rope thongs, she worked among the men. To repel unwanted male advances, she learned to be brusque. In the washing contests, she did not lose. Her pay was twenty-three sen, a woman's full wage. Watching his daughter briskly at work, Sōkichi grew irrepressibly happy.

In early June, when the surface of the newly fermenting soy hardens and rises, Koyoshi unconsciously began trying to avoid Sōkichi's eyes. Sōkichi did not notice it. Even if he saw, he would not understand. At the same time, she began to look both happy and shy. Although she was sunburned, her hands and feet had grown rough, and her fingers had thickened, she acquired a new roundness and beauty. She was feeling the ordinary emotions that everyone experiences. Sōkichi could not imagine what change was taking place within his daughter.

"You have to be careful with young people these days, Sō-san," the senior woman in the kitchen warned him meaningfully while putting the plates away. "You don't know what they'll do out of your sight." Sōkichi had no idea what she was talking about. He continued to work absentmindedly until his wife Okiyo began to snap at the daughter.

In the evening, Okiyo summoned Koyoshi and shouted at her: "This Hatta is a wanderer from God knows where!" Koyoshi was innocently smiling. Sōkichi, returning home having finished his meal, walked in on the scene. Okiyo, daughter of a prosperous independent farmer from a neighboring village, had despised soy brewers when she arrived as a bride through the master's mediation. Her old father had insisted, however, and preserved the honor of the locally influential master. Sometimes even now her manner of speaking betrayed her contempt for soy brewers. It was unpleasant to hear. Slightly out of breath, Okiyo resumed.

"If you keep on flitting around, you'll get to be damaged goods."

"I don't mind being damaged goods."

"Idiot! I can't understand how you can do such things."

"It's all right." Koyoshi continued to suppress her laughter.

It was not in the least unusual for young men and women working in the same factory to pair off. It was only natural. Sōkichi was not particularly surprised. Before long, opposing his wife, he yielded to his daughter: "As long as our child is managing to feed herself, that's good enough, isn't it? It's none of anyone's business!"

Hearing this, his wife pierced him with her eyes: "What, just like that?"

"As long as she's feeding herself, that's good enough, isn't it?" he persisted.

Hatta and Koyoshi began to live together. Early in October, Hatta was suddenly discharged from the company. At the same time, Koyoshi who had said she wanted to earn as much as possible before giving birth, was dismissed from the kitchen. Hatta had nothing in reserve.

"What are we going to do?"

"It can't be helped." Koyoshi did not look worried.

"But we're broke."

"I'll tell Dad. It'll work out somehow."

Gazing at his surprisingly optimistic wife, Hatta felt reassured.

4

The oak grove at the base of the mountain turned red and the west wind blew daily over the cape and through the village. Leaves stripped from their branches were tossed about by the wind and wandered fluttering through the sky. Under the torn thatch roofs, family members huddled motionless like birds warming their bodies in their nests. The cold crept into the houses chilling hands, feet, and backs. Sōkichi's wife turned on him at the slightest provocation. He and his son put up with it in silence. Koyoshi thought about Hatta's feelings and felt uneasy.

Sōkichi did not sleep at night. Even though the wages were low, so long as you worked at the factory you could at least eat all the barley and rice you wanted without worry. Now you had to start worrying about the barley and rice. He helped to row a boat harvesting sea cucumbers and went to work in a salt field some four miles away. Hatta and Senkichi put several types of medicine into cardboard boxes and walked around the neighboring villages trying to sell them. Few wanted to buy medicines from amateur drug vendors wearing quilted jackets that reeked of unrefined soy.

Working on the salt farm and harvesting sea cucumbers were tasks quite unfamiliar to Sōkichi. He found it very hard to acquire the knack of scooping the seawater with a long ladle and spreading it as widely as possible over the salt field without scattering sand from the force of the pouring water. The west wind blew the seawater sideways and drenched his clothing. At times a sudden gust would drive the water backward splashing it over his head and the back of his neck. His neck grew cold and sticky with salt. It was difficult using an ox and gathering the salt that had hardened on top of the sand. Even with great effort he could barely complete half a share of the work.

At dusk, crossing the pass where the cape rose to join the mountains of the interior, he walked the four miles home. Beneath the pass, in a spot sheltered from the wind and giving a lovely view of the entire village below, stood the master's villa with its sculpted gate. Whoever walked by always heard the master's tranquil voice emerge from within, chanting a *nō* song.

Every evening Hatta slipped sideways through a gap in the factory fence and entered the men's dormitory. Sōkichi could not relax. Will Hatta be able to find decent work? Painfully he shifted his body from one position to another and then another. Soon after eating he was assailed by hunger. Like a male animal feeding the choice, tasty meat to the female and the young while eating only the leftover entrails, sinews, and skin, he ate only a minute amount of the barley rice and pickled greens. When it was necessary to leave a portion for the next morning, he kept that in mind as he ate.

He knew as well as anyone that if he went to his wife's village, her family could afford to spare two or three bags of barley. But it was not in his nature to subject himself to the scorn of his wife and mother-in-law by going out to borrow barley. He went to bed, yet could not fall asleep. Heavily he tossed about, stepped outside to urinate, blew his nose. The electric lights of that villa at the pass were glowing incessantly like malicious eyes. The sleepless night was long. As dawn approached, the crumbling house grew even colder, a bitter taste filled his mouth, and his stomach ached from hunger. In the morning frost covered the ground.

They spent New Year's without rice cakes or *sake*. But Sōkichi felt that just staying alive mattered most. A person could reduce three meals to two, and two to one, and survive even on salted greens alone.

Several months passed.

5

In the middle of March the union was finally born. After its formation, Mr. —— and Mr. —— of the Japan Labor——, which the union was expected to join, arrived for the opening ceremony. Taking a seat by themselves near the podium, the corpulent Mr. ——, moving his limbs with difficulty, and the hatchet-faced Mr. —— surveyed the assembled brewers who reeked of soy.

Sōkichi was watching attentively from the rear, nervous lest Hatta, who was delivering the opening address and progress report, should grow tongue-tied before the distinguished visitors. Five slogans writ large on a long strip of paper covered the front wall. When Hatta finally finished speaking and stepped down from the podium, Sōkichi happily drew in a long breath. He nodded to himself as if to say "Good, good!" And he left the youth assembly hall as if the union meeting were already done. He did not want the others to see his welling tears.

A month later, urged on by Yasukichi and Red Loincloth, men from other workshops began to join one by one. Another month or so later, eighty coopers joined up at once. Hatta, who hardly slept for three days around that time, breathed a sigh of relief and felt ecstatic.

"With the numbers getting this high, I guess we'll be all right," said Sōkichi.

"No, no, the great task from now on will be the union members' group discipline."

"And how's that done?"

"You'll see little by little," Hatta cheerfully replied.

6

In January of the third year, 192——, a worker's full annual wage rose from a hundred and twenty to two hundred and eighty yen.

In March the wooden pillows, shining black with grease and the polish of use, were carried to the mouth of the furnace, tossed in along with the coal, and there they burned emitting a human stench.

Barley and rice meals changed from seventy percent barley to seventy percent rice. And the rice was imported at that. Raw sardines were occasionally served with the vegetables, and you could sip all the miso soup you wanted.

Furthermore, in 192——, on a slender part of the cape thrusting into the sea, a site was cleared and a new dormitory began to be built. The mats hanging in the old dormitory, blackened with soot from the open fire, were torn off and flung out onto a vacant lot under an apricot tree starting to wither in the salty air. The mats were ancient and tattered. Pelted by rain, they went on rotting unobserved.

Furthermore, in 192—— wages that had been set by the month were changed to a daily rate of some two yen per day and the workday was reduced to ten hours including rest.

Both Sōkichi and Senkichi were back at work in the factory. Sōkichi no longer took home the hidden hot rice. But the black scars on his belly remained. When he discovered men who betrayed the union in order to ingratiate themselves with the master, or secretly complained and spoke ill of it, he hated them intensely and grumbled persistently. The crumbling thatched roofs scattered about the base of the mountain were replaced by new roofs, sometimes of tile, and even people from neighboring districts moved in.

Along the streets, shops selling apples and bananas appeared for the first time. The shelves on one side of the stationery store were lined with books. Senkichi walked from his house to the factory. When he did piece-work, he finished the day in five or six hours, went to a public bath, and returned home around two o'clock. Since he worked with excessive speed at such times, five hours of labor made him feel as exhausted as a serious bout of fever.

Evenings he read books and attended meetings. Various pamphlets and books lay on his desk, including a volume by Rosa Luxemburg.

7

Sōkichi turned sixty. As he aged, the work grew gradually harder for him. He had trouble falling asleep at night. It weighed on his mind that Ueki the master was scheming to form a company union called "The Sincerity Club" and giving workers time off to have them listen to sermons by a reactionary preacher. In order to assemble everyone for the sermon, the company handed out a free box lunch along with a pint-and-a-half bottle of Masa-mune *sake* and paid their daily wage while exempting them from work. For two or three days Sōkichi did not go to work but bustled feebly all around to keep the union members from attending. When everyone lined up and marched in procession with red flags in the lead, he too sang the songs. At these times hot blood coursed through his veins, and he grew excited with happiness as though he were once again a youth of twenty. Forgetting his weakened legs, he wanted to spring about from place to place.

"You're an old man, so no one's going to mind if you don't go." His wife grumbled about Sōkichi neglecting work at the warehouse to run about on behalf of the union and earning no money. She thought it a waste that he would not go discreetly to accept the longed-for *sake* and box lunches that the club was kindly giving away.

"Shut up!" Sōkichi grew furious. He could barely control the urge to give his wife a beating.

8

A few years later, Sōkichi died.

The master could not forget the men of old who would leap up to work at a word from him and strove to curry favor with him. He yearned to push everyone back into the past. At the factory there were frequent strikes. Even though they were resolved, a year or so would go by and then new demands would bring them on again. In the company's makeshift reasons for rejecting demands, behind all its declarations, there always lurked the intent to crush the union. In time, it appeared openly in the company's actions.

After three weeks had passed during which the soot-stained chimneys —there were thirty of them now—stopped spewing smoke as though dead, the company fired the strikers and hired local farmers who had finished planting the barley. The union members, who had been watching with suppressed glee as the unstirred soy grew hard on the surface and began to rot and mice rampaged through the grain warehouse and the malt room, were suddenly thrown into confusion.

Sōkichi did his utmost to stop the arrival of farmers from nearby villages. Putting his familiar face to use, he made a round of all the villages to dissuade their inhabitants from accepting work at the factory. At the houses whose men were absent and working, he cornered the wives and the old folks and either criticized them harshly or implored their sympathy, all but kneeling before them with clasped hands. The persuading was not only difficult but ineffective. Worn out from the walking, he was disheartened. A long time ago, his flesh had seemed weightless. His arms, legs, and torso had moved almost unconsciously in response to the requirements of a task. But gradually his flesh fell away leaving only the tendons, the skin stretched into wrinkles, and a body that felt heavy and painful. It was especially his legs, grown knotty below the knees when he shouldered heavy loads of soy as a youth, that refused to obey him. Occasionally his legs were seized with sudden cramps and he was paralyzed for a time. This often happened even when he was walking his rounds. This frightened him. Nevertheless, he summoned his energy and rose. We must not be destroyed by the master, he thought, and lashed his painful body onward.

Before dawn he arose and crossed the ridge of the cape while the young people slept soundly—tired out from discussions that lasted past midnight, from keeping watch, from direct action. His legs were stiff and sore. The village was enveloped in stillness and the sun was just beginning to dye red the treetops of the black pine grove to the east. Farmers heading for the factory from a neighboring village were already starting to climb toward the ridge from the opposite direction. There was a group of five or so in overcoats with towels tied around their cheeks and old floppy sports caps hiding their earlobes. Dry grass by the roadside was white with frost.

Sōkichi stopped them at the ridge. The company had given the hired farmers a generous thirty percent increase in wages. Every night it treated them to boiled rice with fish and vegetables, wheat noodles, sushi, and the like. For entertainment it hired a chanter of ancient tales. Having finished planting barley, farmers were now in a bind with no work until next year's rice planting other than weaving straw mats or making rope. Even if temporarily hired by the soy factory, far from being paid thirty percent extra, normally they could only get perhaps eighty percent of the regular wage due to their inexperience. Growing rice and barley brought in a pitiful income, and in recent years they were barely eking out a living. The farmers derived far greater pleasure from gazing at banknotes and silver coins than at Sōkichi's toothless and wrinkled face.

"Are you fellows fixing to let us rot before your very eyes?" Despite being pushed, Sōkichi did not move. He spread his arms and kept the men from passing. "A good time for us is a bad time for the master. And when the master's happy, then we're being hounded by interest payments and can't find anything to eat. It's not a life fit for humans. We just scratch along driven and drooling like cows or horses. See, there'll never come a time that's good for us and good for the master. Just watch! If you let us down, a day will come when the master will work you so hard only your skin and bones will be left."

"Quit your whining! If you want money, scram and go to work."

"Wherever you go, working people throughout the world are linked together like brothers and sisters. Our interests and the masters' interests are totally different. It's no good betraying us and letting yourselves be shamelessly tricked by the master. That's not the way to build solidarity with your fellow workers."

Sōkichi tenaciously held his ground, arms outstretched, and spoke tirelessly on. No matter how many speeches and meetings were held, no matter how many protests were lodged against the company, as long as those farmers went to work and mixed the unrefined soy and packed the finished sauce into casks and shipped them out, the union members were sure to be wiped out just as soon as their funds ran out.

"Are you planning to kill us? Falling for it when the company mumbles sweet nothings?" he continued. "Well, do what you want then! Side with the company and try to kill us! Kill us! Kill us! Kill us! Ha-ha-ha." Suddenly he grew uncontrollably excited.

The farmers, though realizing they would be in trouble if they missed the work bell, inexplicably felt Sōkichi's words twine round them like a snake and could not move. A man in a floppy sports cap had experienced being hired when his field was idle, being lodged in the dormitory, and being paid seventy percent of the regular wage. He knew that this pampering by the company would not last and would soon revert to seventy percent pay. "If they hadn't gone on strike, we wouldn't be getting thirty percent extra for the work," he told his companions.

"Please, I beg you." Sōkichi suddenly joined his hands and turned to the oldest farmer in supplication. "We're all fellow workers. If you simply turn back, we'll win. Help us, help us!"

"What do we do?" The old farmer faced the others.

"Let's not fall for the company tricks!" the man in the sports cap said vigorously.

Every morning Sōkichi went out early, dragging his painful legs, and threw all of his strength into persuading the farmers. One morning, a group of ten or so climbed up to the ridge with hurried steps. Among them were two gangsters the company had brought to a neighboring village in anticipation of picketing strikers. Sōkichi met them below Ueki's villa with its carved gate. When the two spotted him, they rushed forward, kicking up the earth, heads high and arched back like gamecocks. Sōkichi fought them spurred on by a passionate hatred. He lacked confidence in his strength, however, and his body could not do all he asked of it. The gamecocks threw themselves upon him, their weapons sharp as powerful beaks.

Sōkichi was savaged. His cheeks, hands, and lips were ripped open and covered with blood. His head had been gashed by their weapons. Knocked down onto grass white with frost, he groaned. He sensed he would probably die. He had lived for the sake of making his children's lives and his own fit for human beings. He had always sought that with all of his might. At times he had sought for it blindly, at other times with focus. But his quest had never borne victory. And now he would probably die.

When he was brought home on a shutter, past ten o'clock in the morning, he was shouting and roaring with sinister laughter. His ghastly features appeared bereft of reason, as if the gamecocks' weapons had injured his brain.

"Kill us, kill us, kill us, try to kill us! Working people throughout the world are linking up beautifully! Ha-ha-ha, kill us, kill us if you can! Try to kill us!"

"Look at that!" Okiyo glared angrily at her badly wounded husband. "It does no good for you to go out alone, but you go anyway. And this is what happens." Hearing not a word, he waved his arms about and roared with laughter: "Kill us, kill us, kill us! Try to kill us, ha-ha-ha."

For two days he shouted, laughed, and waved his wiry arms about like a man unable to die without getting something in return. But on the third day he breathed his last and was buried in a seaside cemetery. A rough marker, just a roof made from boards, was erected over his grave. Before long, people forgot about him. In time, even if they tried to remember, they could not.

The soot and smoke gushing out of the dirty brick chimneys rose over the village every single day and, stirred by the wind, kept on blowing against the oak grove at the base of the mountain.

Militarized Streets

1

Several single-wheeled carts were rushing full tilt through the slum. A coolie the color of dust was pushing each one. The solitary wheel of each vehicle groaned as if in pain beneath the weight of huge gunnysacks. Across from the slum stood a Chinese barracks with blue roof tiles. The carts, their rhombus-shaped sails inflated, left the slum and disappeared behind the unbaked brick walls of the barracks. The sails vanished from view. Only the wheels continued to groan in the distance. . . .

A child was defecating behind a sorghum straw fence of a slum shanty, squatting surreptitiously as even Mencius himself might have done when young, and poking at the excrement with a slender stick. Heaps of refuse—scraps of paper, rags, straw, broken glass—lay scattered everywhere. A woman with bound feet hurried by looking like an ancient curio from a thieves' market. Coolies with flattened faces were rummaging hungrily through the bits of trash, the peanut shells, the watermelon rinds. Anything that seemed edible—carrot stems, wilted greens, or radish peels—they pulled out and ate.

In the opposite direction from the groaning carts, a match factory's machine saw was devouring poplar logs with a roar as though whittling bones. Four or five White Russian soldiers stepped out of the bluish black interior of the Chinese barracks.

"Need a ride?" A crowd of rickshaw pullers in search of customers materialized and surrounded the Russians. The seats of the coolies' trousers shone with wear. They squabbled noisily, each trying to be the first to grab a customer. "Need a ride?"

The Russians, not so much as glancing at them, walked off with great long-legged strides. Long ago they had fled east from their native land and then from Siberia escaped to China. The only clothes they had arrived in had fallen apart, even the belts. Although penniless, they managed to lay hold of suits and overcoats that were ten years out of style. As in the past, they wore Cossack hats of smudged black fur, leather boots, and gray-blue trousers that were baggy in the seat and tight in the knees. Their heads and shoulders towered above the shorter Chinese. A man walking alongside dressed in Chinese clothing addressed them. It was Yamazaki.

"What did you get paid this month?"

"Not a penny."

"And last month?"

"Last month, too, not a penny."

"And the month before that?"

"The month before, too, not a penny."

"Smack that man!" Yamazaki, a Japanese wearing Chinese clothing, lowered his voice. "To hell with him, smack him! Give that great big Chang Tsung-ch'ang a good smack on his fat blubbery cheeks!"

The White Russian soldiers tossed their heads back and burst into mirthful laughter. Their chief, Mirklov, had sold them to Chang Tsung-ch'ang. After that they were bought by the Shantung Army. Straddling short Chinese horses, their shoes nearly dragging along the ground, they were sent repeatedly into the danger of the front lines. At the front, some had intercepted bullets and fallen. Some were driven back having lost a leg, an eye, or an arm. Some grew tired of the smell of garlic wafting about the Chinese and deserted. Others got into furious fights with the detested Chinese soldiers. When they returned from the front to the Russian bars, the reek of blood and gunpowder had permeated their very flesh.

"Son of a bitch! What's with that Chang Tsung-ch'ang? The whorehouse madam almost bit his lips off! Twenty-seven mistresses he's got! To hell with him! Smack him hard!" The White Russian soldiers tilted up their faces with even more delighted laughter.

Young spring buds were beginning to sprout along the row of acacias lining the tin wall of the match factory before them. Higher up, a flock of little crows flew happily through the sky over the town, their feathers catching the light of the setting sun.

2

The factory smoldered within lavender fumes filled with the scorching smell of dust, sulfur, phosphorus, and resin. Swift as magicians, boy and girl workers lining the workbenches were slapping matches into little yellow boxes, making an endless unbroken sound like the clicking of cowherds' tongues. The bustle and the noise made the teeth rattle. Deftly snatching up fixed amounts of matches brought in from the drying room, they stuffed them into the miniature drawers and shut them with a clap within their labeled outer frames, disposing of each box in a flash. Even playful boys and girls of six or seven were industriously toiling away.

The Chinese, shouldering the smaller children in baskets and making the bigger ones walk, came into town to sell them. About half the workers had thus been bought for seven to ten yuan. Some were barely more than infants. Being so young and small, if seated beside the older workers their hands could not reach the workbench, so trays were placed on the floor for them. On these platforms they put little stools and sat packing the matches with tiny, dimpled hands.

All their faces had turned the gray-yellow color of clay. Black, grimy bandages were wrapped around fingertips burned and festering from the spontaneous combustion of matches and scraped by the pulverized glass glued to the sides of the matchboxes. Once work began, all conversation was forbidden until the rest period. For six hours they only moved their hands like mute miniature robots.

From time to time there erupted a sudden swoosh. It was the sound of the yellow phosphorus matches bursting into flame from accidental friction. At such times children's fingers were burned. Simultaneously, their grimy bodies were obscured by the swaying rise of purplish smoke.

No one uttered a word. And yet a veritable madness of tumultuous grating, creaking noise spilled all around.

Kantarō walked round and round the factory. He was equipped with a whip and a pistol. His subordinate, a Chinese foreman, followed him. The foreman carried a wooden stick. He was entitled to strike any worker with that stick even if it meant breaking young hands or legs. But there was no need at all for either the stick or the pistol as the workers strove to show utmost diligence before the Japanese and the foreman. Kantarō was a youth of just twenty-four. A cantankerous, argumentative man, he disliked making the Chinese work more efficiently and made a poor supervisor. The toxic gases bearing dust and yellow phosphorus had steadily invaded his lungs, too, along with those of the children.

"What on earth are you, Chinese or Japanese?" The sullen manager, angry over the pressure from Swedish matches, had recently with a sarcastic and cutting look accused him of siding with the Chinese. Kantarō's father had become a heroin addict. Recalling that and the manager's words, Kantarō's face grew forlorn. The Japanese did not object to selling heroin. But smoking it like the Chinese was beyond the pale. His father smoked it like the Chinese, and like the Chinese he became an addict. Kantarō was thinking: "The other Japanese already hate us. Will I get kicked out of this factory before long?" In fact, Kantarō felt a greater affinity for the Chinese than for his shrewd fellow Japanese. The workers, too, seemed friendlier and more open toward him than toward Koyama, Morita, or the others.

"How many more have you got?" Kantarō smiled at Fang Hung-chi who was noisily working the planer and placing the matchwood into a wooden crate. Fang's head was white with dust. Under the flat nose grinned big stained yellow teeth. "How many more?"

"Three, three," Fang hurriedly replied. It meant three truckloads.

"Hurry it up."

"Soon, soon." Fang applied a fastener to a crate filled with a forest of little matchsticks. It made a tight squeak. Kantarō proceeded to the station where the dipping work was done. The sweet burning smell of phosphorus, mingled with sulfur and resin, made him sniffle.

From the open door of the rear entrance the machine saw and the bark-stripping machine groaned raspingly as though grinding teeth. Koyama, having picked up and examined a raw matchstick, flung it away contemptuously atop a straw bag and turned back down the filthy passageway. "What do you think of that Yui?" He was pointing at Yui Li-song, an intractable and stubborn worker in Kantarō's charge.

"Nothing in particular."

"His work is always so sloppy, he's turning out trash at the dipping station. You know that, right?"

"That isn't true."

"Well, if trash doesn't look like trash to you, that's all right then."

Kantarō found it annoying to be distrusted for siding too stubbornly with the Chinese, but joining Koyama in denigrating a man in his charge was even less tolerable. Kantarō was in charge of the matchstick storage, dipping station, and drying room.

Koyama's injured pride made him whine. "Let a character like him do what he wants, and he'll be out of control the day the Northern Punitive Army gets here!"

Now that Koyama was angry, Kantarō felt like backing Yui all the more. Koyama's lower jawbone was decayed with phosphorus poisoning; his lungs were afflicted, too, convulsing his torso with coughing. Yui was a proud Chinese who did indeed look down his nose at people. The two walked on.

"Ah!"

Just then, at the spot where matchboxes are paper-wrapped by the dozen and packed into large wooden boxes, a sudden swoosh rent the air. The flat-featured Hung Yueh-wo, considered a beauty by her fellow workers though not by the Japanese, drew back in alarm. The friction of matches touching within the wooden box had triggered a flare-up. As if a cannon had been fired, dark purple smoke erupted from the container packed with thousands of matchboxes and spread in all directions. Hung Yueh-wo, her delicate figure enveloped by smoke, seemed to have burned her fingers.

Koyama pressed a bony hand against his mouth and, choking in the smoke, gazed sharply at her. Painfully clutching her burned hand, Hung raised her face and looked fearfully around. But meeting Koyama's gaze she promptly lowered her eyes to the box which was still emitting smoke.

Kantarō saw Koyama's mouth with its sunken jawbone contort with pain. Hung, with even greater anxiety, now cast a frightened upward glance toward the overseer. Within the thick billows of smoke, Koyama was bent double and went on choking.

Kantarō walked off toward the office.

3

The violence of Chiang Kai-shek's Second Northern Punitive Army and lawlessness of the destitute Shantung Army were throwing the region into a daily uproar. People were making a name for themselves through carrying out anti-Japanese publicity. Asked why they were doing it, they replied it was because they were hungry.

The warlord Chang Tsung-ch'ang, who did not pay the soldiers a single yuan for six or seven months at a stretch, seeing from his car a mother pitifully begging with her child by the castle gate, ordered his attendant to give her three hundred yuan. Chang was this sort of capricious man. "A tear in a devil's eye!" Even the Chinese reviled Chang Tsung-ch'ang as so much trash. The town's atmosphere could not help but affect the factory workers.

Yamazaki, who planned to return to Japan having made a fortune in China, was strolling around, visiting in turn the M Flour Mill, Nikka Egg Noodles, K Cotton Mill, Fu-lung Match, and other firms. He had pocketed as his personal savings the secret funds he had been given. Rather than lay out money and purchase piece after piece of dubious information from the

Chinese, it made more sense to get it all from the business association and make that serve as his report. This is what Yamazaki did. The money he then kept for himself. His pocket contained the business cards of the Fu-lung Match Company employees, as well as those of the Nikka Egg Noodles commercial travelers. He had never booked an order for a single match, of course, nor gone to buy any other materials.

Arriving at the factory entrance, he clapped a long-nailed hand to his nose and faltered before the violent stench of sulfur, smoke, dust, and unwashed workers. He had just parted from the Russian soldiers. He prided himself that his speech, facial features, and manner of walking did not differ in the least from those of the Chinese. Blowing his nose with his fingers, he could nonchalantly wipe the snivel on whatever came to hand. His black brimless hat topped with a button, his clothes, and his shoes were all Chinese. Growing his fingernails long was also in imitation of Chinese taste. The only flaw, one he had not noticed, was his sharp eyes whose whites and irises contrasted too starkly. This alone sufficed to prevent him from disguising his occupation and ethnicity. It set him apart from the heavy, cloudy Chinese look. His occupation of furtively probing behind hidden things had acquired a shape on its own and emerged to the surface. The vain Yamazaki, as we shall learn, knew nothing of this defect.

Just as Yamazaki reached the workshop entrance, Kantarō stepped out of the interior, a fleck of yellow adhering to the tip of his nose. Kantarō suddenly laughed and said something.

"What is it?" asked Yamazaki.

"A very interesting piece of news!"

"What is it?"

"I'll tell you in a minute. And when I do, will you pay me for the information? Five yen will do. A mere five yen will do!"

"Sure I'll pay, if the information is worth it."

"If you don't pay, Mr. Yamazaki, you'll have made so much money you won't know where to put it."

Yamazaki uttered a displeased chuckle. "What is it?"

"Bandits have shown up. When I went shooting ducks at the Lun-k'ou marsh the other day, I saw six or seven bandits openly coming from the direction of the Hwang Ho River." Kantarō began to laugh. The innocent laughter suggested he had been joking about the fee. "I threw away the bicycle I'd been riding and fled. It was a first-class Kent."

Yamazaki suppressed a sarcastic smile. His face seemed to say: here I am searching for information of grave importance to the safety of the state, such as it is, and you joke around with idle nonsense! Noticing his reaction, Kantarō gradually stiffened and the laughter grew strained.

Koyama now came out still coughing his wracking cough. Workers with faded faces, having finished enough work for one day's voucher, began to appear at the exit. Kantarō, together with Yamazaki, walked to the office. The workers had the amount of the day's work recorded in the attendance book and received meal tickets. The commotion and the vying, accompanied by the metallic sound of the Chinese language, swirled around the foreman's desk. It was getting dark.

"Here, as always, obedience rules." So murmured Yamazaki after casting a sharp glance at the jostling workers.

"Far from it," replied Koyama. "There are subversives even among the administration."

"Hmm, it's pretty hard for us Japanese to tell whether or not agents from the General Workers Association have slipped in. We have to be careful."

"Well, if they have, just set a spy on them and you'll soon find out."

"Except that these days things have gotten so dangerous you have to set spies on the spies themselves."

"Huh! Can't figure the damned things out." Koyama went on coughing. He was spitting out phlegm.

The three entered the office. It too had been affected by phosphorus, sulfur, and potassium chlorate: fading all the colors, corroding the wood grain of the desk, darkening it into gray. Uchikawa, one of the partners in buying up antiquated rifles from the government at three yen apiece and selling them by the thousands to Chang Tsung-ch'ang at fifty yen apiece, had taken up position next to the double-glazed window and wore a gloomy expression dark with worry. His face, like the factory itself, was hard and bone-dry. This was the manager.

"Oh, it's you. Whenever you come it stinks to high heaven of garlic." Uchikawa laughed gruffly. Even his laughter was dry.

"That's great to hear. If I smell of garlic this much, I must be indistinguishable from the Chinese. What do you think?" Yamazaki struck the pose of a boasting clown.

"If you think so yourself, that's perfect. You don't need anyone's help."

"Wo ho Chung kuo jen pu shih i yang ma. Son mo pu i yang, na erh yu pu i yang ti yang tzu?" "How am I different from a Chinese?" Yamazaki had suddenly shouted out in Chinese. Yet he clearly said it as a joke, one of

his ways of pleasing Uchikawa. He was trying to wheedle a certain something out of Uchikawa who had so richly profited from the antiquated rifles.
He was expecting him to hand it over at any moment. Kantarō knew it. It
was a truly unsightly spectacle.

Straining every sense, Yamazaki ran sniffing around like a starving,
homeless dog. Koyama, who revealed all of his brutal nature before those
junior to himself, seemed a different man when the manager was present. He
became silent and self-effacing. Yamazaki, not being Uchikawa's employee,
could afford to be comparatively informal. Yet that informality too was
deliberately feigned. It was clearly a way of ingratiating himself.

If the manager showed an interest in it, Koyama mustered his own
interest even in the newspaper discussions of politics of the native land he
had not stepped on in ten years—or put on a show of being interested. Seeing Uchikawa's darkened face, he promptly reacted: "If those characters are
in a much better position now than this time last year, isn't it because Germany is supplying them with new weapons?"

"Mm," growled Uchikawa.

"I wonder how much it is? The volume of weapons." He had unsealed
a letter that had arrived that very morning and stolen a glance at the contents. Having done so, he already knew the volume of weapons. Yet Koyama
pretended not to know.

"The whites say they're here for the churches, the charities, and such.
But behind all that they're doing one hell of a booming business. There's no
comparison with us."

"Free schools and free hospitals are nothing but a trick they use. However you look at it."

"Mm."

"But this time, no matter what kind of efficient weapons Chiang Kai-
shek comes equipped with, Master Chang will fight with his back to the
wall. If anyone can't afford to lose this battle, it's Master Chang." He
believed he had expressed an impressive opinion before the expert Yamazaki. His face looked triumphant. Yamazaki noticed it.

"Someone is planning to have Chang Tsung-ch'ang with his old rifles
lose to the new German rifles. . . ."

"Who cares whether Master Chang wins or loses? That's not the concern of the people who sold him the guns." A sarcastic smile creased Yamazaki's clean-shaven face as if mocking them for fretting about such things.

"In the Northern Punitive Army they've still got quite a few communists who've left the political section," murmured Uchikawa grimly. "They

say that no matter how much this Chiang tries to exterminate communists, they stick to him like ticks. What will happen if communist outlaws take over this town? What on earth will happen?"

"Communists are the air itself. If there's an opening, they'll enter it. But what interests me more is whether or not the Northern Punitive Army has enough strength to get this far. Finding that out, I think, is the first consideration."

"How can you find out?"

"Money," said Yamazaki with a sneer. "To move a large army of a hundred thousand men, even two or three hundred thousand yuan aren't worth a damn."

"Speaking of money, the business association is putting up a total of four million yen at the outset and two million more later."

"Huh! That no doubt is a mistaken report," said Yamazaki with another sneer. But the saliva spraying the faded desk betrayed his delight at having landed a fine fish. "So they've definitely paid out six million yen then. . . . In that case, they won't come. It's all right, they won't come. That's splendid. It's splendid that the business association donated six million yen. Just splendid."

Koyama could not quite make out why Yamazaki was in such absurdly high spirits.

4

Uchikawa was said to be playing a triple game. In addition to running the match factory, respectably and openly, he was conducting two other kinds of business. The first was the trade in weapons. The second was the trade in drugs: opium, morphine, cocaine, heroin, codeine, and the like. In all the dealings, his partners were Chinese.

Many of the foreigners residing throughout the expansive, chaotic interior of China were engaging in the gun trade or the drug trade as their true occupations. The English did it. The French did it. So did the Germans and Spaniards. On the one hand, they drugged the Chinese and destroyed their minds. On the other, they supplied the warlords and outlaws with guns and ammunition. Through their actions they helped to sow bloodshed, plunder, and anxiety among the people.

Uchikawa was a stubborn, headstrong, and cunning man. He could hold his own not only in a dog-eat-dog world but in the world of bandit-eat-bandit as well. When he grew zealous about a project, he had no time to spare even for a half-hour haircut. His graying hair wild and disheveled, his beard tangled, he plunged into work. Coded telephone calls frequently reached the factory. "Of item three, eighteen units arrived in tatters today" meant that less than four thousand yen had been paid. "Cooked ten pig snouts with hodgepodge of boiled rice" meant ten rifles had been sold along with the appropriate ammunition and related equipment.

Yamazaki knew Uchikawa's secrets. Being in charge put Uchikawa in an advantageous position insofar as the factory possessed the facilities for instant reception of a variety of information on daily changes and events. Chinese policemen, railway clerks, and customs officials had long been accustomed to supplementing their salaries by squeezing money from the rich. Uchikawa utilized this tradition skillfully.

"Though you show up at the factory, "said Yamazaki," it's hard to tell what your real job is. If you keep gobbling up the lion's share, sooner or later your stomach'll start to hurt."

"Don't say that, my dear fellow, don't say that!"

Perceiving Yamazaki's hint, Uchikawa strove to turn it into jest by clownishly ducking and shaking his hands. "This is like some acrobatic tight-rope act. If things go wrong, you fall and die. Even just sitting here like this, I often get scared."

"The one who falls won't be you but an errand boy or some other flunky."

"No, no. Not necessarily, not necessarily . . ."

The Chinese—warlords, landlords, coolies, or beggars—could not get through a single day without item one, item two, or item three. Such was the addiction forced on them. Items one, two, and three were the codes for opium, heroin, and morphine. This is what the antinarcotics activists were struggling against.

Importing narcotics was prohibited, and so too was using them. According to the activists, ever since the Opium Wars multinational imperialism had been bringing in opium in a deliberate effort to destroy the Chinese people. They were drowning them in it. Despite the public ban, the laws were not being implemented. The drugs poured in through the gaps in the net. Undaunted by confiscations and fines, they devised other ways of importing. They masked the narcotics with flour, slipped them in among pharmaceuticals, or wrapped them around the bellies of smugglers. There was no way to keep the drugs out. Yamazaki knew that.

Even if Uchikawa did not traffic in narcotics, someone else certainly would. Even if the Japanese did not handle narcotics, the Germans or other foreigners certainly would. This suggested to Yamazaki a reason for assisting Uchikawa. Without someone to satisfy their cravings, the addicted Chinese would probably moan in agony and die. Therefore, it was incumbent upon him to stand by his fellow Japanese. The French, the Germans, and the rest were insolently importing outrageous quantities of the substance. Brazenly they sailed in with fully loaded ships of six thousand tons. Compared to that, the Japanese were excessively timid and honest, as was the way in that fussy country of theirs.

But Uchikawa was exceptionally miserly and did not pay fairly. Yamazaki grew peevish. He knew just how huge a profit Uchikawa and Takatsu of the S Bank had made from the guns. The gun trade was more troublesome than the drug trade. All of it had to be conducted with absolute secrecy. The Chinese authorities were extremely severe. While the exposure of drug trafficking led to no more than a fine or a prison term, trading in guns was a matter of life and death. Being found in possession of firearms was in China a capital crime. This business was a true tightrope act. There were even cases of rag dealers arrested by policemen while casually fingering rusty old rifle bullets they had bought along with the other trash. These men were eventually executed. That is how seriously guns were regarded.

The lesser warlords and outlaws were particularly eager to grab hold of guns even if they had to kill to get them. No matter how expensive, they purchased them. It was very easy to earn a commission by selling to them. So it was well worth laying out five hundred yen or so simply for the sake of removing any hindrance to the sales. The one who took care of all the lower-level preparations for this was he, Yamazaki, was it not? Uchikawa made no effort to reward him for it.

Yamazaki worried that if he left the matter alone too long, he would fail to get any sort of recompense at all. But let Uchikawa spurn him if he will; he had ideas of his own. If by chance he tried to swindle him this time with a measly hundred or two hundred yen, Yamazaki would fling his entire business to the dogs then and there. Yamazaki knew what Uchikawa and the rest were up to. And if he decided to expose them, he could do it. He was only protecting them because they were his compatriots.

It had happened one autumn. A lengthy funeral procession led by long-eared donkeys was passing along a country road far from the city, moving toward the mountains and a deep, dreary forest with dead-colored leaves.

The hearse was being pulled by six donkeys. The donkeys painfully shook their big heads, too large for their small trunks and short legs, and all six streamed with sweat. Vapor rose from their curly, dirty hair. The coffin was somberly decorated with snake images and black cloth befitting the Chinese way of mourning the deceased. The chief mourner, wearing a hat of coarse hemp, was followed by howling female mourners. Apparently someone who had died in the city was being taken back to his native countryside.

And yet why were six donkeys sweating hard enough to raise steam while pulling a single body across what was still level ground? Why was a single body so heavy? The policemen wondered at this.

For a while all went well. Coffins were not customarily pulled by animals but carried on people's shoulders. That too deepened the policemen's suspicion. But the two policemen were no match for the seven or eight sturdy men guarding the hearse. And the procession was drawing ever closer to the forest and mountains. Only one village remained before it would enter the forest. In the center of the village there was a police station.

When the chief mourner and the keening women grew tired of decorously following the coffin, they yawned and strangely laughed. And that caught one policeman's attention. As the funeral procession approached the village barracks, therefore, the situation abruptly changed. The hearse was ordered to halt. Policemen armed with rifles and swords surrounded the cart. The black curtain and the canopy covering the casket were torn off. The lid of the casket was removed. Under the lid they found, not a body, but rather a large quantity of tightly packed rifles and grenades.

"What the hell!"

Yamazaki knew about that too. Uchikawa was the man to do the unexpected.

5

In the vicinity of Shih-wang-tien, the Palace of Ten Kings, there is a squalid, jumbled neighborhood. Kantarō lived there in his father's house. His parents, two younger sisters, and a motherless child lived with him. He commuted to the factory cutting diagonally through a quarter of riverfront shops.

"Is that staggering old man a Japanese?" The local Japanese, asked by their Chinese acquaintances about Takezaburō with his yellowish, clouded eyes, replied in tones of utter contempt: "Of course not, that's a Korean." The Japanese considered manual labor and drug addiction a national disgrace. Even to go buy vegetables a mere three blocks away, the Japanese haughtily ensconced themselves in rickshaws, and yet were known for haggling fiercely with the coolies over the fare.

Of course there were some down-and-out Japanese who had joined the ranks of coolies and lived by selling their labor. Catching sight of one from atop their rickshaws, the others disdainfully spat out: "Huh, that's a Korean." Kantarō's father Takezaburō was one of the people who had incurred such contempt. He could not go on living without his pipe, alcohol lamp, and item number three. Once a day, without fail, he had to consume the drug. If his body was deprived of it, he thrashed about groaning with pain. Like a carp sprung out of water, he had no way of enduring it. Kantarō did not like his father at all.

His father had grown virtually incapable of doing any real work. Instead of the father, it was Kantarō's sister Suzu who handled the family's business. She was presently back in Japan, planning to return with four or five pounds of narcotics. Most Japanese were in the business of selling drugs. The shops advertising bean-jam dumplings, souvenirs, watches, or antiques were nothing but fronts. If Uchikawa was a wholesaler, these were the retailers. No fewer than a thousand people engaging in such a business lived here. Takezaburō was one of them.

Opium was too expensive for coolies and laborers. For this reason a compound containing the cheaper and much more powerful item number three was used. Whereas even three months of smoking opium did not lead to addiction, heroin produced a sickly pallor within ten days. It contained the main ingredient and a synergist. If the compound was not skillfully prepared, the product sold poorly. The proper mix tended to be kept secret and treated as a family recipe. Having failed at various occupations, Takezaburō in the end began to deal in number three as his best final chance. At first he had a hard time with meager sales. Yet he knew that even if he failed at every single thing, he could never return to Japan. He had been driven out.

No matter how fabulously profitable the drug business was said to be, it proved difficult once he had actually begun. "Son of a bitch! This time I'll try smoking some myself to see if it's any good. If I don't have the guts to do that, the business will never succeed." When he said it, neither he nor his wife Osen yet understood the drug's fearsome power.

"Don't be silly. What if you get addicted?" Osen said with a laugh.

"Don't you be so casual about it. There's no way I can go back to Japan!"

And as the product sales gradually improved, his complexion changed to the color of withered pears. The drug had invaded his body cells. He had fallen into the trap. Struggle and flounder as he might, he could no longer live without smoking. It was just two years since Suzu, Shun, and Kantarō had arrived from Japan.

Suzu did everything from preparing K'uai-shang-k'uai—Supreme Pleasure —to replenishing the raw materials and at times selling the goods from the back door to the pale-faced Chinese who would enter with soft stealthy footsteps.

Shun, the younger of his two sisters, played with Ichirō whom Toshiko had left behind. Ichirō was Kantarō's child. Toshiko was the wife who had gone back to Japan hating her husband and his family. And Shun had once been good friends with Toshiko. Suzu, the older sister, had been wholeheartedly devoting herself to the family ever since Toshiko's departure.

It was always Suzu who was sent back to Japan to resupply the materials. Braving the danger, she went. It was much easier for a woman— especially a young, oddly innocent woman—to smuggle contraband past the stringent customs. Takezaburō had pressed Kantarō, Suzu, and even Kantarō's wife Toshiko to strap a pound each to their bodies when they first arrived in China.

Kantarō had been stunned by his father's impudence. Had he asked just the two siblings, he could have tolerated it. But he had also calmly bid Toshiko, Kantarō's wife of only four months, to do the same. Even now Kantarō remained convinced that half the responsibility for his separation from Toshiko after a mere year and a half of marriage lay with his father. There was a limit to people's insensitivity.

But the first time, the embarrassed and nervous Suzu and Toshiko had managed to bring it off skillfully and with ease. It was the father and Kantarō who were delayed at the customshouse facing the landing dock. The women passed through without a hitch. Encouraged by the success, Father took advantage of it and sent Suzu back to Japan. After two or three times, Suzu began to feel the thrill of deceiving the customs.

"What do you feel when you're doing it?" Kantarō, unable to forget the dread of being discovered and his discontent with his father, questioned his sister afterward.

"Nothing. I just feel sorry for our poor father."

"And you were worried sick, weren't you, when you were wrapping that bag of powder around your waist and saying, 'Oh, don't I look three months pregnant?' "

"Sure, I worried. I could never tie the sash properly. . . . But that didn't matter. When I thought of our poor father having to ask such a thing from the children and daughter-in-law he had brought to Tsinan for the first time, I pitied him so much I cried."

"That's what you say now. But at the time you were terrified of being caught."

"And what about you, Brother? Did you know from the start that life here would be so miserable?"

"No, I never imagined it would be as terrible as this."

"I knew it right away. . . . When Grandfather died and Father went back to Japan by himself without even taking Mother along, that made everything clear, didn't it?"

"Hey, you sure know how to make great speeches after the fact."

Ever since his wife had left the child with him and fled, he and his sister had grown very close. An outsider might assume that Kantarō, desiring a better wife, had discarded Toshiko like a worn-out pair of sandals. On the contrary, even if he had been motivated by practical self-interest, to send away the woman he had married was no light matter. For an old-fashioned man like himself, it had meant various sorts of confusion, anguish, and indecision. The only one who knew about that was Suzu. He came to love his younger sister very much. The child was attached to her too. Like the doves of Tokyo's Asakusa district, Suzu was at ease with people. If you tried to catch such a dove, it would fly up alertly and settle a precarious foot or two away. She possessed such a talent. This was already her seventh return to Japan.

6

Rumors of regional turmoil and Chiang Kai-shek's military exploits had grown ever more frequent around the time Suzu reached Japan.

The sole concern of China's Japanese residents was whether the property accumulated over the years—the decorated houses, the rare Chinese utensils—and their very lives might not be savagely and bloodily crushed by the violent Southern soldiers as they had been at Nanking and Hankow during the May 30 Incident. Their anxieties were being encouraged by someone. Worried, they held a meeting of the residents' association. Two chosen delegates set off to petition the consulate. Intimations of great danger had spread fear not only among those who had amassed sizable fortunes but even among the penniless day laborers. Ceaseless skirmishes among the war-lords and the continuous commotion made these intimations even stronger. Indeed, disturbances erupted often in the city. In fact, a Chinese military patrol broke into a girls' school to the east of the amusement park in broad daylight.

There were two soldiers. They entered the dormitory housing the female students and sated their sexual hunger. When a woman teacher humbly pleaded with them to keep quiet about what they had done, the soldiers demanded money. Unable to refuse, she paid. Nonetheless, upon returning to their dark barracks, the two proudly told their fellow soldiers all about it. After nightfall, a band of lustful soldiers stormed the school. The Chinese screams and metallic shouts resounded far in the distance.

Every night, houses in various parts of the city were attacked by armed soldiers. "Is Mr. So-and-So from Wei-san-lu here? It's urgent!" When someone was called out of a movie theater in the middle of watching a film, even the others around him flinched with fear. "What, another robbery?"

The soldiers were short of food. Wrapping black cloths around their faces and heads, they concealed their bodies with large baggy gowns. And they pillaged houses indiscriminately. Unlike ordinary bandits, they did not systematically target houses known to contain cash. This made them all the more troublesome. Even the poor dreaded them. On forcing their way in, they would crash into corner after corner, overturning everything like night-hawks in search of prey. They would leap about, bruising their shins, and as they thrust their hands deep into a closet the edge of the gown would suddenly flip up to reveal the sleeve of an army uniform.

"Ah, soldiers!"

"So what if we are soldiers? Even soldiers can't live without eating. The chief pays us nothing!" They were not about to withdraw just because their true identity had been revealed. *"Wo ti wo ti! Ni ti wo ti!"* What's mine is mine! What's yours is mine!

At the factory, Uchikawa was painstakingly devising countermeasures —not only against the communist efforts at propagandizing and organizing that might accompany the Northern Punitive Army's arrival but also against workers fleeing under cover of the upheaval. The bold and defiant ones were brutally attacked. Workers, including the married couples, were strictly forbidden to leave the factory compound. All were confined to the two dormitories. The gates were guarded by the police. These guards refused entrance to anyone without a company identification card.

To prevent escapes, wages were withheld. The workers received neither the month's pay due to them at the end of March nor any money for the work done since the start of April. Their labor was based entirely on piecework. They earned paltry set sums for filling matchboxes, loading crates, tending trucks, pasting boxes, carrying matchwood, cleaning the yard. All the difficult, dirty, and dangerous work was theirs to do. The Japanese merely carried guns and kept watch.

The matches were designed to be quite indistinguishable from China's domestic products. Even the trademark, printed on yellow paper, read "Ta Chi" (Great Good Fortune) in Chinese style. The four corners of the label conspicuously carried the words "T'i ch'ang kuo huo" (Use domestic products!)—one of the slogans adopted by the Anti-Japanese Committee that had been artfully turned to the others' advantage. In fact every bit of the article had indeed been made by Chinese hands and in China. Therefore it was undeniably a Chinese domestic product. Except for the financial capital.

Facing a fierce anti-Japanese boycott in China, it was infinitely more logical to use inexpensive Chinese wage laborers and sell a "national product" no different from the genuine item than to import unmarketable matches from Kobe and pay customs duties, tariffs, and surtaxes. The Ōi Company had long since set its eyes on this goal. It was not just the matches. The capitalists were utilizing the same method with cotton spinning, machinery, flour milling, oil extraction, and sugar manufacture. In this way they compensated for the profits they were denied in a harsh and deadlocked Japan.

The workers' privation grew steadily worse. They lived on rolls of bread, crackers, and water. All their money was gone. Lacking money, they could not smoke a single cigarette or get their wild hair trimmed. They could not earn money to support their families.

Grimily clad mothers, fathers, and wives, out of food for three or four days, came asking to speak with their sons and husbands, only to be refused entry by the guards. Inside, there were sons and daughters wanting to meet parents, husbands wanting to meet wives, wives wanting to meet husbands. Outside, there were parents and wives waiting for remittances from sons and husbands. Koyama and the rest, not wishing to be annoyed by the tearful cries that would follow their meeting, kept them apart.

The workers went round to the poplar storage yard that was surrounded by barbed wire. Nearby was a narrow gap in the tin fence. There they spoke in metallic, sorrowful voices. Hearing the parents' shouts, other workers quietly left their workplaces and drew close to the barbed wire fence. They met secretly, separated by metal spikes. But the sons had no money to give the parents, the husbands no money to give the wives—painful encounters. Some of the people pressed Kantarō to talk to management and ask that they be paid.

"Mr. Inokawa." Wang Hung-chi hesitantly approached Kantarō who was watching the dipping station. Wang was a timid, diligent worker.

"What is it?"

"Mr. Inokawa."

"What is it?" Kantarō's face showed impatience.

"Mr. Inokawa. . . . Please, would you ask Mr. Koyama to give us at least half a month's pay?"

Kantarō heard a note of subservience in Wang's shy voice. Wang went on: "My mother's here and says that my wife gave birth but they've had nothing to eat for three days now. Until the other day they were getting millet from my young sister-in-law's place, but she doesn't have anything left."

Kantarō looked disconcerted. "It's been decided to withhold wages for the time being."

"My mother's standing outside the fence with my older one strapped to her back and crying. Both of them are crying."

"Whatever I might say to the accountant or the manager will have no effect at all."

Wang Hung-chi looked at Kantarō with wondering eyes as though trying to say something. He was suffering in both body and spirit. His chest seemed too oppressed for him to breathe. In Wang's eyes Kantarō sensed something good-natured and compliant—like a bullock at the instant of being struck on the head by the butcher. Still devoid of resistance, the eyes were innocently pleading as if to say: "Why kill me? I don't understand!"

"Yes, I'll tell them. I'll talk to them!" shouted Kantarō in a sudden burst of anger. "They treat you all as though you weren't human. Damn it. Wait, I'll tell them! I'll talk to them!"

Among the Japanese at the factory, Kantarō had the least experience of the colonial life. The others—Uchikawa the manager, Koyama the supervisor, Ōtsu, Morita, Iwai the accountant—were all men who got tired of their cramped homeland and, yearning for unfettered, untamed territory, had set out for Korea and Manchuria. At home they either could not make a living or else tangled with the law. Staying on grew difficult, so they first crossed to Korea. Growing bored with Korea, they came to Manchuria. Bored with Manchuria too, they came to Tientsin, then to Peking. It did not go well in Peking either. It was such a crew that had settled here.

They had ravaged their way through Dairen, Fengtien, Chingtao, and Tientsin. As for Ōtsu, many Koreans, after being charged a fifty percent fee, had been forced to sell their daughters for seventy or eighty yen to this man whose incessantly grinning face strangely resembled male genitals. Moreover the young girls were invariably sampled by Ōtsu before being handed over to buyers. As for Koyama, no fewer than ten coolies had been caught by his heavy stick and left maimed or dead. As for Iwai, at present he had the face of a man who had accumulated some money yet would not so much as smash an insect. But to obtain that money, he had not hesitated to do away with anyone who stood in his way, Japanese, Korean, or Chinese. Thanks to their evil ways, even men as hardened as themselves found Manchuria too rough. Tientsin got tougher, too, as did Chingtao. And so they had come here.

The factory bred a special kind of candid atmosphere often found in places, like detention cells, where felons gather. Here no one tried to cover up his criminal deeds. Rapes, robberies, thefts—they openly chattered about their experiences. Anyone entering their company felt like a nonentity unless he made up exaggerated stories even of crimes he had no memory of having committed. The more varied and abundant a scoundrel's record of criminal outrages, the more he could command respect, inspire fear, and swagger in front of others.

Koyama had once scooped a ladleful of the melted slurry of phosphorus, potassium chlorate, sulfur, and pine resin from a cauldron where it was being heated—and then splashed it over the head of a worker he did not like. From that day on, catching sight of the ladle gripped in his hand, the Chinese would break into a run uttering earsplitting shrieks. Yet if the workers ever happened to spill any of the mixture, he would roar obscenities at them.

Except for Kantarō, they all regarded the workers as animals. Kantarō was amazed that the workers were capable of replenishing the calories consumed during a fifteen-hour working day merely by eating black rolls and fragments of sorghum crackers and drinking water. It seemed to him no people were as patient and persevering as the Chinese. They never complained. They simply strove to earn money by packing yet another box of matches. The piecework system spurred their desire for money and pushed them to work harder still. It seemed to be a system devised for precisely that purpose.

"Idiotic!" Koyama was sneering. "Even the wretches themselves have never given a thought to whether the calories get replenished or not!" Based on his own experience, Koyama felt convinced that the workers here were even more impertinent and inefficient than the coolies of Manchuria. He had used the services of coolies at the Blue Mountain Villa on the wharf in Dairen.

"You've got to realize that the Chinese are a worthless race. There's never any need to praise them." He spoke in the tone of a senior dispensing information. "They have no sense of shame. No matter how good you are to them, it's never enough. Give them ten yen and they'll say 'Hsieh-hsieh.' Give them one yen and again it's 'Hsieh-hsieh.' One sen and they say the same, 'Hsieh-hsieh.' So doing them a big favor is the height of stupidity. Plus afterward they'll get lazy and won't listen to a word you say."

The manager seconded the supervisor's views: "In Korea and Manchuria both, Yobos and Chinks fear us and cower before us." When boarding a train whose seats were full, these two thought it only natural that the Yobos who had boarded earlier should yield the seats to them. Reminding everyone of this, they proclaimed: "The Chinese in these parts like to put on airs. You can bet it's because there's no Japanese army around here." Wandering through Korea and Manchuria, they had watched with intense pleasure as the insubordinate Yobos and coolies were taught their lessons by a garrison's intimidating maneuvers and fierce application of military force. They regretted that such an imperial Japanese garrison had yet to come here.

"But all things are relative," said Kantarō, trying not to yield simple truth to the scoundrels. "Looking at it from the standpoint of work, the Japanese are no match at all for the Chinese. And what's more, the workers at home have unions and strikes and would never submit to such outrageous exploitation in such horrendous conditions."

"I know nothing about all that. Only a puppy like you would know about that." Koyama despised Kantarō's simple heart. "We came all the way to China, so why should we work like coolies? We're giving these people jobs, aren't we? Right? If we hadn't built this factory here, there'd be no place for them to make money. Even the rickshaw pullers, who'd they get money from if we didn't ride and pay? Why the hell should we lower ourselves to their level and work like they do? That'd be a disgrace to the Japanese!"

"Why is work a disgrace?" thought Kantarō. "What an idiot."

"Grow up some, and even you'll understand!" shouted Koyama.

From time to time, a man from the countryside might happen to enter the match factory in search of work. He would come with a dirty quilt thrown over his shoulder and a worn-out rice cooker hanging from his hand in a hemp sack. The guards, instructed in advance by Uchikawa, would let such a person enter. Kantarō would be called to talk to him.

While Kantarō spoke with the man in his Chinese-lecture accent, Uchikawa would be observing the Chinese from the side. He would decide to employ or reject him based on whether or not the fellow was good-tempered, young, well fed, and capable of unlimited labor. A healthy-looking, but not too clean, young person from the countryside would be hired. And in exchange, an old worker afflicted by the bone gangrene peculiar to match factories, or a laborer who had lost all his teeth due to decayed gums, or a female worker no longer able to pick up small objects because her infected fingers were festering from frequent burns, would be expelled without a penny more wages. On top of the poor nutrition and insufficient sunlight—the work lasted from four in the morning till seven at night—the use of the intensely toxic and universally outlawed white phosphorus caused healthy flesh to be ravaged by poison within days.

The turnover was extreme. For each worker coming in, one was thrown out. Over and over it happened. After a while, Kantarō noticed that the Chinese throughout the factory grew pale with fear and anxiety whenever someone was hired. It was not merely those most likely to be discharged, like the feeble old and the frowned upon. Even the skilled workers indispensable to the factory, and the unseasoned boy and girl workers of six or seven, turned white and gazed with sad heavy eyes at the Japanese as though silently entreating those who wielded the power of life and death over them.

Although Kantarō urged with all his might that the wages be paid, Uchikawa and Koyama refused to permit it. "You're wet behind the ears, but as eloquent as any Chink," Koyama chortled sarcastically, conscious that Uchikawa at his side was holding back.

"Wages are not some gift we bestow upon others," said Kantarō combatively. "It's money that must be paid. Labor's a kind of commodity. Isn't it only natural to pay the price of what you've bought?"

However ardently he appealed to their feelings, they did not seem to listen. "What on earth are you, huh? A Chinese? A Russian? And of the extremist radical kind."

"I'm a Japanese." For a moment Kantarō felt a furious impulse stirring within. He had to do something to these two! Otherwise the pain in his chest would not be assuaged. Yet he understood all too clearly the consequences of actually doing what he yearned to do.

"If you're a Japanese, then act like one!" said Koyama. "Matches won't get made just by arguing."

"Matches will get made even less if you let the workers die before your very eyes." Finally the rage he had been suppressing exploded: "Thieves! Cheats!" He grabbed up the chair beside him. Staggering, he swung it in the air.

But Uchikawa stood up and sprang forward like a leopard to snatch the chair away. "Idiot! Idiot! What are you doing, Inokawa? What are you doing?"

Kantarō was shoved out of the office. Bang! The door slammed shut. "This one's really young," said Uchikawa with a laugh to the rigidly tense and angry-eyed Koyama. "He's good for nothing. I'm only keeping him on out of pity for his mother. His old man's a heroin addict, the son's impudent and useless, but his mother's to be pitied. . . ."

7

The yellow wind howled in the electric wires. This wind rushing in from Mongolia engulfed trees, sandy soil, and houses within the swirl of its speed, seeming about to fling them all up and scatter them about. The sun grew pale. The people, feeling powerless and small, huddled tightly in clouds of dust that rose from the earth to the heavens. Various thoughts coursed through their minds. China, China, something is happening here, but it cannot be contained.

Life seemed easygoing here, yet it was utterly painful—heartbreaking! The people thought of their savagely wounded lives. Some resolved to live on concealing their hurt. Some felt worn down by their own deeds. Only Shun, though surrounded by people immersed in gloomy thoughts, thought of nothing at all as she dandled and played with the two-year-old Ichirō.

"*Ten chin, tian chiin.*" In baby-talk Chinese, Ichirō was asking for sweets. "Ichirō looks just like Toshiko," said Shun, laughing happily. "The cute upturned nose, the eyes, the slender eyebrows . . ." She had been best friends with her elder brother's wife. "Even the life line in his palm is exactly like hers!"

Shun was unhappy that her sister-in-law had been made to leave. The target of her unhappiness was her mother. The mother had pampered her daughter-in-law lavishly, but only while she was a novelty. As time went on and she began to notice flaws in her, she turned to disparaging her mercilessly. Shun hated that. With her fingertips she picked out the bits of straw from the long woolen sweater she had knitted for Ichirō. Supporting his shoulder so he would not stumble, she then led him toward her elder brother.

Mother had been impatiently waiting for Kantarō to return from the factory. Suzu's absence made her lonely.

"What is it?"

Mother's face was tense. "When we aren't looking, Wang is quietly taking out Supreme Pleasure and selling it."

"Hmm."

"Just the other day he took three yen for shoe repair and kept a yen in change."

"Well, pretend you didn't notice and say nothing," said Kantarō. "The drawer needs to be locked!"

Takezaburō, thoroughly steeped in number three, could no longer pay attention to such things. The drug's entrancing scent permeated his body. Lying atop a frayed, slightly faded red blanket with his head on a high pillow, he dozed as though melting. All he craved was his dreamlike ecstasy. Everything else was of no concern to him.

Ichirō drew near, led by Shun, and Kantarō swept the little boy up into his arms.

"They say three bandits were captured the other day."

"Oh, they'll be hanging up heads again, won't they?" Shun laughed happily. This barbarous custom reminiscent of Japan's Tokugawa period appealed to her.

"Only it seems that one of the three used to be a noncommissioned officer of the Shantung Army in the K'uai-shu barracks. Apparently he'd taken enough rifles and ammunition for four men and ran off to join the outlaws."

"Oh, that's so great! A sergeant carries off rifles and becomes a bandit, that's so great. How interesting!"

"Just about every day some disturbance takes place." Mother was offering a votive light at a sham Buddhist altar. The drawer beneath the altar was the hiding place for number three. "It might be a good idea to write Suzu and tell her to stay in Japan until we know whether or not the Southern Army will be coming here. Poor girl."

"Hmm." Kantarō thought for a minute. "But even if we send a letter now, it isn't likely to reach her in time. If by any chance she's gotten on the *Sunbeam,* the ship's scheduled to make port today."

"Maybe so."

Father had been dozing on his red blanket for quite a while. Drops of saliva trickled from his thick dark lips onto the blanket. This happened whenever he entered his state of ecstasy. "Good night! Good night! Sleep well!" Shun shouted saucily, pointing a finger at her father. If anything disturbed his dozing at a time like this, however slightly, Father would give a frenzied start as though a fire had been lit under him. Mother and Kantarō both tried to remain quiet or keep their voices low.

His skin a dark yellowish color, the white blood corpuscles deprived of resistance by the drug, Father was gasping for air like a dying man. "Good night! Good night! Sleep well!" Father would probably die before long, thought Kantarō, hastening to his self-destruction. He thought of his father being forced away from his birthplace. Surely there were more than a few people who had come to the colonies like Father and fallen into the depths.

Who could count them? Those who came here did so because they could no longer remain in their native places: hopelessly impoverished people, people with criminal records, people intent on amassing great sums of money before returning proudly to their villages and lording it over those who had insulted them. This was where they arrived after crossing over to Korea and Manchuria, failing again and again, and being pushed into provinces ever more distant from their homeland. Takezaburō had taken the eight-year-old Kantarō and, leaving behind the four-year-old Suzu and two-year-old Shun, crossed to Manchuria.

Behind his native village, separated from it by a river, the steep mountain range of Shikoku punctures the sky. In front of the village there are hills undulating like waves, before them a waterway facing the Pacific. Kantarō spent his childhood in this village, shunned by the other children. Daily the sun traversed the azure-blue transparent sky cut narrow by mountains. In the spring the mellow yet lively tolling of the bell from a mountain temple, one of the eighty-eight sacred places of Shikoku, reverberated over the village. Pilgrims ringing their bells passed along the narrow mountain paths continuously. Ostracized by all, Kantarō stood alone even as he held out his small hands to receive soybeans from the pilgrims. The reason was that his father had plotted to defame the other children's fathers—who were village assembly members—as criminals, accusing them of corruption despite a lack of conclusive evidence. That was the explanation.

But was there really a lack of conclusive evidence? And did Father really plot to defame the other members of the village assembly?

It happened the year the construction of the new elementary school was completed. Takezaburō was elected to the village assembly. He was both farming his own land and working as a tenant. Such a person was considered unfit even for leadership of the sanitation union, let alone membership in the village assembly. At that time Father had been fearlessly outspoken. He had also been sharply perceptive. None of the other members rejoiced to see him turn up at the village assembly meetings.

About a month earlier, Father had constructed a gate. For timber he had cut down some trees on a hillside. And then he had bought a round of drinks for his neighbors, brother-in-law, and nephew who had helped him haul the trees. That turned out to be a mistake. An influential villager called Matsubaya saw this and reported it as bribery. Although it was customary to treat people to drinks as an expression of gratitude for their help, it was decided after much quarreling that he should be fined for it. Worst of all, it seems he had bought alcohol for a man who just happened to be passing by. When the village assembly members started to grumble, Takezaburō withdrew of his own accord.

A special election was held. Father shut himself up at home in a show of penitence. Even had he been menaced with being burned to ashes, house and all, he would not have had the least intention of becoming an assembly member again. The indignation was more than he could bear. At such a time he was inclined to pull the bedclothes over his head and blunt the pain by sleeping. From the bedding which had grown grimy through lack of airing he would emerge only to eat and then crawl back in again. He spent about three days in such idleness.

Nevertheless, Matsubaya's tenants unwisely voted for Father once again. He was reelected. Father grew mildly ambitious. It happened shortly after that.

The construction of the school, begun two years earlier, was completed. It had cost thirty thousand yen—at the time an astonishing sum for a village. Built in the Western style, the school was thickly painted a bluish color and roofed with slate. The sharp corners of the ridge pointed high into the sky. But the wood of the pillars and beams was old and thin, holes were plugged up here and there, and gaps were hidden with boards. They had skimped on the unseen spots.

Gradually the corruption of the assembly members involved in the new school's construction was exposed to the villagers. Father was definitely feeling vengeful about those earlier accusations of bribery. When Matsubaya, the village headman, and others asked him to withdraw his own charges of corruption, he firmly rejected their overtures.

Kantarō remembered it all as vividly as if it had happened the day before. No one in the village could match Father in strength, fighting spirit, and ability to hoist and shoulder heavy bags of rice. With great clarity the son could still see every single detail of his artless father. The memory, however, dated back a decade or, to be exact, thirteen years. It was March. Along the edges of fields, sporadically planted clumps of horse bean flowers, resembling seashells, were starting to blossom. Father needed to be absent for a short while. His younger sister who had recently gotten married was having trouble with her new relatives and there were quarrels. Father left for his brother-in-law's house, a rigging shop by a seaside road in the city of K.

The corruption case took a bad turn while he was away. Matsubaya, the head of the fishermen's association, and the village headman were all acquitted due to insufficient evidence. And since nine-tenths of the villagers had been bribed by Matsubaya, the uproar abruptly subsided. All the evidence was destroyed.

Now charges of false accusation fell upon Father from all quarters of the village. The village headman began saying that a pine Takezaburō had cut for his gate had stood beyond the property line of Father's grove and indeed came from the hillside belonging to the headman. The pine, stripped of bark and planed, formed the backbone of the recently built gate.

Father was branded a timber thief. The headman began insisting he return the tree. But in order to return the tree, roof tiles would have to be removed, the painted walls knocked down, and the interlocked timber taken apart. In trying to mend matters by saying he had made a mistake concerning the property line, Father lost his last shred of credibility. He grew disgusted with villagers who were susceptible to bribes. They in turn wanted nothing to do with a timber thief and slanderer.

One night in late August, Father left Kantarō and his sisters behind and departed from the village. Crickets were beginning to sing in the road-side bushes. From the drooping branches of the ancient persimmon tree in front of the house hung the tart fruit, still green but enormous. As he passed under it in the darkness, the persimmons struck against his head.

Father crossed a floating bridge at the edge of the village and boarded a carriage. The candles flanking the clouded glass on either side of the cab trembled and waved. "Farewell! Farewell!"

For a long time Kantarō could not fall asleep. Father's downfall began after that. If only that affair had not taken place, the family would never have come to China! He could not, after all, abandon the hope of someday returning to Japan. He too was one of those beaten down by scoundrels and going to ruin. It was the servile types who fawned upon the powerful that prospered everywhere! For a long time he could not fall asleep.

A dog was persistently howling. The yellow wind groaned like thunder high in the sky. Kantarō dreamed that his father, bony as a wooden puppet, was walking lightly through a Japanese-style house. Holding a heavy book, Father stepped out into the corridor. There was a door in the corridor. Inside the dim corridor Father's body jerked upward as though his legs had convulsed. At that moment his head struck hard against the doorframe. There was a resounding bang. It all happened in Japan.

Abruptly Kantarō awoke. Someone was really banging on the door. Mother cleared her throat. He sensed her quietly rising and going to the door. The banging resumed. A Chinese seemed to be standing outside. Wondering suspiciously who it might be, Mother cautiously opened the door a crack and peered out. Then she slammed it shut and returned.

"A telegram, at this time of night."

"Who from?" Kantarō raised the upper part of his body.

"I wonder. . . . Would you take a look?"

He turned on the overhead switch. Although it was not very cold, Mother in her nightgown was shivering. "What can it be at a time like this?" she asked.

"Miss Suzu detained by consular police. Someone please come soon. Hanakawaya."

"Oh, dear, Suzu's been arrested." Mother sat with a thud on the straw mats. Startled by the sound, Ichirō, asleep in his little bed, shifted his head.

"So she did arrive today on the *Sunbeam*. They picked her up at the customs as soon as she landed."

Mother had, chameleon-like, turned deathly pale.

"She's been made to bring it so often, they got to know her face at the customs. That's what it was."

8

Kantarō had to go to Chingtao. He was worried about Suzu.

At present he was living at the strategic point where the Chiao-chi railway stretching westward from Chingtao joins up with the Chin-p'u line. Kantarō would have to endure the nine hours to Chingtao, swaying in a dirty train, surrounded by people who were spitting and blowing their noses with their fingers. He left the house. No trains were as carefree and unreliable as Chinese trains. You could not ride them without being prepared to spend three to five hours waiting at a station.

Kantarō knew that although the manager traded in contraband goods like guns and drugs frequently and on a large scale, he had never been arrested. Nonchalantly the manager imported shipments that were twenty, thirty, or fifty times larger than those Kantarō's father or younger sister brought in. And he strutted proudly about. Yet the powerless, like Father or Sister, were arrested and thrown into police cells for bringing in a mere pound or two! The consulate only protected the rich. The poor making a meager living by trade were subject to strict punishment. Here too, the more rotten the scoundrels, the more they profited.

He emerged onto the T'ai-ma-lu Road. Some bandits being transported by rickshaw to the execution ground in front of the station were passing by, guarded by the police and pouring abuse on the multitude of civilians and unarmed soldiers that swarmed around them like flies. There were three of them. Mounted officers and unarmed soldiers held back the surging crowd and opened a path. Coolies, beggars, Germans, and Japanese were pressing forward in waves.

"A cigarette! Give me a cigarette!" A fat bandit with big dark eyes was sprawling in the middle rickshaw and storming as much at the puller as at the police. His arms were twisted behind him and tied so tightly they seemed suspended from the back of his neck; his legs were locked with large shackles.

The dark rickshaw puller drew out a Hatamen donated by a tobacco dealer and inserted it into the man's mouth. The fat man bit it and spit it out. "What is this cheap junk? Idiot! Give me a P'ao-t'ai-pai! P'ao-t'ai-pai! P'ao-t'ai-pai!" The rickshaw puller looked baffled a while. "Give me a P'ao-t'ai-pai! P'ao-t'ai-pai! P'ao-t'ai-pai! Idiot!"

The foremost prisoner was pale, downcast, head drooping. The third man, his arms trussed up so hard the elbow joints seemed about to snap, was nevertheless managing to gulp down so much wine it dribbled out of his mouth. He was thoroughly drunk. This one appeared to be the sergeant.

Prisoners being hauled off to the execution ground demanded a variety of goods from the stores that caught their eyes along the way. Proprietors could not make any profit by giving things away. Government officials refused to pay for anything the prisoners ate or drank. Yet no one, no matter how greedy, denied the requests of prisoners who within an hour or two would be passing through the gates of hell. Naturally the prisoners did not covet expensive objects they could not take along to the other world. All they asked for was wine, sweets, fruit, or cigarettes. There were pitiful cases of fellows munching ecstatically, their cheeks bulging with wild pears that sold at street stalls for two or three sen apiece.

The crowd of sightseers grew thicker as the rickshaws advanced. They filled the broad street, dusty and littered with horse droppings and trash, and trailed the procession. Even more vast was the eagerly waiting pitch-black crowd squirming in the station square.

No scaffolding, no bamboo palisade, no structure suggesting an execution ground had been erected there. Nonetheless, as the bandits drew near it their expressions suddenly changed and grew stiff. A low, unintelligible cry, like a groan or a prayer, resounded from the rickshaws. Their leg shackles rattled. Only the third man, seeming completely unconscious, was leaning limply to the side, his head bouncing against the vehicle's mudguard.

"What will happen with that drunk?" wondered Kantarō. "Maybe it's better for him if he's too drunk to know when they kill him."

The soldiers pushed back the crowd. The pullers lowered the shafts.

The third prisoner abruptly raised his head. His earth-colored lips, drooling with wine, trembled and tensed. His eyes surveyed the crowd. They looked like the eyes of a dead fish. "Go ahead and do it! I'm not scared! Go ahead and do it!" He mumbled it as though in a dream. His words disappeared in the stir of the crowd.

The fat man in the middle, who had been peevishly demanding a P'ao-t'ai-pai until he got one, spit the partly smoked cigarette onto the head of a policeman next to him. The burning cigarette slid off the policeman's hat and fell on the back of his neck. "What! What the hell?" The young policeman leaped up with surprise. The fat man sarcastically and spitefully feigned ignorance. "Son of a bitch!"

The three were dragged down from the vehicles. The iron chains of the leg shackles rang with a rusty timbre. The prisoners did not move.

The crowd stirred aggressively.

Suddenly Kantarō heard a Su-wu song sung in despair. It was a war song he had often heard as a child. Glancing around, he saw the fat man, his lips contorted, singing to himself:

> So liu yu che pul
> hsue ti yu pin ten
> chun chu shi chu nen
> kain hsue ta ton chen
> chan pei hai pien . . .

"That fat man has some nerve!" muttered a young Chinese beside Kantarō maliciously. "Still singing. Still singing."

But Kantarō was gripped by the feeling he had had when he first learned the Chinese lyrics. For an instant he felt utterly forlorn. The song's final line ran: "The old mother grows weary waiting for the return of her beloved child; the young wife adorned in red keeps a lonely watch over the empty bedroom."

Perhaps the fat man had grown up in a farming village and learned to sing that song as a child, taught by the southern wind that blows down from Mount Li. Whatever evil deeds he might have committed, surely he too had once had a peaceful, innocent childhood.

> Chuan yen pei fong tsi
> ien jun han koan fi
> pai hua niang wang al tsi
> hong tsuang i kon wei

"Sons of bitches! Did I murder anyone, you sons of bitches?"

9

When bandits are captured in China, it is customary to parade them through the city before executing them in view of the crowds as a warning to others. The severed heads, three or four in a row, are hung from the roadside lamp-posts. The heads look dreadful. Some have open mouths, exposing grimy, dirty teeth. Some seem about to laugh. Others are frowning. In the summer, green-bottle flies swarm buzzing over the rotting flesh.

The people cast a quick glance at them, then avert their faces and pass by. Among the outlaws there are, of course, not only robbers but murderers. More than a few Japanese have been cruelly killed by them. They would demand money from village heads and, if they did not get it, storm the earth-walled villages, kidnap women and girls, burn houses, and slaughter everyone else. They did it often. Perhaps no amount of exposing the heads compensated for their evil deeds. Thus the crowds, having suffered their depredations, actually welcomed the brutal executions.

"Kneel!" A mounted officer shouted at the three who had been lowered from the vehicles. The men dropped wearily to their knees. Soldiers roughly grabbed the prisoners' shoulders.

"Turn west, idiots! No one's executed facing that way, idiots!"

Again the chains rattled. The three were made to kneel three yards from each other. A tall fat soldier had unsheathed a broadsword slung over his shoulder and was swinging it through the air with a shout, as if practicing. The only part of the broadsword that was shining was its cutting edge. It resembled a hatchet.

"Bring me pork dumplings! Bring me pork dumplings! I want some pork dumplings!" The fat man who had earlier been demanding P'ao-t'ai-pai cigarettes was clattering his leg chains and flapping his bound hands, insisting he be fed the steamed delicacies.

"Forget it!"

"Hey! Bring it! Bring it! Bring me pork dumplings!" He continued to shake his head and yell.

The fascinated crowd surged ever forward, the soldiers armed with rifles unable to stop them. Kantarō, buffeted by the smell of grease and garlic, pushed his way through.

The prisoners, arms twisted and tied behind their backs, had the ropes removed only from their necks. The pale, dejected man with drooping eyes raised his head covered with long shaggy hair.

"I didn't become a bandit just for the fun of it!" It was a sad, dark voice.

Two soldiers, holding the prisoners' heads and backs to keep them still, prodded the men into straightening up. They were keeping them still to make the cutting easy.

"Give me some dumplings! Some dumplings!"

"That fat fellow is acting like a baby again!" A woman dressed in purple whispered next to Kantarō. Her hair was hanging down over her forehead.

"Do it, do it, do it more! Give them a hard time!" An old man without front teeth standing behind her shouted out with evident animosity.

Jostled by the crowd, Kantarō felt someone poke his shoulder from behind. It was Yamazaki. A balding, large-faced man beside Yamazaki glanced at him and smiled. He was Japanese too: Nakatsu.

"Going somewhere?" Yamazaki asked him, his sharp eyes catching sight, through a gap in the tumultuous crowd, of the suitcase Kantarō was intently clutching while trying not to be trampled by the wave of humanity.

Kantarō explained the situation. Nakatsu stood nearby listening to the story and watching him with an ambiguous smile that might have been either friendly or mocking. This was the tough outlaw who used to make the local Japanese residents shudder with fear. Now he was Chang Tsung-ch'ang's military adviser.

"Hmm, hmm," Yamazaki nodded. "The two of us are off to Chingtao too. So what do you need to do? . . . Hmm, hmm. . . . That was really stupid, your sister getting caught by customs. Hmm, hmm."

"The manager can do business as bold as he likes and they pretend not to notice. But for penniless folks like my old man, it's out of the question."

"Don't sulk like that. . . . So you're off to bring back your sister, eh?"

"That's right."

"Since we're going there anyway, shall we spring her for you?" Yamazaki looked at Nakatsu. "For us it's no problem," the tone of his voice seemed to be saying. Kantarō felt it. He thought it would be a mistake not to make use of Yamazaki at a time like this.

"What do you say? No charge, we'll do it for free." Once more Yamazaki looked at Nakatsu. Nakatsu's bearded face was creased in an elusive smile. Though sensing that Yamazaki was responding to some private joke, Kantarō deliberately pretended not to notice.

Just then a furious delight convulsed the crowd. Two soldiers who had been holding a prisoner's head and back were covered, from heads to arms, with steaming blood. The headless corpse pitched forward with a jerk. The spurting blood gradually subsided as the heartbeat weakened.

"Hurrah! Hurrah!" As each head fell, the crowd roared. "Hurrah! Hurrah!" Some even joyfully applauded. This was an emotion the Japanese could not understand.

In three or four minutes, the three—the downcast man, the drunk man, and the fat man who kept demanding dumplings until the instant his head was struck off—all lay lifeless in similar poses.

A woman whose feet were bound in black ran tottering out of the enveloping crowd. Two or three others followed her. Some men joined them too. Grinning they carried long chopsticks with peeled buns impaled on the tips. Officers and soldiers had begun to leave. Approaching the bodies, the women excitedly pressed the buns against the contracting wounds. The buns were not filled with bean jam. Soaking up the rapidly flowing blood, they turned red as boiled lobsters.

"They're doing it, they're doing it." Yamazaki laughed. "Fanatically superstitious, the Chinese. Always will be." Nakatsu made a face as if to say what else could you expect from them.

"Even Master Chang eats it from time to time."

"His umpteen wives eat it too, right?"

"Of course they eat it. It's supposed to guarantee perfect health."

"Master Chang's a savage. . . . I tell you, if the people back home saw this they wouldn't believe their eyes."

The crowd was still laughing boisterously. They did not seem to feel that three human beings had been killed. Not even that dogs or cats had been killed, thought Kantarō. They were no more affected than if caterpillars or locusts had had their heads torn off.

Only the rickshaw pullers who had transported the prisoners looked disheartened by bad luck. Silently, without a single squawk of the horn, the three vehicles disappeared in the multitude. The pullers had been recruited by force. According to superstition, giving a ride to a condemned criminal brings misfortune for life. They were no less dispirited than Japanese sailors would be at having had a drowned man aboard their ship.

"Don't let her see, don't let her see! Hey, don't let her see!"

Suddenly, from the very direction the three rickshaws had gone, three other rickshaws came rushing to the execution ground at full speed. A woman of thirty or so with bound feet jumped down unsteadily from the foremost vehicle and plunged desperately into the wall of people. Close behind her ran an agitated peasant struggling to draw her back. "Don't let her see! Don't let her see!" The peasant was frantically shouting.

Screaming hysterically, crying at the top of her voice, the woman was shoving her way through the crowd and trying to approach the corpses. The peasant was an old man over fifty. Catching up with the woman with his big strides, he spread out his arms and checked her in an embrace. The woman threw herself against her father's shoulder. Stamping her bound feet, she bitterly wept.

"Yuan-na! Yuan-na!" She dissolved into tears in the peasant's arms. "The master's the evil one! The master's the evil one! The master did this to my husband!"

"Forget about it, forget it! All the crying in the world can't bring him back." The old man soothed his daughter. "There's nothing we can do! Forget about it! Forget it!"

The crowd once again grew tense and began to gather around the woman. She was grieving for the man who had sung the war song, wanted dumplings, and clamored for P'ao-t'ai-pai. Looking at the woman, Yamazaki whispered meaningfully into Nakatsu's ear. Somehow Kantarō grasped the connection intuitively. Pushing people aside, Nakatsu hurried toward the soldiers.

"Isn't the fat man the runner employed by the manager?" Kantarō asked nonchalantly. Yamazaki turned away as though he had not heard.

"He's innocent! He's innocent! The evil one is the boss! It's the boss!" The woman was still sobbing.

"Her husband's no bandit!" the peasant explained to the people flocking around them. "The Japanese boss ordered her husband to do business with outlaws. When the police found them, they grabbed him along with the bandits. First he sends his own employee to do business with them, and then when he's caught the Japanese declares that the man's been fired and he knows nothing about it. The evil one's the boss. . . . The boss is evil! The Japanese is evil! "

When people who deal timidly in small quantities of guns or drugs are discovered, they atone for it with their blood. But those who operate on a truly grand scale grab up all they can and make their underlings pay the price. No one knows how many Chinese runners smuggling contraband under the orders of foreign masters are arrested, tortured with water-soaked leather whips, hastily tried, and sentenced to death.

Kantarō's family belonged to the category of those who pay for their deeds. He could not help feeling incensed. Even if there were incontrovertible proof linking the foreign master with his Chinese runner, the foreigner would merely be tried by his own country's consulate. The runner would lose his head while the master, thanks to the fraternal sympathy of his compatriots, would get off with a fine, detention, or reprimand. This was why the Chinese people cried out for the abolition of consular trials and immunity from local law.

The crowd surrounding the woman and the peasant was dispersed by the soldiers alerted by Nakatsu. The woman followed her husband's corpse as it was borne off to the cemetery. She had asked that the corpse be placed in a casket brought by the third rickshaw, but the soldiers refused her request.

"Well, all aboard! All aboard! We're running late." With an apparent sigh of relief, the engineer who had been mingling with the sightseers started to run toward the waiting locomotive. It was already one hour after the scheduled time of departure.

10

The questioning eyes of the consulate and the Chinese police were glittering in Takezaburō's direction.

A patrolman from the seventh ward police station, armed with a gun and a sword, stood sentrylike on the corner of the street lined with acacias, watching the people going in and out the back door. He was on the lookout for anyone taking advantage of the nighttime darkness to come and buy drugs unseen.

Suddenly Shun became aware of him. Pulling the toddling Ichirō by the hand, she had stepped out of her neighbor Ma Kuan-chih's house and onto the stone pavement. "Why is he standing over there?" Gesturing with her head toward the policeman, she put the question to Ma Kuan-chih's wife. It was the first time she had noticed him.

"Oh, Miss Inokawa, didn't you know?" replied the wife, a young woman with bound feet. The neighbors were on extremely good terms. The woman's voice faltered as if she were having trouble saying the words. "He's been standing there every night for five days now. Your family'd better be careful."

"What in the world does he want?"

"He's keeping an eye on the business. Watching for those who come to buy the stuff." The wife drew a listless sigh. "By standing there he's keeping them away."

Mortified at having her family's trade exposed before Ma Kuan-chih's wife, Shun flushed crimson even to her neck. She lifted Ichirō into her arms and fled into the house. A polished pipe in his mouth, Takezaburō was reclining on the red blanket, gazing at an alcohol lamp and striving to attain ecstasy. Mother was talking with a visitor, an antique dealer from Wei-wu Road. The antique dealer was laughingly telling her of the Shantung Army soldiers moving out to the front that morning carrying umbrellas and buckets made out of kerosene cans threaded with thick wire. "Those characters couldn't even keep burglars out of a house!"

Shun's information filled Mother with fear. The antique dealer's reaction was different: "He'll challenge anyone who comes to the back door, yet the thieves he pretends not to see."

"But thieves would hesitate to come, wouldn't they?" Mother glossed over her fear.

"Don't make me laugh. It doesn't make a bit of difference to thieves whether or not that character is standing there. They weren't born yesterday."

The patrolman was keeping watch at night when darkness obscured the identity of those coming and going. During the day he was absent. But it was in the daytime that the business transactions were completed. From early evening until early morning not a single suspect appeared. Even so, this did not in the least dispel the patrolman's suspicions.

By day Takezaburō took out the scales, the mortar and pestle, and went to work. In the daytime he could feel at ease. Adding various ingredients to number three, he produced the desired compound. The heroin addiction made the hand holding the spoon tremble more than that of a nicotine addict. Along with the hands, the legs too shook as he sat. Through the double doors of the adjoining house reverberated the ear-splittingly high-pitched voice of Ma Kuan-chih's wife singing a song.

Gripped in his quivering hand, the pestle clattered and screeched against the mortar's surface. "One pack of heroin, three thousand yen. . . . One pack of heroin, three thousand yen." Thus rang the mortar as it rattled round the bowl. Or so it sounded to Takezaburō. "One pack of heroin, three thousand yen; one pack of heroin, three thousand yen." Such was the state of his delirious mind.

There came the sound of Chinese shoes. Shun uttered a deafening scream. Turning around, Takezaburō saw a broad-shouldered Chinese plain-clothesman standing before him. There was no time to hide anything.

"What is that?"

A sword rattled under the Chinese tunic. The face was that of the familiar patrolman.

"What is that?"

Takezaburō was cowering and gazing at the policeman with piteous eyes that were begging for mercy.

"What is that, huh? Give it here! I'm taking all of it. . . . There's more you're hiding. Out with it! Out with all of it!"

Takezaburō was quaking with the double blow of heroin and dread. His chair seemed about to crumple to the ground.

Another Chinese, smaller and wearing a similar tunic, nimbly stepped in. Clearly he was a partner of the first. The large Chinese hand mercilessly reached for the mortar.

"Wait, just a second! Wait a second!" Osen who had been trembling and watching from the rear stammered out wildly in Chinese and ran to the next room. She returned clutching silver yen taken from the desk drawer. "*Ch'ing ning teng i hui erh.*" Tremulously she thrust the coins under the plainclothesmen's broad sleeves. Shun was looking at the white faces of her father and mother.

The patrolmen fingered the coins within their sleeves. "That's all? . . . Hand over two more yuan! Two more yuan!" Their voices were menacing. Mother cast a pitying glance at Father. His eyes, which long ago had tried to expose the corruption of village assembly members, were now grown clouded and utterly powerless. The second demand satisfied, the patrolman lowered the mortar back to its place. And then with a "Thank you" they departed. Takezaburō heaved a deep sigh of relief.

After that day he was frequently visited by policemen who had taken a liking to extorting from him. Little by little, the money collected from heroin addicts was taken away by policemen. His facial coloring continued to be drained by the drug. The trembling in his arms and legs grew steadily worse. Totally addicted, he could not endure a day without heroin.

11

Anxious rumors of war gradually spread. The continually retreating troops of Chang Tsung-ch'ang linked up with Sun Ch'uan-fang's units and made a stand against Chiang Kai-shek.

All the barracks emptied out as nearly every unit headed for the front. The deserted buildings were being guarded by a handful of soldiers. Quilts, chairs, and bullets were removed from the dark blue barracks. In town they were exchanged for money. Even tables and miniature lamps with sooty globes were carried away.

It was the work of the soldiers guarding the abandoned buildings.

They hoisted up well buckets dripping with water, fence posts, teacups, and tea jars and dragged them away. All that was left in the end was the immovable edifices themselves. Thereupon they detached the windowpanes and the floorboards and marched off to town with them. Such sights were sporadically seen—and revealed the degree of the soldiers' fighting capacity.

With Suzu back, Takezaburō's house was as fresh as a newly cut flower arrangement. "There's a cruiser at anchor in Chingtao. And four destroyers. Armed marines were coming ashore. Naval guns were banging away. And gloomy-looking Chinese are saying it's a show of force." Such was Suzu's account.

"Mommy, Mommy," Ichirō was innocently calling his aunt Suzu.

Without being fully aware of it, Kantarō missed Toshiko. Toshiko had been sharply critical of his addicted father and of her mother-in-law who respected him blindly. If they left China and returned to Japan, neither Father nor Mother could so much as survive. They were invalids. Toshiko had been right. He now felt nostalgic even about her frequent criticisms of his parents.

Suzu did not go so far as to say it, but she understood how he felt. Nonetheless she did not want her sister-in-law to return but rather aspired to make her brother a success and show Toshiko that she had been wrong about him. Her eager assistance in Father's repellent occupation was motivated by similar sentiments. Kantarō was conscious of this. He considered it necessary to convince his sister that he himself had no desire at all to become a success. Least of all did he wish to grow wealthy by selling heroin.

Just as frequently happens in times of adversity, the brother and sister's feelings were united. Suzu was nineteen. Her younger sister Shun was sixteen. Shun was still of an age when sordid things appear beautiful and trifling incidents seem irresistibly amusing. Both sisters seemed blessed with unblemished physical and emotional health. The way they dressed and wore their hair, the fragments of dialect in their speech, still conveyed a strong flavor of their native land. This was readily discernible when comparing them with other young women of the same nationality who had been born in China and grown up attending the local Japanese schools.

Soon after Suzu's return Nakatsu, who had gone to the trouble of bringing her back from Chingtao, became a frequent visitor to the house. A gambler and a drunkard, Nakatsu was a man whose parasitical gluttony made him troublesome enough as a friend but who as an enemy was terrifying and utterly unpredictable. His leg had been crippled during the Russo-Japanese War. He hobbled heavily when he walked. In appearance he was unobtrusive and reserved. Even wearing a new damask Chinese tunic, Nakatsu managed to look covered with dust and dirt.

Kantarō could not comprehend why such a man commanded authority. More than a few times Nakatsu had recovered Japanese hostages kidnapped by outlaws and held for ransom. He told numerous tales of his cruelty toward enemies.

Whenever Nakatsu came, Kantarō's two sisters danced around the house laughing and shouting, "Cripple, cripple!" Hearing Nakatsu's voice outside shouting to the servant Wang Chin-hua to unlatch the gate, then seeing him from the window as he nimbly crossed the courtyard stepping-stones, the sisters leaped about calling him cripple. Nakatsu kept smiling.

Finally one day Shun playfully brought up the subject, watching him closely to see if he would take offense: "Uncle, how can you cut down and shoot so many people with a leg like that?"

"I don't cut them down and shoot them with this leg, but with a pistol and sword in hand. I use this hand." From the baggy sleeve of the Chinese gown emerged a hairy arm with short fat fingers.

"But with you limping around like that, Uncle, anyone can run away from your sword and pistol, can't they?" Shun's voice was filled with amiable laughter. But her eyes were fixed tensely on his face, like those of a cat confronting a dog.

"What! When I need to, I can run faster than you!"

"I see. . . . Uncle, where did you get wounded?"

"Never mind where. . . . That was a long, long time ago. You girls were still tucked away in your father's balls back then."

This extraordinary ruffian, a man who had joined a den of outlaws, taken part in war, raided Russian houses in the outskirts of Harbin, and killed countless people, struck the two sisters as no more than an odd and rather comical character. In addition to touring the front with Chang Tsung-ch'ang, making trips to Peking, and guarding his head, which had a price of tens of thousands of yuan on it, he dutifully played cards with the two girls. He taught them to play mah-jongg. Endlessly, idiotically, he repeated the Chinese words for one, two, three.

It appeared as though he longed for the fragrance of Japan, which this family possessed so abundantly, and that he was selfishly indulging in it.

After the sisters went to bed, Kantarō stayed up with his father and mother. He began to speak: "Mr. Nakatsu's up to no good. . . . He's after Suzu. And he's also somewhat interested in Shun."

"Foolish boy," Takezaburō said with a laugh. "Nakatsu is my age, so he's already fifty-two. What would a man that old want with teenage girls?"

"No, no. From the moment he comes till the moment he leaves, he's got eyes for nothing else. He stares at Suzu and Shun hard enough to bore holes in them. I've seen it with my own eyes."

"I've noticed it too," Mother bashfully put in.

"That's right. I'm sure he's after them."

"Don't be foolish. Would a fifty-two-year-old man run after girls young enough to be his daughters?"

"But isn't it said that the older a man gets, the more he finds young girls attractive? Besides, he's still a bachelor."

"Foolish people! You two are so suspicious. . . . Nakatsu's a good friend of mine. I know him well. He's not the man to do something so indecent and disgraceful." Father had known Nakatsu for four or five years.

Nevertheless, Kantarō's suspicions were not unfounded. Suzu, who had once danced about in amusement whenever the crippled man arrived, now blushed crimson to the roots of her ears and ran to hide as soon as she heard his loud, forceful voice calling to Wang outside the gate.

Nakatsu's sharp eyes were blazing. It was not only the nineteen-year-old Suzu who could not bear to face that gaze. Her sister and mother were shocked by it as well. And Nakatsu had shaved his hirsute face to a blue sheen, neatly combed the swirl of his curly, dusty hair, and gave off a potent smell of hair oil. He camped at the house throughout the day. It was truly a strange sight to see this past master of banditry, murder, robbery, rape, and sundry other serenely committed crimes so thoroughly smitten by the inexperienced Suzu. He did not seem an old man of fifty-two. He rather resembled an innocent twenty-year-old hopelessly tormented by a young woman's charm.

One morning, Ma Kuan-chih's dog Paipai was barking as if it were on fire.

Kantarō woke up. Suzu too seemed about to awake. The dog continued to bark furiously. After a while Suzu got up to open the window. With tense footsteps, she returned to where her brother lay. "A whole crowd of consular officers is here again." Her voice was grave. She seemed to want to hide somewhere. Kantarō jumped to his feet.

The area was tightly surrounded by the consular police. The house was ransacked pell-mell until it looked like the inside of a trash can. This time a box of Supreme Pleasure that Takezaburō had just sealed was taken away along with the mortar, scales, and other paraphernalia.

Before long, Nakatsu left for Su-chou to join Chang Tsung-ch'ang. The battlefront emergency did not allow him the leisure to disclose the agonies of his heart. He departed by the night train.

12

It was a warm evening, just after sunset, when everything still looks light and gleaming. The daytime bustle and the yellow, ashlike dust were finally subsiding. The countless groups of loitering beggars vanished into the darkness. In the narrow alleys, women with glittering earrings began eerily to smile.

Yamazaki emerged from one of these alleys. He was not wearing his customary black Chinese tunic but the gray uniform of an S University student. The lukewarm city seemed tinged with moisture. The sense of anxiety and peril intensified as the night deepened. Only the beggars wrapped in their gunnysacks felt no fear. Yamazaki's eyes were fretful, as though he were impatiently waiting for something. A certain Ch'en Chang-ts'ai who was secretly prowling the city had not yet returned.

The Northern Punitive Army, of which it had been disparagingly said that it would be a huge success if it could invade Hsu-chou or Lin-ch'eng at most, had already captured K'un-chou and was closing in on T'ai-an. Chang Tsung-ch'ang's defending troops continued to retreat from Su-chou, Hsu-chou, Lin-ch'eng, and K'un-chou. Soldiers wounded in the fierce battle at Su-chou were abandoned where they lay. Worse yet, other wounded men who had become a hindrance to the hasty retreat from the frontlines were one and all buried alive on the spot. At Lin-ch'eng, Yamazaki had shot with his pistol the officers under Chang's command who were collapsing like an avalanche.

From the south, Chang's Shantung Army soldiers were pressed hard by the Northern Punitive Army. In the north their path of retreat was blocked by Chang Tu-pien. They were stranded. Of necessity some of them turned aside along the way, crossed the steep slopes of T'ai-shan, passed through Ming-shui and Kuo-tien, and fled to familiar cities. Others surrendered to Chiang Kai-shek.

The unexpected power of the Northern Punitive Army was due to money. Yamazaki had recently ascertained that the report about the corporate association funding Chiang Kai-shek had been false. Instead it was North American businessmen who were financing him. Thanks to their substantial support it was expected that Chiang Kai-shek would even be able to march into Peking. Bent on a cultural invasion of China, the United States had everywhere established churches, schools, and hospitals. It operated deceptive charity projects. It brought presents. It waived compensation. And it tamed the Chinese.

I fear Greeks, thought Yamazaki, no matter how many gifts they bring. For the Chinese, who are no Romans, mused he, it is the Americans who are the Greeks! The Chinese were being taken in by the gifts. Yamazaki was fully aware, of course, of what all this signified for Japan.

> Tsinan is strategically the most important city in China. Situated midway between the country's north and south, it controls the southern half of the Gulf of Pohai and also dominates Tientsin and Peking militarily. If the land around the upper reaches of the Luan River can be said to constitute Peking's back, then Tsinan has the aspect of its front and belly. Fangtzu, Poshan, Tsuch'uan, and other sites along the way to Chingtao contain deposits of about 1.8 billion tons of coal. Westward also, for well over two hundred miles, stretch the great coalfields of Shanhsi hoarding 680 billion tons of coal—some eighty percent of Asia's total supply—along with virtually inexhaustible quantities of iron ore. If Japan is henceforth to become self-sufficient in iron and coal, it can neither afford to ignore the value of the Shantung coal nor let the global value of the great Shanhsi coalfields slip through its fingers. (*The Special Relationship Between Japan and Shantung*, page 19)

Yamazaki, of course, knew this.

> Japan has made great sacrifices and invested enormous amounts of capital in developing the profitability of Manchuria and Mongolia. It is essential to safeguard these investments at all costs. Some argue that even if circumstances should compel us to relinquish Shantung, the unique profits of Manchuria and Mongolia must by all means be retained. Manchuria and Mongolia take precedence over Shantung. While the nation's power must be staked on the struggle for Manchuria and Mongolia, we might have to compromise somewhat on the issue of Shantung. Such arguments can be heard.
>
> Clearly Manchuria and Mongolia are vast lands involving extensive interests, and the merits and demerits of the general situation are exceedingly consequential. But China's national revolution that started in Canton, as well as the underground campaign of the communists, have now thoroughly saturated central China and are striving to extend their nefarious influence to northern China and even into Manchuria.

As a barrier protecting Manchuria and Mongolia, Shantung is again vitally important. So long as Shantung is safe, Manchuria and Mongolia will be secure. Nor is that all: Shantung's geographic prominence, military significance, and the boundless wealth of the Hwang Ho River basin to its rear are such that for the sake of our national defense and the lives of our people we can never allow it to slip from our sphere of influence. American capitalists and the like, quick to note that the Hwang Ho floodplains are suitable for the cultivation of cotton, have been speeding up the pace of research into the matter. If cotton production in this region is indeed feasible, the day may come when Japan need no longer depend on the United States for its cotton imports.

The loss of Shantung's outstanding advantages would result in Japan's inability to achieve future independence in iron and coal. Even worse, it would likely lead to Japan's withdrawal from northern China and launch an unstoppable national decline under an unenterprising, submissive foreign policy. Though the Chinese continent is broad, the only area over which we must have absolute economic sway—other than Manchuria and Mongolia—is Shantung. Over the past decade and more Japan has expended great treasure and precious lives (in the Japanese-German War), has developed Shantung's resources, and is currently investing some 150 million yen through its residents. It stands to reason that we shall protect, expand, and maintain the economic foundation carved out by the unstinting hard work and diligence of our compatriots. (Ibid., pages 31 and 32)

These things, of course, Yamazaki knew full well. Any Japanese could be expected to feel keenly, even without being told, what the American machinations in China meant. It was his ambition to be ahead of the rest.

Information such as the foregoing was already being printed in books. Everyone was thoroughly familiar with it. But no one knew the real facts taking place on this very ground. And these were important. He was planning to utilize Ch'en Chang-ts'ai, a Chinese recently obtained from Nakatsu, to find out far more.

13

The night grew dark. Few people passed through the streets. Yet in one spot beneath the night sky, blinking with glittering stars, a noisy uproar was taking place. The din traveled through the air from its unseen source.

Yamazaki was restlessly pacing along the street redolent with the captivating fragrance of the white wisteria-like blossoms adorning the long-leafed acacia trees. He was in a bad mood. Ch'en, who was supposed to come out with him, had not yet turned up.

Under the acacia trees children were craning their heads sharply upward and struggling in the dim lamplight to tear off the white wisteria-like flowers using long bamboo poles tipped with hooks. The children had been picking the newly dangling blossoms since the daylight hours. They plucked off the flowers and ate them.

Snagged by the hook, a branch broke off with a snap. "Hey, don't break a whole branch!" The hungry children were distracting their empty stomachs by eating flowers.

"Hello there, Mr. Yamazaki!"

The somewhat surprised shout startled Yamazaki, who had been thinking of other things. The rickshaw stopped, and Koyama of the Fu-lung Match Company got off. Seen in the street, Koyama, who strutted about the factory intimidating workers, was a feeble, staggering figure with a receding chin who reeked of phosphorus.

"The Shantung Army has suffered a terrible defeat." Koyama spoke with a lisp. Bone decay had caused the canines supporting his dentures to fall out, and his lower incisors were missing. "Even the brave Cossack cavalry ran away." It was Koyama's way of eagerly showing that he was an insider. "The way things are going, communism is sure to get here," he said gravely. "If we don't get troops sent out from Japan soon, it won't be just property and factories we'll lose, they'll tear off our heads and pricks as well!"

"The Russian soldiers have retreated?"

"Yes, yes, they came back on foot from the direction of Kuo-tien. They'd run the horses so hard, seems half the horses collapsed along the way. They're coming. Someone must be giving Chiang Kai-shek a lot of backing for him to advance at this speed. I strongly suspect it."

"If I don't wrap up the investigation and send a telegram before the night is out, someone will beat me to it! What the hell is Ch'en doing?" thought Yamazaki irritably. "It has to be tonight. Tomorrow night will be too late. Someone else will have done it." As the state of affairs grew tense, five or six of his intelligence-gathering colleagues were arriving on the scene from various directions.

The clatter of disordered, spiritless, dragging hoofbeats rang out in Erhmalu Street. Many sounded lame. "There, they're starting to arrive. They're starting to arrive." With those words, Koyama walked off toward the sound.

After a few minutes, exhausted White Russian soldiers straddling short dirty-coated Chinese horses came into view in the dim street light, their limply hanging boots nearly scraping the road. "These are supposed to be tougher by far than the Chinese soldiers," grumbled Koyama.

The men who had ridden their horses to death limped by, dragging their feet. The straggling line stretched into the distance toward the train station square. Some seemed to have disappeared along the way. The non-payment of salaries, the shortage of food, and Chang Tsung-ch'ang's reckless fighting had sapped their warring spirit. These were the men who had fled across the mountain of T'ai-shan. They were all that was left. Others had dissolved like leeches in salt. Utterly worn out, bereft of all power to think, observe, or grip their swords, they were walking out of sheer force of habit. If they stopped, it seemed certain they would collapse on the spot.

"These are supposed to be tougher by far than the Chinese soldiers," repeated Koyama. "If they're running away, the city's fall is just a matter of time."

At that moment there was the crack of a shot from a Browning in the acacia-lined street, and someone came flying their way cutting through the disorderly line of White Russian soldiers. Another shot followed. Koyama and Yamazaki stopped in their tracks stunned. The fleeing man was rushing toward them. Instantly they sensed the muzzle of the handgun turning toward them as well.

The dead-tired White Russians were indifferent to the gunshots. They did not so much as turn around.

In a second the sprinting man had reached them. When he was directly before them, Yamazaki recognized him as Ch'en Chang-ts'ai. "What's the fuss, you damned idiot!" he shouted with disgust. "Where the hell have you been?"

But Ch'en sped right past Yamazaki with the agility of a monkey and vanished into a dark narrow alley.

"Damned idiot! You're useless! Son of a bitch!"

"Do you know him?" asked Koyama.

"That one? He's unmanageable. I'm paying him but the clown keeps me waiting for two hours. . . ."

Ch'en Chang-ts'ai was at present indispensable to Yamazaki. It was said that he used to be a coolie on the Shanghai waterfront. Nakatsu had brought him along on the way back from Chingtao and handed him over to Yamazaki.

Nakatsu had summoned Ch'en and laid down the rules succinctly. You scratch my back and I'll scratch yours, he had told him. I'll pay you well. But if you do anything to betray me or my friends, I will kill you. Not only you, I'll kill your mother as well.

"This is a joker who spies for the Southern Army until the day before yesterday and then suddenly switches sides," Nakatsu warned Yamazaki. "Just giving him small amounts of money is best. If you hand him an advance, he's uncontrollable. You've got to squeeze him tight and do it often."

He paused, then went on: "Needless to say, you can't believe what he says. The Chinese will cook up any likely story if they think there's money in it."

"All right, all right. I understand," replied Yamazaki.

From somewhere Ch'en had managed to obtain key material evidence: invoices for the weapons shipped from Germany, photographs of the weapons being unloaded at the docks, and receipts for the accompanying ammunition. When ordered, he even produced passports like the ones issued by diplomatic sections, complete with the proper seals. Hence people unable to get a passport in Japan could have one made here by Ch'en. They could even go to Russia so long as they assumed a Chinese name and identity. Ch'en's flawless brush even supplied them with a visa from the consulate. He was fascinating.

"There he goes again!" When Yamazaki walked with him, it frequently happened that a stranger would suddenly grin at Ch'en before passing by. He encountered two or three such mysterious men each day. This man seemed to have poked his nose everywhere. "Who was that?"

"That man? He's a boatman who used to work with me when I was sailing on the junk. These days he's making loads of money."

"You come across people you know amazingly often. Just how many acquaintances do you have in this place?"

"Hardly any. There are fewer than three hundred people whose faces I recognize."

"Damned idiot! Is three hundred people hardly any?"

No one was as astute as Ch'en at penetrating another's secrets. He was sharper than a pickpocket. In this respect Yamazaki himself had to keep on the alert. Carrying about large sums of money in China greatly increased the chances of being robbed.

Ch'en walked the streets in order to find out about the Southern Army spies and plainclothes soldiers who were increasingly infiltrating the city as

Chiang Kai-shek's troops advanced northward. His sudden flight before the bullets just now was occasioned either by a bungled attempt to relieve a rich citizen of cash or by his intrusive shadowing of plainclothes soldiers.

14

About two hours later Ch'en and Yamazaki were riding rickshaws toward S University in Ch'eng-tung.

By the time of the approaching clash between the Japanese troops and the Southern Army, this university would become a base of vigorous activity by the plainclothes soldiers. Japanese soldiers were to be severely harassed. They operated as guerrillas. Taking advantage of an unguarded moment, they would spring into action and then flee to the safety zone. Three thousand officers and men would pursue them with all their might. But they would never be able to capture a single genuine guerrilla. The guerrillas wore clothes identical to those of ordinary civilians. To the Japanese soldiers, all Chinese looked the same. The safety zone was the American school.

Having heard about their supposed presence from Ch'en, Yamazaki resolved to infiltrate the guerrilla nest and verify the rumor. Seven-tenths of Ch'en Chang-ts'ai's reports were unreliable. This one, however, Yamazaki's intuition told him, was true. He planned to make quite sure of it and send a telegram this very night. If he could do this, he could outstrip his colleagues. A point in his favor was that in words, clothes, and tastes he did not in the least differ from a Chinese. Wherever he went, he had no fear of being discovered. Convinced of the efficacy of his disguise, he wished to cultivate his self-confidence by putting it to a strenuous test.

Besides, playing such dangerous games was a pleasure for him. Surely, he thought, this would be a feat he could boast of all his life. He would creep into an enemy camp—moreover a stronghold of crafty guerrillas. This was certain to be one of the triumphant achievements of a lifetime! His life, in fact, was just beginning. His true work lay ahead of him. People in their thirties and forties still put their hopes in the future. But Yamazaki was fulfilling his lifework at this very moment. Never mind the future, he felt, it is the present that counts!

Ch'en Chang-ts'ai had explained the circumstances that led up to his being fired at. He concluded with a warning: "You'd be smart to forget such a daredevil stunt. These fellows are pretty motivated."

"No, I'm going ahead," Yamazaki said decisively. "Call the rickshaws.

The more highly motivated they are, the more's the need for me to go see what they're up to."

"After they shoot you, it'll be too late for regrets."

"I know that!"

"I want a lot of money for this kind of reckless work. If you're thinking of paying me some measly sum, I'll have nothing to do with it from the start."

"You'll get as much money as you like, I told you. If only all goes well."

Yamazaki had changed into a student uniform. Ch'en put one on as well.

The gravelly, uneven, partly washed away road slowed the rickshaws' progress to less than a walking pace. The two alighted from the vehicles. In the darkness of the ordinarily deserted suburbs near the university there was a sense of people stirring.

"Are you all right?" Ch'en whispered.

Yamazaki did not feel afraid in the slightest. All the same, his legs were dreadfully weak. He feared they might unaccountably give out after walking a dozen yards.

"*Ya song ki cho le, ni!*" (Hey, how's it going?) A dark figure called out passing them in a narrow street. Realizing his mistake, the man broke off and gazed suspiciously after them.

"*Chu-tung-hsi!*" (Idiot!) Ch'en Chang-ts'ai yelled without even turning his head.

In the thick shrubbery that rose to human height by the roadside, more men seemed to be moving. The night air appeared to have grown somewhat colder. They passed by the first school building. Between the third and the fourth building, which were crookedly shaped and surrounded by acacias, a bonfire was blazing. The budding leaves of the acacias were dyed crimson by the flames.

"Scared?" Ch'en Chang-ts'ai whispered teasingly, convinced that his own position was superior should the situation turn ugly.

"Idiot! Stop chattering!" Yamazaki scolded him in earnest.

At the same instant a Chinese voice addressed them from a gap between the acacia trunks: "Who goes there?" A flare-up of the distant bonfire revealed a hand gripping a pistol.

Damn, they're being careful, thought Yamazaki. Try something and you're dead, you son of a bitch! He placed his hand on the Browning at his side.

"Is Professor Taft around?" Ch'en asked the question without slackening his pace. The dark figure stepped out from among the acacias and approached for a closer look at their faces.

"Who are you?" asked the shadow.

"Students at the teachers' college."

"Your names?"

"We have an appointment with the professor tonight," Yamazaki shouted at him in Chinese. "Do you have any objection to students going to school?"

Passing what looked like a sentry's hut and entering the fenced-in campus, Yamazaki fell in one step behind Ch'en Chang-ts'ai so as not to be seen from the bonfire. Marching through this nest of guerrillas Ch'en showed not the faintest sign of fear or discomfort. The two advanced toward a dormitory. Suddenly Yamazaki felt a flash of suspicion about Ch'en. This character might have some link with the Southern Army. Give him money and he will say anything. But when it comes to the crunch, he'll switch to the other side. He might be just that type.

Of all the many dormitory rooms only one was lit. Chinese voices emanated from within. The two passed under the windows and turned into the dark corridor. Approaching the room they noticed that its door was ajar. Someone inside the room was making a rattling noise handling firearms; someone else was counting bullets. Clearly these were not students.

A Chinese dressed in black raised his left elbow until his arm was parallel to the ground, rested a handgun on his forearm, aimed, and pretended to fire. The man squeezed the trigger with a click. "Bull's eye!" Evidently the weapon was not loaded.

"Hey, there are Russian bullets mixed in with the others. These are pointed at both ends." The man who was counting the bullets burst out laughing. "That's because Russia has enemies front and rear." Noticing Ch'en and Yamazaki standing at the door, the men abruptly shut their mouths and fixed the two with suspicious stares.

"*Ya! Chi wan fan le ma!*" (Hello, good evening!) With all the nonchalance he could muster, Yamazaki stepped into the room. At that instant he was struck by the sense that Ch'en and the Chinese in black had exchanged knowing smiles.

A dashing young Chinese who had been fingering the weapons in a dark corner rose at the sound of his voice, walked right up to them, and looked steadily into their faces.

"Where have you come from? . . . They say that times are very good in Shanghai. Is it true?"

No one said a word in reply. They looked at each other in silence with questioning eyes. The false tone of his own words making him regret having come, Yamazaki listened to the blood pounding through his heart.

The room contained about twenty rifles and a box of handguns placed next to a pile of old shoes. On a white wall two posters had been pasted side by side showing the Japanese prime minister, Tanaka Giichi, straddling a map of Japan and Korea and trying to grab Manchuria, Mongolia, and Shantung province with long demonlike claws. "When Chinese people are divided, the Japanese devil gets greedy." So read the Chinese caption along the margins.

On another wall over the window hung a caricature of the Manchurian warlord Chang Tso-lin accusing him of plunder, rape, and treason. Posters denouncing the Communist Party and Soviet Russia as "communist bandits" and "red imperialism" were faintly visible in the shadows behind the electric light. Many similar posters could already be seen around Shanghai.

The United States understands Japan's ambitions most shrewdly, thought Yamazaki as he looked at the posters. If Japan does not take Manchuria, Mongolia, and Shantung province, the United States will take them instead. The Americans are eyeing China with its bestially low wages, inexhaustible raw materials, and virtually no labor unions. They are trying to bring in their huge factories and huge banks. They are trying to turn all Chinese into their wage slaves.

"Did you come to ask us to go buying whores with you? Is that why you're here this late at night?" A short droll-faced Chinese laughed, his eyes twinkling.

Laughing in reply, Yamazaki reminded Ch'en Chang-ts'ai about going to see Professor Taft.

"Professor Taft, Professor Taft!" A long-haired Chinese youth echoed the words. "You two have business with Professor Taft?"

"We have an appointment to see him tonight," Yamazaki hesitatingly said.

"Hmm. The professor will be coming downstairs soon."

"Well, then, our timing's perfect." In facile Chinese he had blurted out the opposite of what he meant. He did not know Taft. Having Taft appear was the very last thing he wanted.

Ch'en sat down next to the Chinese and began asking questions: how many had come from Nanking, how many more were expected tonight, how much was the monthly pay?

Yamazaki extracted a Ch'ien-men-pai cigarette and struck a match. He would smoke it, he decided, and then pull out. It takes five minutes to smoke a Ch'ien-men-pai. He felt that Taft would not appear during that time. His belief that these five minutes constituted a period safe from danger was based purely on superstition. Once he made a decision, however, he carried it out. Yamazaki was that sort of person.

Having lit his own cigarette, he offered the opened pack of Ch'ien-men-pai to everyone present. But except for Ch'en, no one made a move to accept. The long-haired youth inspected him closely from head to toe with a withering glare and inquired once again what his business was with Professor Taft. Aware of the animosity, Yamazaki pretended to be absorbed in Ch'en Chang-ts'ai's comments about the dispatch of Japanese troops. He blew out the smoke and took up the conversation. The Japanese can send all the troops they like, he said with a laugh. Before the Northern Punitive Army they will be like a praying mantis trying to stop an oxcart.

"Wherever those Japanese devils go, they never go home without devouring someone," the dashing youth cut in maliciously.

"No, those . . ." Yamazaki could not manage to refer to himself as a devil. "Japanese troops are only invincible when they're facing an army in uniform. Against guerrillas like us they can't do anything." He seemed to be soliciting agreement. All he received was a doubtful silence.

The cigarette was gradually approaching its end. While casually laughing and chatting, Yamazaki often turned his ear toward the corridor and morbidly listened for the sound of Taft's footsteps. Even the noisy steps of the passing Chinese nearly caused him to leap up with alarm. "Well, time to go," he thought, stubbing out the cigarette butt with the tip of his shoe.

In a hushed voice Ch'en was stretching out the conversation with an account of how Chiang Kai-shek had received twenty million yen from the Americans. Next he launched into related subjects. Was it true that Chiang accepted only Germans as military advisers and would not allow Japanese even as observers? Surely the Americans intend to give more money to the Northern Punitive Army. Twenty million yen might be a fit sum for a beggarly nation like Japan, but it was downright miserly for America.

Three or four men who had edged toward a dark corner began to whisper suspiciously. Yamazaki sensed they were not merely wary of him but had realized exactly who he was. Impatient for Ch'en to wind up his story, each minute seeming to last ten hours, he walked to the door.

He listened for footsteps in the dark corridor. There was a faint sound of someone descending the stairs. Ch'en was still mirthfully chuckling and chatting. The footsteps were drawing closer.

With hardly any time to think, he said something to Ch'en and stepped out into the corridor. Within ten seconds he had flown the thirty yards to the corner. There he stopped. There was no sign of Ch'en coming out.

Though expecting the Chinese to give chase, he paused a while to appraise the situation. Amiably laughing, Ch'en finally came out. The Chinese followed him in a ragged crowd. Suddenly he started. Somewhere an engine growled.

Five seconds later he realized it belonged to a truck, loaded with weapons, driving into the school grounds. The youths from the bonfire and those from the room offloaded the firearms and carried them into the building.

Ch'en and Yamazaki stood on the dark lawn, wet with the night dew, watching them. A tall American with a striking face, evidently Taft, was giving instructions in Chinese. The large truck had been heavily loaded with weapons.

Suddenly the man with the distinguished features addressed the two wearing student uniforms: "Hey! Don't worry about standing guard. It's all right. You two come and help too."

"Sure." Ch'en sprang forward readily at once. Snickering at the humor of it, Yamazaki made himself inconspicuous and drew back.

"There's no two ways about it, this is war!" he whispered to Ch'en as they started back. "But tonight I'm truly grateful to you. Thanks to you, I've managed to render a most distinguished service. . . . What a great feeling!"

"You won't forget about the money, will you?" Ch'en was disappointingly calm.

"Mm. Of course not, how could I forget? I'll reward you for sure. But I tell you there's just no way this won't lead to war." He paused in thought. "This is not a war between the Chinese army and the Japanese army. This is a war between Japan and the United States."

15

The fall of the province was only a matter of time. The so-called "economic foundation carved out by hard work and diligence" was about to crumble to nothing. The settlers were led to believe that their homes, easy chairs, ornamental tables, phonographs, antiques, and safes would all be plundered and trampled by thuggish Southern soldiers. Many vicious communists were said to be hiding within the Southern Army. According to rumors that winged about, they skewered people alive and desecrated graves along their way.

The railway station was jammed full of refugees bound for Chingtao, all weighed down with as much luggage as they could bear. A child of six or seven was being made to carry a trunk large enough to contain him. A pregnant woman rushed about, panting breathlessly, having loaded a Chinese porter's shoulders and arms with two wicker trunks each more swollen than her belly. Wealthy landowners' carriages galloped up, one after another, piled high with mountains of boxes and bags.

Commodity prices mirrored the social unrest. They gave a clear account of the turmoil affecting the city and its population. The exchange rate of ten yuan to twelve yen and thirty sen maintained by the Transport Bank dropped sharply along with that of the China Bank currency. The Chinese yuan fell to eight yen, seven yen, five yen, until in the end foreigners, the Japanese included, would no longer accept Chinese currency. Chang Tsung-ch'ang's Shantung Provincial Bank collapsed. The price of handguns, gold, silver, promissory notes, food, carriages, and carfares shot up. A single pistol might be bought or sold for as much as eight hundred and fifty-eight yen. No one any longer took the slightest notice of costly chairs, tables, mirrors, or silk goods.

The social turmoil was simultaneously reflected in the conduct of countless workers. Male and female factory workers, coolies in the streets, and beggars in their tens of thousands stopped fearing the overseers' whips and pistols. Policemen armed with guns and swords turned into simple scarecrows. At all the factories the owners restrained the workers by continuing to withhold their minuscule wages. This strategy barely worked. The workers started a slowdown.

The rumor intensified that the communists had infiltrated the city at about the same time as the guerrillas. The word got around that they planned to distribute arms to the workers and foment an uprising.

The workers utterly ignored the rules and orders the factory owners had arbitrarily issued. A time like this, they felt, offered a splendid opportunity to demonstrate their power to the owners.

The match factory workers had already suffered all that they could endure. They had been patient beyond the bounds of patience. One evening, they elected five representatives who demanded immediate payment of all the wages owed to the workers.

Wang Hung-chi was one of the representatives. The intractable Yui Li-song was another. Wang had received no news either from his wife, who had borne a baby, or from his mother. The lack of news only worsened his anxiety.

The workers had been duped and despised for a long time. Dozens had had their jaws destroyed by acute white phosphorus poisoning.

The delicate bodies of six- and seven-year-old workers had been ravaged in less than a year. The children were then paid their final wage and thrown out. Those purchased from traffickers for eight to ten yuan were never paid at all.

The people had worked. They had worked only to see their parents and wives starve. Like castrated bulls they had dreaded the whip. But eternal dread of the whip leads to eternal slavery.

One night, under cover of darkness, the child workers who yearned for their parents' homes ran away, even without having received a penny in wages. The children who had been bought from traffickers had neither homes nor families to escape to. Silent and forlorn, they remained in the dormitories, their eyes filled with tears.

In the evening, the five worker representatives, including Wang Hung-chi, had hesitantly entered the office. One way or another, they had to get their wages. Rightfully so! The accountant Iwai and the employee Koyama, however, flatly refused. They put on a show of fierce defiance. The manager had not changed his view that the workers were too dependent on their unpaid wages to flee. Until they got them, they would work submissively and industriously. The Chinese treasured money more than life itself, the manager was convinced. They would even die for money.

The five representatives withdrew. The two dormitories brimmed with a stormy atmosphere. Another meeting began. The workers started planning "an insubordinate revolt," to use Koyama's words. Their indignant voices drifted loudly toward the office.

"What are they making such a racket about?" Koyama shouted irritably at the company-housing servant he had sent to look into the situation.

"They're saying that if you won't give them the wages, that's all right." Liu, who had been employed by the Japanese for eight years and could speak their language, replied timidly as though he had done something wrong.

"So what are they going to do?"

"If you won't give in, then you won't, they say." The workers were planning to occupy the factory by force and run it themselves. They intended to sell the product and take their wages from the proceeds. They would throw the Japanese out the factory gates. And as for the traitorous Chinese policemen who protected them, they would beat them to death.

"You're lying!" Koyama bellowed. Liu trembled. "The lazy bastards are doing nothing except feeding at the company's expense. If their wives and parents are really starving, let them chew raw radishes or carrot stubs! They live like beggars anyway, so what are they getting so high and mighty about?" The worry was that the workers would flee if they got paid. And for the skilled workers there were no replacements.

Having said all he could think of to pacify his subordinates, the overseer Li Lan-pu returned. "This is no good. I don't have the vaguest idea what to do," Li said. "Could you at least pay them half of it? If not, there's just no way of controlling them. In these times there's not a thing they can buy without cash."

"Son of a bitch! You're probably in cahoots with them."

"Mr. Koyama, please don't misunderstand me," Li hastily interrupted. "Please don't misunderstand me!"

"Damn you! Damn you!" Koyama roared. "I won't stand for your impudence! Damn you!" For reassurance, he glanced over his shoulder at the pistol hanging on the wall.

The manager had resolved to confront any challenge that arose. If need be, he was prepared to rely on the force of arms. The wives and children of the Japanese employees slipped out of the company housing after eleven in the evening and hurriedly departed by car for the KS Club.

The workers united instinctively. Signs of an impending eruption grew ever more numerous.

The city was not only in danger of invasion, plunder, and destruction by the Southern Army. There was no telling what atrocities the Northern Army might commit out of spite as it withdrew from the city. The men of that army habitually pillaged and raped as if it was their profession. This time they could truly abandon all restraint. They were likely to rampage to their hearts' content.

The foreigners gained confidence merely from catching an occasional glimpse of a compatriot's face. Linked with others of the same nationality and language, they were determined to join forces and withstand whatever hardships and onslaughts this upheaval inflicted upon them. They were moved by the sentimental, antiquated emotion of ethnic unity. "Ah, if only those soldiers in khaki uniforms would arrive!" all of them wished. Simplemindedly they failed to wonder why and for whose sake the army would be coming. If only the troops got here, they thought, they'd be delivered from their plight.

The twentieth of the month passed. The troops began to arrive. They reeked of sweat and leather. The settlers, having felt as disheartened as castaways stranded on a forgotten island, could not conceal their longing for home. More than anything else, it was the accents of men fresh from Japan that triggered their nostalgic sentiments.

On the twenty-sixth, before daybreak, a regiment arrived at the railway station. Heavy fog shrouded the area. The Chinese houses thickly painted red and blue, the unbroken succession of dusty street stalls of all kinds, the Chinese people shouting in shrill voices—all were hidden and indistinguishable in the darkness and fog. Acacia flowers, seductively enlivening the spring, penetrated the fog to scent the air with fragrance.

The soldiers stacked their arms in the station plaza and lowered their knapsacks. They were waiting for their barracks to be allotted. Their language, bearing, and tempers were already rougher and more menacing than back at home.

"Ukichi!" From among the people come to greet the soldiers with countless little Rising Sun flags, a woman suddenly rushed up to Private First Class Kakimoto. She was a middle-aged woman with black-dyed teeth. She flung her arms around Kakimoto's waist and burst into tears. "Ukichi! I'm so happy you've come, Ukichi!"

"Auntie Nakanojō, is that you?" The soldier looked somewhat embarrassed and diffident before his officer. Yet he soon acknowledged her.

"Oh, oh, oh . . ." Overcome with happiness and gratitude, the woman

Japanese troops arrive in Tsinan.

broke into loud sobs. "You've really come. . . . Oh, oh, oh. . . . Now we're all safe. Oh, oh, oh. . . ." This emotion permeated the breasts of all the settlers who had turned out to greet the troops, even if they did not express it so openly.

The soldiers started a bonfire. The flames blazed up. Kakimoto looked at the pale, haggard, bony face of this woman who was ready to drop to her knees before him. There still remained at least traces of the face familiar to him from their village. Who knew the fears and worries that had worn her out? He thought of this while recalling the way she had looked in the village long ago. She was a cousin of a cousin. Their ages differed sufficiently for him to call her an aunt. In the village they were barely related, but here a possessive emotion surged up within him too as though she were his closest flesh and blood. The woman felt an even more powerful bond with him.

"What do you think? Are we going to be all right?" asked the woman.

"You will be all right. Our entire division is coming. Look, we've got this much ammunition" (he shook his tightly packed cartridge pouch to show her) "and swords with sharp blades."

"Oh, oh, oh . . ." The woman resumed her joyful, grateful weeping.

The soldiers' posts were decided. The units went separate ways. One was sent to the egg noodle factory. One was sent to the Fu-lung Match Company. One was sent to the Shōkin Bank. Shouldering their rifles and form-

Japanese residents welcome the troops.

ing into columns, the men marched off toward their designated posts led by their unit commanders.

Many settlers remained for a long time gazing after the columns of troops departing in the direction opposite to that of their homes. Children happily ran after them, waving the flags. Did the adults, who had run about collecting signature-seals petitioning for the dispatch of an expeditionary force, not feel any anger at being cheated as the long-awaited soldiers marched away to guard factories and banks far removed from their tiny houses?

16

Three hours later the factories were securely fortified with sandbags, barbed wire, and roadblocks. Machine guns had been set up. Sentries in khaki were standing guard. The light yellow soil had been effortlessly dug up.

From high above, the burning continental sun sizzled and glared at the city, the people, and the factories. A fine dust arose. The heat was fiery. The soldiers had taken off their jackets, and sweat drew maps over the backs of their undershirts. Yellow sand turned black and gritty as it stuck to their skins.

"Quit dawdling and wasting time as though you were in the barracks! This is real wartime." Lieutenant Shigefuji strode around fixing the men with his narrowed eyes. "Hey, who's that relaxing over there!"

The yellow earth excavated by one group of soldiers was being stuffed into gunnysacks by another. The soldiers had had no time to wash their faces. They had had no time to take off their sturdy, toadlike shoes and expose their suffocating feet to the air. The work had begun the instant they reached their posts. Gunnysacks bulging with yellow soil were carried to the front of the factories. There they were stacked one atop the other. In no time walls were erected. There had not been so much as a five-minute break. A separate company rammed poles requisitioned from somewhere into the ground before the walls of sandbags and then stretched quadruple rolls of barbed wire around them.

In the street they intertwined the heavier logs and constructed road-blocks. Starting at the factory perimeter, the barbed wire led far down the street, crossed it, and connected with the S Bank where a sandbag encirclement, resembling a fuel tank, had been built. The noodle factory and the Fu-lung Match Factory were both surrounded with sandbags and barbed wire and guarded by armed soldiers. Manager Uchikawa treated the company commander and the accompanying officers with deference. He also approached the diligently working soldiers and, getting in their way, strove to make them understand how indispensable their presence was.

The next project was the construction of an expanded defense zone. Beyond the sandbag walls more walls were put up. The soldiers could never make enough. Lookout patrols were assigned. Sentry duty was assigned. Orderlies were assigned. Kitchen work was assigned. Night watch was assigned.

"Hey, anyone seen my jacket?" With a catlike motion, Kamikawa from Kakimoto's work group flipped up someone's uniform hanging from an acacia fork and hurried on. He had just been assigned to a patrol party. His undershirt had turned khaki with the yellow dust. He moved from one acacia branch to another, looking up with a sweat-stained, dusty face and desperately searching. No jacket. The sergeant waiting for the soldiers to assemble cursed fiercely.

Kamikawa was fingering the insignia of a jacket he had already examined. "Someone must have put mine on by mistake." Refusing to accept defeat, he grew more and more irritable.

"Where'd you take it off? Think."

"I don't know. Around here."

"You're so muddle-headed. You won't get it replaced in a war zone. Soon somebody will walk off with your life."

The backs of the men swinging the pickaxes were unbearably sore. The deeper they dug, the more difficult the digging. The company commander and his officers watched them work. The men packing the sandbags struggled to keep up with the diggers.

"What is the matter? Did you lose something?" The manager trotted over toward the noise.

"Can't find my jacket. Maybe somebody put it on by mistake. And it even has my name on it." He forced an embarrassed smile. The company commander overheard him but pretended not to, and only grimaced in disgust.

"Chinks must have stolen it," said Uchikawa. "Weren't they hanging around here just now?" Indeed that must be it, the soldier realized with a start.

"Look sharp, will you. Getting robbed by Chinks the moment you get here. . . . It's pathetic!"

"You can't be too careful with them," the manager counseled the soldiers with good-natured laughter.

From the day of their arrival they acquired a taste for beating the Chinese. When two Chinese were dragged in from the slum, Kamikawa sprang upon them swinging his fists as if to alleviate his anxiety, anger, and the humiliation of being teased. Afterward the other soldiers pounced on the two beggars, too, punching them, stomping on them, kicking them, and swearing at them in Japanese. But no matter how hard they did it, Kamikawa's jacket was never found.

Army life here promptly paralleled army life in Japan. The men cooked their own meals. They cleaned their rooms, cleaned latrines, mended uniforms, carried out sentry duty and patrol duty. The distinction between first-year and second-year soldiers was somewhat less prominent here, but it did exist. The distinction between enlisted men and noncommissioned officers, and between the noncoms and the officers, was of course strictly observed.

"Sleep, sleep! Sleep is great." Driving the match factory workers out of one of the dormitories, the soldiers spread their blankets onto the sorghum straw mats, made knapsacks or rolled-up tents serve as pillows, and lay down. They had gone a truly long time without sleeping, performing a greater variety of tasks than they could remember. It seemed to them they had spent ten or twenty days in continuous work.

"We're only staying here because there are no other buildings large enough in the area," the officer on duty observed as if it were true. "There's to be no close contact with the Chinese who work in this factory. You are especially cautioned against making unauthorized visits to the match-packing area and the workers' dormitory because there are women there."

"Yes, sir!"

"And since some of the Chinese may be harboring unwholesome thoughts, be on your guard. Needless to say, we can't allow their red ideas to infect our Japanese spirit. If that were to happen, it would ruin our honor as Japanese soldiers."

"Yes, sir!"

Without taking off their shoes, uniforms, or leggings, the soldiers simply dropped their heads onto their knapsacks and, as though pulled into an abyss, succumbed to the tenacious enticement of sleep.

17

The troops merely lodged at one of the factory dormitories, nothing more. They did not interfere with the factory in any way. This was in accordance with Second Lieutenant Bandō's warning. Both the commander and the officers possessed samurai spirit. It was beneath the pride of military men to meddle in the conflict between capital and labor.

Even so, the troops had arrived. From that day on, the factory workers, like horses shown the whip, abandoned their slowdown tactics. The supervisors' and overseers' power doubled. Koyama, with his decayed jawbone and wracking cough, was aware of having a great dependable force behind him. This awareness strengthened the tyranny of his club threefold and fourfold.

The overseer Li Lan-pu was getting just twenty-three sen a day more than an ordinary worker from Uchikawa. For that reason alone this Chinese took it for granted, as though he were Japanese, that the khaki troops would become his protectors—his might—and would crush any insubordinate workers who bore a grudge against his oak club. He placated, cajoled, and threatened the workers. It was he who served as a spy for Uchikawa and Koyama. It was he, too, who served as a stool pigeon.

The soldiers in no way interfered with the workers' activities. They had no intention of doing so. In fact, they were protecting the workers. They protected the factory, too. And yet the workers did not feel protected by the troops, they felt menaced by them.

A view of occupied Tsinan.

The soldiers continued constructing the defense zone. Barbed wire spread like a spider's web throughout the length and breadth of the streets. Angular barricades blocked all the intersections. A telephone line was speedily stretched between the brigade and battalion headquarters. The battalion headquarters and the sentry line too were tightly linked up. The soldiers were ordered to carry arms and be ready for combat at a moment's notice. At intersections, sentries with loaded weapons sternly challenged each and every passing Chinese.

Within just a day and a half, the city had changed its appearance entirely. It was as though it had suddenly buckled on armor and helmet over everyday clothes. Roadblocks projected like bristling horns into the middle of streets. Machine guns poked their barrels, like sensitive antennae, over the sandbag parapets. The factory, the walls, the company housing—all were being guarded by a stiff profusion of spiny steel.

It was not only the Chinese who stared in round-eyed wonder at the remarkable efficiency of the Japanese. Even the soldiers themselves, gazing back at the unbroken spread of barbed wire and the Great Wall of packed earth, were surprised at the results of their own work. Although these works had been constructed to repulse Chinese soldiers and fortify a bourgeois factory, they felt happy looking at what they had built. If only this fortification, they thought, were intended to safeguard a factory of our own!

Captain Sakanishi from headquarters inspected the completed earthworks. He studied the direction from which the enemy would advance. Sakanishi was a man who could not help spotting a flaw even in what was flawless. Perfection itself was a defect. After all, anything perfectly accomplished lacked room for further development.

"This is a straight line from the Chieh-shou station on the Shin-p'u line. We've got to assume that the Southern Army will attack from there in full force." Accompanied by other officers and NCOs he toured the southwest corner of the earthworks. "Lieutenant Suenaga, how many tens of thousands of enemy attackers could this flimsy earthwork withstand? Do you think it could withstand even a thousand? How about it?"

"Sir."

"Enemy is enemy. You may safely assume they will challenge us from over there. . . . Right, do it over! Raise the height by half, double the width, triple the length. And double the number of machine guns."

"Sir."

Beyond the earthwork's southwest corner, a grassy plain with green fields and scattered groves of oaks and acacias unfolded far into the distance. The view was hazy. The herds of goats that always grazed about were absent. Probably the peasants, on guard against plunder, had hidden them. Soldiers must obey orders submissively when there is even the slightest difference in rank. Expressing opinions is not permitted. Lieutenant Suenaga gave the order to the sergeant. The sergeant gave the order to the privates. The privates stripped away the quadruple rolls of barbed wire and began to rebuild the earthworks.

"More, more! Stretch it all the way here!"

Aiming to please the fastidious Sakanishi, Lieutenant Suenaga scratched a mark in the earth with his shoe. If we make this corner exceptionally strong, he was thinking, the enemy is likely to concentrate the assault on a weaker sector. And the breakthrough would occur there.

"Take the dirt from here! That acacia is in the way. Cut it down! Damn! Get those roadblocks over here!" Keeping his thoughts entirely to himself, he continued to direct the soldiers: "More, more, bring the spades and picks. This is the only spot that isn't done! Speed it up! Corporal Shinkaku! No, not that way!"

The conscripts from the training institute had been looking forward to going home on leave after eighteen months of service. Due to the intervention, leaves were postponed indefinitely. Though on the verge of tears, they speedily obeyed the lieutenant's barked orders and worked assiduously. They were model soldiers. Eyeing them, an enlisted man named Takatori smiled sardonically. Kakimoto was working at an ordinary pace.

"That's right! Do it the way Kuraya and Kinugasa are doing it, all of you! Put some energy into those picks!" The special-duty sergeant major pointed to the training institute graduates. "Takatori! Pack more dirt in those bags!"

"Sergeant Major, sir! What should we do about these holes mice have eaten through the bags? Should we pack some straw in them first?"

"Yeah, yeah, do that."

The sergeant major, whose mouth was oddly crooked, nodded with satisfaction at Matsushita from the same training institute. Further off, others were ingratiating themselves with the NCOs too. Takatori, who did not fail to overhear, again smiled sardonically. The fawning was so transparent!

In an hour and fifteen minutes, the colossal defensive position had been completed as ordered. The devil himself was welcome to try to breach it now. Utterly exhausted, the soldiers returned to their quarters. They could not wash their muddy hands, noses, and necks. There was no water. The lunch bugle blared. Another one joined in from the direction of the noodle factory.

"It's still only April but here in China the weather's already like July. . . . Ah, I've really had it. I'm hot and I'm famished." They shoveled down the cold rice distributed into their mess tins. "Every single canteen's empty. . . . Cook! Hey, got any hot water? Any hot water?"

The soldier on cook's duty, wearing an apron over his shirt, was busily running about. There was a shortage of cooking utensils.

"Hot water! Hey, hot water!"

"Forget hot water. I don't even have water to wash the rice with."

"Huh! You want to kill us by making us choke on the rice?"

"Ask me if I care!"

"The Chinks are selling hot water. A kettleful for an igazul."

"What the hell's an igazul?"

"It's like a Chinese copper sen. Worth about two and a half rin."

"Selling hot water. What a miserly business." Kuraya, the training institute graduate, laughed with affected elegance.

Takatori was scowling next to a wall. The wall was peeling with decay. Tamada from the noodle factory asked him why he was making such a face: "Is the rough work getting on your nerves? You're looking sour."

"It isn't that. It's that bunch that disgusts me. Kinugasa, Matsushita, and the rest of the bootlickers," Takatori suddenly said. "We've got so many of that type, the Chinese will get robbed to the bone."

"Those characters, hmm. . . . The buffoons stink to high heaven."

"Even though they're squeezed half to death by factory owners and landlords back home, they can't help bowing and scraping and wagging their tails like slaves. What a bunch." Takatori glanced back at the lecherous Nishizaki behind him. The man was a novelty seeker who claimed never to have paid for the same prostitute twice.

"Their type's the most exasperating. They are sweated, wrung, and tormented by the bourgeois without mercy. Despite all that, they don't feel either resentful or rebellions. They fetch and carry, setting their hearts on getting blessed with the leftovers."

"That's true, but what the hell does it matter? Their bootlicking's nothing new." Nishizaki laughed with a leer.

"Go join them, Nishizaki! You'll fit right in!"

"No, no, that's not what I mean. Don't get so angry. . . . There, look at Kinugasa's face. Doesn't it look like a wet dick? Just like a wet dick."

Nishizaki swerved from the topic. Munching away at canned meat over by the entrance, unaware of being talked about, the thick-lipped Kinugasa seemed indeed to fit the description. Tamada laughed. Nishizaki's lewdness was well known. He was an entertaining comedian. Having come to China, he was hoping for a taste of Chinese women—looking forward to it, in fact, since before his arrival. Even while working, he would steal furtive glances at all the passing women with their bound feet, fringe-covered foreheads, and brown or purple suits. Their hands and feet were quite delicate.

He was drawn as well to the female workers who packed matches at the factory. They were not beautiful. They were grimy with dust, smoke, and phosphorus. But they differed somehow from the Japanese. They possessed something different. And the difference thrilled him.

"They're doing something. Hey, the factory people are doing something." The soldiers had been resting a while following their meal. A man noticed a disturbance in the drying area. A worker was being tortured.

"Torture, it's torture!" Kakimoto spoke in a hushed voice as though confiding a secret. "It's torture, they're torturing someone!"

Yui Li-song, the frowning and sardonic worker, lay twisted under the weight of two overseers like a rooster having its neck wrung, one of his legs desperately kicking the air.

"The supervisor's sticking needles under his fingernails."

Fingernails adhere tightly to the flesh of the fingertips. They were inserting cotton-thread needles into the gaps between flesh and nails. Starting with the worker's little fingers, they thrust the needles into his ring fingers, middle fingers, and index fingers. To immobilize his arms the overseers coiled their own arms around them. The agonizing groans cut through the din of the factory. The soldiers shuddered as though their own nails were being torn. Yui Li-song had always been hated by the company staff. He was disobedient. Even if a supervisor or overseer cautioned him, he reacted with contempt. Such is the man he was. Koyama hated him the most.

Takatori knew that the workers at the noodle factory too were cowering before the soldiers' menace. There too the staff was torturing the workers. The soldiers had seen it. If this goes on, they began saying, they would demand to be relieved from guarding the factories. The company garrisoning the egg noodle factory was famous back home. It had fought to the last man both in the Sino-Japanese and the Russo-Japanese wars. Strangely enough, every year two or three radicals kicked out of active service elsewhere entered this company. Once they understood the factory staff's intent to use the army as a shield enabling them to mistreat the workers, the soldiers of this unit refused to consent.

"Of course, these swine over here are using us as a shield too," thought Takatori. "Shit! They're treating us like idiots!"

"Try acting big now—like when you were demanding wages the other day!" Koyama was shouting. "Quit bawling, and let's hear your arrogant talk again like that night!"

"Hmm. I'd heard there are sons of bitches in China who beat workers to death, and it sure as hell seems true."

Little by little, as if nearing something fearsome, the soldiers threaded their way between the mats covered with matchwood and approached the scene. They had slapped others, they had been slapped themselves, but they had never seen fingers pierced with needles. The rusty needles penetrated to the base of the fingernails. Beneath the translucent nails spread purplish blood.

"There are young fools who pamper this type, that's why they act important." (This was directed at Kantarō.) "Are you a communist agent? Take over the factory if you can! . . . Hey! Give me some more of that insolent talk like the other night!"

Koyama was conscious of the support supplied by the approaching soldiers. His face, twisted with rage, flashed a quick smile at them. Then, turning back to Yui, it instantly resumed its contorted shape.

On the factory floor, the workers kept working in deathly silence, listening intently. The only continuous sound was that of the machinery. Some of the workers stopped operating their machines and, careful not to be seen by the staff, were gazing quietly from behind the windows as Koyama forced a needle into Yui's other thumb. Not surprisingly, the youngest and most vulnerable workers averted their faces as though they themselves were being jabbed.

"You're still acting impudent? Li, get me a wet leather whip! A wet leather whip!" Koyama was roaring with fury.

Even the laborers who had continued to work, feigning indifference, flinched now. They stopped moving their hands and looked at each other. As one of their representatives, Yui Li-song had demanded that their wages be paid. For this the owners were taking revenge. The workers also knew that the torture was not directed at Yui alone but was meant to intimidate all of them. If it wasn't for the soldiers, some sorrowfully thought, we could all rise up!

"How about giving it a rest," said Kakimoto.

The workers stared at the wet leather whip gripped in Koyama's bony hand and pictured bare muscles being ripped to shreds in sprays of blood. It was a frequent sight at police interrogations.

Yui's screams merged with Koyama's snarls. The wet leather whip wound itself round the body. The lashes slapped with a cutting sound. Then a tough, bighearted soldier sprang forward.

"Cut it out! You son of a bitch! Scum!"

The soldier smacked Koyama's sickly face. His powerful arm twisted the rawboned hand holding the whip.

"If you think you can torture the workers just because we're here, you're dead wrong! You damned clown!"

Koyama was stunned.

"I'll beat the life out of you, you damned clown!"

The soldier was Takatori.

18

More units arrived. The quarters grew cramped. Lacking both beds and straw matresses, the men spread blankets on the floor and slept all jumbled together. The sorghum-straw mats were beginning to tear. With a rustle, bedbugs crawled out from beneath. The bedbugs were probably perplexed at suddenly encountering not the malnourished workers' unhealthy skin smelling of sulfur and white phosphorus but fresh skin saturated with sweat and grease.

It had been a while since Takatori had last met the new arrivals. They told each other about their separate journeys. As they boarded the transport ship at Moji, they were picking up fliers. Some of the men folded them and carefully concealed them in their chest pockets as if they were talismans.

"As we're walking along the pier, a rain of fliers comes falling out of the sky," said a new arrival laughing. "We look up and there's our union friend Yasukawa trying to disappear from the window. 'Do it gallantly!' he yells. So we yell back 'Do what gallantly?' and he shouts 'Gallantly join hands with the people over there!' " His voice was carefree and loud.

Special-duty sergeant major happened to walk by. He had come back to call someone. "Gallantly join hands with Chinese females, eh?" he yelled and burst into laughter. His hands, absently plucking at the frayed edge of the mat, were callused and hard as a board.

"Kudō ended up getting killed aboard the ship," whispered Kitani, casting an alert sidelong glance at the sergeant major. "I told him it's no good getting all riled up so long as it's just you, but he had a hot-blooded temper and wouldn't listen."

"This time they're really nervous about opposition from the labor unions and soldiers like us." Takatori lowered his voice to a choked whisper. "It's a different era, not like the German-Japanese War or the Siberian Intervention. Sure, we know we can't let them use us as bourgeois tools. But even the bourgeoisie is alarmed about our opposition to the intervention. On March 15 they carry out arrests, on April 10 they disband the three leftist parties. And then they send out the troops. Everything they've done shows that the bourgeoisie is far more thoroughly prepared and systematic."

"They'll shove any obstacle aside. Because what they really want is to occupy this area."

"That's right, that's right. That's what they want to do in order to seize China."

"But we'll do all we can to sabotage their plans and disrupt them. Even if we're told to shoot, none of us will."

And yet, though they hated their rulers and opposed the intervention, not all of them shared the same view: "We're not in a position to take our division home and leave China alone. That, for the present, is asking too much. Nevertheless, we've got work to do. No matter how much we hate the way the army is being used, we can't simply give up military service. To bring about the day when we can truly start to live, we'll learn street fighting. We'll learn to drive armored cars. We'll fight for the sake of that day." Kitani spoke quietly. Takatori alternated between nodding and shaking his head.

"For the sake of that day? All right. You always have been patient. But what about the Chinese workers who are being crushed right now, right before our eyes and with our hands?"

The two had worked in the same factory until entering the military. Kitani, methodical and energetic, had become a private first class. On the first day of his second year of service, Takatori had abandoned his guard post in pursuit of a duck. He was court-martialed for it. It was around dusk when he spotted the sluggish bird on its own and tried to spear it with the bayonet fixed to his rifle. Then he chased it. For five hundred yards he ran after the duck, from the drill ground to the brush-covered hill at the foot of the old castle, before cornering his prey. The duck nimbly dodged him with its awkward webbed feet. Unable to stab it, he ended by trampling it. Relieved, he picked up the long-necked bird by its feet and rose. At this moment he was discovered by an officer on patrol.

Becoming a mere soldier had not made Takatori feel ashamed or unworthy. He liked handling machines, especially light machine guns. Even when firing blanks he imagined mowing down a crowd of attackers with a rain of bullets pouring from this single gun barrel. His somewhat foolish, eccentric character made him widely popular.

Together with Takatori and Kitani, Kudō had gone naked through the military inspection, entered the gloomy barracks, eaten the festive red rice. Together they learned to aim a gun. They learned to attach a bayonet, learned to shoot. Kudō had been killed aboard the transport ship. There was no need to ask why. They recalled his sweet tooth and fiery eyes with affection. His killing had infuriated them. In the stifling dormitory with its low roof and rough walls, each man was absorbed in his own thoughts.

Nasu, the man next to Takatori, had even had his inner pockets searched. When the fliers were found, he had been beaten so severely by Lieutenant Shigefuji that his cheeks were torn. Nasu kept completely silent. "They can confiscate fliers and bark at us as much as they want, but they can't yank our brains out of our skulls!" someone said. "That's right!" Nasu silently thought. "I can think whatever I like. And do whatever I like!"

The wisteria-like acacia flowers were spreading their fragrance. Nearby Kakimoto was worrying about his aunt's family. There hadn't been time enough to inquire after them. Once a person leaves home and crosses the sea, even distant relatives can feel as close as parents or siblings. In the name of protecting the settlers he had been rushed overseas with such haste he did not even have time to visit an aunt recovering from appendicitis. Now he could not so much as visit, let alone protect, his nearest blood relations and other compatriots who were eking out a living scattered about the city. He was protecting a factory. This is what he sweated and slaved for.

Dripping with sweat, he continued the defense work. The factory environs were solidly fortified with embankments, roadblocks, and barbed wire. The men stood watch with fixed bayonets and loaded rifles. No construction work was being carried out anywhere else. Having come as a soldier all the way from home, Kakimoto could not budge beyond this heavily guarded enclosure. Supposedly the settlers will be ordered to come inside this guarded area. And supposedly they will be protected within these ramparts. So why had he come to China?

"Hey! You can strike these matches on boards, or stones, or anything."
Three soldiers returned from the factory floor, each excitedly holding a little box of yellow matches. It was Matsuoka, Motooka, and Tamada. They lit the matches by striking them against pillars and floorboards.

"These are different from the matches back home."

"I think we saw matches like this when we were kids. They were called Boss," Nasu said glumly.

"'This a white phosphorus match'—that's what the Chinese is saying. He can speak a bit of broken Japanese," said Tamada, still smelling of wheat flour from the noodle factory. "He says, 'This have much poison. Other country factory do not make. Our body soon get bad. This chemical bad, have much poison, bad.' These white phosphorus matches are poisonous and cause lots of fires, so they're banned in every other country. That's what they're making here."

"'This have much poison. People die.'" Tamada continued imitating the Chinese worker's words. "'In country village no train, no poison, so drink this for suicide. Man, woman, husband and wife fight. Wife want to die. She take off this match chemical and drink. She drink ten of this box. She die. Japan, rat poison. China, white phosphorus match.'"

"Hmm. . . . If he knows that much Japanese, we can talk with him," said Takatori, showing no concern over who might hear him. "Let's bring that Chinese here and talk. It'll be interesting."

19

Daytime duty was followed by nighttime duty. Nighttime duty was followed by daytime duty. There was hardly time to sleep. The soldiers grew muddy with sweat and dirt. There was next to no water. It was muddy in any case and could not be drunk unboiled. If anyone tried, the stomach and intestines would rumble like thunder. They had not bathed in a long time: a week, no, more than fifteen days. The day before leaving Japan they had washed off the sweat and dust at the bath adjoining the kitchen. That had been the last time.

The dark, windowless Chinese-style dormitory was heavy with an all-male stench. The factory was being protected by means of continuous duty, privation, overwork, and suffering. And the bourgeoisie for its part was scheming to ensure that this resource-rich province of Shantung would fall into its own possession. To enrich the bourgeoisie exploiting them in Japan, the soldiers were being tormented and abused in China too. There was hunger, abuse, and exploitation in Japanese workplaces as well. There was the hell of unemployment. Coming to China, it was the same. Regardless of place or time, the soldiers—originally workers and farmers—could not escape agony. They could not live full, undamaged lives.

"How can we break these heavy shackles holding us down?" thought Takatori. Unbidden he frequented the match factory workshop. An exposed electric fan was cooling the muddy phosphorus. Its spinning blades seemed about to behead the unconcerned workers. The officer on duty had said a few words on the subject of entering the workshop. Obediently the soldiers had listened. But after two or three days they began inquisitively to wander about the workshop and the Chinese quarters. They could not understand each other's words. They spoke with their eyes. Their faces expressed their emotions.

Antagonism toward the officers deepened imperceptibly. Prior to landing, Kudō had been killed. That made it much harder to trust the officers. They were the nearest enemy. There was a clear distinction in baths, meals, hours of duty, even the beds they rested in. Soldiers ate barley. Officers ate rice. Soldiers shared their joys and sorrows only with each other. They had not bathed for a long time. Officers had a bath prepared for them daily at the Chih-ping Company. The company employees indulged them with beer, sweets, and tea while the officers engaged in interminable chatting. Even if the soldiers tried to take a bath later in the day, the officers' endless chatter prevented them. By the time the officers were done, it was too late in the evening.

One time Kamikawa, who had lost his jacket, returned from the bath with a wet towel and freshly washed pink skin. Stealthily he had taken a bath before the officers. He was delighted. "It makes no difference to the lady at the Chih-ping Company whether those stripes are shining or not. Even to a private, she says it's open so go ahead. Because when it comes to protecting the settlers, both the brass and buck privates deserve equal credit. See, I was the first in the bath."

"Nobody there?"

"Nobody."

"The lady at the Chih-ping Company is young, isn't she?"

"Not only young but pretty good-looking."

"Right, I'm off to wash away the dirt."

"I'm going too."

"Me too."

Savoring the joys of theft, they leaped into their shoes without tying the laces. Fourteen of them grabbed their sweat-soaked towels and, without a single piece of soap among them, rushed out of the match factory and cut across the weed-smothered lot opposite the slum. There are a bit too many of us, someone observed, but holding anyone back meant that none of the fourteen would go. A colossal water tank perched atop the red roof. That was the Chih-ping Company. It was just over a block away.

The place was near the unit that had gone to guard the noodle factory. They entered the gate. The pump was moving. Suddenly, from within the red brick building, came a shout from a cuttingly cold officerlike voice. A private first class they knew by sight came flying out stark naked and red as a boiled octopus. Pinched between his fingers like a pair of cats were his uniform and underwear.

"What company's this joker from?" The cutting voice rang out from behind the door. "Hasn't he got any consideration for people? How dare he annoy a family at this early hour!" The last words rose to a pitch of fury.

"What happened?" Takatori who knew every face in the regiment coolly asked the stark-naked PFC.

"It's the brigade major."

"What's the matter with him?"

The fourteen halted before the door. What now? Violently the door was shoved open from within. The aristocratic face of an officer with a remarkably straight nose and brigade major's badges aslant his shoulders confronted the soldiers. His sword unbuckled, the brigade major glared with narrowed eyes at the pressing throng of fourteen men. What the hell? What is this brazen bunch doing here?

"His Excellency is here! Get lost! Get lost!" he bellowed in his cutting voice. "Insolent fools! Get lost! Get lost!"

The fourteen were slashed by the icy shouts. "Damn!" Takatori was stunned. Like a traveler prevented from boarding a ferry at a crossing, he gazed ruefully at the bathhouse before his eyes. Then he looked back at the weed-covered lot they had crossed.

"Damn! What happened?" he muttered. "Shit! We hate feeling slimy from sweat and dirt just like everybody else! Damn! Looks like it's back to putting up with it again."

The private who had entered the bath ahead of the officer had been thrown out in anger. In a moment, the grime floating on the water was cleanly scooped out. The water temperature was adjusted. Two sentries with fixed bayonets were posted to guard the entry to the bath. They were flanked by roses and acacia bushes. Splashing sounds emanated from the bath. The water was ladled out, heated up, cooled down. A soldier on duty seemed to be washing the officer's back. Then he seemed to be giving him a shave.

Afterward, for twenty or thirty minutes, there was not a sound. Thinking the officer might have gotten dizzy or fainted, the sentries peered through a gap in the door. His head rocking on the rim of the tub, his bearded excellency was napping. From his body rose faint snores of contentment.

Bored, the sentries kept pacing before the door. The backs of their dust-covered sweaty necks felt unpleasant, irritating them. Stones jutted out of the ground beneath their feet. The two were guarding a personage on whose head the watching guerrillas had put a price of a hundred and fifty thousand yen. They struggled to suppress their tedium and stifle their yawns.

Wristwatches indicated the passage of one hour. A further twenty minutes elapsed. At long last a footman came in respectfully bearing a fresh pair of shorts. The officer demanded a dry towel.

"Just for one night I'd like to wash off the dirt and sleep in a clean bed!"

"Keep dreaming. Such things are not for the likes of us."

In the room housing the ice-making machinery, soldiers with callused feet in shoes that resembled yellow dust-covered toads were growing numb waiting their turn. A whitish twilight was approaching.

20

A canary was singing in its cage under the eaves. At nightfall, temperature on the continent suddenly fell. Underclothes felt clammy against the skin. Although they were starving, the workers treated the little bird with great affection. It was an intriguing hobby.

"Hmm, I see, I see. Interesting!" Takatori nodded. "Come on, keep talking!" He spoke gruffly. As ever, he did not care who heard him.

"Mussulman people bad. Not good. Winter, day short. Get dark soon. No turn on electric light. Factory dark. Cannot see face. Man and woman always start play." The worker's nose was congested, and his Japanese difficult to make out. "Mussulman people, when man and woman play, take other people matchbox, have many matchbox. Make much money."

The worker's name was Shih I-li. He was pale, slender down to his bones, and seemed old. Asked his age, he said he was thirty-one. He was still young.

"Hmm, when it gets dark the male and female workers start flirting.

Taking advantage of that, the Muslims snatch the matchboxes they'd filled. I see. Interesting, interesting." Takatori nodded. "Come on, keep talking!"

The worker had gradually lost his fear of the soldiers. They formed a circle around this man who smelled of garlic, fat, and strange tobacco.

"Over there near barrack is English hairnet factory. My young sister work there, every day she breathe only hair dust and trash." Shih I-li resumed talking. "Young sister smell like hair and trash. Her chest bad. TB. Hairnet hair, broker go country village, pay three sen, four sen, people cut pigtail hair, broker bring hair sell to factory. If no cut pigtail, people pay tax. Factory beat down broker price fifty percent, sixty percent. Broker ask high price. My father old time man, pay pigtail tax. Father no want cut pigtail. Broker come with police, say cut, if no cut must pay tax. This tax not true, broker and police make it. But if no cut pigtail, they force give money. English company, broker and police rob people. . . . English, American, German, Ja—" (Shih I-li stopped himself) "All make suffer China farmer, worker. Our life hard!"

"Ahem!" A thundering cough and the rattle of a military sword and shoes rang out right behind the soldiers. Lieutenant Shigefuji had come up undetected and was standing behind them. They started.

Shih I-li fell as silent as a deaf-mute. The lieutenant was glaring at him with steely eyes. Like a criminal, his head sadly bowed, the Chinese stood up. Weakly shrugging his shoulders, he left without a sound.

"So he's come to fill your heads with propaganda. Even in this factory there are Reds. Letting someone like that brainwash you with communist propaganda is a stain on your honor!"

"Lieutenant, sir, he was just telling us funny stories. That Chink knows a little Japanese," Takatori said.

"Don't you lie to me! I heard him!" The lieutenant's face turned suddenly fierce. "Stay away from them, funny or not! Break it up! Break it up! Break it up and go to sleep! You'd better be careful!"

"Sir. We will."

The soldiers were drawn to Shih I-li's story and had gathered around him. The lodgings were always dark. The walls were crumbling. The place felt like a cave where none but the oppressed and tormented gathered. Were the soldiers and the workers not twins with the same destiny? The harrowing daily labor drove them both to utter exhaustion.

By bullying these Chinese workers we're tying a rope around our own necks. Bullied workers only make the Ōi Corporation happy, nobody else. Takatori spoke of it simply. Some skeptically shook their heads. Takatori spoke again. He elaborated. We come here thinking we're serving our country. We think we're protecting our national interests. So what policy does the fat bourgeoisie adopt? A strategy that will fatten the bourgeoisie. They'll profit and squeeze the workers' necks even harder. They might slip some money to corrupt labor leaders. But the best workers get choked more and more.

"What fools soldiers are," Takatori said with profound emotion. "Though we're poor farmers and workers ourselves, just because we're wearing uniforms with stand-up collars we're trying to break the workers' and farmers' resistance. We've been sent into a colony and we're risking our lives to make the bourgeoisie richer and richer. We're so blind we don't understand what on earth we're doing! We're actually strangling ourselves with our own hands!"

All grew serious and thoughtful. "Perseverance!" Kitani thought to himself. "We've got to duck the whip and rise up from below." Life here seemed just as painful as life in the factories and farming villages back home, maybe worse. They knew that for a full month now the workers had been forbidden to take a single step outside the factory compound. They were not receiving wages. Among the youngest child workers, seven of them were just five years old. Five of them had been bought in perpetuity for ten or twelve yuan. Removing their jackets from thin chests with ribs sticking out, diligently the children were filling the boxes with matches. Their hands were too small to wrap around a matchbox. Unless there was an extra platform beneath their seats, they could not reach the worktable.

"Come to think of it, we too grew up with our parents telling us to work from about the age of five or six," thought Tamada, recalling his childhood when he used to get up around one in the morning to work in the noodle shop. "But we were never sold to anyone!"

Many of the Chinese workers had come from the countryside. They had quit farming and begun working in factories. The life of a peasant was even more miserable than that of a worker. Taxed extortionately by the ceaselessly feuding warlords backed by various imperialist powers, plundered by outlaws and runaway soldiers, the peasants could not make a living no matter how hard they tilled the soil and watered the livestock. There were droughts. There were plagues of swarming locusts. Entire harvests were seized by armed men.

Some people sold off their land, houses, and livestock and emigrated to eastern provinces. Migrants were everywhere. In the course of migration many were set upon by soldiers on the march and robbed of what little they had. They could not proceed to their destination. Such people became factory workers.

Some people left their families in the villages and came in search of work. The families that remained behind gnawed on tree roots and chewed blades of grass. Some even died eating powdered stones.

"Even my mother, back in that sooty house on the edge of town, barely gets enough to eat by selling gloves," thought the normally cheerful Takatori. "She is sixty-two already. . . so covered with wrinkles even a horny old man won't come near her! She has no one! How can she keep her stomach full just by selling gloves?"

The soldiers found themselves comparing their lives at home with the lives of the workers here. Some recalled that wheat would soon be ripening in the villages and wondered how their fathers, starting to get slightly muddled with age, were managing.

"Wang Hung-chi wife give birth woman child," Shih I-li told the soldiers, pointing to the good-natured Wang whose face looked rather slack, despondent, and bitter.

"Oh, she gave birth."

The eyes of more than twenty soldiers concentrated on Wang. Wang's expression turned timid as though he were eager to hide.

"Wang, no money. Wife, no money. Boss give no money."

"Hmm. The factory's not handing over the wages."

"Mother Wang carry big child, come to factory and cry. Factory man say mother cannot meet Wang."

"Hmm."

"Cannot give money, have no money."

"Hmm."

"Wife, no rice, cannot eat. Milk no come out. Baby cry."

"Hmm."

"Baby cry six day. Wife hungry. Only drink hot water, hot water not enough. Cannot walk. Ten day, morning, baby no cry. She look. Baby dead. Mother run to factory. But police say cannot meet Wang. Mother talk outside fence. Wang listen inside. Wang cannot go home. Boss say nobody go out one step."

"Hmm!"

Wang Hung-chi did not understand Japanese. But he realized from the soldiers' and Shih's strained expressions what Shih I-li was telling them.

"Factory buy children, more more bad," Shih I-li resumed. "Children work, work, get nothing. No haircut money. Cannot buy towel. Only New

Year get fifteen sen. Children work one year, two year, three year. Always work. Always only New Year fifteen sen. Always cannot go out. Three year, eighteen children not go out one day. Only work. Have no hope. Hope no more. Child, only eight, nine, think better die. Take phosphorus, drink. February, two children dead. March, four children dead. Drink phosphorus, burn inside. Much pain. Small children body, only skin and bone, leg kick, kick. . . . Factory man, boss laugh. Say China people have no pride, die because spite. Have no pride. . . ."

"Hmm!"

The soldiers groaned, barely able to breathe.

21

Kantarō was now deprived of any opportunity to associate with the workers. No longer in charge of the dipping work and the drying room, he had been transferred to the office and became an accountant. He buried his head in the account books. From morning till evening he fingered the abacus. This was the magnanimous treatment he had been given. More than ten days had passed but his father had not yet been released from detention by the consular police. Deprived of heroin, his body suffered hellish agonies. He kept moaning with pain, past caring about shame and scorn.

At the factory, Kantarō was frowned on for having sided with disorderly workers. The manager, the foreman, and the senior staff all hated him. Had he been Chinese, his head would have rolled long ago. He was tolerated for being a fellow Japanese.

Agitators from the General Workers' Association had infiltrated the city. This was no mere rumor. It was a fact. Events multiplied both inside and outside the factory. Suddenly leaflets were posted all over fences and electric poles. Leaflets bearing caricatures were scattered throughout the noodle factory. The match factory was on guard—especially the factory gates—against infiltration by agitators. Not only was no one allowed out, no one was allowed in either. The boundary line between inside and outside was doubly defended by armed soldiers and hired policemen.

"One way or the other, I'll get the ax before long!" muttered Kantarō looking forlorn. Since the army's arrival, he had witnessed Koyama torturing the workers he disliked one by one. The dislike was directed at him too.

Workers were not just lashed bloody with wet leather whips or pierced with needles. A worker had been making a phone call. Suddenly he was shoved violently from behind toward the bugle-shaped metal mouthpiece.

The wall telephone clanged loudly. The speaker's nose slammed into the transmitter like a bean-jam bun. The bridge of his nose broke in the middle and a circular dent appeared in the middle of his face. Drops of blood trickled from the wound. Another worker was tied to the trunk and branches of an acacia, as though crucified, his legs dangling in the air.

"I'm impertinent, lazy, cunning, bad. . . . This is a warning . . . this is a warning." Bound to the tree, hanging from its branches, the worker was made to repeat this one thousand times. A child worker with a face resembling a green stunted tomato stood under the tree and counted. The rope was cutting into the man's torso and limbs. The more he struggled, the deeper it bit. The worker on the tree was gasping for breath. "I was impertinent . . . bad . . ." Panting like gusts of wind, the worker spat out the words along with white foam.

Ever since the soldiers discovered the practice, torture was carried out only when the men were on duty away from the dormitory. This was done at the request of the special-duty sergeant major. The soldiers were busily occupied with defense preparations prompted by the reports of the Southern Army's approach.

At the factory Kantarō was avoided and ignored. He could not help being aware of it. "They're getting rid of me after all. Their attitude is telling me to get out at once," he thought, feeling an eerie awkwardness in the presence of the manager and Koyama. "Get out before we fire you, they're saying." He knew the cause: Father was a heroin addict like a Chinese, and he himself had demanded on Wang Hung-chi's behalf that the workers' wages be paid.

From time to time he would slip out of the office. As if intent on checking the volume of piecework, he would enter the workshop. Very carefully he observed the workers. Slightly bent over the clattering machine planting matchwood in crates, Yui Li-song fearfully and hastily bowed his head.

"Don't be so nervous."

"Yes, yes." Once arrogant and proud, Yui Li-song had quite come to resemble a terrified child.

"Just as I thought, the medicine works!" Koyama's gratitude for the military presence, as well as his pride in his methods, grew more conspicuous by the day. In proportion to repeated applications of torture, the workers' demeanor became obedient. As though currying favor, they cringed and bowed before the staff.

"Damn! Even when they sink this low they're forced to work hard. Animals! These are obedient animals, no balls at all!"

Yet Kantarō felt that he himself was an obedient animal, no longer capable of effective resistance. To him it seemed that his father's prolonged detention, the homes left defenseless while factories were being so solidly protected, and the repeated beatings of starving workers who were simply demanding to be paid, all stemmed from a single principle: only the great grow fat—and at the sacrifice of all the countless ones who are small. Long ago, Father had tried to unmask the village assemblymen who had diverted the funds intended for the construction of a school into playing with geishas. For that he had been shoved off the plank and his fall began. He had to keep falling until he could fall no further. It had nothing to do with fate. The little people fall to protect the big. For their sake we must all fall down all the way to rock bottom! But the time will come when the whole gigantic structure itself will be shaken from its foundation stones and collapse. It most certainly will.

Passing the cutting floor where a machine saw sliced up poplar wood like radishes, converting it into a mountain of splints, he walked by the timber storage and peered into the dark and empty soldiers' lodgings. There was a disorderly profusion of knapsacks, blankets, tents, and overcoats. Empty cans swarmed with cigarette butts like maggots. The workers' smell of garlic and spring onions, mingled with the soldiers' smell of sweat and leather, seemed to adhere to the thick, heavy walls of the dormitory.

Walking on tiptoe, he moved toward the eastern entrance through which acacias were visible. His feet rustled against something scattered on the floor. He saw that they were leaflets. Startled he looked around again carefully. Pieces of paper were inserted into the creases of similarly folded overcoats, blankets, and tents. Some were entirely hidden within the creases; others showed their edges like tongues. He took one and looked at it.

These were the leaflets that were feared like scorpions. "Well, well!" Kantarō marveled that such leaflets had been smuggled in unobserved past a most stringently guarded boundary. He read the following words:

Japanese soldiers, brothers!

Japan's imperialistic bourgeoisie has rushed you to the province of Shantung armed with rifles and cannons. And so the military partition of China has already begun.

Have you really come to protect the lives of the Japanese residents? Have you really come to protect the residents' property? No! Absolutely not! Look for yourselves: you are actually protecting neither the lives nor the property of the impoverished residents scattered along the waterfront.

You are only protecting factories, banks, and hospitals. And who owns the factories, banks, and hospitals?

Brothers! You who have been workers and farmers! You must not be misled by words about protecting lives and property or respecting the flag. In the farm villages and factories of Japan you were exploited by the capitalists and landlords. And in China they are asking you to risk your lives fighting a bloody war for the benefit of the imperialistic bourgeoisie. Who will pay the huge cost of the intervention? Every cigarette you smoke, every packet of sugar you consume, every pair of underpants you buy is indirectly charged to you without fail and paid for by your taxes.

Having drowned the national revolutionary movement of China's workers and peasants in blood, the imperialist powers are trying to shift from intervention to land grabbing. Utilizing its advantageous strategic position in order to be the first among the land-grabbers, imperialist Japan has dispatched you to this province. Japan is attempting to turn Shantung into an enslaved colony as it has done with Manchuria. Have you gotten even a penny of profit from the South Manchurian Railway Company or the Fushun Coal Mine? Have your lives been made the slightest bit easier by the South Manchurian Railway Company or the Fushun Coal Mine?

Manchuria is only making big capitalists and big landowners even larger. The big fat capitalists are buying out class traitors like Suzuki Bunji and Matsuoka Komakichi to make exploiting you even easier—impoverishing your wives and children until they go hungry, consolidating a reactionary stronghold that will strangle you too.

To crush China for the sake of partitioning it—that is the imperialists' policy. The imperialists have already realized the first phase of their despicable plan through the combined military intervention against the national revolution. The military occupation of Shantung marks the opening of the second phase of this plan. There is a serious possibility that an imperialist war may break out over colonial repartitioning.

Think, brothers! Tanaka, the general and despot who is sending you to Shantung, is your worst class enemy! He is exploiting and crushing Japan's workers and farmers. He is imprisoning your brothers and fathers, mistreating your wives, your children, your mothers.

Japanese soldiers, brothers! Stop obeying orders to invade Shantung! Stop brandishing bayonets against the people of China! Join hands with the Chinese workers, peasants, and soldiers, and spare no sacrifice to attain an unbreakable union of revolutionary solidarity. Let us cut through the counterrevolutionary front from both sides. Combine forces with China's workers, peasants, and soldiers for the sake of defending the Chinese revolution!

"Hey, hey! What's this? This was stuck in my jacket." Returning from duty, the soldiers noticed the strange pieces of paper. One such leaflet caught the noodle-maker Tamada's eye too as he unwound his leggings and approached his knapsack. Nasu picked up a slip of paper too.

"Hey, we have to report this."

"Wait, wait! Can you report something if you don't know what it is?" Takatori's authoritative voice stopped the training institute graduates.

Evening had come. In the dim dormitory they began reading the leaflets. When they had finished, they looked at each other. Then, hiding their faces in the shadows, they stealthily smiled.

"This is really something. . . . There are some pretty interesting people around."

"Huh, this is the Chinks' work."

"Nothing special. Even I know this much!" The taciturn Nasu was intently rereading the leaflet.

"'Spare no sacrifice to attain an unbreakable union of revolutionary solidarity.'" Takatori reread the closing section aloud. "'Let us cut through the counterrevolutionary front from both sides. Combine forces with China's workers, peasants, and soldiers for the sake of defending the Chinese revolution!' That's right, that's absolutely right!"

In no time the dormitory and the factory were thrown in an uproar. The soldiers were made to stand at attention where they were. The manager, the staff, the company commander, Lieutenant Shigefuji, and the special-duty sergeant major all ran around in consternation. Pockets were searched, faces were slapped. Mats, blankets, knapsacks, personal belongings—all were turned upside down.

The source of the smuggled leaflets was investigated rigorously. The two hundred and fifty or so workers were stripped naked one by one. Even women workers were stripped to the skin. Suspected workers were bound to pillars like Christ himself. The workers' dirty flat-bottomed shoes kicked repeatedly and painfully against the air. The leaflets might as well have been smuggled in by the legendary ninja Sarutobi Sasuke. However thoroughly they searched, they never found out who had done it.

The soldiers' battered cheeks were still smarting. Takatori, always a prime suspect in cases like this, had bumps on his head like horns. They cleaned up the mess and went to sleep. Despite the thrashing, inwardly they were amused. Seized with an unbearable desire to laugh, they found it impossible to fall asleep. No sooner did one fit of laughter subside than someone else would helplessly burst out laughing. "Pf-f-f-f! . . . Let us cut through the counterrevolutionary front from both sides!"

They were delighted to see the superiors rushing about in confusion with their masks off, delighted that the perpetrator was never found, delighted that it was none of them. Takatori had pulled the blanket over his head and repeatedly tried to fall asleep. But soon he would be distracted by someone's words or by childlike laughter ringing out through the cavelike quarters.

It was past eleven. They were still awake. Suddenly, with a wild clatter of shoes, the noncommissioned officer on duty barged in.

"Get up! Get up! Everybody up!"

"Another inspection?"

"Idiot! This is no damned inspection. The Southern Army's entering the city. Chang Tsung-ch'ang just flung open the gates and took off. All-night watch!"

"Pf-f-f-f-f."

Bursting with more laughter, the soldiers got up.

22

Chang Tsung-ch'ang and Sun Ch'uan-fang had abandoned T'ai-an without a fight. They tried to hold the front briefly at Chieh-shou. But pressed hard by Ma Yu-hsiang's cavalry units which had bypassed the Hwang Ho River to squeeze them from the flank, and Ch'en Tiao-yuan's overpowering forces which had threaded south of T'ai-shan to emerge onto the Ming-shui plain, they abandoned Chieh-shou and the Hwang Ho, once again without a fight.

The defeated army had poured into the old city of Tsinan. Next, having blown up the railway bridge over the Hwang Ho, they withdrew toward Tientsin by the Chin-p'u line. Fearful of being left behind, the Shantung Army soldiers strove to be first in line to flee. Placing ladders against freight cars they scrambled up onto the roofs. The train roofs were swarming with soldiers. They seemed on the verge of tumbling off.

About six hours later, having spent the night at Wang-she-jen-chang, Ku Chu-t'ung's Third Division of the Southern Army began to enter the city at dawn. The next to enter were Ch'en Tiao-yuan's Thirteenth and Twenty-second Divisions. The station master of the Chin-p'u line, who had only just equipped Chang Tsung-ch'ang with a splendid locomotive, respectfully ushered Ku Chu-t'ung into the station and the radiotelegraph office. The place was promptly occupied by Ku Chu-t'ung's troops.

An hour later Ho Yao-tsu's units arrived along the Chin-p'u line. Three hours after that, Fang Chen-wu arrived. His soldiers had been pressing in from the flank along the Hwang Ho. All told, the troops numbered about twenty thousand men.

Night fell. Near midnight another marching column, followed by cars and then by porters carrying huge trunks loaded with pots and pans, reached the vicinity of the station. On the running boards either side of a fine limousine stood two boy soldiers, pistols drawn, attentively gazing about. Despite their desperate efforts to stay alert, the boys' heads kept nodding from time to time and they seemed about to succumb on the spot to the relentless pressure of sleep. The limousine was being protected front and rear, left and right, by mounted cavalrymen. Other cars were following it.

The procession's advance was obstructed by roadblocks. Both horses and cars slackened their speed and squeezed past them with difficulty. From a car window flanked by a boy with a pistol, a man with a long face and somewhat sunken cheeks suddenly thrust his head out. "What is this?" the man angrily shouted.

"This is what the Japanese army put up."

"Why do something so provocative?" the man said, surveying the surroundings with sharp, black, rapidly moving eyes. "There are sandbags, too, and barbed wire everywhere."

"Yes."

"And soldiers, even machine gun emplacements. . . . This is tantamount to an act of hostility toward our revolutionary army! Why didn't you demand that these be removed?"

"Well, . . ." The mounted man alongside the car seemed to be a staff officer or division commander.

"We must immediately issue a strong protest demanding these things be totally removed!"

Once past the roadblocks, the limousine accelerated. The nodding heads of boy soldiers banged against the car, startling them awake. The procession sped off toward the walled city.

A year earlier, the leader of the newly arrived party had received a letter from Moscow, written by his son Ching-kuo, which said in part: "You have now become an enemy of the Chinese people. Father, you are a hero of the counterrevolution, the new leader of the militarists. You massacred the workers in Shanghai. For that, of course, the bourgeoisie of the entire world will hail you with words of praise, the imperialists will shower you with innumerable gifts. But never forget the existence of the proletariat! Father, through a coup d'état you have become the hero of the day. But I believe that your triumph will be short-lived. Father! Day by day, the communists are preparing for the struggle."

This bitter letter was addressed to the man whose military headquarters had now moved into the city of Tsinan, the traitor Chiang Kai-shek.

23

Surrounded by crowds of demonstrators wearing nationalist uniforms, Chinese officers were stuffing their mouths with melons. The city was an exhibit of miscellaneous leaflets. Fixed to a slender pole atop the peeling red-lacquered gate, the huge Sun in the Blue Sky flag billowed in the wind.

The limping Nakatsu had changed from a Shantung Army uniform to a Chinese tunic. He had left Chang Tsung-ch'ang's stronghold, but instead of boarding Chang's fleeing train had gone no further than the waterfront settlement.

Recently Chang Tsung-ch'ang had been turning his fat head to avoid meeting Nakatsu's eyes. The Russian Mirklov was no good either. Only the fifteenth wife's younger brother Chi Te-shu treated him well. Since parting reluctantly from Suzu to go to Su-chou, Nakatsu had confirmed a long-held suspicion: "Just as I thought, he no longer likes me."

Chang did not speak to him. Even when Nakatsu told him why he came, Chang merely nodded. I don't care if he doesn't like me, thought Nakatsu. People's likes and dislikes are beyond their control. That's true for me too. It's an obvious fact. Nevertheless, it did get on his nerves. His true character reasserted itself. Without so much as consulting Chang, with his pistol he shot down the retreating officers and men who came to Lin-cheng. He gave orders that any soldiers who were hopelessly wounded should be killed.

The wounded soldiers pleaded for mercy as they were being covered with soil. "Have pity! We've been wounded fighting for Master Chang. And you want to bury us alive?"

"You were wounded for Master Chang, and you'll be buried for Master Chang. You are big idiots!" The same words could be applied to himself.

"Have mercy! Have mercy!" the wounded desperately wailed. The gruesome work soothed his savage emotions.

Without any semblance of a strategic plan, Chang beat an undignified retreat to the old capital. He gave up the government office he had held for a full two and a half years. Giving this up meant total ruin. It alienated people. He was rebuked by the Manchurian warlord Chang Tso-lin. There was no way out. Nakatsu could see that. "Shit! Now's the time to be done with him."

Nakatsu switched to being a masterless samurai of times past. Retiring from the front, he wasted no time in stopping by the Inokawa house. Take-zaburō was groaning away in detention. Except for Kantarō, there was no man in the house, and Kantarō himself was away in the daytime. This was exceedingly convenient for Nakatsu. His separation from Suzu since his departure for the front, far from cooling his feelings, had in fact whipped up the fifty-year-old's passion.

Sometimes his feeling for Suzu was the love of an old man, born out of a desire that old age cannot extinguish, for an inexperienced girl who might be his grandchild. But no sooner did he start to feel this way than he decided that love could go hang. Such a genteel and tedious approach was nothing but a nuisance. Should he adopt the rough approach instead and simply take her without warning? That would be more interesting! He shuttled back and forth between the two alternatives. It was delightful to savor his own leisurely feelings. While savoring them, it was delightful to daydream about what he should do next.

Nakatsu's reappearance did not greatly alarm either Suzu or Shun.

A river ran along the edge of the city. Its water, gushing since time immemorial from the spring inside the city fortress, made no sound. Unarmed Chinese soldiers immersed their heads in it like a herd of hippopotami, muddying its flow. On one side of the city, soldiers in gray nationalist uniforms were moving about everywhere like ants. On the other side, encircled by sandbags, khaki uniforms were shining. It was like a pair of roosters glaring at each other before a fight, watching for an unguarded moment. Beggars and vagabonds, having nothing they could be robbed of, were fearless.

Suzu, Shun, and their mother knew that their house stood alone amid a swarm of ants in nationalist uniforms, beggars, and vagabonds. Knowing this, they were afraid. Everyone around them was Chinese.

The Shantung Army accompanied their retreat with mischief: plundering money and valuables from numerous places, firing their weapons indiscriminately. To nationalist eyes this appeared hostile. Anxiety grew even worse.

The visits from Nakatsu, a bandit turned warrior, eased the women's anxiety and fears somewhat. Nakatsu was good with the pistol. He commanded respect. His presence reassured them.

Suspicious-looking Chinese came and went like stray dogs through the paved, trash-strewn alley. Although the Inokawa house was built in the Chinese style with heavy stones and thick walls, it was easily distinguished from a Chinese house by its windows and the roofed stone fence of the Shikoku countryside. Whenever Suzu, Shun, and Mother saw a Chinese wearing the long and loose traditional garb, they had a sinister feeling that he was concealing a pistol in his pocket. The anxiety that seized them at such times made them yearn for someone to depend on.

Nakatsu feasted his senses on the Japanese girls' simple bright garments, their Shikoku dialect, and their alluring flesh, soft as the breast of a baby bird. At the same time, he sympathized with the family's anxiety, appeared concerned, and spoke reassuringly. Osen unstintingly emptied her meager purse so that Nakatsu would eat breakfast, lunch, and dinner and then stay on late into the night. Shun suspected nothing.

Whenever Suzu tried to approach Nakatsu with the same open and friendly attitude with which she addressed others, he grew tense. For some reason, his face flushed red. Nakatsu had robbed, killed, and raped. He was hated and dreaded by many as a fearsome scorpion. Nevertheless, he remained in fact the same comical, amusing character with a cheerful smile he had been earlier. This struck Suzu as simultaneously strange and pleasurable. But from the moment he appeared at the entrance until the time twelve or fifteen hours later when he left through the double doors of the gate, glancing backward once more, Nakatsu did not for a single minute lift his smiling, eerie eyes from her face, neck, or hands. That made Suzu feel confined and stifled.

His stubborn gaze stayed fixed on her even when she was busy with chores. She sensed it. At times she worried he might brazenly embrace her from behind with thick hairy arms and lick the back of her neck like a bear. She shuddered. When her brother was absent, this fear was even stronger. If her mother was away, too, she felt the pressure of fear and danger intensify sharply. Suzu began to look for support to her younger sister and toddling nephew. She cowered in corners like a small bird.

Kantarō was aware of the double fear assailing the household. Although his sisters' and mother's obsession with the threat of the Chinese soldiers' violence was strong enough to make them tremble, it seemed the women were almost unaware of the terrible danger posed by Nakatsu. Mother was especially heedless. That frustrated him. Mother seemed to be inviting Nakatsu into the house deliberately. He squabbled with his mother. His fear might have crept into his words unawares and affected her.

One evening he told her that he could get a six-mat storeroom at the match factory's company house cleared out. They could find refuge there, he suggested, taking along only their valuables. Mother abruptly retorted that she was not inviting Nakatsu into the house because she found him attractive. Kantarō felt himself under attack.

"Why is she twisting my words? Have I ever said there was anything between her and Nakatsu?" Kantarō thought. "Stupid, she's got it all wrong!" But as was his habit in such cases, he fell silent.

"If you don't like the idea, you don't have to go anywhere," he simply said. Nothing more. Mother became hysterical. Ever since coming here as a bride, she shouted, there had not been a single day when she had not worried about Takezaburō and the children. Since coming all the way to China there had been nothing but pain—and whose fault was that? With these words she burst into wild tears.

The situation within the household grew strangely discordant. The following evening, in his sisters' presence, Kantarō said: "I wonder how long Mister Nakatsu is thinking of staying in the city. If he doesn't flee, he'll be captured."

"He says he's given up on following Chang Tsung-ch'ang."

"Why?"

"I don't know why," Shun answered. Her brother had returned from the factory after being challenged by numerous sentries along the way.

"He says he'll stay here for good."

"When did he say that? When did you hear that?"

"He said it the day he got back from Chieh-shou. A week ago now. Didn't you hear him?"

"What! Why were you hiding that from me?" Now he too was shouting hysterically. "The reason he's hanging around here," he insisted, irritated beyond endurance, "is because he's trying to get into Suzu!"

"That's disgusting." Even Shun flushed scarlet. "Don't talk like that."

"Fools! Fools! You're probably happy Father's still in detention!" For some reason, even Kantarō took leave of his senses. He glared at his sisters and raged as if he were kicking them. "That scum is only acting important because Father and I aren't here! Don't you understand that?"

"*Tiya! Tiya!*" Ichirō innocently trotted up to Kantarō's knees.

24

Street stalls had been set up in a section of a dusty street. The Chinese, like the street itself, were covered with copper-colored dust. The stalls were their entire property. Half-completed Chinese-style houses rose emptily behind them.

A throng in gray nationalist uniforms sauntered by. The copper-colored vendors dubiously watching them were surrounded in a flash with no time even to fold up their shops. Cries, curses, hands and feet struggling frantically as if drowning, overturned stalls—roaring with laughter, the nationalist uniforms scattered. Of the plates and baskets piled high with food, not a single boiled egg remained, not a single slice of fried pork.

Nationalist uniforms chewed merrily as they wandered through the city. In the streets on the opposite side, khaki uniforms continued to work stretching the thorny wire. They glared at each other. This side glared. That side glared. Stones flew.

Just then, in a western outskirt, on a narrow street obstructed by the solid triply reinforced sandbag walls, a Japanese accompanied by a Chinese was being challenged by sentries with fixed bayonets. "You don't look Japanese to me," said the sentry, pointing the bayonet at him. "Your Chinese is too good."

"I am Japanese, I tell you."

"Are you really?" the dirt-covered sentry said with surprise.

"Yes, I really am Japanese." The man's lower front teeth were missing.

"And that Chink?"

"He's, uh, a stubborn worker who sneaked away from the factory this morning. And now . . ." The absence of teeth muffled his voice and blurred his pronunciation. Two bayonets glittered before his chest. Koyama mopped away sweat. This only deepened the sentries' suspicions. It was wonderful to have the troops on hand. But make a single mistake and they were terrifying. Koyama nervously explained that he was a foreman at a match factory, that he had gone to catch a worker who had tried to run away, and that they were accommodating soldiers at the factory too. His explanation was confused.

"Well, then, let's go see the commander of the guard," said one of the sentries, a man with a decisive air, and led him to a cramped dark Chinese house at the head of the street. Apparently the sentry's suspicions had not been dispelled. The lantern shone on off-duty soldiers lying about.

"Sergeant, sir! This one may be a Southern Army spy. His face and words are very suspicious."

What an unpleasant mess this has turned into, thought Koyama, feeling an odd sense of contradiction. He was taking such good care of the troops at the factory. . . .

"Hey, what's the matter?" A familiar voice called unexpectedly out of a dark corner.

"Aah, Mr. Yamazaki!" Koyama instantly recognized the spy Yamazaki. He was saved! Spitefully flaunting his friendship with Yamazaki, he stepped arrogantly over the soldiers' fidgeting bodies to shake hands with him.

Wearing a black Chinese tunic, Yamazaki, together with the similarly attired Nakatsu, was sitting on a long bench in a corner before a sleepy sergeant.

"What's the matter?"

"The soldiers here are nothing like the soldiers we're looking after so kindly at my factory," declared Koyama in a tone strongly suggesting that the soldiers' function was to serve as his shield. He told the story of chasing an escaped worker since early morning and grabbing him as he crouched behind a stack of straw bags filled with dried manure.

"That's him. That's him." He pointed to a pale, grimy Chinese shivering near the entrance and glancing around. He was twenty years old. There were three lumps on his face. They were stained red with fresh blood.

"What an imbecile. Even Chang Tsung-ch'ang's soldiers aren't so stupid that they run away only to get caught," Nakatsu jeered. "Why don't you kill him? It'll be a splendid lesson to the others." Nakatsu's bloodthirsty eyes were shining as though he were about to start licking his lips. Koyama narrowed his eyes and did not object. The soldiers raised their faces and looked at Nakatsu with amazement as if seeing him for the first time.

A shot rang out from the direction where the reciprocal glaring and stone throwing had been going on. All pricked up their ears. Yamazaki and Nakatsu hurriedly stepped out. Yamazaki reminded the sergeant of what he had ordered him to do a little earlier.

"Yes, sir." Within the darkness, the sergeant bowed toward Yamazaki's back.

In the street, inquisitive vagabonds were running in the direction of the gunshot. Women with bound feet were fleeing from the same direction. Another shot rang out. Presently a gray armored motorcar sprouting a horn-like machine gun roared up with an earthshaking tremor as though bent on crushing the opposing side in this petty clash. Dogs nonchalantly loitered.

"Damn it! This is exactly the wrong thing to do!" Coated with dust by the armored car, Yamazaki clicked his tongue like a master exasperated by a disciple's blunder. He had deep plans of his own. He worked hard to realize them. Anyone he could utilize toward that end, he used. Nakatsu was another asset being utilized. "This is exactly the wrong thing to do. If you want to win, first lose!" he muttered to Nakatsu.

"It's not a matter of winning or losing. Those ants have brought a cannon! We should wipe them out!"

"No. . . . If a just cause is absent, then the winner will be the loser."

"Your way of doing things is always such a bother!"

Yamazaki liked Nakatsu's boldness and his widespread influence among the Chinese. Those were properties he could utilize. But this complicated thug was absorbed in his own daydreams and paying him little attention. This he did not like.

Ku Chu-t'ung was occupying the Chin-p'u line train station and the radiotelegraph office. That was extremely dangerous. It caused Yamazaki severe anxiety. The information sent to his home country and everywhere else had to meet with his approval. He did not mind if this entailed some degree of fabrication. The means of communication were in Ku Chu-t'ung's grip. Moreover, Chiang Kai-shek could not be allowed to continue his advance toward Tientsin and Peking. That was absolutely impermissible if Manchuria's security was to be guaranteed. Thus a just cause was required. You might also call it a false accusation. To manufacture it, it was best to use thugs like Nakatsu as agents.

An officer came running out of a side street. The skirmish quieted down. Pretending to be foolish sightseers, the two walked toward the Tung-hsing pier.

"Hey, quit your daily visits to that little girl and help me out a little," Yamazaki jokingly said.

As he walked the street, Nakatsu was dreamily visualizing Suzu's hands, feet, shoulders, nose, mouth, and her other points of beauty. He was enjoying drawing up fanciful plans for abducting her. Neither the absurdity nor the consequences of such plans concerned him. It was the thought of forcibly snatching the girl that brought him pleasure. Since Yamazaki had brought up the subject of Suzu, Nakatsu revealed his plan with a merry smile.

"Just how old are you?" Yamazaki asked.

"Fifty-two." Nakatsu did not think it particularly odd.

"That girl's young enough to be your daughter. She's probably only a third your age."

"That's the way I like it. You don't understand how I feel. I just can't resist that soft innocence, so what the hell. Until I got to be this age, I'd never met a girl like that. How should I put it. . . . It's a totally indescribable feeling that's taken over my whole existence."

"You're too old to be talking like a silly teenager!"

"It's nothing frivolous, believe me. Whatever you say, I can't give up this resolution."

"F-f-f," Yamazaki snickered. "Sure, she is a cute girl . . . but it's her mother who'd be ideal for you. If you married the mother, it'd be a perfect match. How about it? Her old man is a heroin addict locked up at the consulate, so how about going after her? If you do that, I'll help you myself."

"Don't make me laugh. I'm tired of old hags. Anyway, my woman's got to be a virgin! I won't get another chance to lay my hands on a girl like that!"

Koyama directed an offensive grimace at the soldiers in the Chinese house and left. The captured worker followed.

25

Takezaburō left the detention cell of the consular police and entered S Hospital. He had severed his little toe with the edge of an enameled basin. That act had enabled him to leave detention. A young Foreign Ministry policeman newly arrived overseas escorted him unhappily to the hospital.

At the match factory, the manager was worrying more than the army itself about the removal of roadblocks prompted by Chiang Kai-shek's protests, as well as the danger of a clash between the Japanese troops and the Southern Army. The factory staff had been fidgety since the morning of the day. There was no guarantee the workers would not collaborate with the radicals in the Southern Army.

Around ten o'clock, Kantarō learned that his father had been taken to

S Hospital. His mother and a baggily clad Chinese with a stand-up collar, shoving aside a policeman about to stop them, burst into the office. Kantarō jumped. Breathless, and with the frantic eyes of a child in shock, Mother was unable to utter a word. Seeing her, Kantarō was struck by the fearful thought that Suzu had been kidnapped.

"Quick, S Hospital, go. Your father hurt. Bleeding. Come quick." The affable-looking Chinese spoke in a jumble of Japanese and Chinese. He fretted to communicate his message with all possible speed. Creases appeared between his broadly separated eyebrows. In the end he gave up and blurted it all out in Chinese. Kantarō understood.

Suppressing his indignation over the derisive smile that the manager exchanged with Koyama, Kantarō briefly excused himself and hurried toward the hospital. In the streets soldiers were dragging heavy road obstacles out of the way.

"Wait a moment," Mother called after him.

Kantarō made no reply.

"Wait a moment!" Mother repeated.

"What is it?" he asked brusquely.

"You must take him this." Mother was standing tearfully before a Chinese policeman at the gate. "He must have this." She pulled out a small paper parcel from behind her sash. "It's Supreme Pleasure."

"Is everything all right at home?" Kantarō's anxiety over Nakatsu outweighed his reluctance to speak.

Mother remained silent, unable to understand the question.

"Are Suzu and Shun all right?"

"Oh," Mother said innocently. "Mr. Nakatsu was coming just as I was going out. They're all right."

"Nakatsu's there? You don't know what he's going to do!"

"..."

"Go right back," he said resolutely, abandoning his earlier tone of annoyance.

"What about Father?" Mother hesitated.

"You can't be careless about what he might do to Suzu and Shun."

"But . . ."

Clearly she was worried about her husband. The hell with it! He could not press her further. Mother and the Chinese with the stand-up collar followed as he hurried on to the hospital.

He was vaguely aware of Nakatsu's dangerous plot. Even while he was quarreling with Mother, he kept hinting that she should try not to leave home. And now Nakatsu had slipped in just as she was leaving. The image of Nakatsu's obscene, complacent smile flashed through Kantarō's mind. His anxiety grew even sharper.

Takezaburō had put up with heroin deprivation as long as he could. But twenty-nine days in detention were beyond his endurance. Groaning like a dying man and thrashing about, he writhed in agony under the young policeman's contemptuous smile. Not a trace was left of the gallant assemblyman who had once tried to unmask corruption. That was Kantarō's first thought as he found his father rolling violently about in the sickroom's white bed, his morbidly yellowish body held down by nurses. Who had made him like this? No one protects us! The privilege of being Japanese has no meaning for the poor!

A handsome young Chinese doctor was bandaging father's emaciated right foot. Father moaned while the wound was being dressed. The physician gave the impression of being Japanese. Blood, wiped away with gauze, welled up again from Father's mutilated toe. The red seeped through the white bandage. A Chinese orderly was looking on with a vexed expression. When Kantarō entered, two young consular policemen with maroon hatbands exchanged glances and stepped out of the room. Kantarō had brought the "Supreme Pleasure" to give to his father. Knowing this, the policemen withdrew. Kantarō sensed that.

Father was gasping and moaning, his protruding cheekbones and sunken eyes like those of a corpse dead from starvation. "I'd better keep the drug away from him and just end the terrible habit," thought the son.

As soon as the father's hollow eyes caught sight of the son, he asked for "Supreme Pleasure" like a fretful child, heedless of being overheard by the policemen outside the door.

"Damn! There's no help for it!" The drug was handed over.

Ecstatically and greedily Takezaburō sucked it up, ingesting the contents of the entire packet. "It was so damn painful I couldn't stand it, so finally I pulled a stunt like this. If I hadn't cut off my toe, I couldn't have gotten out. No matter how much I squirmed, they just laughed."

Mother and the Chinese arrived. As the drug took effect, Takezaburō forgot about the pain in his foot. He grew cheerful and beamed foolishly at the people around him.

"He's become a total slave to heroin," thought Kantarō. "Even if he has to chop off his toe, he's got to have it! A toe for heroin! This would never have happened if he hadn't come to China! If only he hadn't been driven out of that village, it would never have come to this!" He shuddered with horror.

"Is it already gone? . . . Isn't there more? Let me have it! Let me have it!" Like a child, Father began to plead again.

Untold numbers of people in China have, like Takezaburō, become captives of opium, morphine, and heroin brought in by foreigners. Thanks to the narcotics, millions of people are addicted and being destroyed. . . .

26

A lame man, balding and shabby, stepped onto the broiling dusty paving stones of an alley. Outwardly his movements were jerky and unsightly. But in fact he was walking briskly and with ease. After a while he retraced his steps along the same stone-paved alley. His walk was even sprightlier and his lame leg seemed to fly. Presently he summoned a rickshaw and leaped in. "Run!" The rickshaw was swallowed up by the dusty, scorching streets.

At the back of the alley, in a house circled by a stone fence, Suzu sat before a cheap sewing machine, sewing a dress, unsewing it, and sewing it once again. She was dissatisfied with the seams, which refused to run parallel and straight.

Ichirō's eyes dominated his button-nosed face. His eyes were big and bright, just like those of his vanished mother. He crept up to Shun. With his small hand he tried to snatch away a flier Shun was reading. It was one of the fliers Chiang Kai-shek had put out. Its style was rather different from the classical Chinese reader used in school, and Shun had trouble reading it.

"Wait, will you." She handed Ichirō a toy dog and shooed him away. . . . "The nationalist government exempts this province from all taxation. . . ."

Ichirō flung away the dog, spread out his arms, and resumed his attack. The flier got crumpled. Shun smoothed it out and continued to read: ". . . Chang Tso-lin, and Chang Tsung-ch'ang, robbing, raping, treasonous . . ."

Suddenly Ichirō knocked the paper from her hands with both of his. Only half-read, the flier was reduced to ribbons. Shun did not mind. She was thinking about something. Suzu was concentrating intently on the sewing machine. The needle moved rapidly and methodically up and down. The stitches roughly advanced.

"That man seemed very strange today."

"What?" Suzu blankly replied.

"He seemed up to something. It wasn't just that he was staring at us and all around with those angry-looking eyes of his. There was something terrible in the way his eyes and mouth were smiling."

"I wonder."

The catlike Shun was recalling various aspects of Nakatsu's behavior over the past few days. For at least two or three days he had been showing signs of something terrifying.

"Sister! Sister!" Shun called out to Suzu again.

A room in a Chinese inn on Tung-hsing pier was the gathering place for Nakatsu's companions who had stayed on in the city, disguised, after Chang Tsung-ch'ang's withdrawal. There were four or five of them, and they treasured wild, violent work more than food itself. T'ang, short and fat, would fall upon enemy sentries barehanded, bite through their windpipes, and come away with rifles and bayonets. All had kidnapped a number of rich daughters and wives for ransom. The room was piled high with furniture, flower-patterned tea jars, trunks, and silver.

Now that Nakatsu was ready to put into practice his abduction scheme, having endlessly refined it in fantasy, he grew bewildered. Would it not be better just to give it up altogether? It was good to love the girl as though she were his granddaughter. Maybe this is what he should do. Never before had he felt so confused. But he never breathed a word of this to his companions. Instead he discussed the best way to execute his plan. Dividing his companions among three cars, he negotiated with Yamazaki to make certain they would not be challenged while driving through the sector guarded by the Japanese troops. It would be troublesome to have the sentries discover a girl in Japanese clothing being held by force. When approaching the sector where the Southern Army was stationed, atop the cars he would hoist the Sun in the Blue Sky flags he had already obtained. Such was his decision.

Two cars would cruise down the street. Nakatsu would stroll by and lure the girl out of the house. The car in front would suddenly stop. Instantly men would jump out of the car and bundle the girl in. Nakatsu would follow in the second car. Thus it had been resolved. If the younger sister and the child came out of the house, as well, all three would be taken. The cars would speed some ten miles without stopping until reaching Luo-k'ou along the Hwang Ho River; from there they would flee toward Tientsin. This was the plan. If Suzu refused to be lured out by Nakatsu, five men would force their way into the house. She would have to be dragged away violently. He had five hundred yuan in silver and three thousand five hundred yuan in the obsolete paper currency. Nakatsu needed to raise about a thousand yen more.

Yamazaki, who was staying at the same inn, tried hard to talk him out of it. He was a miserly man. Nakatsu interpreted his opposition as unwillingness to lend him money. That was hitting a tender spot. The more he was opposed, the more obstinate he grew.

"Won't you give up such an idiotic scheme, eh?" Yamazaki said. "If you were snatching a rich woman I might understand, but what are you going to do with a penniless girl? Be serious, will you?"

"Shut the hell up!" The closer the time drew, the harder Nakatsu strove to hide his disquiet and appear supremely calm.

"If you've got such a flaming passion for her, then forget about kidnapping her. Just propose marriage. There's no need for barbaric violence. Just take the girl properly as a wife, and I'll be on your side."

"Don't talk nonsense!" Nakatsu laughed. "When Master Chang caught sight of a beauty on the way to Tung-an market in Peking, he just had her grabbed on the spot and bundled into the car, so what's the difference? Elegant schemes like marriage proposals don't suit our character. It's much less troublesome and much more pleasant just to grab what I want without hesitation."

Nakatsu's companion Hei Fu-kuei narrowed his clouded eyes and nodded in agreement.

"Well, I suppose you people can't rid yourselves of your outlaw ways."

Nakatsu laughed. "In this whole wide China, it's only you and that argumentative brother of hers who talk like that."

"No. I'm saying it seriously. For your sake."

"I don't give a damn how you're saying it! If I like her, I'll grab her and marry her. And if I get tired of her, I'll sell her and get rid of her. It's simple, it's easy, and it feels great!"

"Don't start acting too big! I can't guarantee that you'll get past the sentry line."

"Ho, ho. . . . If you won't do it, I don't care. You might have some trouble of your own when I let slip some of this treasure of information I'm holding." Such was his threat.

The five assembled men drank a cup before departure. Compared with them, Yamazaki seemed vaguely Japanese. Offered a cup, he declined with a frown. From the slight bulges under the men's tunics it could be seen that each was armed with five loaded pistols: two at chest level, two at the sides, and one in the right hip pocket.

"This miser is just piling up money, he's not about to lend out any!" thought Nakatsu with disgust. "Son of a bitch! This one hasn't come to China to enjoy a life of uninhibited freedom. He's here to accumulate a minor fortune! What an idiot! Shit!"

The cars arrived. Once more Nakatsu thought of getting properly married and loving his bride as though she were his grandchild. That would be peaceable and good, but he had already stepped into the river. Even if the current was violent, he was determined to cross to the other side.

"Well, shall we go?" He stood up. The shortage of money weighed on his mind too.

"Boy, where's the blanket?" shouted Nakatsu's agreeable companion Hei Fu-kuei. "Put that Russian blanket in the front car." Once again Hei cheerfully narrowed his eyes. "With today's impressive state of high alert, our job might be a trifle difficult if we don't wrap up the woman from head to toe when we're driving through the city. Let those sentries in khaki discover a gagged woman and it'll be the end of us."

The five men got ready and stepped out into the corridor. Through the second-story window could be seen a soldier in a gray uniform thrusting his hands into the pockets of a passerby. The young manservant brought the blanket.

"Not that one! I said the Russian blanket," Hei bellowed.

Nakatsu lavishly distributed money all around. A different manservant, pretty as a girl, ran up with a reddish brown Russian blanket in his hands.

"Yes, this one, this one." Hei took it at the staircase. It was an elaborately made, thick blanket, somewhat worn. Hei bent his arms a little and suddenly swept the blanket over the pretty youth's head.

"*Aiya!*" the young man cried out in surprise.

"See, this is how it's done." Proud of his skill, Hei looked around. "Do this and she's yours." Nakatsu laughed with satisfaction.

Yamazaki gazed after the five ruffians as though reluctant to see them go. Hurrying over to Nakatsu, he whispered something in his ear. Nakatsu nodded. Some money was transferred to Nakatsu.

The cars emerged from T'ai-ma-lu Road onto Fourth Street, which was free of roadblocks and barbed wire, and turned at Ch'i-ma-lu Road in the direction of Yung-sui-men. They were making a detour that steered clear of both the Japanese-held zone and the sector holding the Southern Army. Nakatsu rode up to Shih-wang-tien by rickshaw.

Having lured the girl outdoors, they would kidnap her at Kuan-i-chieh. The arrangements were complete.

Nakatsu alighted from the rickshaw. Once more he walked nimbly, as if flying, through the same paved alley he had entered and exited so swiftly just an hour ago. Green leaves of acacias rustled in the wind. Underneath the leaves, he was pressing forward. Despite the limp, he had the spirited stride of a youth. His feet scarcely touched the ground.

The gate was closed. Nakatsu called Wang Chin-hua. Someone seemed to be inside, yet there was no reply. He called again. After a few threatening words from Nakatsu, the bolt clanked open. The young Chinese servant was standing nervously inside.

"What's going on?"

"Ah. . . . Welcome."

"What's going on?"

Suzu's half-sewn dress was still there but Suzu, who only moments before had been sewing at the machine, was gone. Shun and Ichirō were gone too.

"What's going on?"

Nakatsu rapidly inspected each of the familiar rooms. The occupants seemed to have fled in haste, taking nothing along. "They sensed something! They've hidden somewhere. They've run away!" For some time he hovered about in confusion.

His companions, unable to wait in the cars any longer, barged noisily into the house. They loved plunder and violence. They knocked over the Buddhist altar and yanked out the drawers. Narcotics and utensils scattered across the floor.

The neatly arranged interior of the house was thrown into utter disarray. Anything attractive that the hands of the five picked up, they hurriedly stuffed in their pockets. The grabbing of a girl was transformed into the grabbing of household goods. That too delighted them greatly.

27

Kantarō and his mother boarded a rickshaw to return home from the hospital. Five or six rifle shots rang out from somewhere. They sounded like firecrackers.

A company of fierce Mongolian cavalrymen galloped southward

through the city, flying like the wind and raising clouds of dust. In their wake scattered groups of soldiers in khaki appeared carrying rifles with fixed bayonets. The crackle of rifle fire, like bursting beans, grew intense in every direction. As they neared Sixth Street, the rickshaw puller hesitated in fear.

"Hurry up! We must make sure our family's all right!"

They came to Fifth Street. Bullets fired from the second story of a thick-walled Western-style building flew whistling all around the street. Soldiers were running. A barefoot Japanese was running with his shirt unbuttoned. A woman in red satin and with fringed hair was running unsteadily.

From there, the rickshaw dashed to Third Street. By now even Kantarō could not help feeling imperiled.

"Hurry up, will you! What are you waiting for!"

"Sir, it's dangerous. We could get killed."

"I don't care. Go, go!"

But the man would advance no further.

Events had suddenly accelerated following the plunder of Kantarō's house. The great beams and pillars of a house on the verge of collapse will break into pieces all at once if even a single wedge is removed. To trigger a fight, just lightly touching somebody's sleeve provides enough of a pretext.

Nakatsu's pillaging had sparked street fighting. Witnessing Nakatsu's vandalism, the gray uniforms swarming in the neighborhood rushed in. The house was knocked to pieces. Hearing the racket, the khaki uniforms ran up. Soon the exchange of gunfire began. In the twinkling of an eye, it spread to the entire city. It was as though they had been ready and looking forward to it. Thus was triggered the vehement and notorious war of the streets.

The earth-floored hall of the KS Club was packed with people who had narrowly escaped the fighting. More refugees kept crowding in. Among them was a man who, blocked from leaving his house by the gray Southern soldiers, had broken through the wall to an adjacent house, borrowed Chinese clothing, and fled disguised as a coolie, pushing a passing rickshaw. There was a man who fled after seeing his wife dragged away by Southern soldiers before his eyes. Some came clutching blankets and cloth bundles. Some were in their underwear. A young sick-looking child with eyes red from crying was carried on its father's back.

Most refugees were silent. Only the fat proprietress of a drapery store was proudly and shrilly chattering away: "I'm telling you, my Momo is great. When we were running away I asked him 'What will you do if the

234 / Kuroshima Denji

Southern Army grabs you?' and he says 'I'll cut my throat with a razor together with Mother.' Isn't he just great? True Japanese man." She lifted the flat-nosed nine-year-old up high and showed him to people. "I'm telling you, this is a true Japanese man." Whenever she saw a familiar face, the fat woman proudly repeated her words, unmindful of the others' concerns.

Squeezed by the crowd, Suzu and Shun were cowering in a corner of the earth-floored hall. Ichirō had been taken by the Southern Army! It was only when they saw the red-eyed child fretting on its father's back that they realized it. Where did they lose him? They had no clear memory of it. Going back to search for him might cost them their lives. They only had the strength to protect themselves.

A great number of barefoot women rushed in. They were the prostitutes from Yung-hsien-li. Chinese soldiers had poured into the red light district, throwing the prostitutes into a panic.

Unable even to sit on a mat, a man in a torn shirt and trousers stood by the blanket-draped window biting his lip, one hand thrust into a pocket, staring ahead with shining eyes. His body was restless with agitation. The man had lost sight of his wife and child.

"Mrs. Koide! Listen to this. My Momo . . ."

The fat woman resumed her boasting.

When Nakatsu and companions forced their way into her house, Suzu, together with Shun and Ichirō, was crouching beneath the hemp-palm chairs in their neighbor Ma Kuan-chih's house. That much they remembered. The unfamiliar Chinese smell permeated the bed, the bedclothes, and all around.

From their own house they could hear the raging of many violent footsteps, shouted curses, and noises of destruction. Boards creaked and snapped as they were pried away. Cupboards crashed, glass broke, walls thudded.

Terrified, they crept out from under the chairs and approached the window. Cautiously they raised their eyes just enough to take a peek. The stone-paved alley was swirling ominously with soldiers in gray uniforms. A dirty-looking man was vanishing down the opposite alley, Suzu's sewing machine under his arm. A wire birdcage lay trampled underfoot. How fortunate that Ma Kuan-chih's wife had hidden them!

Someone banged on the door. The girls were sure they were coming to kill them. They crawled under the chairs again and tucked in their heads. Rough footsteps drew near. They held their breath and pricked up their ears.

It was Ma Kuan-chih. "It's dangerous for you here. Quick! Hide in the lavatory." Ma Kuan-chih was kind.

They fled to the lavatory. They were not safe there either. They were in a bind. Another Chinese house stood close to the lavatory. There was a gap between the buildings. Shun madly clambered up the six-foot wall and jumped down into the intervening space. She felt safer there. Suzu jumped down after her.

From the other side of the wall they heard five or six men noisily kicking chairs and boxes about. They seemed to have entered the lavatory too. The girls listened alertly. The voices spoke Chinese. Was it Nakatsu? Or the Southern soldiers? In either case, if discovered they would be stripped naked or murdered.

The gap between the houses opened onto a different alley. Through the narrow space they could see frantically fleeing barefoot people flitting past. Khaki uniforms ran up with fixed bayonets. There was no time to think. They jumped out into the alley. Next they ran as fast as they could in the same direction as everyone else. They ran pushing the slower people aside. Ichirō was forgotten.

More and more refugees kept pushing their way into the KS Club. When did this enormous disturbance begin? The girls marveled at it. They had no idea that their own house had touched off the fighting. It was the Southern soldiers who were to blame. This is what they were led to think. Many other people, of course, thought the same. Incidents are always created as needed by reactionary thugs like Nakatsu. That, of course, they did not know.

Artillery and rifle fire sounded, now far, now near, now intermittently, now continuously. Each time a cannon fired, windowpanes rattled. A man with a badly gashed head walked in. Hours passed.

Some of the men went out and washed rice. When the rice was cooked, the men distributed it only to the people they knew and to the prostitutes. These ate their fill, but the others were not given a single bowlful. Suzu and Shun were gripped by a forlorn feeling of being excluded. If their brother were here, thought Suzu, they would be allowed to eat. Although the prostitutes in their crimson kimonos were protesting that they were full, each was being pressed to accept one more rice ball.

At last the leftover food, adhering to the bottom of the rice tub, was passed around. They were angry at being treated as inferiors. But if they balked at eating now, there was no telling when they would get another chance. Everyone jostled to grab the rice with dirty hands. It was a miserable spectacle: they looked like hungry demons.

In the evening, they received orders to move to the S Bank company housing. They were told they could not be defended where they were. Suzu gripped Shun's hand tightly. Staying close to the walls to avoid being hit by bullets, they emerged onto the main road. The invariably lively main road was deserted, not even a stray dog in sight. From time to time a rifle shot rang out.

"Look at that! Over there. . . . They got a lot of those Southern troops." A bearded man running with a child on his back pointed to the post office grounds.

"What?" Suzu glanced in the direction he was pointing.

Encircled by a barbed-wire stockade, disarmed soldiers in gray uniforms were groaning and crying like animals, their arms tied behind their back. There were dozens, even hundreds, of them. Four or five khaki soldiers with fixed bayonets stood scattered about.

Suddenly Shun screamed, tugged hard at Suzu's hand, and fell to the ground.

"What is it?"

A stray bullet had struck her leg. Blood was spreading across the whitish muslin.

"What is it?"

Chinese nationalist soldiers captured.

Awareness of having been hit by a bullet overwhelmed her strained emotions even more than the pain of the wound itself. Shun simply could not get up. Other people ran rapidly past them. Suzu lifted her younger sister onto her own back and rose. The two had fallen far behind and now were alone. Suzu often stopped to hitch her sister's heavy body higher. Cold drops of blood trickled steadily onto her hurriedly moving calves.

People spent the night sitting on mats in S Bank's company housing, thirteen families sharing two mats. There was no physician. Suzu tore up her handkerchief and bound up Shun's purple, stricken thigh. The two did not even sit on the edge of a mat. They sat on wooden boards.

"That must hurt. Sit on this."

A small middle-aged woman with black-dyed teeth spread out her own nightgown instead of a mat. Suzu did not know her. She stretched out Shun's leg taking care not to stain the nightgown with blood. The sisters lay down side by side on the woman's nightgown.

"Ah, how terrible. Who knows how many people have killed, and been killed, today."

Sighing the woman chanted the name of Amida Buddha. "How many have lost all they had. . . . Certainly more than a hundred. How many have had their homes destroyed! . . . Ah, ah! How horrible! How horrible!"

"Hail Amida Buddha."

"Hail Amida Buddha."

The night grew late. Clenching her teeth, Shun tried to withstand the pain but moans escaped of their own accord. Artillery was still thundering in the distance, rending the silence. People snored and dogs barked. Only the electric lights were growing ever brighter. The shoes of MPs banged loudly in the corridors.

The next day, after noon, the two were taken to the hospital where their injured father was being treated with Mother staying beside him. There Shun received medical care.

28

Slaughter and plunder are inseparable from armies and wars. Whenever a war is waged, looting, robbery, and murder are invariably committed. Depending on their merits, such events are either reported with exaggeration or, conversely, passed over in silence.

On this day, fourteen settlers were massacred, counting the nine disinterred two days later. Japan's bourgeois press gave the number as two hundred and eighty. The newspapers wrote that women had been stripped naked, treated with unspeakable savagery, and subsequently butchered. Young girls had had stakes thrust into their vaginas, arms broken by clubs, and eyes gouged out. This is what the papers wrote. The public was informed about a person whose skull was smashed before the correspondent's very eyes, spilling the brains onto the dusty road.

Similar reports were printed concerning the looting. According to one survivor, not only were valuables and clothing stolen but floorboards, mats, and ceiling planks were ripped away and even elementary school textbooks carried off. Gold chains, gold watches, and two hundred forty yuan in coin and three hundred eighty in banknotes were pillaged as well. This victim's story was published.

Reading such accounts, no sane person could fail to detest the Southern Army. No one in his right mind could fail to grow indignant and conclude that such vicious troops deserved to be annihilated. So great was the power of sensational reportage. The nation's public opinion and animosity, the soldiers' reckless courage and fury, are inevitably manufactured out of this sort of information.

Yamazaki understood this. And he utilized it. On the third day he discovered mutilated corpses buried in a field northeast of the railway bridge on the Chin-p'u line. The freshly raised mounds of earth had looked suspicious.

They were dug up. A woman and two men lay within, giving off a powerful sour stench. Six more bodies were hidden in the vicinity of a water tank just a short distance away. Their ears had been sliced off and the stomachs of some had been stuffed with stones making them swollen and hard.

Both in Shih-wang-tien and Kuan-i-chieh, many houses had been looted and vandalized beyond all recognition. Attired in Chinese clothing, Yamazaki strolled about inspecting the ruins. This must be made known, he thought. To the soldiers, to the settlers, and to the people back home.

Thanks to his professional sense, he fully understood what would happen when this information was broadcast. This man was well aware of the enormous effects of inflating the number of victims from fourteen to two hundred and eighty. A war cannot be prosecuted without guiding a nation's people into a state of excitement and frenzy. The enemy must be advertised as fiendishly evil. The public's sympathy must be aroused! This he knew well. . . .

The house in Shih-wang-tien that his friend Nakatsu had been the first to break into and loot was now a shattered empty shell. That this had set off the fighting was to him a stroke of unforeseen good fortune. Inside the house there were beggars. They were stealing the smashed chairs, mats, a girl's broken umbrella, and other objects strewn about. I have certainly put this to excellent use, thought Yamazaki.

"That's right, this was the Inokawa house," he muttered nonchalantly. "The sacking of this place by the Southern Army started the war! That's right! The Southern Army's to blame!"

This willful man halted before the house. Behind the thick wrecked walls, beggars were stealthily moving about.

"Hey, Mr. Yamazaki!" An unpleasantly familiar voice reached his ears from behind.

"Aah, Master Ch'en!" Yamazaki glossed over the momentary jolt. It was Ch'en Chang-ts'ai, the man with whom he had infiltrated S University in the guise of students. Despite promising to reward him, he had been repeatedly dodging him ever since and had not given him a single yuan.

"So. How are things?" Ch'en eyed Yamazaki with an ambiguous smile.

"Aah, about that-- next time. With this confusion, it's impossible."

"Next time? Next time?" Ch'en repeated. "It's dishonorable to keep saying that!" He took a step closer to Yamazaki. "Who helped you learn what the Americans were really up to?" his eyes seemed to be saying. "Who helped you to distinguish yourself?"

"A troublesome bastard to be stuck with!" thought Yamazaki. "I'd better take advantage of the confusion to get rid of him." He started to walk.

Ch'en followed him. He went on trailing him like a shadow. They went to Kuan-i-chieh. They came to the corner of First Street. Yamazaki glanced all around as his right hand moved to his tunic pocket.

The following instant a pistol shot rang through the street like a bursting bean. Almost simultaneously something nickel-plated flashed in Ch'en Chang-ts'ai's hand too. But Ch'en had no time to squeeze the trigger. The arm with the pistol jerked up toward a ruined roof, a shudder ran through his body, and he fell with a heavy thud onto the trash-strewn street.

"Good riddance!"

Yamazaki walked off. With this single pistol shot the three hundred yuan he owed Ch'en rolled into his own pocket. Thinking of it, he felt a thrill.

It was essential to inform the soldiers, the refugees, and the public back home about the settlers' pillaged houses, the dead woman with her ears sliced off, the dead men with their stomachs packed with stones. This is what he was thinking. It was essential to tell the entire world!

He emerged before the headquarters.

"Halt!"

The sentry's voice did not enter his ears.

"Halt!"

He walked on absorbed in thought.

Since before the withdrawal of the Northern Army, this checkpoint had been heavily guarded and conducted rigorous body searches. Even the warlord Sun Ch'uan-fang's car had been ordered to stop. Its owner had been dragged out. His pockets had been searched. "I am Sun Ch'uan-fang!" The gold-braided balding old man had stamped on the ground with rage. "I am Sun Ch'uan-fang! How dare you!" He could have been the supreme commander of the Soviet Red Army for all the sentry cared. It made no difference to him. He was only carrying out his duty. "Huh! Sun Ch'uan-fang, is it? All I see is some unknown joker in a fancy gold-braided uniform!"

It was this sentry line Yamazaki was passing. The sentries glared at this man who was dressed Chinese and looked Chinese.

"Halt!"

Forgetting his Chinese clothing, Yamazaki was reveling in the pleasure of being Japanese. Dreamily he was imagining the storm of popular passion whipped up by the reports of atrocities. I will tell them! I will let them know! ... He was vaguely aware of a Chinese being challenged by sentries. He assumed it had nothing to do with him.

"Halt!"

Still he noticed nothing.

There was a burst of rifle fire. Yamazaki, five pistols and a bankbook registering eight thousand yen as close to his heart as ever, dropped on the spot. Off to the devil at last!

29

The airplanes appeared. Approaching the city airspace, they dropped one black lump after another like birds shitting in flight. The objects streaked through the air and shook the ground with detonations. Air raid!

There were three aircraft flying in a V-formation. They flew in a wide circle over the city as though searching for an old nest. They reached the western suburb. Suddenly one of the airplanes burst open like a glass bead. A shower of sparks shot from it. Spitting black smoke, blazing, wings breaking apart, it plummeted to the ground.

The street fighting was over. The exhausted soldiers received two and a half days of rest. They drank *sake* and in two days smoked up the cigarettes they had gone without for a week.

Chinese corpses lay sprawled throughout the streets. A sour stench fouled the air. Countless flies buzzed. Shaggy-haired stray dogs and beggars, both licking their lips, wandered cheerfully among the corpses, the dogs wagging their tails. The sky-piercing antenna of a blown-up radio station was broken in the middle, leaning, about to fall. No one turned to look. No one repaired it. People black as earth were scraping into buckets the brain matter from skulls that lay beneath it.

Suddenly: moving out! It was four in the morning, a time when weariness starts to give way to sensuous desire. The soldiers were roughly awakened.

Kakimoto had scraped his shin jumping into a Chinese factory through its stone window. His sock, pressed by the legging, rubbed against the festering wound he had daubed with iodine. He limped into line. The eastern sky was just starting to grow white. They were to attack ramparts forty feet high, forty feet wide, and seven miles in circumference: orders from a bitterly cold company commander; invisible faces. Lieutenant Shigefuji walked gripping his military sword. Some of the barbed wire having been shoved aside, the soldiers passed through the narrow opening and marched in a column along the line of telegraph poles.

The road was wet with dew. There was utter silence. Only the rhythmic crunching of the men's shoes broke the stillness and was swallowed up by the dark sky. On the western side of S Hospital, responding to quiet authoritative orders, artillerymen were placing guns into position with a clatter of wheels. Silently the soldiers marched on. Bluish clouds dyed purple by the red sunrise were drifting gently. It grew bright.

The house whose roof had been smashed by the downed aircraft crouched like a crab with a crushed shell. There was no one around but soldiers. The house looked devoid of life. The surrounding grass had been trampled out of recognition.

Gradually the faces of Takatori, Kitani, Nasu, and others grew distinct. They were walking like wooden dolls, shouldering rifles, knapsacks and mess tins clinging to their backs. Kakimoto, in addition to dreading the war, felt sick with worry that his aunt Nakanojō might have had her child killed, her house plundered, and been left homeless and hungry. To have come all the way here and then been unable to help her in any way! Takatori and his comrades had a reason for walking like mindless wooden dolls. They were putting up with a great deal.

The company entered a devastated street. Windowpanes, doors, walls, roofs—all had been destroyed. A military shoe struck a woman's rattan clog. The soldiers turned past a tall solid stone house and wall to emerge onto a broad and desolate grassy plain. Obliquely they cut across it. Once more they passed through the rubble of what had been houses. They wound along the narrow streets.

Suddenly the sun rose radiantly bright among the jagged ruined roofs. Fragments of cloud that had been scattered throughout the sky vanished without a trace. Again it would get hot! The entire wreckage stood out illuminated intensely by the sun.

The company came out onto a main road. This led in a straight line to the outer gate of the stronghold. A Sun in the Blue Sky flag fluttered from a structure beyond the gate.

From somewhere a signal was heard. Far to the rear, from the vicinity of the artillery emplacement, gunfire roared out. Shells moaned through the sky and exploded ahead. In response, continuous gunfire commenced from the opposite, eastern direction. Kakimoto's calves twitched and trembled. Then his entire body began to shiver.

That is when it happened. Suddenly the company column was fired upon from the flank. The company commander heard several shots crack just above his head. They came from the second floor of T Hospital. Kakimoto heard them too. The shots ceased.

"Oh, no! What a place to be ambushed from!" the special-duty sergeant major exclaimed sadly, taking cover behind an acacia. The soldiers looked at each other. Wry smiles spontaneously creased their faces. At the same time, they heard the company commander's startled order to spread out.

"Now he'll be ordering us to attack this place too."

Takatori grinned meaningfully at the stocky Tamada. Kakimoto heard him too.

"And what the hell for? No one will be there."

Tamada raised his head and surveyed the two-story hospital. While he was still eying it, the right flank, headed by Lieutenant Shigefuji, broke through the doors and with bayonets and rifles thrust out before them charged into the interior, which reeked of disinfectant. Other soldiers poured in after them. Nurses in white flickered before their eyes. Patients were lying in beds. Pleurisy, nephritis, gastric ulcers, cardiac valve disease—separate departments for internal medicine and surgery. The doors dividing the many rooms were banged open one after another. Muddy shoes jumped atop beds. The operating table's thick glass shattered into a web of cracks.

In the record written at the time, this incident was described as follows: "Regiment number XXX, steadily approaching fortification gate under cover of darkness, was suddenly subjected to heavy Chinese fire from T hospital to north, placing it in extreme danger. But considering said building's nature as hospital, temporary dilemma ensued concerning appropriate countermeasures. Situation growing acute, however, and cognizant hesitation would inevitably result in numerous casualties from random fire. Captain N employed section of unit to destroy enemy elements. In view of acute conditions, measures taken were truly unavoidable." And so forth.

Thirty minutes later, the soldiers pulled out of the hospital, unpleasant memories seared into their brains. Throughout the following day they could not stop thinking about it. The next day too, they could not stop thinking about it. Kakimoto's movements were sluggish and seemed reluctant. He was absorbed in thoughts he himself could hardly understand. "A sick child was stabbed against the wall. And then with the blood gushing out of its chest, the child wobbled and crouched on the floor. Can such things be done! Can such things happen!" He was tormented by something like remorse. "That pale woman was sleeping in bed, mouth open, knowing nothing. . . . A small triangular hole opened up in her blanket. And the woman is sleeping, never to awaken. . . . My hands trembled then. My arms were suddenly drained of strength! The things we were made to do!"

Once more they formed a column and proceeded toward the fort. The assault was now at its height. *Bang! Ta-ta-ta-ta-ta-ta-ta!* Machine guns inside and outside the fort hailed each other and rattled away in rapid succession. No sooner did the noise stop for an instant than it rang out once more. Howitzer shells were bursting against the walls.

The faces of Takatori, Tamada, Matsushita, and the others were looking sullen. Even Kuraya from the training institute was glum and sunken in thought. "That's right, they're all weighed down by unpleasant memories!" thought Kakimoto. These members of the lowest class, the ones who held the blades and did the killing directly, were unable to fathom for whose sake it was that they killed. They had been possessed by someone.

Their fellow Japanese had been massacred. Their homes had been stripped down to the last plank. To them, this seemed to be the only issue. And so they felt a passionate anger and thirst for revenge that demanded multiple retaliation for every person killed. It was undeniable that the passionate anger and thirst for revenge were a prominent factor in the killing of the "enemy." It was this anger that impelled them to kick the corpses of the slain Chinese—slain Chinese whose numbers exceeded those of the Japanese killed in the street fighting by about fifteen to one.

What did they do it for? Whom did they do it for?

30

Morning after the next: six o'clock. The continent-scorching day was already beginning.

The soldiers lined up in the corner of the match factory's poplar wood storage house. The sensitive Lieutenant Shigefuji fixed his attention on the expressions of the men who seemed to be avoiding their superior's direct gaze. He saw unrest, loss of morale, reluctance, irresolution. For a long time he had been aware of a dangerous atmosphere brewing among the men. Immediately he had thought of someone hiding in the shadows and plotting something!

The brave, simple, emotional Shigefuji possessed an acute talent for intuitively perceiving the needs and instincts of the soldiers he was managing. This sense let him know when the soldiers were surreptitiously doing

Civilian victims of the intervention.

something behind his back—something of a bad nature. Clearly they had grown disloyal. Takatori had struck a factory supervisor, resorting to violence so that the workers would get all their wages. Since then at least five or six soldiers had lost the ability to distinguish between arriving at the front to fight for their country and coming here to join workers in committing outrageous acts. Among them it was especially Takatori he was keeping an eye on. All the more so as many of the soldiers found Takatori's statements appealing. The lieutenant knew that too. There had to be a reason for it!

The special-duty sergeant major in charge of personnel had noticed this too. The sergeant major was gravely concerned that the men might be conspiring with the Chinese communists. But Shigefuji made light of the matter. He was convinced that whatever they set out to do, as ordinary soldiers they were incapable of accomplishing much. Noticing the unrest, unease, and certain lack of pride in the eyes of the lined-up soldiers, he was swift to attribute the cause to scheming by Takatori and his ilk. He resolved to break them this very day. There would be countless casualties. They would commit a major blunder! He frowned.

Having rewound his leggings, Takatori, dragging his shoes, was trying to fall into line after everyone else. The officer drew close to him. From the side, he struck him a hard blow on the cheek. He did it deliberately in such a way that all the soldiers could see it.

"Hey, Takatori! Don't loaf!"

". . ."

"You don't like serving your country? Those who don't are traitors." And he struck him three more times. "Is that clear?"

". . ."

Takatori's eyes were jutting from their sockets and burning as if about to lunge forward. He had no idea why he had suddenly been hit. The lieutenant did not like the way Takatori was staring at him. He could not tolerate an insolent attitude.

"Watch it! If you don't shape up, you'll be sorry!" he shouted.

"What have I done?"

"Watch it! Cut it out, Takatori!" He rattled his sword. "I can see right through you. I know exactly what you're up to. You have no idea what a terrible thing you're doing."

"I'm not doing anything."

For an instant, Takatori hesitated. But instantly he fixed the lieutenant with his shining eyes.

"Quit it!" Shigefuji said solemnly. "I know everything!"

"Know what?"

As an enlisted soldier he had been hit a number of times in the past. He had been kicked. He had been beaten with the sword enough to bend it. Countless times he had endured it. Other men had received much the same treatment. "What are we actually being made to do? To wring our own necks! Nothing less! Soldiers are the most good-natured fools in existence."

The soldiers felt that Takatori was not being beaten alone. They were all being beaten. The officer was doing it to intimidate them. Their faces darkened.

Like an accurate barometer, the sensitive Shigefuji soon noticed it. His eyes registered the soldiers' growing agitation and strange restlessness. If he continued the beating, it would achieve the opposite effect from that intended. The entire unit would be affected. And his tone of voice betrayed this awareness. Takatori looked up and tried to say something. The lieutenant cut him off.

"What on earth are you men starting to think of? Eh? Just what kind of things are running through your mind?"

"We don't want to do all this work just to be harassed."

"Hmm. . . . He doesn't want to be harassed, he says." The officer deliberately twisted the soldier's words. "In that case, obey orders properly! If you just obey orders, everything will be fine."

Shigefuji pushed it no further. Intrepid as he was, he was outnumbered. Glancing at the soldiers' expressions, he held his tongue. From his experience of handling soldiers he knew he must never show the slightest doubt that his orders might not be obeyed. Before the men an officer had to display absolute conviction that his orders would be carried out without question. He understood this was essential. And this is the stance he took. He was far from satisfied with Takatori's attitude. Nevertheless, acting as if he were through with the admonition, he drew himself up to his full height and faced the line of soldiers.

31

Soldiers were falling in quick succession like puppets of straw.

Within the fort, Fang Chen-wu was doggedly holding his ground. He demonstrated a fighting spirit that would not rest without pushing north to storm Tientsin and Peking whatever the obstacles. The gates were sturdy and could not be broken through easily. The walls were thick. The Sun in the

Blue Sky flag continued to fly vigorously within. The defenders were far from weak, and their weapons were new.

Chiang Kai-shek, willing to accede to any Japanese demand, merely proposed that he be allowed to pass through the area and attack Tientsin and Peking. This proposal was not accepted. The Japanese commanding officer knew that Manchuria would be threatened. Thereupon the Chinese soldiers grew stubborn.

As the other units stormed the various sectors of the fort, the officers of Kakimoto's unit strove desperately to break through the segment assigned to them. The casualties were mounting. The officers' ambition and rivalry weighed heavily upon the soldiers. Kakimoto and his comrades could see that clearly. There was no time even to untie their leggings. They were dead tired. It was too much. They dozed unawares while aiming their rifles.

Within the confusion, men lost track of their comrades-in-arms. The city was as hot as under a rain of hot tongs. Torn off by the yellow wind, young acacia leaves mixed with dust flew blindingly through the streets. That evening the gray uniforms ceased firing. The soldiers returned to the factory and stretched their legs. Around two in the morning they were assailed by a fearsome nightmare. Some two hundred warriors simultaneously gasped for breath, groaned, and awoke. Hands clawed at the air in distress.

This same phenomenon had taken place in Japan on a night after a new conscript, roundly rebuked and beaten by an instructor for failing to keep up with a double-time march, had hanged himself from a pine branch before an old castle. That time too the entire company had gasped for breath. They had groaned. And they had awoken simultaneously. It was inexplicable.

"Something sinister is happening."

"I thought I was being strangled. . . . It was awful, I just couldn't breathe."

"Somebody's actually being killed! Brutally killed for no reason!"

They were fully awake.

"Is Takatori here? Takatori? Is Takatori here? I have a feeling I saw Takatori with someone!" Kakimoto looked as though he were still staring at a phantom. He felt himself dragged into a deep icy pit.

The next morning they learned that Takatori, Nasu, Okamoto, Matsushita, and Tamada had not come back. Everyone wondered but nobody said anything. They spoke to each other with their eyes. Kitani and Kakimoto inquired at the hospital casualty wards and morgues: not there. Evening came. Still they did not return. The following morning came. Still they did not return. Relieved sentries, pale with lack of sleep and with dew, returned to quarters. There was no news.

Takatori's commander, Lieutenant Shigefuji, came back from somewhere looking exceedingly odd. In a corner of the room, Kitani and Kakimoto caught sight of the lieutenant's highly unnatural smile suggesting he was concealing something. Kitani's intuition latched onto that smile. The lieutenant's state of mind was so plain he felt he could touch it.

"How about it, today we're attacking the Le-yuan gate. . . ."

"Is that so." Kitani's response to the lieutenant's shamefaced, ingratiating overture was cool and brusque.

"If you men give it your best shot today, it's sure to fall."

"Is that so. . . . Lieutenant, sir! What happened to Takatori and the others? They've been gone since the day before yesterday. We can't find them anywhere."

"What do you mean by asking me that? Kitani! What do you have to do with Takatori?" Lieutenant Shigefuji, his eyes and voice furious, suddenly closed in on Kitani. His attitude evinced a readiness to shoot Kitani too.

"We have plenty to do with him. It's only natural to worry about our comrades!"

Kakimoto, who had been watching the exchange from the side, abruptly grabbed his rifle and rose, resolution and anger etched between his eyebrows. The soldiers who up to now had been winding their leggings or smoking grew tense as well. Some, taking up their rifles, rose from the opposite corner, breechblocks clicking as they chambered rounds of ammunition.

"Look here, Kakimoto, what do you mean by that?" demanded the lieutenant.

"No need to say what I mean, is there?"

Lieutenant Shigefuji found himself in a genuine confrontation. The lieutenant had been under the impression that he possessed the power to command the platoon. Yet now, before Private Kakimoto's rifle, he was nothing but a single living creature—just as, the day before yesterday, the disarmed Takatori, Nasu, Okamoto, and others had been nothing but frail living creatures. And so all of a sudden, he cunningly played his best remaining card. Falling back from Kakimoto five or six steps, he shouted: "All right, fall in! Fall in! Everyone take your rifle and out!" and rushed out of the dormitory as if fleeing.

"Son of a bitch! Disgraceful shit of an officer!" The enraged soldiers cursed him in unison.

Kakimoto was thinking about the slightly foolish, reckless Takatori. Where had that honest, genial fellow gone? He seemed foolish but in fact was anything but a fool. It was Takatori who had approached the workers before anyone else. He had made friends with them. Soldiers had thrown away their lives in the Russo-Japanese and Sino-Japanese wars. Now they were risking their lives to protect the settlers and their property. But those were bloody lies. It was Takatori who had pointed this out before anyone else.

"In truth, all they're making us do is kill the Chinese," he had said. And then he had sympathetically asked Kakimoto about his aunt's family. At that time Kakimoto did not yet know that his aunt had barely managed to flee to the S Bank, nor that her five-year-old daughter had been killed. The silver hidden beneath the floorboards had vanished too. He did not know that either.

"The P'u-li-men neighborhood suffered the worst damage."

"So it seems. I still can't go to see it."

"What did we come here for?...We've come all this way yet we can't protect our own relatives or even see them.... Let's hope they're all right."

"Hmm. I'm awfully worried about them!"

"All the way here they send us," resumed Takatori, "and we wouldn't even be able to protect our own parents.... This is the truth. This is the true picture of our present situation. Only those with a pile of money get protected. And it doesn't matter in the least what kind of sacrifices we ourselves have to pay.

"While guarding the factories here, we torment the workers. We drive off the Southern Army. This way, they're thinking, they'll get their hands on the Manchurian interests. Because for them Manchuria is the grand prize. We get paid about seven yen a month. Our lives get thrown away for free. We get nothing out of it. When we go back, we get nothing unless we go out to work for it. We may be their Manchurian bulwark, but they won't give us any time off or free food for it.... If we're truly here to protect the settlers, why do they put us in this dirty, uncomfortable, bedbug-infested factory dorm? There are plenty of cleaner, bigger buildings like the elementary school, the club, and the like. And they're much more convenient. What's the reason for putting us here other than to oppress the workers and guard the factory?"

Kakimoto felt deeply moved, quite out of keeping with Takatori's bold speech.

"We're being used to beat China down. And the more we hinder the workers' and peasants' movement here, the harder our own lives at home will get."

That, too, Takatori had said.

"It's only the wealthy who smile while crushing China. The wealthy will get even wealthier from it. . . . They'll profit, and they'll use those profits to keep us pinned in our place. In any case, we can never win alone. Unless the Chinese do their damnedest, our own task at home will be really tough!"

And now Takatori had vanished. It was only his final words that Kakimoto did not yet understand clearly.

What worried the officers far more than any outlaws or Southern troops holding out in a fort were those ninja leaflets, and the likes of Takatori, and the possibility of a revolutionary alliance between the workers and the soldiers. It was that they feared the most. There was no defense against that.

32

This day again a desperate and vicious assault was launched. At three in the afternoon, surrounded by trash, Kakimoto was shot through the shoulder by a bullet come flying from behind the fort wall. Along with a jolting truck full of wounded men, he arrived at a hospital.

All the hospitals were overflowing with casualties. More kept steadily coming in, on stretchers or on foot, and were crammed into the already crowded rooms. Even parts of isolation wards were occupied by the wounded. Kakimoto was put into a room in the charity ward whose Chinese patients had been driven out. It contained iron beds stripped of white paint, stained straw mattresses, and blankets stinking of pus. There were no sheets. It was worse than the ordinary rooms. Screams of thirst, pain, and death struggles were calling to each other as if from cages. The ferocity of the fighting was fully manifest in the number of the wounded and their unrestrained cries.

"Infantry close to the gates are getting killed by shrapnel. Our artillery's firing like mad but their aim's all wrong. Our own shells are exploding over our heads." A stretcher bearer bringing in the wounded grumbled bitterly beside the beds.

"They must be using the shells the Southern Army left behind."

"Maybe so. That's screwing up the range and so they're killing the infantry with friendly fire."

"Damn! That's all we need. As if the war didn't stink from the start!"

No sooner was one truckload of the wounded brought in and the clatter of the stretcher bearers' shoes subsided than the next truck drove groaning up before the doctors could attend to even a third of the wounded. Again the stretcher bearers stamped noisily in weighed down by the casualties.

"The X regiment is getting hit the worst. Nine killed already. It's because the CO is trying to outdo everyone else." The stretcher bearer newly arrived next to Kakimoto's bed was whispering in a deep voice to the wounded man he had brought in. "The officers' ambition can only be satisfied by using us as their stepping-stones! At Lushun they piled up a mountain of corpses. And the general responsible is worshipped as a god!"

Kakimoto was vaguely listening. The X regiment was his. Turning he saw that the man being lifted into the bed was Kuroiwa from his company. His trousers had been removed, and the tourniquet bound around his leg was stiff with black blood. He and his comrades had been forced into a reckless charge for the sake of the commander's ambition and competitiveness. They were falling before their comrades' eyes. "Occupied by X's battalion!" "Seized by Y's company!" Such reports ignite the vanity of people called "commanders."

"It's because they do the impossible. They're hotshots showing they can pull off what nobody else can do!" The anger in Kuroiwa's voice was even stronger than the pain from his wound.

"They're squeezing the last drops of energy out of the soldiers in all the units, aren't they?" Kakimoto suddenly put in from the side.

The stretcher bearer looked at him with quiet surprise. Kuroiwa, recognizing Kakimoto, smiled faintly. "That may be so."

"Of course it's so! All these countless wounded.... Wars are where commanders compete to see who's more ambitious. Wars are designed that way. So we drive out all the Chinese soldiers. So we lose our arms and legs serving as the commanders' stepping-stones. Ha! And the commanders, in turn, are incited from above by their hunger for medals. On top of the high and mighty you've always got those who're even higher and mightier."

"While we're the ones at the very bottom."

"Right. And heavy rocks are piled threefold and fourfold on top of us! Sons of bitches!"

A cheerful army doctor was calmly treating the wounded, smiling pleasantly at their pain, their screams, the thrashing arms and legs. Using scissors, he cut through a shirt stuck to the skin with clotted blood. "'A general triumphs, ten thousand men fall.' Is that it?" Overhearing the soldiers' complaints, he lightly hummed the proverb as though chanting a Chinese poem. Kakimoto was treated by this doctor. Next he was dressed in a new white hospital gown.

The fort was captured the following day before noon. He heard about it while sitting up in bed. The pain from the wound had gradually eased. The injured shoulder did not in the least keep him from walking. On the third day, Kitani and Yamashita came to visit him.

"Hey, Kakimoto, how goes it?" Kitani shouted in a rough, husky voice. "Sure enough, Takatori and the others were murdered! All five were found on the bank beside the Hwang Ho, eaten by dogs, their bones sticking out."

Kakimoto had sensed that such a thing might have happened. Yet actually hearing it stabbed at his heart. "So that was it. There was a reason for the nightmare that night!"

"All five have now been brought to the morgue."

"Who the hell were they killed by?" Kuroiwa asked. "Who did it? Is the murderer known?"

"Quiet! What's the use of asking?" Kitani gravely waved his arm. "We know without being told. He did it!"

"He?"

"He did it!"

For a time they remained silent.

Kakimoto, his arm slung from his wounded shoulder like a toy, walked to the morgue with Kitani and Yamashita. Kuroiwa with his shattered thighbone could not move. The city, visible from the hospital courtyard, was devastated. Even so, the trampled, muddied grass was trying to rise again. The acacias, in spite of the wind, were greener than ever. A large crowd of nurses, doctors, soldiers, and townspeople was gathered outside the entrance and windows of the morgue. Rising on tiptoe, they were trying to view the gnawed remains of the five.

The bodies of Takatori and his comrades were already decomposed from the heat. The unbearable sour stench of decayed flesh, mingled with incense smoke, assailed the sense of smell. It was impossible to tell which was Takatori, which Nasu, which Tamada. They were covered with white cloth. The men had been shot and abandoned. Until the search party's arrival, their bodies seem to have been feasted on by packs of shaggy stray dogs.

"So that's what those damned hands brought them to!" muttered Yamashita. "But how could these bodies have let us know that this had been done to them?" he asked bewildered.

"That's something I can't explain at all," said Kitani. "But the officers were scared of our guns turning against them so they fired first! To safeguard their interests, they'll sacrifice anyone and never look back!"

The three crossed a grassy bank and came to a meadow with a trench dug in it. In the shade of a large acacia a funeral pyre was being prepared.

"One wrong move and we might have been killed too," whispered Kitani, jumping across the trench. "They're afraid of us. But next time, the day we pick up the sword, we won't let them fire the first shot. We'll skewer their hearts before we let that happen!"

33

POSTCRIPT

The five soldiers—only half of their flesh remained—were declared "heroes fallen in battle." Their bodies, placed in coffins and doused with petroleum, turned to stinking smoke amid the cremation flames and evaporated.

Their parents back home are probably convinced that their sons were struck down by the bullets of hateful Chinks. But among all the soldiers their murders have kindled a new and passionate hatred for officers.

As a consequence of the military intervention, China's anti-Japanese, anti-imperialist movement has grown all the more powerful. Words like "We vow to wipe out this shame," written across the ruined Le-yuan-men Gate, have inflamed people's hearts. Japan's bourgeoisie largely achieved the expedition's original goal, "security of the Manchurian colony," at least for the time being. Through such acts as blowing up the shrewd warlord Chang Tso-lin and shooting Chiang Kai-shek's ally Yang Yu-t'ing, the Japanese bourgeoisie committed itself to maintaining an armed grip on Manchuria and Mongolia and is devoted to their complete territorial takeover. It is concentrating all its energy to that end.

The workers of the Fu-lung Match Factory subsequently joined hands with the soldiers and rose. As before, wives from the company housing boarded cars and fled to the KS Club. They never returned. The workers' strength was impressive. Consequently, Uchikawa combined his capital with that of Jui Tien who was planning to consolidate the global match industry. Once again the workers were facing a powerful enemy.

And as for Inokawa Kantarō, who in the course of this upheaval lost his house, his job, and his child, he was fired from the match factory. He had no idea what had happened to Ichirō. Perhaps he had been killed by the Chinese. He grieved for him. He had lost the child who had closely resembled Toshiko, and that was painful. All the same, he resigned himself to the inevitable. Until one day something happened.

He was wandering aimlessly around the neighborhood of Shih-wang-tien where his house had once stood. The aftermath of the destruction had not yet been cleaned up. There was even more dirt and dust in the streets. The Chinese were gnawing on ends of raw radish.

"*Tiya! Tiya!*"

Suddenly someone trotted up to his legs. It was a child dressed in dirty Chinese clothing. The child's head was shaved in the Chinese manner, leaving a fringe and sidelocks.

"*Tiya! Tiya!*"

The child had left its playmates and run up to him. He was looking at Ichirō.

Ma Kuan-chih's wife was standing on the street corner beside an acacia with torn branches. As if dreaming, he lifted the child into an embrace. Ichirō had been rescued by Ma Kuan-chih.

NOVEMBER 1930

Bibliography

Aaron, Daniel. *Writers on the Left: Episodes in American Literary Communism.* New York: Columbia University Press, 1992.

Beasley, W. G. *The Japanese Experience: A Short History of Japan.* Berkeley: University of California Press, 2000.

Buhle, Mari Jo, Paul Buhle, and Dan Georgakas, eds. *Encyclopedia of the American Left.* Urbana: University of Illinois Press, 1992.

Ch'ae, Man-Sik. *Peace Under Heaven.* Translated by Chun Kyung-Ja. Armonk, NY: M. E. Sharpe, 1997.

Coiner, Constance. *Better Red: The Writing and Resistance of Tillie Olsen and Meridel Le Sueur.* Urbana: University of Illinois Press, 2000.

Conroy, Jack, and Curt Johnson, eds. *Writers in Revolt: The Anvil Anthology.* New York: Lawrence Hill, 1973.

Denning, Michael. *The Cultural Front: The Laboring of American Culture in the Twentieth Century.* London: Verso, 1998.

Fitzpatrick, Sheila. *The Cultural Front: Power and Culture in Revolutionary Russia.* Ithaca: Cornell University Press, 1992.

Foley, Barbara. *Radical Representations: Politics and Form in U.S. Proletarian Fiction, 1929–1941.* Durham: Duke University Press, 1993.

Hane, Mikiso. *Modern Japan: A Historical Survey.* Boulder: Westview, 1992.

———. *Peasants, Rebels, Women, and Outcastes: The Underside of Modern Japan.* Lanham, MD: Rowman & Littlefield, 2003.

Harlow, Barbara. *Resistance Literature.* New York: Methuen, 1987.

Herbst, Josephine. *Pity Is Not Enough.* Urbana: University of Illinois Press, 1998.

Hicks, Granville, Joseph North, Michael Gold, Paul Peters, Isidor Schneider, and Alan Calmer, eds. *Proletarian Literature in the United States.* New York: International, 1935.

Hsiung, James C., and Steven I. Levine, eds. *China's Bitter Victory: The War with Japan, 1937–1945.* Armonk, NY: M. E. Sharpe, 1992.

Hunter, Janet E. *Concise Dictionary of Modern Japanese History*. Berkeley: University of California Press, 1984.

Inagaki Tatsurō. "Kuroshima Denji no rinkaku." In *Puroretaria bungaku*, ed. Nihon Bungaku Kenkyū Shiryō Kankōkai. Tokyo: Yūseidō, 1971.

Keene, Donald. *Dawn to the West: Japanese Literature of the Modern Era*. Vol. 1. New York: Holt, 1984.

Kisaka, Junichiro. "Detour Through a Dark Valley." In *Japan Examined: Perspectives on Modern Japanese History*, ed. Harry Wray and Hilary Conroy. Honolulu: University of Hawai'i Press, 1983.

Kobayashi Shigeo. *Puroretaria bungaku no sakkatachi*. Tokyo: Shin Nihon Shuppansha, 1988.

Kobayashi, Takiji. *The Factory Ship*. Translated by Frank Motofuji. Tokyo: Tokyo University Press, 1973.

Kuroshima Denji. *Kuroshima Denji zenshū*. Edited by Odagiri Hideo and Tsuboi Shigeji. 3 vols. Tokyo: Chikuma Shobō, 1970.

———. *Nihon puroretaria bungaku shū 9: Kuroshima Denji shū*. Tokyo: Shin Nihon Shuppansha, 1989.

———. *Teihon Kuroshima Denji zenshū*. Edited by Satō Kazuo. 5 vols. Tokyo: Bensei Shuppan, 2001.

Kuroshima Kazuo. "Chichi." Monthly Bulletin 1, April 1970. *Kuroshima Denji zenshū*, vol. 1.

Le Sueur, Meridel. *Salute to Spring*. New York: International, 1989.

Lippit, Noriko Mizuta. "War Literature." *Kodansha Encyclopedia of Japan*, vol. 8. Tokyo: Kodansha, 1983.

Marx, Karl. *Karl Marx: Selected Writings*. Edited by Lawrence H. Simon. Indianapolis: Hackett, 1994.

Marx, Karl, and Friedrich Engels. *Marx and Engels on Literature and Art: Selected Writings*. Edited by Lee Baxandall and Stefan Morawski. St. Louis: Telos, 1973.

Mitchell, Richard H. *Censorship in Imperial Japan*. Princeton: Princeton University Pres, 1983.

Morales, Alejandro. *The Brick People*. Houston, TX: Arte Publico Press, 1988.

Moroi Shirō. "Kuroshima Denji nenpu." In *Kuroshima Denji zenshū*, vol. 3.

Nekola, Charlotte, and Paula Rabinowitz, eds. *Writing Red: An Anthology of American Women Writers, 1930–1940*. New York: Feminist Press, 1988.

Ngugi wa Thiong'o. *Penpoints, Gunpoints, and Dreams: Towards a Critical Theory of the Arts and the State in Africa*. Oxford: Clarendon Press, 1998.

Nihon Bungaku Kenkyū Shiryō Kankōkai, eds. *Puroretaria bungaku*. Tokyo: Yūseidō, 1971.

Oguma, Hideo. *Long, Long Autumn Nights: Selected Poems of Oguma Hideo.* Translated by David G. Goodman. Ann Arbor: Center for Japanese Studies, 1989.

Ohara Institute for Social Research. Hosei University. www.oisr.org.

Olsen, Tillie. *Yonnondio: From the Thirties.* New York: Delta, 1974.

Prawer, S. S. *Karl Marx and World Literature.* Oxford: Oxford University Press, 1985.

Rabinowitz, Paula. *Labor and Desire: Women's Revolutionary Fiction in Depression America.* Chapel Hill: University of North Carolina Press, 1991.

Rabson, Steve. *Righteous Cause or Tragic Folly: Changing Views of War in Modern Japanese Poetry.* Ann Arbor: University of Michigan Press, 1998.

Rideout, Walter B. *The Radical Novel in the United States, 1900–1954: Some Interrelations of Literature and Society.* Cambridge, MA: Harvard University Press, 1956.

Rubinstein, Annette T. *American Literature: Root and Flower.* Beijing: Foreign Language Teaching and Research Press, 1988.

Shea, George T. *Leftwing Literature in Japan: A Brief History of the Proletarian Literary Movement.* Tokyo: Hosei University Press, 1964.

Shulman, Robert. *The Power of Political Art: The 1930s Literary Left Reconsidered.* Chapel Hill: University of North Carolina Press, 2000.

Smedley, Agnes. *Portraits of Chinese Women in Revolution.* Edited by Jan Mackinnon and Steve Mackinnon. New York: Feminist Press, 1994.

Wald, Alan M. *Writing from the Left: New Essays on Radical Culture and Politics.* London: Verso, 1994.

Wray, Harry, and Hilary Conroy, eds. *Japan Examined: Perspectives on Modern Japanese History.* Honolulu: University of Hawai'i Press, 1983.

Wright, Richard. *Uncle Tom's Children: Five Long Stories.* New York: HarperPerennial, 1993.

A young Kuroshima Denji, in his army uniform, sits in a Russian forest.
(From *Kuroshima Denji zenshu*, Tokyo: 1970)

About the Author

One of the most consistently antimilitarist intellectuals of modern Japan, the proletarian writer Kuroshima Denji (1898–1943) produced numerous literary works potently expressing his passionate opposition to armed force as an instrument of imperialism. Best known for his "Siberian stories" of the late 1920s—vivid depictions of agonies suffered by the Japanese soldiers and Russian civilians in the course of Japan's invasion of the newly emerging Soviet Union—Kuroshima also wrote a number of powerful narratives dealing with the hardships, struggles, and rare triumphs of peasant life. His only full-length novel, *Militarized Streets,* a shocking description of economic and military aggression against China by Japan and other powers, was censored not only by Japan's imperial government but by the US occupation authorities as well. The present collection marks the first rendition into English of much of Kuroshima's most highly acclaimed work.

About the Translator

Zeljko (Jake) Cipris obtained his doctorate from the Department of East Asian Languages and Cultures at Columbia University and is presently an assistant professor of Japanese at the University of the Pacific in Stockton, California. He is the coauthor with Shoko Hamano of *Making Sense of Japanese Grammar: A Clear Guide Through Common Problems* (University of Hawai'i Press, 2002). His translation of Ishikawa Tatsuzō's formerly banned novel *Soldiers Alive* was published in 2003. An inveterate traveler, Jake is the happy fellow-parent of a writer and a musician.